Also By Dannika Dark:

THE MAGERI SERIES
Sterling
Twist
Impulse
Gravity
Shine

NOVELLAS
Closer

THE SEVEN SERIES
Seven Years
Six Months

ACKNOWLEDGMENTS:

Thank you for taking this journey with me.

Dying isn't the hardest thing you'll ever do—living is.
—*Sterling*

"Fate brought us together for a reason; there are no accidents. Everything that happens in our lives leads us to a greater destiny, even if we don't always understand the purpose."
—*Twist*

CHAPTER 1

"Do it again, Peaches."

"Don't call me Peaches," I growled.

Justus, my Ghuardian, circled the mat in our training room like a predator. "I'll do whatever it takes to get you motivated enough to try harder."

A bead of sweat trickled down his temple and he locked his cobalt eyes on mine. Brilliant flashes of light sparked in his irises as he leaned forward, bracing for my attack. I tried not to allow his physical appearance to intimidate me. His broad shoulders were impossibly strong, his body conditioned from rigorous training, his thighs as powerful as a rugby player's and built for running. Justus had the commanding appearance of a warrior, all the way down to his chiseled jaw and menacing stare. He didn't have any hair I could grab during our training sessions because he kept it closely shaved, which drew attention to his masculine features.

I flashed at him with concentrated speed and before contact, I bent to the right and tried to kick him in the face with my left foot.

Justus grabbed my calf and swung me around.

"Is that the best you can do?" he mocked.

Even though I hung upside down, I defiantly shouted, "No!" and yanked down his track pants.

Laughter pealed out of Simon, who was watching from the sidelines as Justus stood helpless in a pair of silk boxers.

Justus dropped me on the floor and when he bent over to pull up his pants, I sprang to my feet, grabbed the back of his head, and shoved his face into my knee. He fell on his side like a bag of concrete, blood splashing across the mat.

"Atta girl!" Simon applauded from his spot on the floor, legs stretched out and crossed at the ankles. He wolf whistled at Justus, who clumsily reached down and pulled up his pants.

When I tried to touch his face, he jerked away.

"Your nose is bleeding," I said regretfully. "Let me heal you."

Training was serious business in our world. We could heal our injuries by borrowing energy from sunlight or another Mage, but Justus preferred not to. His motto was the "suck it up" kind. Maybe he perceived the injuries inflicted upon him in the training room as "deserved" and thought they should serve as reminders of his mistakes.

"It will heal," he murmured, stripping off his tank top and wiping the blood off his mouth and chin.

Justus had taught me to ruthlessly take him down and then run. Logan had watched our sessions a few times, but with great difficulty. He not only took issue with seeing me suffer injuries, but had also rebuked Justus for not showing me how to fight offensively. But deep down, my Ghuardian still believed a woman was incapable of becoming a warrior. His lessons were more extensive than they used to be, but the end move was always to flee once I weakened my opponent. If escape proved impossible, he'd instructed me to juice them.

That meant stealing their light by joining hands. The core light within a Mage is the source of our energy. Juicing is comparable to draining a battery, weakening the victim so he can't flash and keep up. It was a last resort since Justus never wanted me juicing from another Mage.

Light can be addicting.

"Disrobing your opponent will not be a move that wins battles," Justus advised, rising to his feet.

Simon lurched forward and swaggered to my side, then draped his arm over my shoulder. "I don't know, mate. That looked like a battle of the britches to me, with ten points awarded to your Learner. Good thing you had your underpants on or I might have had to skip lunch."

I rocked on my heels and my lips eased into a playful grin. "I don't know, Simon. Call the fire department because that would have been totally *hot*."

Justus turned beet red and spun on his heel, reaching for a lethal dagger on the wall. I often riled him up to see him crack a smile on his stern face.

Justus had become emotionally distant over the past few months since his falling-out with Page, my Relic. We'd been communicating through phone and Internet, but her life had become too chaotic for socializing. The number of clients Page handled had doubled after Justus put a dagger in her ex-partner's chest. Her Council hadn't assigned her a new partner, so poor Page was working crazy hours to make all her appointments. I appreciated the playfulness she had once brought out in Justus, but his personal affairs were none of mine. You can't decide what's best for someone else—we each have our own path to follow.

Justus faced the wall, gripping the dagger tightly in his right hand. I became apprehensive of his motives. With lightning speed, he twisted around and threw the dagger at Simon. I raised my hand and knocked the weapon away with a sharp pulse of energy.

"Bloody hell!" Simon exclaimed, watching the blade skid across the floor. "I swear, Justus, you haven't been able to take a joke since 1905 when I put glue in your hat."

"What was *that* about?" I shrieked.

A smile spread across Justus's face and he absently stroked his Creator's mark located above his navel. It resembled a Chinese symbol, much different than the one I had on my ass. *Lucky me.*

"You have other skills we should be working on in here," he suggested in a baritone voice. "I know nothing about telekinesis, but my observations indicate you have more control when acting on instinct. Do you recall the knife fight with Adam and Samil? Your emotions and split-second decisions show you have the potential to master your gift, but it is conviction you lack."

"I told you I'm still working on it."

One of my gifts as a Mage allowed me to move certain metals recently touched by another Mage. This was a rare gift, one I couldn't talk about because the only ones capable of this feat were Uniques. Page knew about Uniques because her ancestors had specialized in working for them. I was still a Mage—the only difference being that my light was stronger. Uniques had become an urban legend, and with good reason. In ancient times, they were feared and massacred. So if any still remained, then like me, they were in hiding. Page didn't think Uniques were a fluke; she believed a Creator could make a Unique if the first spark occurred during an electrical storm. No one but her ancestors had ever connected the dots. She'd never shared that information with anyone because in the wrong hands, a Creator could make an army and start a war.

Justus knew I was a Unique, but he didn't know the details Page had revealed to me about the *kind* of Unique I was. Maybe she believed he was duty-bound to HALO and the secret would leak. Page knew of four types of Uniques and, based on my specific traits, revealed I was a Shiner. She'd been able to tell from the silvering that sometimes occurred in my pupils and my ability to move metals.

Justus wiped his nose, checking for blood. "You don't work enough on refining your skills. Opening locks and grabbing the keys off the table is not sufficient practice."

I pinched my damp shirt between my fingers and circulated some cool air by tugging at it. "I don't really know what else I can *do*, Ghuardian. Novis had me break a lock and I can move knives around. Seems more like a carnival trick than a gift."

Simon swiped the knife off the floor and twirled it between his fingers like a pro.

Justus stepped forward and regarded me with a stern gaze. "All gifts are nothing more than a sideshow act unless you learn how to properly use them."

"Tossing daggers at Simon's head is not the way I want to learn."

"Perhaps it is the only way to make you *react*," he countered.

I crossed my arms and felt a sting of annoyance. "So why not throw it at *me*?"

Justus dropped his hand on my shoulder and tilted his head to the side. "Because, Learner, you would have taken the blade. I'm impressed you chose to use your gift to save your friend instead of stupidly jumping in front of him. *That's* what I had expected you to do." His mouth quirked and he lowered his eyes. "You astound me more with each passing day. It's a sign that you're maturing into the Mage you have the potential to become. Self-sacrifice is a *human* trait."

"It's a noble one," I pointed out.

His hand slid away. "Perhaps. But in the end, you leave the person you saved alone with your enemy. Then who wins? It may be noble to die for another, but it's not always the best move."

"Sometimes it's the *only* move."

"And those are the choices you will face," he said quietly. After a deep breath, Justus turned away. "You may have the shower first. I'm going upstairs to put ice on my nose."

Justus triggered the button that lowered the lift, and I watched him ascend through the ceiling and into the upper level of our home.

"Well, buttercup, looks like it's just you and me."

I glared at Simon's white T-shirt which said *I Perform All My Own Stunts*.

What Justus didn't know was that Simon had been secretly teaching me a few things on the side. He not only had a reputation for being a skilled strategist, consulted by the Mageri in high-profile investigations, but also as a skilled trainer in fighting techniques and weaponry. Justus trained me because that was his job as my Ghuardian, but his tactics differed from how Simon taught me, which was no-holds-barred.

Where Justus held back, Simon let me have it.

I wasn't naïve enough to believe I'd become one of the most lethal warriors in Mage history. I had weaknesses. I wasn't as physically strong as a man, so letting him get too close exposed my vulnerability. Every situation differed and the real thing never played out like in the training room.

"Bring it," I dared, curling my fingers inward.

With a jerk of his head, Simon shook his tousled brown hair away from his eyes. His kissable lips turned up in a fiendish smile, deepening the dimple in his cheek. When he stripped off his shirt, I belted out a laugh.

Which deflated his ego. "For pity's sake, what now?"

"Sorry. Your nipple ring threw me off."

"Now I know why it never worked out between us."

I turned up my nose at him. "Maybe it's because you tossed me off the bed."

"Love, I only seduced you to taste your light."

My face heated. "What did you just say?"

He scratched his smooth jaw pensively. "The truth would have come out eventually. If you want to know, you'll have to take this knife from my hand." He spun it once between his fingers.

Well, that just pissed me off. Simon smiled wickedly and gripped the sharp blade. I flashed across the room and he crouched low, keeping a watchful eye on me.

"Are we dancing?" His question dissolved into laughter.

Simon was a smidge taller than Justus, but not as built. I felt more confident taking him on physically, but disarming him was impossible. I'd only done it once and that's because he'd been drinking.

I stopped behind him and before he could turn around, I twisted his arm around his back.

Simon leaned to the left and fell, forcing me to let go. In a move too fast to track, his right leg swung around and swept my legs from behind, causing my knees to buckle and sending me to the ground. As soon as I hit the mat, I rolled away and leapt to my feet before he could grab me.

"Simon, you better tell me what you're talking about," I threatened, wiping a strand of dark hair away from my face. My ponytail had come loose three fights ago.

Simon hopped to a squatting position and gave me a cheeky grin. "If you really want to know, then come and take it," he sang.

"I hate you. We both know I can't take the knife from your hand."

"You're a clever girl; figure it out."

Just then, it hit me. All those stupid training sessions on disarming my enemy and it had never clicked.

Not once, because I'd been fighting him the way *Justus* had taught me.

I could see in his eyes that he sensed my moment of epiphany, and he tightened his grip on the handle.

With my right arm extended, I pulled the knife clean out of his hand using my power. As the blade sliced toward me, I swung my arm and altered its direction. A muffled crack sounded when it punctured the wall behind me.

"Spectacular!" He panted, folding his arms as he stood up. "I've been wondering when you would figure it out. You still need to find a way to gain control of the knife and put it in your hand."

I flashed forward and knocked him onto his back, then seized his throat. "What were you saying about our time in the bedroom?"

"Oh, that."

"Yeah, *that*."

Around the time when we first met, Simon and I had engaged in some lascivious kissing in my bed. We were drunk and once he initiated the binding of our light, it became hard to stop. In my defense, Simon's a handsome man and I'd never felt sexual energy from another Mage.

"Em," he began, his brown eyes skating off to the side. Simon was too pretty for his own good and tried to use it to his advantage.

"You were saying?"

"About that," he began, his British accent becoming thicker. "The only reason I came on to you in the bedroom is so I could taste your light."

"*What?*"

I sat up, straddling him.

"I'm a curious chap. This should come as no surprise. When you hurt your ankle, it gave me an opportunity to start something up and drink your energy without getting slapped. Sharing a little light can give you an idea of how powerful a Mage is. I didn't know you were a Unique. *That* came as a surprise."

"So you just made out with me to sample my light?" I stared at him incredulously.

God, *no wonder* he'd jumped off so fast and never started it up again. He'd gotten the answer he wanted.

Nosy bastard.

"What made you think I was different?"

He sat up and leaned back on his palms. "Didn't say that."

I rested my hands on his shoulders and squeezed. "You're not telling me something."

"And that's news? Your energy on the dance floor was oozing out of you."

"I don't ooze." I twisted my mouth, growing impatient.

Simon snorted. "A Learner lacks the control to keep it contained and the skills to shut it off. That's what makes you so attractive to all these manky bastards who would like nothing more than to make you one of their pets. Your energy made me thick in the pants."

"A light breeze makes you thick in the pants."

"When Samil had custody of you, I fought with Justus. Your Creator would have never let you go once he discovered what you were. I knew this, but Justus was naïve. He's also a man who upholds the law and abides by it. I have my own thoughts on all these sodding laws. Maybe I could relate to your situation and that's why it was harder for me to accept." He bit his lip and averted his gaze.

I reached around and caressed beneath his hair, smoothing my fingers over the tattoo on the nape of his neck. "Someday I hope you open up about what happened to you, Simon. You can't hold it in forever. Pain like that becomes a black hole that'll consume you with fear and hate."

"Now you're starting to sound like Justus."

He leaned away and my hands slid back to his shoulders. The silence was cut short when a throat cleared.

The lift had returned and Logan stood to my right with his arms folded, golden eyes watching us. I was sweaty, Simon was shirtless, and we were in a position that could have been splashed on the cover of any adult magazine.

Simon winked at Logan. "Just showing your girl a few moves."

"I'd like to show you a few of my own," Logan said obliquely. He reached to the wall and lifted a dagger with a black handle and serrated edges.

"Boys, do we have to do this now?" I sensed a challenge.

Logan swung his eyes at me and smiled.

"You don't get off that easy," Simon said, tossing me to the side.

"No, but I bet *you* do," Logan suggested.

Game on.

CHAPTER 2

OVER THE PAST FEW MONTHS since Tarek's death, much had changed, and yet life stayed the same. I had accepted Logan Cross to be my mate, but we hadn't decided on when to make the leap. My accepting him was all the claim he needed, but a ceremony would make it official in my eyes. The problem was, we weren't the same Breed, so it wouldn't be legal.

Logan and I had been intimate on several occasions. It could hardly be helped in his presence. What had begun as a noble gesture when I had temporarily gone blind had continued in our relationship. Logan immersed us in darkness so he would not see my body, even going so far as to install thick shutters and drapes in his condo for privacy. Not a great way to boost a woman's ego, but on the other hand, Logan had the skilled hands and mouth of a god. I tried to convince him that sex in the dark wasn't necessary now that I could see, but Logan said he didn't want to know all of me all at once. He liked unwrapping his gifts slowly, admiring the ribbon, feeling the silky wrapping beneath his fingertips, and knowing there was more to come.

I still lived with my Ghuardian, whom I still *called* Ghuardian, despite his proclamation that by accepting Logan I would no longer be under his care. With Justus in the house, it felt more like sneaking my boyfriend in after Dad went to bed, so Logan and I were only intimate at his condo.

Justus came from a different time when women probably didn't have sex until marriage. It didn't deter *him* from having sex all over Cognito, but he believed a respectable woman should make a man wait. I wondered what he thought of Page since they had wrinkled the sheets rather quickly. Maybe after developing feelings for her, he'd begun to regret having treated her like all his other concubines. Maybe that's why it ended between them.

Logan insisted that I continue living with Justus. Nero remained a threat. He had formed an alliance with Tarek, a Chitah Lord, in hopes it would make him privy to inside information. After Tarek's violent death at Logan's hand, Nero had retaliated by killing Knox and trying to finish off Sunny in the process. The Overlord had offered Tarek's family a settlement for their loss, but they'd refused to be compensated. Without closure, the investigation remained open, although no arrests had been made.

Logan felt it wouldn't be dignified to take me from my Ghuardian. He abided by the laws of my Breed and said I needed to learn as much as I could—that I was still too inexperienced to be cut loose in the world.

As frustrating as it was, I respected Logan even more. I worked harder in the training room and listened to my Ghuardian when he imparted his wisdom upon me.

Although most of his words of wisdom had to do with my toiletries hogging up the bathroom sink.

While sitting at the desk in our study, I glanced at the photograph of me on Justus's desk. The picture was one Adam had taken a million years ago of me sitting in a patch of tall grass back in Memphis where I first met Justus. I reflected on that time—that naïve girl who couldn't have imagined the fate that lay ahead of her. Justus had swiped the photo from Adam's bag during a visit and kept it in his private study. Now he seemed less embarrassed by it and prominently displayed the photograph on his desk.

Justus and Simon had left the house a little while ago to pick up some equipment for tree cutting; some of the branches near the garage had split due to the recent heavy snow. Simon had suggested hacking down all the overgrown trees near the driveway and garage. After they left, I'd sent Logan out to pick something up for me.

Something *very* special.

The study had a chair in the corner, a foldaway couch, and Tiffany lamps. The soft glow from the light against the dark brown walls gave the room a tranquil charm. Amid the small collection of antique books, one book was glaringly absent from that room—a weathered book with red leather binding that contained the records of HALO's investigations. After retrieving the book from our old house and giving it to Justus, I'd never seen it again. They used it to document evidence that would incriminate the outlaws they hunted. HALO worked independently of any higher authority, but they respected the law. They made excellent money, and the men who represented the organization were comprised of different Breeds.

But that wasn't the life for me. I worked as an apprentice for Novis—a Councilman who served under the Mageri. Novis was also the official keeper of the records. As his apprentice, I was tasked with relaying information; he didn't trust the privacy of electronic devices. There were also times when Novis meeting with someone would raise suspicion, so I acted as his messenger. During those meetings, I wore sunglasses to deter any Vampires from charming me for information. Something about the reflective lens covering the eyes thwarted their gift.

In any case, I still had Christian as my bodyguard, and he kept a tight watch on me. If anyone got too close, Christian would step in and tell them to *saunter on*. For a Vampire, he seemed to tolerate guarding a Mage just fine.

I clicked a few keys on the laptop and smiled when Sunny appeared on my screen. She looked radiant with a rose tint on her apple cheeks. The sun filtered through the window beside her and picked up the vibrant color of her blond hair. She kept it wavy and stylishly above her shoulders. I had plans to give her a surprise baby shower in another month or two. I had asked Simon for help finding a baby mobile with disco balls. It was a joke, of course, but knowing Sunny, she'd hang it up proudly.

"Hi, Sunshine. How are you feeling today?"

"Bloated," she replied with a twist of her mouth. "Novis is probably wondering what the heck is going on with me lately. All I do is *eat*."

"Well, you have two mouths to feed in there. Can you feel them moving?"

Her expression brightened "At first it was just flutters and wiggling. Novis calls it the quickening. I call it *gas*." She laughed melodically and twirled her hair between her fingers. "Now I really feel something going on in there. I'm over five months along, so I guess it only gets worse from here."

"I don't see why you won't stay with us," I argued, tapping my fingers on the desk.

She leaned back and adjusted her monitor. "You know I love you, girl. But I need to figure out how to get on with my life again. Novis isn't going to keep me around forever, and I seriously doubt Justus could handle two screaming babies."

A laugh burst out of my mouth. "The offer stands and we have a guestroom upstairs if you're worried about the noise. You'd be close to the kitchen and I could help with whatever you needed. Two babies? That's a handful, Sunny. How are you going to manage it?"

She shrugged. "Women worse off than me seem to manage just fine. I guess I'll figure it out soon enough. Knox bought some books…" Her blue eyes glittered and she looked down wistfully. "I still can't believe he's gone. Sometimes I roll over at night and think he's lying next to me. I can feel his warm chest against my back and the way he'd trace his finger over my shoulder when he thought I was sleeping. I'd give anything to just have one more moment with him."

"Please don't make me cry, Sunny," I said, wiping away a tear.

She rubbed her face and blew out a breath. "It's hard, that's all." Her fingers laced together in front of her face and a knock sounded. She looked to the right and a voice murmured in the distance.

"Is that Novis?" I asked.

"I'm fine," she said, still looking up. "No, I had a glass of milk a little while ago. Really, I'm good."

A door closed and she sighed heavily.

"Well?"

"Novis checking on me for the millionth time. He must think I'm about to give birth at any minute. I don't know how he feels about all this. Sometimes it looks like it freaks him out, and I catch him staring at my belly. Which, by the way, is getting fatter by the day. Ugh! I can't fit into my clothes anymore and the ones he's been buying me are hideous!"

"Well, who's gonna see you?"

"*I* see me, and I look like a float in a parade. I asked for stretchy jeans, but he keeps buying me these long, flowy dresses. Do I look like a flowy-dress kind of girl?"

"You'd look beautiful in a tablecloth, Sunny. Seriously. Have you had any luck finding Kane?"

Kane was Sunny's brother. He always showed up for birthdays and made sure she had money, but he traveled a lot. They'd fallen out of touch and she wanted to track him down. Sunny needed family with her, and maybe she hoped Kane would settle down and take care of her for a little while.

"No," she said in a disheartened voice. "I don't even know where to begin. He always knew how to find me, but it was never the other way around. What if something happened to him?"

"I'm sure he's fine. He's probably looking for you now that you moved away from Texas."

"I left a phone number with some people down there that he knows, but it's like he just disappeared off the face of the earth."

"Maybe I'll put a bug in Justus's ear and see if he knows anyone who could look for Kane."

"Would you?" Her brows slanted pleadingly.

"Absolutely." My phone vibrated. "Hey, I have to run. Logan is back," I said excitedly. "I'll call you tomorrow and we'll talk longer. I want to hear some ideas for baby names."

"I already told you, Silver, I'm calling her Zoë and that's final."

I sighed. "Please don't give her my old name because you feel some kind of guilt—or Knox did—for what happened to me."

"Jeez, I like the name," she bit out. "Now shut up about it. By the way, will you just *look* at this!"

Sunny held up her delicate hands to the camera with her nails facing out. I snorted as her mouth twisted to the side.

"He won't even let me paint my nails."

"Novis? Maybe he's right. Those chemicals can't be good for the babies."

"My mother used to dye her hair, paint her nails, and probably chain-smoked until I was born, and I turned out perfectly fine."

"On that note, I'll talk to you soon."

I caught a glimpse of Sunny poking out her tongue as I shut the lid to the laptop.

Without missing a beat, I dashed upstairs to let Logan in the garage. He looked handsome with his choppy hair styled every which way. His black sneakers squeaked on the polished floor as he spun around and slammed the car door. The garage door lowered and when I leapt into his arms, he swung me around.

"Mmm, I like it when my female greets me this way," he purred.

I nuzzled my face into his neck as he slowly set my feet on the ground. Logan Cross was six and a half feet of divine maleness. His smell always reminded me of an oncoming storm, and I still got butterflies looking at his unearthly amber eyes, sharply lined with black rims around the irises. Nothing compared to the predatory stare of a Chitah, and it put goose bumps on my arms.

"Did I ever tell you how much I love you, Mr. Cross?"

"No, Little Raven," he murmured against my ear. "I'm afraid you will have to say it *again* and *again* until I can remember."

His mouth was on mine and his hands slid down my back and cupped my ass. I nibbled on his bottom lip and a small growl rose from his throat. My hungry kisses crossed the line of his smooth jaw, my lips moving to his throat as I stood on my tiptoes. I lightly licked his Adam's apple and Logan gripped me tighter. It was a Chitah thing, and I no longer fought my instincts.

A deep vibration rose from his chest. Logan backed me up and the next thing I knew, I was lying on the hood of Justus's sleek Porsche. What was once a vast collection of exquisite cars was now a collection of three, aside from the Ducati, which he rarely drove.

Logan's ravenous tongue found a sensitive spot on my neck that made me crave his skin against mine. I slipped my hands beneath his shirt, scratching at his strong back. I loved the way his body felt. The taut muscles along his abs, the baby-fine hair on his arms and legs, the masculine cut of his jaw, and especially right now, the thick press between my legs. The hood of the car dented from our weight and Logan's heated breath stirred a voice within me that wanted to say "to hell with it" and have sex right on top of my Ghuardian's one-hundred-thousand-dollar Porsche.

"Wait, Logan. We're going to mess up his car."

When his tongue entered my mouth, the complaint was forgotten.

Until the garage door lifted up.

"Learner!" Justus bellowed. "I can feel your energy. You better not be doing what I think you're doing in there."

"Oh shit!" I said, pushing Logan away and scrambling off the car.

The garage door rose, slowly revealing Justus's ankles, knees, and tightly clenched fists. I flashed to the door and once the vertical crease in his forehead came into view, I lifted my arms.

"Surprise!" I shouted.

He incinerated me with his molten gaze.

Simon ambled past us and didn't utter a word.

"Your energy was bleeding all over the driveway. Do you think that's how a lady behaves? I don't care if you have accepted Cross. A man of worth wouldn't—"

I gripped his steel jaw and angled his head up. "Happy birthday, Ghuardian."

All color bled away from Justus's face. His jaw went slack and his eyes darted back to mine. "What is that?"

"That," I said, waving my arm, "is your very own Mercedes-Benz Roadster. The salesman said it's a limited edition. I can't remember all the SLR stuff. I chose an onyx finish because you already have a silver car, and the doors are really cool the way they lift up. There's no back seat—this is all for you. Turns out the guy running the place was a Mage, so I got a Breed discount and a choice between cars he doesn't offer humans."

Without moving his jaw, Justus spoke in a low voice. "How did you pay for this?"

"I've been saving up all my paychecks. In case you've forgotten, I'm an apprentice for a Councilman. We make pretty good money. There was a better model, but I couldn't afford it and your birthday was around the corner. Simon told me the date of your creation, so I wanted to do something special. I still feel responsible for your destroyed cars and I know this isn't as good as them, but…"

"I need everyone out of here," Justus ordered, his voice reverberating off the walls.

"Well, Logan, that's us," Simon said with a disgusted arch of his brow. "Let's leave the Ghuardian alone to chastise his thoughtful Learner."

"If you utter one cruel thing to her, I will not let it slide," Logan promised, pointing his finger at the floor. "Do not test me on this. You may be her Ghuardian, but I am her mate and I will not allow another male to beat her down for thoughtfulness." He slowly turned around and joined Simon in the elevator that led to our underground home.

I wrung my hands anxiously, not having envisioned this reaction. I hadn't prepared for anything but laughter and a haughty thanks. Justus valued expensive things and although it wasn't the best model on the lot, it was the classiest one I could afford.

Justus approached the car with a heavy gait. When he reached the front end, his finger drew a circle on the glossy paint.

"Logan went to pick it up while you guys were shopping for chain saws. I couldn't figure out a way to get you out of the house, so Simon hatched a plan that involved manual labor—something he knows you like."

Butterflies swarmed in my stomach because I couldn't see his face. *Was the vein in his forehead sticking out? Was he mad?* Maybe I'd insulted him by giving him the cheaper model.

When he knelt down on one knee, I nervously turned around and closed the garage door. The frosty air was filling up the room and making me shiver. Or maybe Justus was the one making me shiver.

I approached him from behind and glanced around the room. There were no windows, the floor was spotless, clean tools hung from the walls, and the space was large enough to accommodate twenty cars. Instead, the only vehicles he owned were the motorcycle, Porsche, Jaguar, and his beloved Aston Martin. Maybe that was enough for most men, but Justus wasn't most men.

"If you don't like it, the salesman said I could return it right away. You can keep the money and do what you—"

"Learner," he interrupted.

I fell silent, studying the lines on the back of his neck as he lifted his head to look at the car. I walked around until I faced him and knelt down on both knees, sitting back on my calves.

Justus lifted his right hand and touched my face. I felt warmth not only in his touch but in his gaze.

"I have no words for how honored I am by your gift. You could have given me a plant and I would be as equally moved that you thought to mark this day."

"You have a black thumb and Max would probably eat it," I said softly. "This seemed like a better idea."

He shook his head and retracted his arm. "My Learner bought me a car," he said to himself. "I have given you nothing of this value..."

"No, no, no. Don't you dare start up. You've not only given me all those expensive dresses, but a beautiful bedroom. Not to mention a roof over my head and taking on the impossible task of protecting me."

"Impossible indeed," he said with a subtle smirk. Justus rose to his feet and looked down at me with tenderness. "Why don't you take one of my other cars," he offered.

"I like my car."

He glared behind me at the beat-up silver car that had become an eyesore in his pristine garage. The bumper had a ding and dirt coated the hood. "You want to give me a car worth fifty times the value of yours and expect nothing in return?"

"Pretty much, yeah."

"Are you always going to be as stubborn as you are now?"

I smiled and rose to my feet. "Pretty much, yeah."

"Why do I suspect Novis does not pay you a salary the equivalent of this car's value?"

"Um..."

"Yes?"

I grimaced a little. "I asked Novis for an advance on my salary. In about four months, I'll be getting my paycheck again. But the car is yours, free and clear."

He ran his hands over his shaved head and made a low sound.

"Please don't take it back," I begged. "Not unless you hate it."

My lip quivered and I stared off to the right. He meant so much to me, and this was the only way I could think of that would impress him. I would be mortified if I had to drive the car back to the lot.

"Learner, if one tear falls from your lashes to this floor, I'll make you mop the entire garage. I accept your gift, with honor."

I laughed and blinked the mist away from my eyes. As much as I wanted to throw my arms around him, Justus would only stiffen and back away. "Well, she's all yours. The keys are in the car if you want to take her for a spin."

"Would you join me?"

"I can't right now. I'm going with Logan to pick up Finn, plus I know you have something already planned with Simon. Finn's not going to stay with Lucian anymore. They're still going to tutor together, but I think Finn's having issues sleeping there. Lucian is an insomniac and he's not giving Finn the privacy his wolf needs. Leo can't take him right now because he said he's working on an important case and will be traveling a lot."

"Yes, that is correct," Justus confirmed.

"Finn wanted to stay with Logan again. I think he looks up to him more than the others. Anyhow, we're going to head out and pick him up. Do you want me to bring you home a cake? I know you don't really care for those, so I thought the car was a better choice."

Justus strolled toward the Porsche. "And will you be away… all evening?"

Well, *that* was a little personal.

"I haven't decided yet if I'm going to have sex with Logan tonight."

I watched the back of his neck burn scarlet and I bit my lip to keep from laughing.

"Why don't you polish the smudges off the hood of my Porsche and then you can make up your mind."

Damn. He'd noticed.

"You can take me for a spin in it tomorrow, even though your driving scares the crap out of me. Simon said he's taking you out on the town for your birthday, so you two have fun. Don't do anything I wouldn't do."

CHAPTER 3

I DROVE LOGAN BACK TO THE dealership to pick up his car and then we headed to Lucian's apartment in separate vehicles. I glanced in my rearview mirror at Christian trailing behind on his motorbike, struggling to avoid the patches of ice left on the road from the last snowstorm. I couldn't wait for summer. In fact, I was thinking about planting some flowers on our property to brighten it up.

Lucian lived downtown in a high-rise apartment building similar to the one Simon resided in. I patiently waited in the empty lobby while Logan went to help Finn carry his bags. When the elevator doors parted, I sprang to my feet from the red leather chair, my eyes wide.

"What on earth are you wearing?" I exclaimed.

Finn's elfin smile was pure mischief. His skinny black jeans were low-rise and too tight, not to mention a size too long. Normally he wore khakis, preppy shorts, or oversized sweatshirts. Finnegan was a handsome fellow with innocent hazel eyes and wavy brown hair. He looked like any other kid coming out of college, except this young man had been to hell and back. He dragged an oversized laundry bag behind him and paused at my reaction to his jeans.

Logan walked by and leaned in to whisper privately, "It's a Shifter thing. He took something with Lucian's scent to remember him by."

"And he wants to smell Lucian's crotch?" I murmured.

Logan's eyes brightened. He covered his smile with a fist and glanced over his shoulder at Finn. "Separation anxiety, perhaps. Little Wolf only wore my sneakers for a week."

I rushed at Finn and wrapped my arms around him, nuzzling against his shaggy hair. He was always embarrassed that his ears stuck out a little, so he kept his hair long enough to cover them.

"Feels like I haven't seen you in forever," I said. "I'm so glad you've decided to stay with Logan."

Finn sniffed out a laugh and I stepped back. His eyes dropped to the ground and his lips remained pressed into a smile. "He's coolio. At least he gives my wolf some space."

Logan grabbed the bulky sack from Finn and tossed it over his shoulder. "I'll go put these in the car and pull around front. It took forever to find a parking space, so give me a few extra minutes. Silver, I'll drive you back to your car. You two wait here."

"He's not kidding," I said. "I had to park in the south forty. I think I'll ride with you guys and pick up my car tomorrow."

I strolled to the front doors with Finn and leaned against the cold glass. Finn pulled a red yo-yo out of his pocket and showed me a few tricks.

"You two getting married?" he asked, winding up the string.

"Well, we made a verbal agreement between us, but you know we can't make it legal."

"Doesn't mean you can't have a ceremony."

I hugged my arms. "I guess."

"There are no laws that say you *can't* have one," he said. "The laws only point out the rights you *are* and *aren't* entitled to. You know that, right?"

The glossy yo-yo swung around and settled on the floor, then rolled forward before he snapped it back up.

"Have you thought about going to school?"

Finn snorted. "School is for humans. We don't have Breed school. Professions are learned either on the job or through training, but I've heard of private tutors."

"And?"

He shrugged, tucking the yo-yo in his pocket. "You need money for that."

"Logan would—"

"Feels weird taking his money, you know?" Finn turned to look at the street. "I'll read whatever books they give me, and that's just as good as any class where someone drills their personal beliefs and values in my head. There are still assholes out there who think owning a Shifter is okay. You know that?"

The anger on his face was palpable, putting a mottle of red on his cheeks that made me notice he had a few tiny freckles. He tucked his hands in the pockets of his dark blue jacket and sniffed, twitching his nose as a lady rushed in. A blast of cold air followed behind her and she jogged to the elevator with two plastic sacks and went upstairs.

"There's Logan," I said. "Come on."

I hooked my arm around Finn's and he lowered his eyes to the ground when we stepped outside.

Christian appeared before us, his black trench coat flapping in the wind as he stood between the street and us.

"Get back inside," he said in clipped words, his Irish accent so dark and sinister it made the hair on the back of my neck stand up.

"What's wrong?"

"Your puppy's jeans are going to get him arrested by the fashion police. Do you want to have this conversation now? Get inside the fecking building."

I backed up and we hurried into the lobby. Logan stepped out of the car and approached Christian. I was a bundle of nerves—if this was an attack, we couldn't risk doing anything in daylight that would expose us to humans.

Logan's eyes scanned the street, his nostrils flaring to pick up emotional scents. I watched impatiently while Christian stood with his arms folded, staring at his dirty black shoes. He was using his Vampire hearing to filter through sounds—he must have heard something that caused alarm.

"Finn, maybe you should go back up to Lucian's apartment," I whispered.

"He's not home. You want me to sit up there by myself while you guys are attacked? No, thanks."

"Finn…"

When his eyes met mine, I actually blinked.

"I can take care of myself," he said in a voice I rarely heard. In that moment, I felt the power of an alpha wolf in his words like a current. Nero had whipped him into submission and a lifetime of slavery had reinforced that mind-set to such a point, I feared Finn would never become the man he was born to be.

When I looked outside, Logan and Christian were gone.

"Where did they go?"

My heart thumped wildly and I glanced at the empty lobby behind us. Suddenly, being inside didn't feel so safe.

"Lookie what we got here," a voice cut in from a hallway on the other side of the room. A man about my height with wavy black hair and a thin mustache rubbed his hands together. I could feel his Mage energy and he wasn't doing anything to conceal it.

"Do I know you?" I asked the man.

He puckered his lips and made a kissing sound. Finn stepped in front of me, holding his arm out. "What's your business?"

The door violently crashed in and Christian stumbled into the room, slightly hunched over and staring between all of us.

I glared over my shoulder as he stepped on broken glass. "You couldn't just walk in like a normal person?"

"Woo-hoo! We got ourselves a party!" the man chanted, doing a jig and clapping his hands once. He opened his jacket and revealed weapons, one of which included a stake. "Afraid you're not who I'm looking for, Vamp. But if you want to play Pin the Tail on the Bloodsucker, we can do that later."

Christian stood upright with an apathetic expression. "You can either deal with me now, or we can have a friendly conversation later on while I'm feeding your bowels to the sharks."

"There's no ocean in Cognito," the man pointed out.

Christian strolled forward, scratching his short beard. "Aye. You're a bright little battery, aren't you? Well for your information, I have a season pass to the aquarium."

The man coughed into his hand and cleared his throat. "Why don't you go fuck off for a little while so I can do my job?"

"You're not touching her," Finn said in a caged voice.

The Mage snorted, stretching out his arms and wiggling his fingers. "You got *that* right."

A rush of adrenaline entered my veins and I flashed to my left and then several feet in front of Finn. "You lay a hand on Finn and I'll—"

"You'll what?"

Christian glanced at me expectantly.

"I'll make a necklace out of your teeth."

A burst of dark laughter flew out of Christian's mouth and he bent over, holding his knees. "*Jaysus wept*. You call that a threat? Just *look* at his teeth; they look like barnacles. They're practically falling out of his mouth."

"*Will you shut up?*" I hissed.

"Are you langered?" he said with a straight face, implying I was drunk. "I think you need to stop watching Hannibal Lecter movies and take a few lessons in the school of Poe."

"Look who's talking! You wanted to take him to the zoo and feed him to a whale."

Christian tipped his head to the side and stood up straight. "A shark is not a *whale*. For your information, lass, a shark has about three hundred teeth in multiple rows around their mouth," he said, pointing to his face. "They're sharp and sink deep into your flesh. Their black eyes roll into the back of their head when they get hold of their prey."

"Sounds a lot like you. Do they also get a boner?"

The man looked between us. "Are you two married or something? Why don't you both shut the fuck up?"

Christian gave him a mechanical smile. "One more word and I'll drain you."

I flashed at the Mage and punched him in the face. Before he could grab hold of me, I leapt out of reach. Finn's expression darkened and I knew he was moments away from shifting.

"I got it, Finn. Don't worry," I reassured him.

The Mage touched his cheek and flashed at me, getting a grip on my neck. I performed a maneuver Justus had taught me to twist my body around and elbow him in the back. Before I could complete the move, Christian knocked the Mage to the ground and pinned his wrists.

"Quite the collection you have in there," Christian said, looking at the weapons strapped inside the lining of the man's open jacket.

"I had it, Christian."

He glanced up at me. "To be sure, lass. But what kind of guard would I be if I weren't *guarding* you?"

The Mage lifted his legs and managed to kick Christian in the back of the head.

"Mommy!" a little girl cried out from an open elevator to our left. She was a little thing, maybe three years old, clutching a stuffed bunny. "Mommy?"

Finn rushed over and took the girl by the hand. "Stay very still," he said in a powerful voice that gave me chills. There was authority in his tone that made you want to submit. She obediently looked up at him with expressive blue eyes and a small pout on her face.

The Mage kicked Christian again.

"Stop doing that, you dolt. Now, who sent you?" Christian leaned in close and the man's eyes glazed over as he was charmed by Christian's spell.

"Nero."

"Why?"

"To take out the wolf."

"*Bastard*," I whispered.

Arms gripped my shoulders and I whirled around, seconds from throwing my energy into Logan. He held my wrist and looked down at me with concern brimming in his eyes.

"Are you all right?"

I nodded.

"There was another one outside, but he's taken care of."

That gave me the shivers because I knew what Logan meant. "Did you call the cleaners?"

"I hid the body and they're on their way. Did you get any information from him?" Logan asked Christian. His eyes darted briefly at Finn and the little human child with brown pigtails.

"Nero sent him," I said. "Who else would pull this kind of stunt?"

"Could have been Tarek's family," Logan muttered under his breath. "It seems our enemies are coming at us from all directions."

The third time the Mage kicked Christian was the last. Christian leaned in and murmured darkly, "I told you not to do that, you fecking *cocktail*."

Then his mouth was around the man's throat. The Mage struggled at first, but his limbs weakened and then he grew still.

Christian slowly stretched out his body on top of him and moaned, drinking deeply. The Mage's eyes fluttered and finally closed. His skin blanched and Christian gently twisted his head more to the right.

Finn had lifted the little girl into his arms and was distracting her by pointing at a picture of horses on the wall.

"Christian, you can't do that in here."

I could rebuke him all I wanted for his behavior, but Christian was uncouth and did what he pleased, *whenever* he pleased.

I heard the smacking sound of his lips unlatching their hold. He slowly licked the man's neck with a long stroke of his tongue, healing the puncture wound. Not a drop of blood spilled.

"Who's to know? They'll think he passed out from hunger on his way to the pizza shop." Christian licked the corner of his mouth and stood up. "Wasn't really in the mood for Italian today, but I never turn down a free meal."

"Are there any cameras in here?" Logan asked, scoping out the room.

Christian stood up and grabbed the Mage by the hand, dragging him toward the men's room. "Be right back. Someone has to go to the toilet."

Logan clasped my trembling hands, his eyes brimming with concern. "Are you sure you're not hurt?"

"He was after Finn. I thought Nero would have been satisfied with taking out Knox, but he's just waiting until we let our guard down."

Logan's mouth formed a grim line. "He couldn't have known you would be here. Otherwise he wouldn't have sent an incompetent fool."

"Unless he wanted me to watch."

"Nero's the kind of man who calculates his attacks. These were amateurs. Lucian has a routine schedule and Nero knew when Finn would be left alone."

"Emma!" a shrill voice cried. A frantic woman who looked to be in her late thirties flew out of the elevator with her arms outstretched. Some of her stringy wet hair dangled from the white towel wrapped around her head. Her flowery, satin robe clung to her wet body. She snatched her daughter away from Finn and hugged her tight.

"Emma, you had Mommy so worried. I told you to stay in your room and play while I took a shower."

"I wanted to go zoom on *that*," the little girl said, pointing at the elevator.

The mother skeptically glared at Finn, who folded his arms and stepped back, lowering his eyes.

"We kept an eye on her," I said. "We were trying to find an attendant."

A blast of cold air blew in from the demolished door and the woman quietly got inside the elevator, eyeing us as if we were a gang of criminals.

"We need to get out of here," Logan said. "Walk with us, Little Wolf. Stick to me like glue and we'll head back to my apartment. I'll call Leo. HALO took the hit on Knox personal and they'll want to know Nero isn't backing down."

"What about Christian?" I asked.

A toilet flushed and my guard stepped out of the restroom, brushing air off his shoulder. "Shotgun."

"You can't call shotgun in *my* boyfriend's car."

Christian unwrapped a piece of butterscotch and tucked the noisy wrapper in his pocket. "I believe I just did," he said, waltzing over broken glass and out the front door.

I narrowed my eyes and before I knew it, Logan lifted me straight up. I stared down at his face and frowned. "I'm perfectly capable of walking, Mr. Cross. I seem to have these two limbs dangling from my torso that work amazingly well."

"Wrap your legs around me, female," he said in a hoarse whisper.

I got those little butterflies as I looked into his eyes and ran my finger over the tiny laugh line near the corner of his mouth. Obediently, I slowly lifted my thighs and locked my ankles behind him. Logan savored physical contact and created every opportunity he could to touch me. Maybe I felt silly with my long legs wrapped around a dangerous-looking man, but I quickly decided what other people thought about us didn't matter.

"Oh brother," Finn said, walking through the open door.

Logan reached out his hand and gripped the back of Finn's jacket. "Hold up, Little Wolf. We walk *together*."

When we arrived at Logan's condo, he closed the shutters and drapes, locked the door, turned on the security monitors in his hidden room, and made a private call to Leo. We'd had a discussion not too long ago that we wouldn't live in hiding because of Nero. And yet here we were… hiding.

Christian was standing guard in the lobby downstairs, scrutinizing everyone who entered the building.

"Finn, promise me you won't go out by yourself," I said firmly, taking a seat beside him on the sofa.

Logan was a minimalist, so we stared straight ahead at a wall that divided the kitchen and living room.

"Where's the little TV he used to have?"

"Remember the attack a few months ago? Smashed. Logan only bought that for you; he's not big on television, just movies on occasion."

Finn lifted the woodcarving of a cheetah from the end table on his right. "I liked the couch better when it was over there," he said, pointing toward the wall. "I don't like my back to the window. I have to sleep here at night."

"We'll move it a little later. Before Logan bought drapes, he thought we'd have more privacy from prying eyes if we faced away from the street. When's the last time you let your wolf out?"

Finn cleared his throat and I could sense his unease. He was jittery and kept wringing his hands together. "A month."

"Is that a long time?"

His eyes briefly flicked to mine and he set the cheetah down. "Probably. I don't know many Shifters, remember? I used to let my wolf out at least four times a week, so we had a routine and I'd let him roam at night. Now it's *all kinds* of messed up because of Lucian. My wolf might be aggressive now and Logan should probably lock himself up for a couple of nights."

"Do you want to come stay with me?"

He scratched his right arm where Nero had branded him. "I don't know Justus all that well, so that wouldn't work."

"You could have the upstairs area all night and we won't bother you. Our house is underground and safe."

He stretched his left arm on the sofa behind me and I liked how at ease Finn felt with me. "So now you think I can't take care of myself? Some asshole Mage wants to rough me up and now I'm supposed to be a groundhog instead of a wolf? No way. I wasn't a coward when I had to live in a barn as a slave—you think now that I'm free on the streets I'm about to start running?"

I pulled my legs up and picked at a tiny hole in the knee of my faded jeans. "Have you thought about finding your father?"

Finn leaned forward on his elbows and lowered his head. "He's dead to me. What kind of man sells his own child to pay off a debt? That's not the kind of man I want to know." He rose to his feet. "That's not the kind of man I want to be."

The closet door in the front hall cracked open and Logan emerged through the coats. He pulled a stick of gum from his pocket and removed the wrapper, then folded the piece onto his tongue.

"What did Leo say?" I asked.

Logan strolled into the dimly lit room and sat in the chair to our right. "Leo expressed concern about Nero's persistence. He's informing his HALO brothers tomorrow."

"Why tomorrow?"

When Logan gazed at me ardently and gave me a wolfish grin, I felt a flurry of tingles. He kicked off his sneakers, never once removing the indulgent look from his eyes as his tongue swept over his bottom lip. "Because your Ghuardian would be over here in ten minutes to take you home, and I want to have a meal with my mate."

God, I loved it when he called me that. Even better was when he said *my female*. I'd never met a more confident man, one who was absolute in his feelings for me despite any obstacles, including my own reluctance. But that had changed in the last few months and now my feelings were tattooed all over my lower belly in the shape of cheetah paw prints with Logan's initials.

"I hope you're not cooking Chinese food, because that's all Lucian ever brings home," Finn complained, rubbing his nose. "If I eat one more egg roll, I'm divorcing this family."

I laughed and watched Finn walk to the bathroom. Logan quickly took his place on the sofa, stretching out his impressive legs and smacking his gum.

"You seem to be in a good mood," I said, curling up against him.

Logan wrapped his arm around my shoulders and lifted my left hand, staring at the mood ring on my middle finger. "You seem to be in good spirits as well, my little Mage."

"I swear that thing only changes colors when you're around."

He chuckled enigmatically. "I never told you, Little Raven, but since the day you put it on, I've noticed the color changing in my presence."

"Have you now?"

The crook of his finger touched my chin and tilted my head up. Logan possessed unique features. His brows were heavy over his golden eyes and he had a distinct appearance—someone you noticed. Not the chiseled features Justus had, but animalistic and soft all at once. He could hold a tranquil expression one minute and the next, something fierce and formidable. Perhaps his wide smile could look menacing at times, but I knew the one hundred different smiles of Logan Cross, each with their unique little meaning. Every inch of his body was lean muscle, even though he could eat up a storm. Chitahs were built for speed, displaying impressive muscle tone when they used their running abilities. But what I really loved was when Logan would get excited, causing a flurry of spotted colors to mark his smooth skin.

Touching him was like an appetizer for my fingers. I slipped my hand beneath his shirt, resting my palm on the flat of his stomach.

He shifted a little and the fabric of his shirt rustled against the back of the sofa. "What troubles you?" he asked. "Your scent changed."

"If we hadn't showed up, something might have happened to Finn. That scares me, Logan. It's been calm these past few months and I thought Nero would leave us alone. Doesn't he have better things to do, like terrorizing some small country or pulling the feathers off a baby chick?"

"I don't want you hunting him," Logan said in a low voice.

"I'm not."

"You're lying to me. Do you think I can't scent a lie? I know you've been looking for him, Silver."

I retracted my hand and stood up, then paced across the room. "Nero *ruined* my best friend's life by taking away the one thing that meant something to her. I never thought I'd see her fall in love with a man, and Knox came along and proved me wrong. How can I just sit here and do nothing?"

"Because if you hunt him down, then you will have my congratulations on becoming the old me."

I swung around. "What's that supposed to mean?"

Logan rose from the sofa and crossed the room. "If you thirst for revenge above justice, then you will become no better than the man I once was. Revenge will blind you more than Tarek's venom ever did. Let HALO do their job. Nero will eventually fall—men like him get greedy and make mistakes. We have enough to consider with my elders not dropping Tarek's case. A magnifying glass sits heavily on top of us—one speck of light and we will burn like ants."

"Your elders wouldn't care about my business," I argued. "Nero is a Mage and Chitahs don't give a damn about Mage business."

"Maybe killing Nero would be a mark on your character that you will never wipe clean. You can become so blinded by your target that you won't care what it takes to get what you want. Perhaps you'll sleep at night, but at what cost? I will never remove the shadow upon my name for my past deeds. I have been doing investigative work on the side, but few trust me. My word means little because of the reputation that precedes me. Don't let that be your fate, Silver."

I stepped back and shook my head. "It's so easy for you to say, Logan. What if the circumstances were reversed? What if Nero buried one of your brothers and was now after me? Would you be able to sit on the sidelines and let justice prevail?"

A muscle twitched in his cheek as he stood with languid arms at his sides.

"It's a chess match, Logan. He's picking off the weak pieces and coming after my king. I've pissed him off something awful, and he's not going to rest until he's ruined my life and won the game. Nero is an ancient Mage—time is irrelevant to him. He could sit around for five months or five decades, but he's not letting this go. Simon has chastised me for the way I used to play chess. He once said I spent so much time protecting all my pieces that I ended up on the run and getting cornered. All those stupid lessons," I said with a soft chuckle. "I used to hate him for all his game-related words of wisdom, but he was right."

Logan cradled my head in his hands, softening the sharp edge in his voice. "Your life is not a game."

I touched the back of his hands and sighed, wishing I could somehow make all this drama go away. "I just want this to be over. I want my life back again."

He offered me a stunning smile. "You are the apprentice of a Councilman. I suspect you will always have danger nipping at your heels."

"Trouble loves me," I said playfully.

Logan slid his arms around me and I melted into his warm embrace. "Trouble never felt so good." His lips touched mine and they were hot and pliant. "If you want to hunt Nero, then we do it together. I am against this, Silver, but you are my female and I will stand by your side."

"Thanks." I stepped back and put space between us. "I gave up the search about a month ago when I hit a wall, but I'll think about what you said. It just gets harder every time I see Sunny. I think she's going to have the ceremony for Knox soon. I have a feeling she'll release his ashes before the babies come."

A clicking sound from behind startled me and I peered over my shoulder. A red wolf with large ears stalked into the room, head low and hazel eyes leering up at us. The fur on his face had silver tips and he was larger than an average-sized wolf.

Logan's arm swept around me and he stepped between us. Finn growled and bared his teeth, eyeing Logan like a meaty prize.

"Let me go," I insisted, kneeling down and crawling around Logan.

"Silver!"

He reached out to snatch my shirt and Finn's wolf lunged. I wrapped my arms around his neck and held him back.

"Shhh." His ears were soft between my fingers and I kissed his snout. "Hey there, pretty boy. I missed you so much."

I couldn't begin to explain why I trusted his wolf unconditionally, why I never felt fear in his presence. He snorted and sat down, then began licking the side of my face. We'd bonded on the night Finn's wolf protected me from a guard in Nero's compound. We had developed an unbreakable trust from the beginning, and Logan said it perplexed even him. He reasoned that alphas instinctively sought to form a pack and Finn must have subconsciously thought of me as one of his own.

All I knew was that I loved that kid.

CHAPTER 4

ADAM PATTED OUT THE BUTT of his cigarette in the dirty ashtray and glanced around the crowded bar. Human establishments were safer bets for business chats and dirty dealings. Adam kept his Mage light concealed, not worrying about the risk of another Mage finding out what he was. He had other things on his mind tonight.

One of which was meeting up with Knox's ex-partner, the one he'd worked with before leaving the Special Forces.

Adam had spent months searching for the Mage who murdered his twin sister long ago in an alleyway, an event he'd witnessed that had scarred him more than the marks on his face, arms, and chest. One he relived on the night his best friend was murdered in front of his eyes, when once again, he was powerless to help. Maybe he'd never find his sister's killer, but he felt an obligation to close a case Knox had been working on before he died. Brotherhood meant something to him. Knox would have wanted him to honor a fallen brother—that's what real men did.

"Here's your card, Mr. Lucan Riddle," the bartender said. "You have an open tab, so just shout if you want something."

"I appreciate it."

The bartender stole another glimpse of Adam's scars and walked away, shaking his head. Adam caught his reflection in the mirror behind the liquor bottles. He touched one of the marks that carved down his temple and stopped at his cheek. There was a gap in his eyebrow where the hair had stopped growing in. He kept a scruff on his face, although it grew in patchily because of the scars. They were deep and ran along both sides of his face. One crossed over his left temple and eye while the other sloped down his right jaw. He'd tried a beard for a while, but it made it more obvious he was hiding something, so he decided *to hell with it*—let 'em look.

Maybe he wouldn't be the same guy he once was, but it never helped when women constantly rejected him. It had once been easy for him to charm a girl into having a beer and light conversation, but now they grimaced and found someone else to sit next to.

A man has needs. Adam had thought about taking a prostitute up on her offer once but decided that was a road he didn't want to travel down. He'd rather be alone than have to pay for sex.

The last woman he'd felt in his arms was Cheri, and that stung. She'd deceived him in the worst way a woman could.

The speakers pumped out a ZZ Top song and the men bobbed their heads while checking out the women. None of these humans had game compared to Breed men. After a few hundred years, immortal men had refined those skills based on trial and error. Most just got right to the point.

"You're Adam Razor?"

Adam nodded.

A young man sat on the stool to his left. He had long skinny legs and the ugliest damn shoes Adam had ever seen. They were bright orange running shoes and he wore them with no socks. His jeans were short enough that his ankles showed when he relaxed his feet on the barstool footrest. He waved at the bartender and ordered a strawberry daiquiri.

"We can do the formalities if you want. I'm Oliver. Everyone calls me Ollie, but that's a dumbass nickname, so do me a favor and call me Oliver. Now you can tell me why my partner is dead."

"*Ex*-partner," Adam corrected. When Adam left the Special Forces, Knox had paired up with a new guy. You only partnered with people you trusted, and even though Knox couldn't stand Oliver, he was a genius with modern technology.

"I think you owe me an explanation as to what the good goddamn is so important up here in Cognito that my *ex-partner* wanted to leave behind a decent job where men respected him." Oliver glanced up as the bartender set the tall glass in front of him.

Adam leaned on his elbow with his index finger holding up his head, watching Oliver gobble up the strawberry garnish. He sure didn't look like Special Forces material. Adam wasn't even sure if he was in his thirties. The frames on his glasses were black, and it looked like he used some kind of gel to spike up his strawberry-blond hair.

Oliver sucked down several sips and began swirling his straw in the drink. "Knox was one badass mother. How did it happen?"

"We got jumped by the wrong kind of men," Adam said, not elaborating. "Look, I appreciate you coming all this way for a face-to-face. I don't know you, so this isn't the kind of conversation I feel right about having over the phone."

The music continued to blast and Adam leaned in close enough that their words were private. No one in the bar invaded their space, maintaining at least a fifteen-foot radius. The humans were either playing pool or watching hockey on the television screens.

"Yeah, well, least I could do. Knox hated the piss out of me, but he had enough good sense to keep me as his partner. You know how it is—guys like me are given a lot of shit. Not everyone can be the Terminator. Computers are where it's at, and if more of me aren't brought in, then the unit will become obsolete. Can't run into every scenario with your dicks swinging. Sometimes you need a guy who can crack any security password or come up with an elegant solution to a clusterfuck."

"Knox said you got a look at the Trinity files."

The Trinity files were documented proof the Special Forces had an agenda to research and destroy the Breed.

Oliver arched his right eyebrow and glared over his shoulder. "I know you two were tight, but that shit is not something you need to be posting as your status update on your public profile page, if you get my meaning."

Adam leaned in close. "Have you heard the name Zoë Merrick?"

By the look on Oliver's face, that was an affirmative.

"I've been giving it a lot of thought," Adam said. "I'd like to know how one of our guys knew about Zoë and what she was. If you've seen the files, you know what else is out there," Adam said, knowing Oliver had access to detailed information about the Breed world.

"She's just part of a list of names they've been tracking down. I don't know where they came from, but I don't see anything special about them. Apparently, someone higher up does. Knox actually flew ahead of us to save Zoë when we got the orders to deliver a bullet. He never admitted it, but I knew he wasn't about to take out a woman."

Adam still wasn't clear on something. "Why was her name in the files?"

It didn't make sense, but Silver had held back on telling him a lot of things lately. He knew something was going on, but she was keeping tight-lipped about it.

Oliver sucked down half his drink and then stuck his finger in his shoe to scratch his foot. "'Cause men in suits and ties always have a list tucked away. They probably bought it… or stole it. Maybe they didn't know what the hell it was. Around that time, some guy named Samil was a big case. They were tapping his calls and following him, so maybe some of those names came from him. It's like finding one of those arrowheads in a field. You know what it is, what it's used for, what it's made of, but fuck if you know what it's doing in the middle of the field and who put it there. We can sit on our asses and guess all night, and you can buy me three more of these," he suggested, dipping the same finger he'd used to scratch his foot into the icy drink.

Adam could see why Knox thought this guy was a real dick.

"I thought you'd want to know about the metal shit more than some chick," Oliver murmured.

The music quieted and a few shouts sounded from the front of the room. Adam surveyed his surroundings, taking mental pictures of the faces and their locations.

Oliver discreetly hooked his pinky finger in his nose, scratched, and then studied his fingernail. When the music cranked on, he angled his body toward Adam. "I know who the buyer is."

If that didn't make Adam's heart stop in his chest, nothing would. He took a calming breath and rubbed the back of his neck. "Who?"

A few seconds passed and the human computer geek widened his eyes thoughtfully and stared at the napkin adhered to the bottom of his glass. "For the right price—"

In a flash, Adam snatched him up by the collar and gave him a close-up view of his scarred face. "We're not playing *The Price Is Right*, feel me?"

"Some guy named Cedric."

Adam let go and rubbed his jaw. *Why did that name sound familiar?* "Who's selling?"

"That I don't know." Oliver cleared his throat and took another drink. "Someone got sloppy and I found Cedric's name and phone number in a hidden file. Could be anyone, but it doesn't matter. That metal they're manufacturing has defects, but they're not telling the buyer. Guess it's a matter of time before they find out. Kind of like the carriage that turns back into a pumpkin. Speaking of," Oliver said, glaring at an oversized watch on his wrist, "I have to bail."

"You just got here, and we're not done," Adam pointed out. This guy was working his last nerve. He'd paid for the plane ticket to fly him up here and now he thought a ten-minute conversation in a bar would suffice?

"This was the 'getting to know you' date. We'll get to first base on the second date if you treat me right, but I'm not that easy."

Adam glared at Oliver as he stood up and hovered over his glass, sucking down the rest of the fruity drink.

If they had tapped Samil's phone, they might have overheard conversations with Marco. That's probably how they'd gotten some of the names in their files. Marco had found Zoë and offered her to Samil—maybe it piqued the interest of the men in charge. As much as he wanted to know all the facts, Adam had learned a long time ago that life doesn't give you all the answers on a silver platter.

"I'm five blocks up at the Brooks Hotel. Call me tomorrow, but not before noon. I stay up late and like to sleep in. Next time, why don't you put me up at a place that serves continental breakfast," he said, not really asking. "Adios."

The rubber on his sneakers stuck to the floor and he stumbled before making his exit.

Adam finished off his beer and felt listless with the new information. Oliver knew more than Adam had thought he would. Despite how he felt about the guy, he trusted him on the simple basis that Knox had. This was HALO's case, but without an inside connection to the human world, it would quickly become a cold case. Once Adam put this to bed, he could focus on hunting the Mage who'd killed his sister. All he had to go on was a memory and the location of the Creator's mark on the Mage, the same one that Silver carried, making him one of Samil's progeny.

Adam lit up a cigarette and blew out a steady breath of smoke. He spent the next few minutes watching it burn without taking another drag until he heard a familiar hyena laugh.

His eyes slid across the room and caught sight of Simon and Justus emerging from one of the adjoining rooms. Each had a woman ornamenting his arm. Simon was three sheets to the wind, and the tall blonde walking beside him had her eyes all over Justus. The man had a Mage ability that attracted women, and Adam wondered how that didn't bug the hell out of Simon.

"I still think you cheated," the blonde teased, pushing out her plump lips and batting her lashes at Simon.

"Love, if it's one thing I don't do, it's cheat." He snorted. "And tell me exactly how one cheats at darts?"

This wasn't the kind of bar that drew in men like Simon—he stood out in his leather pants, sleeveless shirt, and studded collar. A few men turned their heads, sizing him up like they wanted to beat the shit out of him.

Justus spotted Adam at the bar and froze as if deciding what to do. The woman on his left arm brushed her skinny fingers over his shaved head, tugging at his earlobe. Justus distanced himself from her and approached Adam.

"What brings you here?"

"Weak beer," Adam replied, holding up his empty bottle of import.

"Simon, take a walk," Justus requested, sliding onto the stool to Adam's left.

"Let me just take this off your hands," Simon said, touching the arm of the other woman who clutched Justus like he was a walking lottery ticket. "Here, love. Try one of these." He held out a bright red lollipop. Adam recognized it as a Sensor pop—candy spiked with different emotional flavors to give customers a sample.

"I'm on a diet," she complained.

Simon curved his arm around her back and leaned in close to her ear. "I promise if you lick my lolli, I'll return the favor."

As they drifted off, Justus ordered an entire bottle of cheap wine. He handed a large sum of money to the bartender and set the unopened bottle to the side.

"How is your training going with Novis?"

Adam considered the question. "He's a fair Creator."

"Does he know his Learner is getting drunk in a human bar?"

"Like I said, he's fair. I'm not a man who requires a babysitter."

Justus grunted, staring ahead at their reflection in the mirror. He leaned forward, the tribal tattoo on his arm standing out since he wore a tight shirt with short sleeves. Adam would bet his entire outfit cost him a fat penny, including the expensive cologne wafting over.

"How's Silver?"

"You should come over and ask her yourself," Justus said.

"We talk."

Justus rubbed his jaw. "I remember when I first met you, I didn't think she was a woman you'd ever let out of your sight again. Silver looks up to you, and that's a weight of responsibility on your shoulders."

Adam didn't care for Justus's judgmental tone. "We can turn the tables and talk about your shortcomings as a Ghuardian, or we can sit here and have a friendly drink," Adam suggested humorously. He often butted heads with Justus and they both chuckled. "How are things with HALO?"

"Overcoming a deep loss. Knox would have been an outstanding addition. His head was in the right place, and I've seen few humans so passionate about doing the right thing. A man requires more than connections to be invited into our group—he requires a solid amount of integrity. He'll be missed."

Adam squeezed the glass bottle. It suddenly hit him how much he missed hanging out with Knox and the banter they'd shared. Over the past few months, it had been a struggle to live in the same house with Sunny. Seeing her was a daily reminder of the loss. On a number of nights, he stayed in a motel. But most of the time, he avoided her. She wouldn't accept his apology, and frankly, that's all he really wanted. She insisted nothing could have prevented Knox's death, but Adam would always carry the weight of regret in his heart.

A waitress with a bright smile and short hair leaned between them, setting a piece of paper on the bar. "Be sure to stop in tomorrow night. We're having half-off cover charge to see the show."

Adam liked the casual atmosphere in Northern Lights. He hadn't returned here since the night Knox had been slain in the parking lot. He'd spent thirty minutes pacing around the spot where Knox had taken his last breath. Putting ghosts to bed was necessary to move on.

A few women made meowing sounds, screaming excitedly. Adam and Justus peered over their shoulders at Simon, who was dirty dancing with the blonde. She had the white stick from the sucker poking out of her mouth; her arms snaked around his neck as they engaged in a lascivious dance that was going to get them kicked out. Simon's face was buried in her neck and his hands spread across her ass like explorers in a new land.

Justus tapped his finger on the bottle. "You're invited to dinner. I'm extending the invitation to Novis, if he cares to join us. Bring Sunny if you wish. I'll let Silver know to prepare something this Saturday; she's become quite competent at cooking steaks."

Adam snorted and shook his head. Silver tried, but she adamantly disliked cooking. She would swear at the food and hurl utensils into the sink. If someone helped her, she was fine.

"Sounds good. I'll pass the message to Novis. I can't guarantee he'll come; he's been wrapped up with the Mageri lately. They've been reaching out to all the Councilmen in the territories for their usual check-in, so he's been traveling on the weekends. I'll have to borrow one of his cars since Sunny can't ride on my bike in her condition."

"If it is too much to ask of your Creator, you may borrow one of mine," Justus offered.

As much as Adam wanted to dislike Justus for being such an arrogant bastard, he had his moments.

"Won't be necessary. Novis will agree, but he'll send a guard with us."

Novis allowed Sunny out of the house on a few occasions, but only if she was heavily guarded.

"We look forward to it." Justus rose from his seat and placed his hand on Adam's shoulder, lingering for a moment. "There's nothing you could have done."

Then he walked off.

A hot coal burned in Adam's stomach. Despite the words of comfort Justus offered, Adam had replayed that fateful night in his head a million times. He could have done so many things differently. At least Sunny survived, because it would have killed Knox to know she hadn't lived.

"You want another beer or can I bring you the menu? If you're not hungry for dinner, we've got appetizers and desserts," the bartender said.

"Got any pecan pie?"

CHAPTER 5

After a brief confrontation between Finn's wolf and Logan, it became evident the two needed to stay apart. Finn hadn't shifted in weeks and it was apparent by his restless behavior. Only I could get near him, so Logan retired to his hidden apartment next door. Finn's wolf raced around the condo, chewed on a pillow until the stuffing came out, and finally relaxed near the window. Wild animals should be allowed to roam at night, but we'd never keep up with him.

My phone vibrated. I lifted it from the end table and read Simon's message.

> Simon: Your Ghuardian bailed.
>
> Silver: What do you mean?
>
> Simon: While I'm shagging a sweet young thing, Justus pulled a disappearing act.
>
> Silver: Did you try calling him?
>
> Simon: Affirmative.
>
> Silver: Maybe he's putting on his birthday suit for someone.
>
> Simon: All the hotties are accounted for in the bar. He left me high and dry.
>
> Silver: You need a ride?
>
> Simon: Catching a cab. Call him for me. He's in one of his PMS moods. Pissy Mage Syndrome.
>
> Silver: Maybe getting him laid wasn't the best birthday present.

Simon: Love, a woman is the only birthday present worth unwrapping. Ciao.

I sent a message to Justus, but he didn't reply back. Then I tried calling. After it went to voice mail, I thought about who I could contact. I decided not to wake Novis up in the middle of the night to tell him my Ghuardian had gone to a bar to get laid and then taken off. Justus would be mortified because he admired Novis.

So instead, I sent a message to Adam. We kept in touch, but something was occupying his time lately.

Finn's sleeping wolf whimpered and flapped his tail once, eyes fluttering as he dreamed of whatever wolves dream of.

Adam sent me a reply that he'd seen Justus leave the bar with a bottle of wine, clearly not feeling as spirited as Simon. That put me at ease a little, although I was not my Ghuardian's keeper. Maybe he was taking his new car for a spin and testing its limits.

I approached the coat closet in Logan's front hallway and turned the brass knob, then stepped inside. It looked like an ordinary closet filled with sneakers and jackets. But when I shut the door behind me, the back wall opened up, revealing a spacious room with computers on the left and a seating area in the middle.

Logan wasn't at his desk. I'd begun to turn my head and I gasped when a pair of strong hands forcefully pulled my arms behind my back. He held them so tightly I couldn't touch him with my fingers, which were dripping with Mage light.

My senses heightened, I stretched my body as much as I could and kicked him in the leg. He groaned and before he could react, I kicked him again and knocked him off balance. When Logan's grip loosened, I jabbed him in the ribs with my elbow. Once free, I spun around and slammed my palms against his chest.

"Gotcha."

A grin slid up his handsome face. My energy was contained, but had it not been, he would have been toast.

"Impressive, Little Raven." With heavy breaths, he lightly held my wrists and moved my hands down. "Next time, don't hold back."

I suddenly gripped the waistline of his pants, pulled him forward, hooked my leg around his, and pushed him to the floor with my left arm. I fell on top of Logan, straddling him as I pinned his muscular arms.

"Who said I was holding back, Mr. Cross?"

"Then throw your power into me," he dared.

"Since when did you become masochistic? I'm not charging you up."

"How can I teach you to defend yourself if I don't know how strong you are as a Mage?"

I nuzzled against his neck and straightened my legs, relaxing on top of him. "Take my word for it when I tell you I'm strong. You've had a small dose of my light once or twice before and even that was enough to knock you down."

"Anyone can be knocked down, Silver. But I want assurance your attacker won't get back up."

My lips tasted the warm skin of his neck and the next thing I knew, Logan flipped me onto my back and tightly gripped my wrists. He stared down at me with animalistic eyes, caging me with his body and his scent.

"This is how a Chitah male will pin a Mage. He'll restrain your arms just like this, and you won't be able to throw your light into him. So tell me how you're going to escape?" he asked in a textured voice.

I gave it some consideration. "Well, I could probably start with telling him my life story up until the age of ten. That should bore him to tears."

He frowned, unimpressed with my suggestion. Logan didn't like how Tarek had overpowered me—that without being able to use my Mage energy, I'd been helpless against him. In my defense, I'd gotten a couple of good hits in, but I simply stood no chance against a man who outweighed and outmuscled me.

"Maybe I wrap my legs around him, like this," I said, slowly spreading my legs and locking them around the back of his strong thighs.

Logan's eyes hooded. "If that's the game you play, then get him so worked up that he'll let go of your hands and trust your scent. A

Chitah will know if you're leading him on. If he trusts your intent, then he'll let go. That's when you attack."

The fact that Logan was giving me advice on how to make out with another man to save my life left me nonplussed.

"What are my other options?" I asked. Honestly, I was only kidding and merely being flirtatious with him to see if I could get a little action going in our private room.

He blinked and lowered his gaze, easing back and sitting on his knees. "Provoke him so he bites you. Fake your death. Fake the pain by reliving the bite that almost killed you. Trick his senses, because a Chitah will never expect a Mage to survive if they are bitten with four canines. If you're bitten with less than that, then fake paralysis. Get him off you and then strike when he's least expecting it. But don't get amped up on adrenaline before you spring on him. Put aside your human instincts and remember you are fighting Breed. We all have special skills, and you must always remember what they are with anyone you're up against."

I sighed and rubbed my face. "I'm just so tired of learning how to fight. This isn't the kind of person I was raised to be. I shouldn't have to fight to survive."

"You must fight for anything worth keeping, and that includes your life." He brushed his fingers through his blond, disheveled hair and rested his arms on my bent knees. "I can't teach you how to fight a Mage, but you will never again be a helpless female at the hands of another Chitah." His upper lip twitched angrily and Logan blew out a controlled breath.

"Stop worrying, Logan. I don't want Tarek to overshadow our relationship. And please, can I just walk into a room without being pinned by my boyfriend?"

His brows angled disapprovingly. "I've told you before—I do not wish to be called a *boy*."

A laugh bubbled up and I tried to contain it. Pointless, since Logan could scent my amusement. I locked my eyes with his and he tensed. "Lover sounds like we're having an affair." A smile played on my lips. "Mr. Cross, I would greatly appreciate it if I could walk into a room without being pinned to the ground by *my male*."

In seconds flat, he smothered me with his body. "Whatever pleases *my* female. Now tell me what you came in here for."

"Justus took off and Simon doesn't know where. It doesn't sound like Justus. He's never avoided my calls before."

"Perhaps he is tied up."

I smiled, running my hands along his strong back and kissing his chin. "That I don't doubt. But if he's not at the house in the morning, can you help me find him? I'm sure he'll be there, but now Simon has me worried."

"Your Ghuardian is an old Mage who can take care of himself."

He brushed his lips close to mine but pulled back, leaving me craving more. Before I could protest, his mouth was against my ear. "Can I look at them?"

"My bosoms?" I snorted, knowing exactly what he was asking to see.

His hand slid down between us and the button on my pants popped free. I was beginning to think I should charge Logan a fee to look at my tattoos.

When my zipper came undone and he kissed me salaciously, I lost the thought.

During the three months that had passed since Justus last saw Page La Croix, she'd made no efforts to contact him. Silver and Page had forged a friendship, keeping in touch through phone and Internet. He'd tried to forget her as easily as she had him, but for whatever reason, he couldn't let go. Justus had *never* slept with the same woman twice, and yet he found himself thinking about her in the late hours of the night while lying in bed.

The very bed he'd made passionate love to her in and held her close as he watched her sleep.

Justus had been ordering an arrangement of orchids that were delivered to her door every Tuesday and Friday. He was certain they'd ended up in the trash, but that didn't prevent him from selecting the finest flowers the city had to offer. Prior to that, he had been sending her dresses and elegant blouses. He knew his efforts had been squandered when he'd paid a visit to his friend, Remi, for advice. Remi had no insight he could relay to Justus—only that Page had someone new in her life whom she would never give up. With another man in the picture, she would never wear the clothes he sent, so Justus began sending flowers instead. Modern men gave up easily, but men from his time pursued a woman, wooed her, and showed what he could offer.

It didn't take Justus long to find Page's new apartment building. She had moved out of her old one and, much to his relief, rented a brownstone in a safer area of town.

He rang the bell, but no one answered. Two hours later, the cap on the cheap bottle of red he'd bought at the bar had been unscrewed. Justus polished off most of the wine while sitting on the steps, watching the humans walk their dogs.

What did he know of women? He knew nothing of what made them tick—one reason he stayed out of Silver's personal life. Trying to understand the decisions she made was an exercise in futility. Then again, who was he to talk? Here he was at the doorstep of a woman who was not even his own Breed.

A biting chill hung in the air, but it didn't affect him. He wore nothing but a T-shirt and dark slacks, utilizing his Thermal abilities to regulate his body temperature. None of the humans that walked by had called the cops on him for loitering, but most people didn't like to get involved.

Justus sat on the gritty step, the soles of his shoes crunching over the rough concrete with each slide of his foot. His left leg was extended and he leaned against the wall on his right shoulder—half asleep.

It bothered him that Page had stopped coming around. Whatever had started between them had been snuffed out faster than he could draw breath, but time hadn't quelled the insistent need he had to know she was safe. There was no rational explanation for his behavior, and it shamed him that he couldn't get it under control. She invaded his thoughts on a daily basis, and he was concerned that without a partner, she was overworking herself. Page was much like him and allowed work to consume her.

He felt her presence before she even spoke.

"Mr. De Gradi?"

A shiver snaked up his spine. It was her impersonal use of his name that gave him pause. He wanted to know why she didn't find him a worthy male, but pride kept his mouth wired shut and prevented him from seeking the truth. Why should he care? Justus could have any woman he wanted without all the strings to get tangled in.

"Apologies," he murmured, not lifting his eyes to meet hers.

"Are you drunk on my stoop?"

The glass bottle scraped against the concrete as his foot knocked it to the side. He couldn't keep his eyes focused and rubbed their corners. When he lowered his hands, Page came in to view.

She was wrapped up in a large black coat, watching him with her bewitching brown eyes. Her skin glowed, and he remembered how smooth it had felt beneath his fingertips and how sweet it had tasted against his tongue. Brown hair peeked out from the edge of the beige knit hat that flopped over loosely in the back. Had he forgotten how radiant a woman she was?

"What are you doing here? And why are you drinking outside my apartment?"

"Will you speak with me?" he asked. "Privately."

Her eyes darted around and she stuffed her bare hands in her coat pockets, sniffling as a gust of wind chilled the air.

"We can talk here, but I'm calling you a cab."

"Where is your car?"

"It's… Mr. De Gradi, this isn't about—"

"Don't call me that," he said harshly, rising to his feet.

"I'm sorry. I didn't want to get too personal."

He looked down at Page, who was holding on to the brick wall that led up to the doors. "Are you well?"

She smiled coyly. "I'm well. And you?"

"Inebriated, but well. You're right. We shouldn't have this conversation while I'm in this condition." He stumbled to the step below and she began to reach out to help but retracted her arm.

"Justus, please. Sit down and I'll hail you a cab. I think you're intelligent enough to know you're in no condition to drive."

She was right. The Mercedes Silver had bought him was parked a few paces up the road. He felt guilty about leaving it unattended, uncertain if it would send her a message that he cared little of her gift.

As if Page could read his mind, she made an offer.

"I have a reserved space in the indoor garage you can use. The parking in this city is just horrendous, but we're pretty lucky to have a five-story garage at the end of the street. I'm paid up through the year and my space is empty. I'll move your car."

"And walk home unescorted?"

Page tugged at the end of her hat and shivered. Her bulky coat didn't look warm enough for this weather, so he cranked up his internal thermostat, even knowing she'd feel none of it because she stood several feet away from him.

"Have you been able to manage your cases?"

Her inky lashes fanned down and she studied his shoes. "The Council offered me a partner and I turned them down."

"Why would you do that?" Justus took a few steps toward her and Page moved behind the wall that divided the space between them.

"Well, I went out to dinner with him so we could get to know each other."

The air must have heated up ten degrees. The thought of another man buying her dinner and putting his hands on her body lit a fire in Justus.

"Go on," he said in a placid voice.

Page rubbed her nose and shrugged with her eyebrows. "We didn't get along. He's a bright guy, but way too controlling and opinionated. I can see why his last partner left him. Most of the time, partners are male and female. Not really an arranged marriage, but a suggested one. He's been married for ten years and I think he was hoping the Council would pair him up with another man so his wife wouldn't get jealous. I got the vibe he doesn't think women are as intelligent as men. He told me he made his wife quit her job after they got married."

Fool. "And have you put in a request for another partner?"

"They offer their best candidate and if the match doesn't work, I'm on my own. Maybe it's better this way. I have a few connections and I'm going to see if anyone knows of a good lone Relic in need of a partner. I've been managing my cases, but I had to give up a few of my clients. It was tough."

That piqued his curiosity. "Who did you let go?"

"I thought about cutting the difficult ones I don't get along with, but they're my best-paying clients. So I made the decision to cut the ones who paid the least."

Justus set the bottle down and leaned on the wall. "I thought money didn't matter to you?"

Page worked her jaw a little and looked up at the building. "Things change. I'm a single woman and I was living on the wrong side of town. There were ten robberies and two rapes that happened in the old building while I lived there, but I couldn't afford to move anywhere else. Do you know why? I found out Slater was underpaying me. He controlled all the finances. I *knew* we had to be making good money, but he said after sending a cut to the Council and investing a portion of the money, it didn't leave us with much. I didn't know any better because I'd never had to deal with the finances. That asshole stole from me. Now I'm left with…"

"With what?"

Page shook her head and pulled her hat off, revealing a tangle of honey-brown hair. She threaded her fingers through the straight locks and brushed it away from her angelic face. He admired her delicate features, including the Cupid's bow of her upper lip. He'd never seen dark eyes so mesmerizing, and her creamy complexion appeared as if it had not been acquainted with the sun. Intelligence brimmed in her expressive eyes, and that was a bigger turn-on than he could have imagined.

"Answer the question, Page. What are you left with?"

"No future. No savings. I'm trying to rebuild what he stole from me. I'm not going to lie, Justus. Money intimidates the hell out of me. People are consumed by it—controlled by it. I've watched it happen, and those are the people who are the most dangerous. They think they can buy anything they want and that everything is replaceable."

"Is that why you severed our relationship?" he accused rather than asked.

Her words grew sharp. "I had my reasons. But yes, it bothered me to know how much you make. I got a glimpse at the real man beneath all that, but I've also seen the side of you that's controlled and influenced by materialism. How much is that watch on your wrist?" she asked, pointing at the gold Rolex accented with diamonds. "You're a Mage, and that means you're able to sense time without looking at a clock. So why buy a trinket you have no use for—one that probably costs more than a month of my rent? Haven't you ever considered alternative uses for that money? There are orphanages in the city, women's shelters, people who are struggling to make ends meet. Why not put your money to good use?"

"You assume I do not?"

Page immediately covered her face. "I'm so sorry. I have no right to judge you. I just didn't expect to see you sitting outside my door tonight and it took me off guard." She raised her arm and a cab slowed down. "I'm so glad to know you're doing well, Justus. I really am. To be honest, I don't know why you showed up here."

That was the moment Justus wanted to lay it on the line—tell her how consumed he was by the thought of her, and yet, his feet were cemented to the sidewalk. The words tangled in his throat and he knew his actions must have appeared irrational.

"Do you not have a man to care for you?"

"Talk about déjà vu," she said with a wistful grin. "No, I do not."

Perhaps she was lying, or maybe she didn't want to talk about her personal life with a drunk. Justus wanted to know who the other man was in her life that she was keeping a secret.

The brakes on the cab squealed as the car rolled up to the curb and parked, smoke billowing out of the exhaust pipe.

"Can I have the keys to your car? I'll make sure it's taken care of," she said, holding out her hand. When he didn't move, her fingers curled inward and she suppressed a grin, but he still caught it. "Promise I won't take it for a spin all over the city. This is a safe neighborhood and it's a short walk. If it'll make you feel better, my neighbor won't mind if I call him down and ask if he can walk me, although his wife might. She's sweet, but retirement doesn't suit her."

Justus fished his hands in his pockets and gave it some thought.

This would mean he'd have to see her again and he wasn't sure how he felt about that. Jealousy stirred in him when he considered asking if she had been intimate with another man. It wasn't his place, but maybe what he was feeling toward her was a sense of claim on something no other man had known. *Irrational indeed.*

"It's a black Mercedes. I want you to go upstairs and have your neighbor drive you to the garage in my car before escorting you home. Do you understand?"

"Of course," she replied, her gaze steady. Page took the keys from his hand and tucked them in her coat pocket.

The wall separated them, but it felt like more than distance stood between them.

An awkward pause hung in the air as Justus staggered and rubbed his face. He didn't have to sober up to recognize he had made a spectacle of himself.

"I'll have Simon pick up the car tomorrow. My apologies for interrupting your evening; I will keep you no longer."

It was an arduous walk to the cab, but once inside, he stole a glimpse of Page walking up the steps as the car sped away.

Silver would soon be leaving him. It was only a matter of time now that she had accepted Logan's claim. A moment of independence Justus had once looked forward to was now met with an unexpected sense of loss.

He would be alone again.

CHAPTER 6

After Logan fell asleep beside me in the hidden room, I slipped into the Grey Veil and called for Justus. It was a place he'd once showed me that existed in the subconscious—a place he'd created. My Ghuardian possessed quite a few gifts, this being one of them. He'd once told me not all rare gifts serve a valuable purpose, but I disagreed. Going to the Grey Veil had once saved my life.

The ability to visit was easier when I'd recently taken some of his light, which I'd done during a training session a few days prior after breaking my finger during a maneuver. Anyone he'd shared his light with could visit, provided Justus had shown them the way.

It required concentration to enter this realm. I don't know what I was expecting to find—Justus lounging around on top of the black rock, fishing in the crystal waters? I admired the calm beauty and bathed myself in sunlight.

It seemed like ages since I'd last visited, yet nothing had changed. I wondered if this place held any significance. The trees were tall and whispered secrets as the wind tickled their green leaves. The early morning light filtered onto the clear water, capturing its reflective qualities and creating a ripple of sparkles across the surface. In the distance, I could hear woodpeckers and other strange sounds from within the forest.

"Ghuardian?"

"Silver?"

I whirled around and blinked in surprise at Logan. "What are you doing here?"

"Dreamwalking, I suppose. Why did you come here?"

Logan had the ability to dreamwalk but couldn't do so with

everyone. While the Grey Veil had restrictions on who could visit, the doors weren't locked for my inquisitive Chitah.

"Logan, you're not supposed to be here."

He folded his arms and it was then I noticed his long hair. I felt rueful looking at it, remembering how I'd cut it off in an attempt to sever our relationship.

"Female, you were turning in your sleep and I sensed distress."

"I'm trying to find Justus. I'm worried."

He chuckled softly and touched my shoulders. "And is this how it will be when you move away from him? Am I to worry that each night he doesn't answer your call, you will be here looking for him?"

A gust of wind lifted my raven locks and Logan stepped forward, capturing a strand of hair between his fingers and leaning down to take in my scent.

"He'll always be my Ghuardian. That doesn't go away if I move out."

Logan cocked his head to the side, staring down at me with bright, animalistic eyes. "If?"

"You want me to stay with Justus temporarily, but he's the one who makes the call on when I'm ready for independence. I'm a Mage, first and foremost. I still need to learn to protect my light because five hundred years from now, I'm still going to be a Mage. I'm not sure if one or two years is sufficient for me to learn what I need to know."

Logan gently bent down, as soft as a whisper, and brushed his lips against my cheek. "I will wait for you."

"Rubbish," Simon said from the edge of the woods where he was leaning against a maple tree. I laughed at the long johns that snugly fit his body. He waved his arm at a monarch butterfly that landed on his crotch and began spreading its wings.

"Simon, what are you doing here?"

"Better here than where I was. Brought home a lovely little strumpet last night who just so happens to be a marathon runner. Now there's a woman with stamina."

I snorted. "So you left her alone to hang out in the woods?"

He looked away and I caught a flash of his tongue ring as he yawned. "As it turns out, that girl is sexual napalm. She's the kind that'll wear you out so you have no energy to fight her when she starts moving in. She's in the other room now, actually making breakfast!" He made a gruff sound and approached us with his arms folded. "I don't do domestic."

"Then kick her out instead of following me around," I suggested.

His voice rose an octave and his hands became animated. "I knew she was at the club shopping for a husband based on the hints she dropped in conversation, but bloody hell, she had the best set of knockers. I feel like such a prat for bringing her home—I have somewhere I need to be."

Logan cleared his throat and stood with his arms at his sides. "Perhaps if you found a female of worth, you would have no need to put your cock in every hole it finds."

I covered my mouth to keep from laughing and Simon flashed him a peevish glance. "Bugger off."

"Simon, have you heard from Justus?"

He stretched his arms and his long johns slid down his narrow waist just a little. "Your Ghuardian's at home with a hangover. Serves him right."

Relief washed over me and I relaxed my shoulders. "Logan, I want you to drive me back to Lucian's to pick up my car. I need to head home and make sure everything's all right."

Simon stepped between us. "And why is your car over at Lucian's house?"

"Because we were attacked," Logan said before I could stop him.

Without taking his eyes from mine, Simon said, "By whom?"

I bit my lip and glanced at a butterfly caught in the breeze. "Nero's men. They were out for Finn."

He drew in a sharp breath and held it for a minute. "Nero wants you to surrender to him. I thought he was out for revenge at first, but that's not his style. He's the kind of man with an agenda. Getting back at a woman by stalking her friends is not something an ancient Mage would do. He still wants you, Silver. He wants your addictive light because it's strong. I gather he's trying to make sense of the documents he stole from the truck and hasn't quite pieced it all together yet. The boxes will only titillate his feeble mind but not provide him with all the answers he's seeking. I suspect he's still collecting humans to turn into one of us."

"Adam told me that during Nero's attack, he revealed he had an Infuser."

"Fancy that," Simon said sarcastically.

Merc, the former Councilman who had betrayed the Mageri and died, had possessed the ability to pull core light from a Mage, rendering them human. But he could never hold on to it and the light would dissipate within a day. We'd found out he was working with Nero, but without an Infuser, they weren't able to seal core light into Nero's light.

Now that he had an Infuser, all he needed was someone with Merc's ability. If Nero found a way to steal gifts from a Mage, there's no telling how powerful he could become.

"Nero has quite a harem," Simon murmured. "Not likely any of them is a Unique, but it's possible they have extremely rare gifts due to the method by which Samil created them, in combination with their unusual genes. Their light must be strong if he paid for them."

"If he finds someone with Merc's gift, then we're all in trouble. Knowing Nero, he would have the light of a Creator put in him so he can weed out the middleman," I said. "The lab documents he stole may not tell him much, but he'll notice the names and piece together what Samil was up to. If he gains the ability to make his own progeny, then nothing will stop him. I don't know if he's keeping them long enough to find a way to steal their powers or if he's trying to build an army."

Simon laughed and walked to the edge of the water where he dipped his toe in the stream. "I wager he was trying to find a way to absorb their gifts. Maybe his initial intent was to build an army, but it would take years of brainwashing to get a man of free will to join his little camp. Maybe he's been doing just that. Do you remember Ray?"

"Ray?" I thought about it and Simon glanced over his shoulder. "The guy I helped from Nero's compound? That Ray?"

"The very one. Three months ago, he was arrested by Enforcers and is now facing punishment by the Mageri."

"Holy shit. What for?"

The last I'd heard, Ray wanted to start a new life. I'd found out Samil had kept Ray as his progeny before turning him over to Nero. Perhaps that early influence made him weak.

Simon hitched up the back of his white long johns and scraped a hand through his messy brown hair. "Attempted murder of a Councilman. *Attempted* murder won't get noticed by the Mageri unless it's against one of their appointed leaders. They hired me to do a little investigation and computer hacking. Looks like Nero had gotten to him after all. Whether he was with him all along, blackmailed, or Nero paid him a substantial fee, Ray was a man with an agenda."

"But why kill someone on the Council? What does that accomplish?"

Simon shrugged. "They're looking into it; my job is done. If I had to guess, I'd say the man he tried to assassinate was interfering with Nero's plans, either directly or indirectly. Highly doubtful it's a plan of revenge, but your former captor is a man with a purpose, and I suspect his ultimate goal is to dismantle the justice system."

I rubbed my face in frustration.

"Ask me to hunt him," Logan said in slow words.

I peered through my fingers and saw he wasn't talking to Simon but looking down at me. "What?"

Logan stepped closer and the hairs on my arms stood up.

"If you ask me to hunt him, I will. I've offered my assistance with the investigation, but no one has specifically asked me to—"

"No. Absolutely not." I shook my head and Simon gave me a look with the tilt of his head. "Logan, I thought I'd lost you when you fought against Tarek. I can't go through that again."

"And I can't stand here knowing my female and my brothers are being hunted down like prey. Turn the tables and let me sink my teeth into that Mage's neck until his blood runs cold."

"Silver, it's not a bad idea," Simon interjected.

"You get back to your bacon-frying trollop and leave us alone! I don't want you putting any ideas into his head."

The next thing I knew, I was shaken awake and lying on the sofa in Logan's secret room. Only the corner lamp was on, but I could see Logan's face clearly.

I blinked a few times and stared up at him with wide eyes. The black rims around the amber looked engorged. "Finn's hurt."

Startled by his words, I vaulted off the sofa, gripping the back of his sweats as Logan hurried out the door. The light from inside the apartment blinded me and I squinted as he tugged me toward the living room.

"What happened? Is he okay?"

"I scented distress and forced myself awake," he said, circling behind the couch.

I carefully stepped around pieces of glass sprinkled across the floor, but the windows weren't broken out all the way. They looked like the cracked windshield of a car after an accident. The shutters hung askew, and the curtain rod had fallen down. In the center of the window was a hole big enough to put your head and arm through, blood all around the surrounding glass. There were spatters of it everywhere and puddles on the floor.

"The laminated glass was punched out," he said, pointing to the bloody hole. "This wasn't a Vampire—one of them would have knocked out the entire window."

"Chitah?"

"I can't tell, but it's a good thing they didn't make it inside. I didn't see a body outside the building. If he fell, it wasn't to his death."

The door crashed in and Logan whirled around, protectively shielding me with his body.

Christian strolled into the room and flicked his eyes around. "If either of you lost a fecking Chitah, he's tucked away in the dumpster downstairs."

I glanced around, looking for the wolf. "Where's Finn?"

Logan touched my shoulder. "He's in the kitchen. I got him to shift once but he needs to keep on—"

I flew past him and Logan snatched my arm.

"Let me go!"

"Silver, he's hurt. He might also be in human form without clothes."

I looked at him incredulously. "I hate to break this to you now, but I've seen a naked man before." I jerked my arm free and quickened my pace toward the kitchen. The lights were bright, illuminating the gruesome display on the tile.

Beside the kitchen island, Finn's wolf lay on his side, unconscious and bleeding from the neck or shoulder—I couldn't tell which. Blood was caked in his fur and streaked across the floor.

Logan held a rag beneath the faucet and then placed it over his wound.

"Can't you heal him?" I begged. Chitahs could heal superficial wounds by use of their saliva.

"Not as a wolf," he said. "There's too much fur. I found him in human form and worked on his neck a little, but the wounds are too deep. I think his wolf fought off the attacker and the glass cut him up bad—unless the man had a knife. He needs to shift."

I glanced up at Logan while holding Finn's paw. "He's unconscious, Logan. We'll never get him to shift, and Finn once told me it's easier to make a human shift to a wolf than vice versa. We need a Relic."

Logan's fangs punched out and his face contorted in anger. "The man who did this will pay."

"He already did," Christian said.

I shook my head in disbelief. "We don't have time for this."

Logan's voice rose to a shout. "He could have killed Finn! When I'm dreamwalking, I'm not as attuned to what's going on around me. He could have slaughtered us in our sleep!"

Blood soaked the rag Logan held against Finn's neck and my heart raced like a hummingbird in my chest. I scrambled to the hall and dug frantically through my purse.

"Who are you calling?"

"Page. She'll know what to do."

"You called the right person," Page said, pulling her hat off her head. "Where is he?"

"Follow me." Logan opened the hallway closet that led to the adjacent apartment.

Page looked apprehensively at the kitchen on her left, noticing the blood smears all over the floor. When the closet door closed behind us, the wall opened up. Logan kicked aside some of his sneakers and we stepped into the room. Christian stayed behind so he could call the cleaners to take care of the Chitah.

I switched on a few desk lamps and Page knelt in front of Finn's wolf with her medical bag. He was sprawled out in the center of the room in front of the sofa. "I've treated all different kinds of Breeds and try to keep my clientele diverse, but Shifters are who I specialize in on a daily basis. Slater never wanted to deal with them and always took our Mage or Vampire clients because they paid better."

A Relic served as a consultant—not unlike having a doctor, therapist, and researcher rolled up in one. Relics provided insight to the abilities or limitations of different Breeds. Page sometimes dealt with Mage clients, but what she knew of them was basic. There were too many gifts and nuances she hadn't learned in detail. Her ancestors had specialized in Uniques, a rare type of Mage. It might be comparable to knowing a little about Ford cars in general but being an expert when it comes to Ford Mustangs.

While hunched over Finn, she opened her black bag and pulled out an injection needle and a few other items.

I bit my nail and nervously watched as she shaved a small area on his leg. "What are you giving him?"

"Can I ask Logan to leave the room?"

Logan strolled toward her and leered down. "And what is your reason for suggesting I abandon my brother to bleed out on the floor?"

She peered up at him with doe eyes. Logan could intimidate the hell out of anyone, even if it wasn't intentional.

"Because if you flip your switch in here, Chitah, I could get hurt. This is a precautionary measure to protect the person who is trying to help your brother. He'll have a reaction to the injection, and I can't afford to take any chances. Do you want to risk harming a woman because you couldn't control your impulses?"

Logan pressed his lips together tightly, conceding defeat. She was right; if Logan lost a grip on his emotions, it could be dangerous for Page because she'd be the one administering the shot.

"I'll come right out if we need you," I promised. "Can you call Justus and let him know what's going on? He'll probably reach out to Leo, but my Ghuardian needs to be aware of the danger we're in. I'll take care of Finn; maybe you should clean up."

Logan had blood smeared across his bare chest and stains on his grey sweats from carrying Finn's body. His bare feet had picked up some of it from the floor and tracked it around.

Without a word, he quietly left the room and looked on the verge of erupting in anger. It was a good thing Page had asked him to leave because I was certain he would have flipped his switch and gone primal. I knew Logan wouldn't have hurt me, but no matter how protective Chitahs are of women, I couldn't guarantee Page's safety.

I stroked Finn's fur and tears stained my cheeks. "This won't hurt him, will it?"

After pushing out the air bubbles from the tip of the needle, she flicked the end with her finger. "No. I came up with a solution that forces a Shifter to change. It helps when they're unconscious or unwilling and need to heal. I'm not sharing this solution with anyone outside of a few trusted Relics. It's helpful to us for obvious reasons, but people always seem to find a way to use good things for wicked deeds. Stand back, Silver. Sometimes there's a dramatic reaction."

I stood up and stepped back a few feet. "What do you mean by dramatic?"

With lightning speed, Page inserted the needle into his leg, pushed the plunger, and yanked the syringe out. She'd begun to get up when Finn's wolf flipped onto his feet in a violent motion and knocked her down. Finn thrashed and snarled as if attacking an invisible entity only he could see. Within seconds, his body moved like liquid and transformed into his human form.

I grabbed the red throw from the sofa and draped it across his lower body. "Finn, are you okay? Can you hear me? It's Silver."

He moaned and coughed, rolling onto his back. I smoothed my hands around his neck and shoulder, noticing the wounds were no longer visible. His eyes rolled back and he lost consciousness again.

"Page? Is he…"

When I looked over my shoulder, Page was still on the floor, lying on her side.

I crawled over and moved some of her hair away from her face. "Are you hurt?"

"Is he healed?"

"Yes, I don't see any wounds on his neck."

"Good. He'll sleep for about six hours. There's a strong sedative in the solution."

Page still hadn't moved and her voice sounded off.

"Here, let me help you sit up."

I pulled her to a sitting position and she unzipped the front of her coat. A bead of sweat rolled down her temple and her cheeks were flushed. Without asking, I pulled her coat away because she hadn't bothered to take it off when she'd come flying through the door.

"Wait, Silver. It's fine."

"Don't be ridiculous. You're going to burn up in that thing if you—"

I froze. All the blood drained from my head and rendered me speechless. The jacket fell halfway off her shoulders, revealing an unexpected and shocking revelation.

She moved her arms away from her body and exposed her swollen belly.

Page was pregnant.

CHAPTER 7

Once Finn had shifted and healed himself, Logan carried him to the living room sofa. I brought in a couple of soft blankets and a change of clothes. Logan knelt down beside Finn and washed away the congealed blood from his hair and neck.

I left the two alone so Logan could care for the young Shifter he considered a brother. When the cleaners arrived, Christian went outside to show them the dead Chitah and give a statement. These men were legit and would report their findings to the authorities.

After sweeping up glass and mopping the kitchen floor, I put on Logan's brown sweater and went to the kitchen to make cocoa. Page carefully sat on one of the stools and rubbed her tired eyes. She kept her coat on and wanted to talk with me privately about her condition.

"When did this happen?" I began. "You seem so... big."

She smiled and set down her green coffee cup. "Thanks. That's what every woman wants to hear."

"I just mean you're bigger than Sunny, and she's got twins. How far along are you? And how the hell have you managed to keep this a secret?"

"I'm not even four months."

I gasped, bumping my drink as my arm flew out. "That's impossible! Are you having sextuplets or something?"

She took a long, unsteady breath and another sip of cocoa. Her unpolished fingernail pushed a marshmallow beneath the frothy surface.

"It's Slater's baby. As far as the accelerated gestation, I'm not sure what's causing it, but I think it has to do with whatever Slater injected me with."

"What can you remember about the kidnapping? Maybe I can help."

"Only Slater knows what he did to me, and now Slater's dead. The secret is buried with him and I'll never know. Whatever he injected me with, the other two men weren't aware of it. They collected information from me for testing, but at night when they left, Slater pumped me up with a concoction of his own. When the doctors began giving me their own injections, I just lost it. I screamed and struggled so much they had to sedate me. I tried to get Slater to talk to me, but he wouldn't give up any information. He just said he was sorry it had to come to this."

That bastard, I thought to myself. What kind of low-down, dirty man would do something like that, all for the sake of getting a woman pregnant with his baby?

"What did he say when he showed up at your apartment before the kidnapping?" I asked.

She tugged absently on the straight tips of her brown hair. "He said he wanted to help me. I tried to talk reason into him, but he was going to do what he wanted regardless."

"But why you, Page? Why go through all that trouble just to have a baby with someone who isn't even a willing partner? Couldn't he find someone else?"

"It's a Relic thing. There are those who come from esteemed families, and mine is one of them. He wanted to combine our genetics. If you want to call it anything, call it ego."

"Great way to bring a child into the world."

She covered her face and sniffed. "I'm so scared, Silver. I'm afraid of what's growing inside me. I can't pinpoint the exact day, but based on the accelerated growth, I'm probably just a few weeks away from going into labor. God, what did he do to me?"

I caught her wrist and lowered her hand. "You're not alone, Page. Is this why you broke up with Justus?"

She turned her head and appeared emotionally spent. "I saved him the disgrace of knowing the kind of woman he took into his bed. He would have never wanted me with another man's baby. Aside from that, it's too dangerous to raise children among Breed. Relics still live in the human world—our kids go to school and the only interaction we have with immortals is through our jobs. It's not the same as with Chitahs, for example, because they have healing abilities. Relics accept the risks that come with raising children because we ourselves are mortal. It would never have worked out between us, Silver. A Mage has no desire to raise children; it's something they choose to give up when they enter this life."

"You don't think Justus would accept the baby? He's a man who would do the right thing," I offered.

Although, I said it with hesitation. Justus had professed it was an honor to be a paternal figure, but that didn't mean he wanted a baby. Aside from that, he would realize the danger. The wrong amount of energy in his hands could kill her child. Justus was also a member of HALO, and that placed him in a respectable position. Many opposing forces, such as Nero, perceived HALO as traitors for sharing information among different Breeds. That put anyone he cared for in danger, including myself. I didn't know if he had the kind of commitment it would take to protect a mortal child, let alone the ability.

"It's not fair to ask that of a man you've only known for a night or two."

"He cares for you, Page."

She wrung her hands together and placed them in her lap, glancing down at her belly. "I couldn't ask a man to love me *that* much."

"Maybe you should give him the choice. You changed him, whether you realize it or not. He's a great man, and you brought that out in him in the short time you were together. Who am I to judge when it's love? Five minutes, five decades—in your heart, you know when you love someone."

Her voice trembled and fell to a whisper. "I have too much to deal with right now."

"Have you seen a Relic?"

"Not since the night I left Justus. Remember when I became ill at your house? The Relic came by and after an examination, she revealed I was pregnant and how far along. I was just sick to my stomach and needed to get away from everyone to think it through."

"So you haven't seen a Relic since? Maybe you should call the old bat."

Page chuckled softly and her eyes brightened. "She's not so bad. She just takes the bitter pill in the morning."

"She's a pill all right."

"I'm afraid someone might try to hurt me or the baby if they find out. You know how the Breed condemns those who are different, and genetic testing has always been a nasty rumor. If people knew the truth, they would hunt and kill us out of fear. That includes you too, Silver."

"Well, they can join the club," I said with a smirk. "They'll have to stand in line with everyone else coming after me these days." I got up and dumped my cocoa in the sink, then rinsed out the cup.

"That's the life I'm trying to save this baby from. I'll love him no matter what, but I want him to have a normal life. Can you keep this between us for now?" she asked, easing out of the chair and supporting her lower back with her hands. "This puffy coat can pretty much throw anyone off, and lately I've been seeing my clients through the Internet. I think some of them have grown suspicious, but I told them I've been ill. I probably won't be leaving my apartment much until the birth."

"I just can't believe this," I said in a breath, watching her zip up her coat and pop a marshmallow into her mouth. "You need a Relic. Who's going to deliver the baby? Don't you know someone you can trust?"

A worry line formed and she touched her hair. "If you want to know the truth, I have no idea what to do. I haven't had enough time to really figure out the answer because of how fast the pregnancy is moving along."

I stepped forward, holding out my hand. "Is it kicking?"

A smile relaxed her face and it was mischievous, with a little hook at the corner of her mouth. "Just the last couple of weeks it started all of a sudden. At first, I thought maybe the baby wasn't alive because I didn't feel anything. Now he's running a marathon in there."

"That's a good sign."

She unzipped her coat enough for me to place my palm on her

firm belly. Page moved my hand to the left. "Here," she said.

I felt a hard push against my palm. "Wow! He's going to be a kickboxer."

Page's smile waned and she zipped up her coat. "He's my little fighter. I just hope he won't have to do it all his life if he isn't normal."

I laughed and jutted out my hip. "Haven't you heard? Normal is out. Mutants are all the rage. Just look at me; I turned out okay, right?"

The door to the closet clicked open. Logan rubbed the back of his neck and walked past Page, then eased up beside me. "Can I make you breakfast?" His soft lips touched my neck and I playfully pinched his earlobe.

"After all that drama, I don't think I'll be hungry for a while."

"Mmm, but I seem to have an appetite for lemon cake all of a sudden," he growled in my ear.

Page looked away, a blush rising on her neck and face. "I should be going. Finn needs rest after he wakes up, but make sure he eats plenty of protein and greens. If he shows any unusual symptoms or behavior, please call me right away. I've never had any adverse reactions from the injection, but just keep an eye on him."

She glanced down at her bag on the floor and I realized she was going to give away her secret if she tried to bend over and pick it up.

"Here, let me get that and I'll walk you out. Did you drive?"

A melodic laugh flew out of her mouth and she handed me a key. "I borrowed your Ghuardian's car, so I'll go ahead and leave it here with you. Just let him know that Simon doesn't need to come get it. I'll hail a cab."

"Do you need an escort?" Logan asked.

His nose twitched and his tone seemed off. I also noticed his brow was pushed over his eyes and he wasn't acting himself.

"No, I'm fine," she insisted. "I hope you find a safe place to stay. I'm sorry to see this attack happened, but the Shifter will heal. You know how to reach me, and I'm always available. Have a good morning."

Page saw herself out and as I was lifting her cup from the kitchen island, Logan captured my wrist and set the mug down.

"What ails that female?"

Damn, that man could scent a lie. I could tell he was reading my emotions—tasting them on his tongue and interpreting every layer.

"She's just getting over something."

Logan narrowed his golden eyes and drew in quick puffs of air. It was animalistic the way he'd pull in a scent, from the intense look in his eyes to the movement of his tall and powerful body. I stepped back and Logan corralled me against the cabinet, placing his arms on either side of me.

"Is that female with child?"

"Logan, you can't tell anyone. There's no sense in me lying because you'd figure it out on your own, but Page swore me to secrecy. It means a lot that she trusts me, and I've already broken her trust by telling you, but it can hardly be helped. Please don't say anything. I can't go into the details because it's not for me to tell."

He cupped his large hands beneath my jaw and slid them back until his fingers slipped into my hair. I could never tire of feeling that man's lips on mine, of his gentle approach, the sweet taste of mint on his breath, and the moment his grip tightened on the back of my neck as he slid his tongue in my mouth. Logan wrapped his arms around me and lifted me onto the cabinet, but I didn't give him my mouth. He leaned in and when I pulled back, his lips twitched in amusement.

"On my word as a Chitah, your secret is safe."

"Thank you, Mr. Cross," I said, intoxicated by his presence.

I leaned back on my hands while he explored the slope of my breast with his nose, taking in my scent.

"Do you know what attracted me to you on the night we met?" he asked.

"You mean the night you kidnapped me?"

Without missing a beat, he ran his tongue along my neck and kissed the soft patch of skin beneath my ear. I melted a little, hooking my ankles around the back of his legs.

"Your tenacity. I hadn't felt desire for a woman in years until the moment you talked back and challenged me to a fight. Keep the fire within you burning and always be honest with me. You have no idea what a turn-on it is to have your trust."

"So whenever I tell you the truth, it works like an aphrodisiac?"

A subtle scent wafted in the air and had an immediate impact on my body. My breath hitched when his fingers unexpectedly slipped beneath my shirt and gently smoothed their way up my back. His mouth found the curve of my jaw and he worked his delicate kisses all the way down to my chin.

"Are you going to let me go?" I whispered.

His mouth hovered over mine and desire licked over my body. "On one condition."

My breath bounced back against his and the energy between us was fierce. The butterflies returned when I caught him staring ardently into my eyes. A vibration rose deep within his throat.

"What's that?"

His lips lightly brushed against mine. "Kiss me, Little Raven."

Logan had connections and called a professional to repair the living room window. We were lucky the attacker hadn't been able to get inside through the main door, but that hadn't deterred him from scaling the outside ledges and crossing over some of the neighboring balconies.

I drove the new Mercedes home and Logan tailed me in his car, Finn asleep in the back seat. Levi was at work and Lucian didn't seem to be a reliable option. In any case, Logan felt responsible for what had happened and said it was his job to make sure Finn was taken care of. Passing him off to someone else would set a bad example.

Logan wasn't amused when I pulled up to a drive-through and ordered breakfast. These men were going to be starving by the time we reached the house, so I decided to grab a few sacks of biscuits, sausages, hash browns, and pancakes. I cracked the windows so Justus's new car wouldn't smell like fast food. I paid the cashier using my Ember Gates card, which connected to a shared account with my Ghuardian. Justus denied it, but I knew he still monitored my charges daily.

The temperature was ten degrees above freezing and hardly noticeable, thanks to the intense heat from the sun. As soon as I pulled up the driveway and neared the garage, the door lifted and Justus ducked beneath it. He walked toward my car with a powerful stride.

"Uh-oh," I muttered.

He passed my car and approached the driver's side of Logan's car behind me, then leaned in the window. I drove the sleek black Mercedes into the garage and parked farther down to the left. His massive garage could fit an airplane.

I gathered up the sacks of biscuits in my arms and got out of the car. Logan pulled in and parked behind me. Before the engine shut off, I saw Justus carrying Finn to the elevators.

"What's going on?" I asked.

Logan was supposed to go back home and check on the guy repairing his window.

He slammed the door and stuffed his hands into the pockets of his black jacket. "Your Ghuardian wants us to stay here for the night."

"You are kidding me."

Justus had slowly been warming up to Logan, but he'd never offered to let him sleep over. The times that Logan had stayed, it was at my request.

"Novis is on his way over."

My heart did a flip-flop. "What's going on? Is there something you're not telling me?"

"I guess we'll find out."

I peeled off my coat, hung it on a hook, and walked through the quiet house.

"Ghuardian?"

Justus came out of the guest hall on the left. We never used the rooms off that hall—they mirrored our living quarters so an intruder wouldn't suspect a lower floor.

"How long will he remain that way?" Justus asked.

Logan unzipped his jacket and slung it over a chair. "The Relic said a few hours. I want him locked up in that room until I'm certain he won't shift." Logan lowered his voice and leaned in toward Justus, so slightly it was barely perceptible. "You have my gratitude for offering your home to us for the night. The windows will be repaired by morning."

Justus rubbed his hand across his tattoo and dragged his eyes over to mine. There was a pregnant pause as he folded his arms and stepped in front of Logan in a confrontational stance.

I tensed.

"This will be your new home."

My jaw slackened.

Logan looked at me sideways. I shook my head to confirm my disbelief.

Justus continued. "You have proven yourself as a man of worth, one who has stood by my Learner's side and who has put your life on the line so that she might live. I cannot sit idly by while your life is at risk; it is not the honorable thing to do. You've had more than my gratitude over the past year, for I have been in your debt."

Those were heavy words. Monetary gain held less value than collecting on debts. Favors were paramount among Breed—we all honored them and you could collect at any time. That's a valuable coin for an immortal to have in his pocket.

Logan stood up straight and glowered at Justus. "I did not save her life for the purpose of placing you in my debt. This is not something that requires payment."

Justus had inadvertently insulted Logan. It was subtle, but Logan's reaction had been immediate.

"This is nonnegotiable," Justus countered. "I'm not making this offer as a friendly gesture, but as a preventive measure. Yes, I am in your debt and this will clear that away. But there have been some recent developments that have put us *all* in immediate danger."

"And you think hiding away in a bunker like a cockroach is the dignified thing to do? I'm sorry, Justus, but this is where we disagree. If you run from something, you only become prey. Maybe you manage to save your own life, but at what expense? Your dignity, *that's* what. Life is full of peril, and at any moment we could be taken."

"Had the Shifter been killed, would you still feel the same?"

Logan pointed his finger in my Ghuardian's face. I stood speechless, uncertain of how to defuse the situation.

"That Shifter had lived his entire life in slavery. He'd never known freedom until we released him from captivity. The only life he'd had was one of fear. He was too afraid to escape, knowing the punishment would be severe. Now he has tasted freedom, and freedom always comes at a price. Can he be snuffed out by some maniacal traitor with an agenda of war? Yes. But for the first time in his life, he knows what it feels like to have a choice about something as simple as an ice cream flavor. He's discovering his identity through his clothes, and his mind is opening because of an education he never had access to. Finn has become a man who can think for himself, make decisions, and put his footprint on this world. Those are the fundamental things all men strive for and die for. If you take that from a man, they are no longer alive. What is the value of a life unlived—of a person who refuses freedom only so they may draw another breath? Had he been taken last night, I would be proud of the life he's lived in the short time he's had with me. I would not regret that I didn't shove him away in a closet to protect him. Life is more than a heartbeat, Mage. It's the essence of our souls and the fiber of our beings. It is the breath of imagination within our souls; it's the fire in our hearts that burns for change and progress. Extinguish the fire and you have killed the man, even if he still draws breath."

Justus cracked a smile and chuckled softly, stepping back and dragging his eyes to mine. "I always knew I liked him for a reason. We can continue to argue about this, or you can wait until Novis arrives. There is much to discuss." His eyes flicked down to a paper sack I still held in my hand—the others I had put on the kitchen counter.

I swung my eyes between the two men. "Um, anyone feel like pancakes?"

CHAPTER 8

Adam relaxed on his black motorcycle outside Northern Lights. Tonight's act was attracting a sizeable crowd and the parking lot had quickly filled up, including a gang of bikers who had given Adam the once-over when he drove by them. He shut off the engine and removed his helmet, running his fingers through the tangles in his hair. Adam kept his thick hair a little long on top because it had a slight wave and never looked right if he kept it closely trimmed.

Oliver had asked to meet outside the club. He said he didn't care for crowds, but Adam suspected that as a human, he felt the parking lot was neutral ground that would allow him to bail more easily. He'd adamantly refused when Adam offered to swing by the hotel.

To be fair, it was a smart move. Men with information should never be in a situation where they're not in control.

A group of men made catcalls at two young women sauntering toward the main door. The men leered while adjusting their packages. The girls must have left their jackets in the car, and they wore slinky dresses and swung their hips like pendulums. Adam parked at a respectable distance from the front entrance, close enough to hear the chatter.

"Fuck off," one of the girls said, her middle finger proud and high. Laughter erupted from the crowd and they cheered as the girls made their way inside.

The bar had a classic appeal with its brick exterior and dark windows. The sign had Northern Lights written in off-white italics on a panel that shifted colors from green to purple, just like the aurora borealis. Someone had attempted to decorate one of the windows with yellow twinkle lights, but half of them were hanging askew.

Adam scraped his black boot along the gravel and kept his hands tucked in the warm pockets of his leather jacket. A few flecks of snow swirled in the air but melted as soon as they hit the ground. The smoky aroma of flame-broiled hamburgers filled the air and made his stomach growl.

"Razor, you gotta be shitting me. You ride that thing out in this weather?"

Adam turned around and watched Oliver hop onto the open bed of a pickup truck. He sat down on the tailgate and wiped his hands on his black jeans.

"It's Adam. I don't go by Razor anymore," he said, inching up to the edge of the truck.

Oliver swung his legs, drawing attention to his bright orange running shoes.

Good thing Knox isn't here, Adam thought. *He would have yanked them off his feet and hurled them into the sewer.*

"Adam Shmadam," he replied. "Not a very tough-guy name for someone who's Breed."

"I suppose Oliver is about as badass as it gets," Adam said, leaning against the truck on his right arm.

"Damn skippy. Look, I'm still working for the SF and you know they run a tight ship. Meaning no leaks. My ass is on the line by coming here, although they think I'm on vacation in Maui, which is where I *should* be. Instead, I'm sitting in the sinkhole of Cognito—metropolis of paranormal and freaky-deaky shit. Did you know this city is more populous with Breed than anywhere else in the nation? Cognito doesn't stack up to a few countries in Europe, but I'm about as comfy here as a piglet in a smokehouse."

"Look, I know the deal. You feel like your ass is on the line, and in some ways, it is. But if you get busted, then it won't be because of me."

"Can you guys read minds?" Oliver took off his glasses and nervously polished the lenses. "I keep going around humming this irritating '80s song to block my thoughts—the stuff I know could start a war."

"No, we aren't mind readers," Adam said, pushing away from

the truck and pacing in a circle. He kicked a few pebbles and glanced up at Oliver, who was looking at Adam's scars. His eyes quickly sailed up at a streetlamp and then back down to his shoes.

"Is it safe out here?" Oliver asked with a nervous smile, tucking his glasses in his shirt pocket beneath the windbreaker he wore.

Adam glanced around. "Some of us have exceptional hearing, but no place is safe. Inside or outside, it doesn't matter. I can't take you into a Breed bar that has private rooms because you're a human. I also don't have the authority to put you on the list. It's doubtful any Breed are lurking about in this area; most of us prefer to hang out with our own kind. If anyone is listening, then he won't know what the hell he's hearing anyhow. To be honest, Oliver, most don't give a shit about other people's affairs. They've heard it all and tend to tune out anything that doesn't directly affect them."

Which was the truth. Vampires could hear a pin drop across a room, but he'd come to realize that half weren't listening. A guy had once told him that after four hundred years of hearing people's conversations, he could give a rat's ass if they were revealing the location of the lost city of gold. Vamps worked as guards or were hired to spy on specific individuals, but most were aloof and the majority were assholes.

Oliver lifted his legs and stood up on the tailgate of the truck. "If that's the case, then *all you fuckers can go to hell!*" he shouted into the darkness.

Adam yanked him down by his shirt and Oliver hit the ground hard. He didn't have time for this shit. Adam knelt down and gave him his scary face. "Keep that in check. Just because they don't care what comes out of your mouth doesn't mean they won't skin you alive for insulting them. And don't ever throw out a challenge unless you're ready to accept the consequences. Now get up before those bikers come over here and chain your ankles to the back of a city bus."

Oliver dusted off one of his shoes as he stood up. "I'm only here because Knox was a guy I respected. I know he hated my ass, but he was someone I could trust. When he left, he said it wasn't too late for me to check out before I got in too deep. But you know what? I worked my ass off to get where I am. Yeah, maybe it's corrupt, but you'll find that everywhere. If all the good guys bail, then what are you left with? It's a stepping-stone and maybe that's why I don't feel warm fuzzies about putting my ass on the line by talking to you. But I'm here because it mattered to Knox. I won't be square with him until I give you everything I would have given him. Run with it and do what you want, I don't care. This is my closure, and I'm still pissed as hell a guy like him went down." His nostrils flared and his lips formed a grim line as he kicked the ground hard.

"Knox died saving his woman. He died for the one and *only* thing that mattered to him."

Oliver's face softened and he tipped his head to the side. "Guess that counts for something then."

The door to the club flew open and a swell of laughter made them turn around. It looked like the bikers had gone inside and a few girls floated out, lighting up cigarettes. An angelic voice sang a Rolling Stones ballad—her voice floating on the breeze and echoing through the parking lot. It made Adam shudder with the haunting memory of Knox. He pushed those thoughts aside and pulled a pack of smokes out of his pocket.

"Tell me about Cedric."

"I did some sniffing around, but I can't find anything else on the guy. Knox thought the seller on our side was dealing directly with someone he knew on your side. Didn't tell me his name, but I guess you probably know. He guessed wrong and it looks like Cedric is acting as the middleman, either dealing to your big honcho or selling on the black market. I don't know, the black market theory would mean more buyers and more of that shit floating around in your world, which it's not. Knox didn't seem to think anyone else was getting their hands on the metal except his guy, so that means Cedric must work for him. The name doesn't ring a bell?"

Adam's finger involuntarily ran along the groove of his scar that cut across his jaw. "I don't know. I've heard the name, but it doesn't mean anything. There could be a million guys named Cedric."

Oliver watched him take a long drag from his cigarette and tuck the soft pack inside his jacket.

"That metal is what some of *our* weapons are made of. You knew that, right?"

Adam nodded. He knew. While he hadn't known it at the time, the Special Forces had specially armed them to take out Breed. They were the guinea pigs for using some of that experimental weaponry.

"Didn't take me long to figure out something wasn't right with the stuff we were issued," Oliver said proudly, sitting on the bed of the truck again. He took his glasses out of his pocket and slipped them onto his face. "They're not all the same. Someone is still refining and trying to make improvements. It nulls some of your gifts, but it doesn't work the same on everyone. And I'm talking from an individual basis, not just by Breed. Some are immune. Did I mention the strength wears down over time until it's nothing more than a scrap of metal? Maybe that's what those douchebags are trying to remedy. They'd probably love nothing more than to sell this shit to you guys so you can kill yourselves and save them the trouble."

Adam flicked his cigarette and it landed beside a tire. "And we'd probably do just that. You can't find out who's selling and stop them?"

He shrugged. "Could be one guy or maybe a whole bunch. It would take time for me to dig, and the problem with snooping is sometimes you get your nose too deep in someone's crack. Worry about who's actually creating the shit—that's who we need to put a stop to. But you can bet they're protected and if someone goes after them, that someone is going to end up paddling in the middle of the Pacific Ocean wearing shark bait as a floatation device."

"Were the exchanges on a regular basis?"

Oliver scratched the patch of dark blond hair on his jaw. "Cedric's name came up on one file and nowhere else. What I *can* give you is the information included in that entry."

Adam folded his arms. "How much?"

Oliver grinned sheepishly. "Look, it's a favor for Knox that I'm even here, but I wouldn't mind tucking away a little cash on the side for a trip to Maui. How about ten grand and I'll give you a license plate?"

"Deal."

Adam didn't hesitate to answer. He had the funds and that

license plate number was enough to track down the vehicle, even if Cedric no longer owned it. He couldn't have asked for a better clue aside from the man's last name. Cedric could be a false name or an alias for all he knew.

"Sweet. We're doing this in cash because shit gets found out when you start moving large sums of money around. You got that on you?"

"I can get it."

Oliver hopped off the truck and the door to the club swung open again. This time a rowdy gang of men stumbled out and disappeared around the left side of the building.

"Tomorrow?"

Adam hesitated. "I have plans tomorrow night." *That damn dinner with Justus.* "How about Sunday?"

"Your call, but I'm heading back Monday morning, so get it together. You know my number. Adios."

Oliver hustled out of there and vanished around the street corner. Adam looked at the cars around him, crammed in like sardines. Some had illegally parked and he guessed the overflow went to the back of the building.

A flare of energy made the hair on the back of his neck bristle. A Mage was on the premises. Adam concealed his light and hustled toward his bike. The music inside the bar changed to a steady beat, the kind that garnered a flood of cheers and clapping.

Rock music blared from the open door. Adam threw his leg over the bike and before he put on his helmet, he caught a glimpse of a blond woman flying out the main door. Her boots stomped down the wooden steps and the figure disappeared around the side of the building. Someone had pissed her off.

A sound catapulted him off his bike and he tossed the helmet on the ground, heart pounding against his chest. It was a muffled squeal—barely audible. Adam never dismissed something that caused him alarm, so he jogged in the direction the woman had gone.

His throat became dry and his palms sweaty as he neared the left corner of the building. A dilapidated fence ran along the outer edge, the wood so old part of it was rotting away. He could only hear his motorcycle boots crunching on the gravel, so he paused for a moment and cocked his head.

He heard the sound of low murmurs and someone making a hushing noise. It could be that he was about to interrupt someone having a good time, but it didn't feel right.

Adam turned the corner and walked up on a scene that made his fists clench. He could barely contain the Mage energy surging to his fingertips.

It was *her*.

The girl with the acoustic guitar he'd once seen marching onto a stage the same night Knox was murdered. It was *her* angelic voice that had filled the parking lot during those last moments. It was *her* voice he often heard in his dreams before they turned into nightmares. It was *her* voice that had sung just moments ago—the wavy-haired girl who'd stormed out the main door.

A guy with a black goatee was balancing on one arm and unzipping his pants with the other. Two men were holding her arms, eyes ripe with wicked intentions.

Her lovely hair was splayed across the dirt. She wasn't struggling.

Adam's lips peeled back and he approached with wrath burning his veins like venom. A dull roar filled his head as he saw their mouths moving, but all he heard was the pounding of his own heart.

"Get away from her!" he shouted. His body trembled with the urge to rush them, but they outnumbered him and were too close to the girl. It was against the law to kill a human or to reveal he was a Mage, so the ass-kicking that was about to ensue was going to be nothing but fists and fury.

"Why don't you mind your own goddamn business," the man on the left said. "Take a walk."

Adam shucked off his coat and the winter air nipped at his arms. Without missing a beat, he stalked forward and the three men rose to their feet.

The girl did not. The closer Adam got, the more he could see her swollen face; they had knocked her unconscious. The wind blew up her turquoise dress, and to the right, he noticed a guitar propped against the brick wall.

The big guy with the goatee stood astride the young woman while the men on either side of him began to spread apart.

Adam moved to the left like a torpedo. He spun around, bent low, and delivered a solid kick to the face of one of the thugs. It knocked the man back with such force that he hit the wall and collapsed.

The dirtbag on the right moved in, pulling a switchblade from his pocket.

"You got big fuckin' balls to be walking up on private business. Now I'm going to take this knife and add to that collection you got going on all over your face."

Maybe that would have scared most men, but Adam didn't blink. His heart rate slowed down to a steady beat as it always did before a fight. It's how he kept calm and thinking clearly.

The man lunged and swiped his blade, cutting Adam's arm. Blood oozed brightly to the surface and trickled down to his fingertips. Adam seized the man by the wrist and snapped back his arm, forcing him to drop the knife. He threw a series of violent punches and the human bent over and vaulted up with a surprising right uppercut. Pain exploded in Adam's left eye.

"Sonofabitch!" the man shouted, leaning to the right and spitting. "I think he broke my tooth."

Adam swept out his leg and knocked the weakling off his feet. He picked up the blade and seized the man by the throat, pressing the sharp knife against his fleshy cheek.

"You think my scars are funny?" With a slow stroke, Adam pressed the cold blade against his face, penetrating the top layer of skin and drawing a little blood. When the man's eyes went wide with fear, Adam stood up and watched him scurry backward until he hopped to his feet and ran.

He blinked a few times, feeling a throb radiating across his cheekbone.

"I see you're badass with a knife," Goatee said.

Adam flicked his wrist and the knife punched through the dirt. "You think having your friends pin down a young girl while you force yourself on her makes you a man?"

The deviant stroked his goatee and glanced indifferently at the unconscious woman. "You think I give a shit about her? That little whore may have the crowd wrapped around her finger when she's on stage, but I know all about girls like her. She thinks she's too good for everyone when she's nothing but white trash."

"Musta hurt like a bitch when she turned you down," Adam growled, circling to the right to draw the man away from the woman.

The man stepped forward. "What's it to you? I suppose you think you can get a piece of ass like that on your own? Think again," he said, raking her over with his eyes. Then his voice lowered and he raised his sharp eyes to Adam. "You can have a turn; I won't judge."

He was serious. This sonofabitch thought he could tempt Adam to join him in his sadistic game of rape.

That's when all reason went out the window. Adam didn't care about Mage rules anymore, he flashed forward and knocked the guy out with a blast of energy to the chest. Adam refrained from a deathblow, but the strike was powerful enough to make it feel like a truck had hit him.

"What the... umph," Goatee grunted, unable to speak through his groans and rapid breaths. He'd received the equivalent of an electric shock with CPR paddles, but he still staggered to his feet.

"Want more?" Adam shoved him in the chest with more power, charging up his light for another strike.

With a shaky hand, Goatee pulled a switchblade from his back pocket and when his lecherous eyes fell on the girl, Adam didn't hold back.

He laid his fist into Goatee's face and heard bones crack. The knife dropped to the ground and when Adam held out his hands to give him another painful shock, the man stumbled backward and staggered toward the parking lot.

Adam dropped to his knees and cradled the girl's neck. She looked young, maybe in her early twenties, but it was hard to tell in the dim alley. Adam was a Healer and while his gift worked on most Breeds, it didn't work on humans.

He had never seen her face up close because when they'd first met, she'd been crouched on the floor beneath him. But he remembered with perfect clarity when she took charge of the stage with her guitar.

Adam had noticed how expressive her features were—she'd radiated life. Her full lips were tinted with the palest of pinks and her most noticeable attribute was her hair—beautiful, carefree waves with a few braids woven in, and not the color women got from a bottle but a warm shade of blond. The cut on her lip and the fresh bruise marred those features only a fraction.

With the gentlest of ease, he pulled her up to a sitting position. Her head rolled to the side and she sank against his chest. He thought about calling the police and leaving her in the alley, but that was out of the question. No way in hell was he going to leave her this way. He hadn't done it with Silver and he sure as hell wasn't about to start now. If he stayed at her side until the cops arrived, they would question him and want a statement.

That's when things could get sticky. Novis had warned him that getting involved with humans left fingerprints. Even though the report would go under his alias name, Lucan Riddle, it would flag Breed authorities. If someone ran an investigation, it would bring trouble right to Novis's front door and jeopardize his position on the Council.

Adam cursed under his breath. He glanced around and noticed a ring of shiny keys with a blue, Earth-shaped ball attached to the end. There were only three keys on the chain and the car key looked like it belonged to an older model. She must have parked her car in the back.

Adam tugged the hem of her dress down until it covered her legs, then he got up and grabbed his jacket from the concrete. After draping it over her chest to keep her warm, he lifted the girl into his arms and walked toward the back of the building. Adam began testing the key in a few of the older cars without success.

"Surely not," he murmured, staring at a VW van that looked like it had traveled to the future in a time machine. It had a white top and lime-green bottom.

The key slid in the lock and he opened up the back doors. Wide cushions covered the floor and a pea-green blanket was neatly folded by the door.

Adam carefully laid her down in the back and wrapped her up

in the blanket. He found a pillow and tucked it beneath her head. Anger flared at the idea of her sleeping in the back of a van. By all the personal effects tucked in corners and the boxes of food, it looked like home sweet home.

"No, no, no," she mumbled.

"Shhh." He brushed her silky hair away from her face until she no longer stirred.

Maybe he should have called the cops or left her in the van to freeze, but that's not how it all went down.

A gust of wind blew from behind and he slammed the doors shut, twirling the keys in his hand as he lifted his eyes to the sky. The low clouds were breaking up and he could see a few stars blinking from behind. It made him think about all the events in his life that had led him here. Had he never chased down Silver the night they'd met, he would have never become a Mage. Knox wouldn't have died. Then again, Silver might have. What was the purpose of his life, and why was he standing in an empty parking lot, putting an unconscious woman into a van?

Fate was a moody bitch, indeed.

Adam walked around to the other side of the van, got in, and drove away.

CHAPTER 9

WHILE I GOT THE HOUSE ready for the dinner party, Logan drove back to his condo to pack a few things for his stay. Justus had mentioned Novis would be late, but it slipped his mind to tell me until the last minute that Adam was also invited.

Great. Thanks for the heads-up.

I spent the afternoon cleaning the house and brushing my cat so he wouldn't shed his black hair all over our guests. Max didn't like strangers, but he became quite affectionate when he noticed someone in a nice pair of slacks. Maybe that's why he seemed to love Justus so much. Finn decided he wanted to stay in his room, so I took him a plate of reheated sausages. Page said it would be best if we didn't overstimulate him for the next twenty-four hours. He was listless and agitated, which she said was a common side effect from the injection.

Panic ensued. There weren't enough main ingredients and nothing was thawed out. I spat out a few curses and stared in the fridge.

I contemplated the pros and cons of making BLTs for our Councilman and finally opted against it. Instead, I thawed out chicken in a bowl of hot water and then put it in the microwave. Baked with picante sauce and served with Spanish rice on the side, we'd be rolling. It *sounded* good, and I was pretty sure it was a legitimate recipe.

The silent alarm flashed in the house and Justus went into the security room.

"Be right back," he said, heading out the door.

After polishing the hammered surface of the dining table, I sat down in the dark room and held up my hands, transferring threads of blue light between my fingers. I had a firm grasp of my abilities as a Mage, with the exception of balling up my energy and using it in one shot like Justus could. Novis had said a long time ago that I *was* potential, not that I had it.

But he was right; my gift was an absolute. Whether or not I would learn to use that gift was my choice. Therefore, I truly *was* the potential.

The front door opened and Justus flew down the hall and toward the training room where he'd been working out. I held my breath when I heard the sound of heavy footsteps approaching.

Apprehensively, I stood up. "Logan?"

Levi shadowed the entranceway of the dining room and stood motionless. I could only make out his silhouette. He didn't stand as tall as Logan, but Levi had a fuller frame and more of a tough-guy appearance. His short blond hair was about an inch long, and he had an irresistible chin dimple.

Butterflies flitted in my stomach at his uncharacteristic behavior. "Is something wrong, Levi?"

He stalked forward and kicked over one of the chairs blocking his way. Without a word, Levi wrapped his thick arms around my waist and lifted me up into a bear hug.

"Hey, I'm fine," I said against his temple. "It's Finn who was hurt."

He flashed his amber eyes at me. "You were attacked twice, and nobody comes after my sister."

I melted a little at his words. Levi had bonded with me more than the rest of Logan's family had. I didn't know Lucian very well, and Leo had a serious personality and wasn't the kind of guy you go around hugging. Levi, on the other hand, *was*.

Not wanting to blow off a special moment with a man I cared about, I wrapped my arms around Levi's neck and gave him a generous hug.

"I'm fine. The Relic said Finn has to stay in the bedroom—"

"Shut up, Silver. Can I just enjoy my hug without the verbal intercourse?"

I snorted and leaned back, scratching at his stubbly chin. A smile wound up his tough face and it was criminal.

"Why are you here?"

He loosened his grip and my feet touched the floor.

"Logan called about the break-in, but something else is going on with HALO. Some major shit is going down and Justus invited me over. We'll talk about it later. You sure you're okay?" The pad of his thumb stroked my eyebrow and I touched his tatted arm.

"I don't think I have enough chicken if you're going to eat over."

"Girl, I'm not into breasts and thighs. Got any sausages?"

I slapped his chest and walked around him. "Do you want something to drink?"

"I could use a beer, honey."

I pulled a couple of cold ones out of the fridge and joined him in the living room. Justus had an awesome house and every room felt like home. Large monitors filled the left wall and gave us either a surveillance view of outside or a screensaver. They were currently watching the property and Christian was nowhere in sight. He somehow managed to stay out of view. The main wall had a faux fireplace, and the furniture ranged from leather and swivel chairs to a charcoal-colored rug and matching sofas. Justus had expensive taste when it came to his masculine furnishings. Levi made himself at home, lying on the rug with his fingers laced behind his head and ankles crossed.

I set his imported beer on the table behind him and collapsed on the sofa. "Are you living here with us too?"

He rubbed his nose and reached around for the beer. "Trust me when I say that you wouldn't want to live with me. I snore, I don't clean up after myself, and the TV stays on day and night."

"Even when you're not home?"

"It makes people think I'm home."

I took a swig of my beer and tore at the label. "What exactly do you do for a living?" Something Levi was always evasive about answering.

"Thug patrol." Levi sat up with a knee bent and his arm draped over it, holding the bottle. "I used to be one of the RSF, but I didn't like the corruption. Without proof, I couldn't get any of those traitor assholes out of there, so I split. Breed jail is all about taking down the sharks, but the streets are swimming with piranhas."

"What's RSF?"

"Regulators of the Security Force. They work for the higher authority."

I knew a little about Regulators. They carried out orders given by the higher authority within each Breed but were not the governing law themselves. When someone needed to be brought in, a Regulator served a warrant and they went to Breed jail where the higher authority would determine their punishment. Not all Breeds had their own form of police. An arrest could only be made with a warrant or substantial evidence. Justus had explained that Regulators only worked hot cases and crimes against humans—unlike HALO, which spent years gathering evidence against high-profile criminals. The Mageri was more advanced when it came to social order and had been the first to establish a police force—the Enforcers. They were preferred in sensitive cases where the Mageri needed to review the case before the other Breeds became aware of the details.

"So you're not a cop but you're like what—one of those Guardian Angels that patrol the streets? Is that legal?"

His Adam's apple bobbed up and down as he swallowed the rest of his beer before setting the bottle on the table. Levi belched and scratched his chin. "Most crimes that happen on the streets stay on the streets. The Breed decided we didn't have enough room to build jails to hold everyone, so they turn a blind eye to a lot of shit. Most have little jurisdiction outside their own, but there are some basic fundamentals. Shifters have a right to protect their property and seek revenge on someone who hurts one of their own. For instance, if a female Shifter is uh… assaulted, her family has full rights to go after the attacker. So I work with an independent group that hunts down the riffraff."

"And then what?"

His brow arched slowly. "Well, we've got our methods. Believe it or not, some of the Breeds fund our organization because we're doing everyone a service, but they do it under the table. It's also kind of like PI work; someone might hire us to investigate an unpunishable action committed against them."

"Wow. All this time I thought you were a bouncer in a bar."

Levi snorted. "I've done that on the side for extra cash, but now I'm legit with my job."

"Learner," Justus barked from the hallway to the right. "Do you have enough food in there for tonight's meal?"

I leaned around and glared at him. "I didn't know you were inviting half the city. Anyone else coming I should know about? Sunny? The Council? The King?"

"It's five thirty-two," he said without looking at his overpriced watch. "I want the food on the table before they arrive at six."

"Six!" I shouted. "You didn't tell me that. I thought you said later tonight."

He folded his arms. "That *is* later."

I stared in panic as Levi circled around the couch and stood between us, almost obscuring my view. "Ghuardian or not, I don't like the way you're barking orders at Silver. A female shouldn't have to serve a male, but as that's your repugnant custom, I can't do shit about it. But keep it up and we'll go toe-to-toe in your training room."

Justus dragged his eyes over to mine and I could feel the energy in the room spike.

"I'll get it done, Ghuardian. Next time give me a heads-up. The chicken alone is going to take a half an hour to bake, and I haven't even preheated the oven," I grumbled, stomping into the kitchen.

As I cursed and flung pans on the counter, Levi came up behind me and I felt a vibration against my back from the thrumming in his chest. "Be calm, female."

"He is fully capable of cooking for himself, but he chooses to live in the Stone Age where he thinks it's a woman's job. Why is ordering a pizza so damn difficult?"

"Female," he whispered. "*Be calm.*"

I relaxed, succumbing to the inflection in his voice combined with his purr. It was in my genetic makeup to respond, and now I understood why I had behavioral characteristics that weren't normal for a Mage. My surrogate mother was a Chitah human, and the egg was from a Chitah. That made me more than half, even though I didn't have any physical characteristics.

Levi cleared his throat. "Throw the chicken in the oven if you want, but let me have a look at what you've got in here and I'll help."

"Novis is coming over, Levi. This calls for more than bologna sandwiches."

He rocked with laughter and studied the contents of the fridge. "You *do* have sausages. I can work with this," he said, pulling the package out and waving it in his hand.

"That I don't doubt," I said with a suggestive wink, patting his shoulder.

"Find me a serving spoon, will ya?"

I reached in the utensil drawer and snapped my arm back, hissing. "Dammit! I told Justus not to put the knives in there!" The gash on my index finger was deep and painful.

Levi grabbed my wrist and before I could argue, wrapped his lips around my finger. His tongue slid along the skin, mending the cut with the healing agent in his saliva. It tickled a little and became numb as the pain vanished.

"I could have gotten a Band-Aid, you know."

He smirked fiendishly and my entire body stiffened when a voice spoke from behind.

"Any reason I should be concerned about my female's finger in your mouth?" Logan said in a threatening voice.

I couldn't deny I loved seeing the jealous fire in his eyes when we all knew Levi was no threat.

Levi's mouth made a kissing sound as he pulled my finger out and winked at Logan. "She wanted to see if the rumors were true about what I can do with my tongue. It's a good thing she didn't cut her breast is all I'm sayin'."

"It's a shame Sunny was feeling over the weather. This is a splendid meal, Silver. You have outdone yourself." Novis complimented me, wiping his mouth with a cloth napkin.

"Under the weather," Levi corrected.

I flicked my contemptuous eyes toward Levi who smirked at his plate.

The chicken had never made it to the oven. Instead, Levi had prepared macaroni mixed with slices of sausage. I'd had faith that Levi could somehow pull gourmet out of his ass with pasta shells, but once he mixed the cheese in, there was no turning back. I realized it was an epic fail when I set the bowl in front of Justus and felt the heat rise in the room ten degrees. Justus dragged his eyes up to mine and obliterated me with his gaze.

It didn't seem to be a catastrophe with Levi and Logan, who each devoured every bite on their plates and went for a second helping. Apparently, the Cross brothers hadn't raised the bar on their culinary skills.

I sat in my usual spot with Justus to my right at the head of the table and Novis sitting opposite him. Levi and Adam sat across from me, while Logan cozily scooted closer on the bench to my left.

We avoided weighty conversations until Novis finished eating—he didn't care for serious chatter while enjoying a meal.

Adam had been uncharacteristically quiet throughout dinner and didn't engage in the usual banter. He seemed restless and anxious. I'd caught Logan staring at him a few times during dinner and I'd nudged his shoulder so he'd quit. The way Logan glared at him unsettled me.

"I am here tonight with some unfortunate news," Novis began. As he pinched his lower lip, his clear blue eyes focused on the center of the table as if he were lost in a distant fog. If it's one quality Novis had, it was riveting blue eyes that stood out against his black hair. A person could easily get distracted by his gaze. "Months ago, an assassin attempted a hit on a Councilman in one of the neighboring territories. The attack was thwarted by a stealthy guard who had a gut instinct. Unfortunately, the attacker was someone who worked closely with a Councilman, and you all knew him as Ray."

The man I saved from Nero's compound.

"Two nights ago, I received a call from Levi."

I glanced up at Levi, who licked some cheese from his thumb as if he already knew the whole story.

"As you may already know, Levi once worked within law enforcement and still has inside connections. Ray was discovered dead in his cell."

"Inside job," Levi confirmed. "Nobody gets in and out of those floors; they're heavily monitored. Someone was covering their shit."

After a short sip of wine, Novis placed his palms on the table. "What you are not aware of is that this morning, a coordinated attack was executed against key Mageri Councilmen across all territories."

Everyone gasped and Justus tossed down his fork.

"HALO uncovered the plot a week ago, but we didn't have enough information to go on as to when the strike would occur."

I turned my head slowly toward my Ghuardian and saw color bleed into his neck and the vein pulse in his forehead. He kept his eyes low as he laced his fingers in front of his face.

"This was no fault of your men," Novis said as if reiterating something he'd already discussed privately with Justus. "We heeded your warning and took what precautionary measures we could."

"And your guards are here?" Logan asked, pushing his plate away.

"Yes. My trusted guards are outside the entrance."

Adam wiped his hand over his mouth. "Was anyone hurt?"

After a short pause, Novis lifted his sharp eyes and took his time looking at each of us. "Twelve died. Each Council is comprised of no less than three and no more than six. A total of thirty-five attacks took place, all occurring at precisely the same second."

"Including you?" I anxiously held my breath.

His voice softened. "Yes."

"Does Simon know? Maybe he has an idea of what Nero is trying to accomplish."

Novis lightly touched his lip. "Simon is the one who saved my life. I am in his debt."

"I was not aware of this," Justus cut in.

Novis sharpened his gaze at my Ghuardian. "You are not aware of all matters of the Council, and nor are you entitled."

"Apologies." Justus lowered his head respectfully.

"Accepted," Novis said, leaning back in his chair. "I was meeting with Simon on another matter when I was rushed by two men. They incapacitated two of my guards with weapons made from that metal. Simon had only one stunner on him, but he needs very little to get the job done. He took out both attackers while my remaining guards escorted me to safety."

"Did you question them?" I asked.

"Let me reiterate that Simon *took them out*. An attack on a Councilman does not earn a man any rights except death."

Once again, laws I didn't agree with. "You don't think you might have learned something by detaining them?"

"Learner," Justus said, warning me in a quiet voice.

Novis hid a private smile. "Perhaps we can continue this conversation another time as it strays from the matter at hand."

"What does this have to do with Ray?" I couldn't make the connection, but it looked as if he knew.

Novis refilled his wineglass and the sound of tiny gurgles and splashes filled the quiet room. Candles flickered on the table and brought out the sparkling beauty of the crystal glasses. Several bottles of wine were open and each sat beside bowls of chocolate mints wrapped in delicate foil.

Justus eased back in his chair, causing the wood to creak beneath his weight. "HALO kept an eye on Ray when the Mageri granted him independence. While there was no reason to suspect anything, we hired an investigator to watch over him and report suspicious activity. We have no concrete evidence, but we're certain Nero got to him. Ray's attack against the Councilman was sloppy. We think Nero might have tried calling off the attack and Ray went ahead with it anyway."

"What made you think Nero was behind it all?" I asked.

Justus slanted his cobalt eyes to mine and his jaw tightened. "The attack earned Ray a cot in Breed jail, but for reasons unexplained, the Regulators weren't allowed to question him at the time. We believe Nero paid someone on the inside to help keep his hands clean. It wasn't until last week that we were finally granted permission to have a Vampire question Ray."

"And that shit is why I fucking left," Levi announced, pressing his finger against the table.

Justus threw his weight on his forearms and his biceps hardened. "The interrogation was cut short, but it was enough to give us Nero's name. Ray turned up dead, as did the interrogator."

"How did you know there would be another attack?"

"Ray gave up the name of a man he was working with. It took a day to track him down. The details *he* provided led us to believe something big was about to go down. We sent word to the Mageri, uncertain if Nero knew we were onto him."

Novis tapped his finger on the rim of his glass. "You have our gratitude, Justus. Your perseverance saved lives. Had we not received a warning, more lives would have been lost as many increased their security upon the Mageri's recommendation. There is no way you could have known the attack would occur so soon, if at all. Not every plot discovered is realized."

"Why would Nero attack your leaders?" Logan inquired, gripping my leg beneath the table. I glanced up at his strong profile and admired the man who had once considered a Mage his enemy. Now here he was by my side, genuinely interested in our affairs.

Novis flashed his teeth as he tore the wrapper away from a mint. "Nero craves what all outlaws want: power. They will never have power as long as there is organized law. These ancients have tasted the freedom of lawlessness for centuries—now they are struggling against conforming to a higher authority. Social order limits what they are capable of achieving. This is true even among your own kind, Chitah."

Logan nodded and I caught his eyes on Adam again, his nose twitching. I gripped his wrist and he looked down at his wine, lifting the glass and swirling the liquid inside.

Adam looked at Novis with concern. "Was anyone on our Council lost?"

"No." After chewing his mint, Novis rolled up the silver wrapper and placed it on his plate. "I was the only one attacked. It leads me to believe he is targeting the most influential leaders—that seems to be the only commonality. What troubles me is finding out he had already bought his way in with Merc. It makes me wonder how many more he has bribed and what is going on in that ambitious mind of his," Novis said, his words trailing off.

Adam slanted his eyes toward Levi. "You should have stayed in."

Levi rolled something between his fingers. "How 'bout I shove this cork up your nose so you'll quit sticking it where it doesn't belong?"

"I know a guy in the same situation, but he chose to stay and do the right thing. If you leave corruption, then corruption takes over. Don't get mad at me just because you pussied out."

Levi slammed his fist on the table and rose to his feet, two of his canines sliding out. "Wanna take it outside?"

"Sit down, Levi," Logan said. "We both know he's right."

"That doesn't mean shit," he growled through clenched teeth. "It's none of his business."

"Levi, *sit*. We've discussed this at length."

With a hard sigh, Levi sat down and shoved his plate out of the way, leaning toward Logan. "Well, I can't take it back, now can I? There's no returning once you leave. You don't think I wonder about it? I have nightmares about what kind of man I might have become if I'd stuck around."

"Gentlemen," Novis interrupted. "We're going off course. Adam is correct. A man should stand his ground against all obstacles, even if it seems justice will not prevail. It's why I will retain my position on the Council, despite the corruption, despite the dangers. But I respect where you are, Levi. The service you provide is invaluable and perhaps there is a greater purpose to your life."

The tension in the room made me sick to my stomach. Just knowing that Nero had played a hand in dividing these friends and brothers caused my energy to spike. I thought about Sunny, who'd lost the love of her life. With Novis as a target, she might be in more danger than ever before. And now he was going after Finn!

"Learner, level it down," Justus said between clenched teeth.

My eyes darted up to his and I caught Adam craning his neck to look at my silvering eyes. Logan was no longer touching me, and everyone at the table ceased their talking. Anger funneled through my veins and more than ever, I wanted Nero dead. The man who'd chained and beat me. The man who'd taken lives and continued to slay anyone who mattered to me. A man older than the time of

Christ, who sought to divide and conquer. A man of wealth. A man of power. Untouchable.

"Learner..."

My hands were shaking as threads of blue light leaked onto my lap. I couldn't level it down. Overcome with emotion, I was seconds away from the energy spiraling into a black hole and sucking me into unconsciousness—right there at the dinner table in front of everyone.

A chair scraped back and hit the floor. Justus grabbed my wrists and yanked me out of my seat.

"Get your hands off her!" Logan roared.

"Stay out of this, Chitah. She's about to lose control if I don't draw out her energy."

Adam cleared his throat. "I don't know if that's a good idea. Have you ever tasted her light when she's *that* juiced up?"

No, he hadn't. My power had gradually become more potent since the time of my creation. I yanked my hands back and heard a low-decibel hum in my head as a buzz tickled my palms.

"Give me your power," Justus commanded.

"Justus," Novis said, rising from the table. "Let it consume her. It could do more harm than good if—"

Without warning, Justus jerked my hands forward and placed them on his blue button-up shirt. A loud crack sounded and he flew back and hit the wall.

"Jesus!" Levi shouted, standing up with the rest of us.

I shuddered as an icy wave chilled my bones from the energy loss. Before I could move, bodies were rushing toward Justus, who was slumped on the floor with smoke rising from his chest.

"Damn," Levi said, ripping the buttons free on Justus's shirt. "It singed the fabric all the way through."

Adam remained seated, wiping his face and looking toward the door.

"Are you all right?" Logan asked from behind me, his fingers tense around my shoulders.

"I'm fine," I said, breathing heavily.

He turned me around and examined me with intense eyes,

lifting my chin with the crook of his finger. "I'm not kidding around, Silver. Are you all right?"

Logan turned my palms up and brushed his hands over them. I shuddered and my teeth began to chatter. He pulled me against his warm chest and wrapped his arms around my body, talking to the men who were busy helping Justus.

"Is he conscious?"

"Worry not, Chitah," Novis said.

When the room fell silent, I struggled to turn my head and see what was going on. Novis rolled up the sleeves of his black shirt and placed his slender fingers on Justus's chest. I could see bright red marks where I had burned him.

"Oh my God," I whispered in a horrified voice. Nothing like that had ever happened before.

Threads of blue light emanated from Novis's fingertips as he brushed them against my Ghuardian's chest, moving in slow circles.

"I don't get that shit," Levi said. "She just blasted him with the same light and you're putting more in him?"

"This is healing light," Novis explained. "Our energy comes in different forms and it requires concentration to pull the right kind out. What Silver released into him was her full power."

"I thought that juiced up another Mage," Levi said, his tone more a statement than a question.

"Normally, it would. But her light exceeded what a Mage would take when juicing another."

Novis carefully tiptoed around the truth that I was a Unique. It was something neither Levi nor Adam was privy to and not a fact we advertised in the local paper.

Justus coughed several times and sat up, taking in a few ragged breaths.

Novis laughed softly and turned to look up at me from his squatting position. "I'd say this was a splendid dinner, Silver. Well done. Perhaps next time you'll throw us a barbecue?"

Levi hammered out a hard laugh, wheezing into his fist. "I have to get back to work. We'll keep our eyes and ears on the streets. If I come across any information, I'll let you know."

"I appreciate that, friend," Novis replied.

Adam threw his napkin on the plate. "I'll head out with you."

"And where are you going?" Novis tilted his head to the side and an uncomfortable tension hung in the air.

"To find a job."

Novis squinted and I wondered what was going on between those two.

"Then I wish you luck and hope you will consult with me on any offers you receive."

Levi raised his hand. "Later, Lo. Call me when Finn is feeling himself. I'm sure he doesn't want everyone bugging the shit out of him." Levi swaggered out the door, grabbing a handful of mints on his way and Adam following close behind.

I pulled away from Logan and knelt in front of Justus. He clumsily tugged his shirt off and gripped the table to stand up before exchanging a private glance with Novis and nodding. Novis touched his shoulder and kept eye contact for a nanosecond before turning away.

Justus towered over me like the Hulk.

It was that *oh shit* moment where I was about to get reamed by my Ghuardian for having embarrassed him in front of a Councilman.

"Get changed, Learner. You've been holding back on me. I want you downstairs in the training room in five minutes."

CHAPTER 10

ADAM RETURNED TO THE MOTEL without delay. He should have declined Justus's dinner invitation, but Novis had important information about the recent attack. The girl had tossed and turned most of the day, which he'd felt was a good sign. After healing his cut arm, he'd had no choice but to leave the unconscious girl alone and attend Justus's gathering. But his mind had been on her the whole time and he'd taken the first opportunity to return.

His cheap motel room was paid up through the month. Outer stairwells and walkways led to the rooms like any motel, and each room included a television and coffee machine. It became Adam's retreat when things got crazy. Now he finally understood how Silver felt when she'd begun living with Justus. A human spends their adult life alone, making their own decisions. To have all that suddenly stripped away—where decisions are made *for* you—was a difficult life to adjust to. Novis was a fair Creator, but Adam was feeling stifled by the dependent lifestyle.

When he entered the room, the young woman was still asleep in the bed nearest the bathroom.

Adam had been in his fair share of scuffles—one had knocked him out for three days. Of course, he'd been in the medical unit under observation. When he awoke, he'd overheard the doctors saying he was lucky he hadn't gone into a permanent coma.

Coma. Man, did that word scare him.

Adam adjusted the heater in the room, impatient for the girl to wake up. Maybe it wasn't a good idea to let her sleep this long.

So she wakes up, and then what? *"Hi, I'm Adam. You don't know who I am, but I brought you to my motel room."*

He shook his head and looked around the room. The bedspreads were mauve with zigzag patterns in pastel blue. The beds were on the left side and the television sat atop the dresser on the right. It didn't get more basic than this. Adam usually ate dinner at the wooden table by the exterior door. He tossed his wallet and keys by the ashtray and flipped on the bathroom light, then knelt by her bed in the dark room. The light from behind him allowed Adam to get a closer look at her face.

His heart skipped a beat when her eyelids fluttered and she turned her head toward him.

"Hey," he said, brushing a long strand of blond hair away from her face. "Time to wake up."

The swelling on her left eye didn't look as bad as it had earlier. She had a nasty cut on her lower lip in the center, but nothing that would require stitches. The knot on her head told him they must have slammed her against the concrete until she stopped fighting.

God, did that burn him. In all kinds of ways any decent man would feel.

"Hey, you need to wake up now. Can you hear me?"

He touched her right cheek with his rough hand and rubbed it a few times until she moaned. Then he remembered as a kid how his sister would pinch him in the same spot until he'd wake up.

Adam continued rubbing his fingers across her face until her hand suddenly flew up and slapped his wrist.

"That's it, Kitten. Keep fighting until you wake up. You can do it, just open your eyes. I won't hurt you—you're safe. Open your eyes, come on," he said, coaxing her and still running his fingers along her jaw.

"Mmmrrr, stop," she mumbled. "Stop it." Several grunts and groans vibrated in her throat as she swatted at his hand.

Adam wouldn't stop. Not until her eyes opened.

She suddenly turned her head and bit his hand.

"Ow! Why the hell did you bite me?"

"'Cause I told you to stop," she complained in a raspy voice.

Her eyelids fluttered and she touched her face with her right hand. Then she hissed when her tongue swept across the cut on her lip.

Adam backed up because he knew what was next. She was going to remember.

The young woman swallowed a few times and moved her mouth around, her hand exploring the bruise on her face. She finally rolled onto her back, quieting for a moment.

Adam waited for an outburst of screams when the memory of what those bastards had done slammed into her thoughts. He sat motionless as her chest began to rock. She lifted her arms with the elbows up in the air, palming her eyes.

Crying.

It broke his damn heart. "I found you," he began in a soft voice. "I took care of those animals and brought you here. You've been unconscious for about a day now, but the bruise on your face seems okay. How's the knot on your head?"

She sniffed her stuffy nose and gasped in quick succession as she tried calming down. "It hurts a little."

"I'll run downstairs and grab a bucket of ice. Is there anyone you want me to call to come get you?"

He already knew the answer to that. A woman living in a van didn't have a place to go. No decent person would allow a friend to live in her car.

"No. My things… my guitar."

"Your van is in the parking lot, locked up tight," he said.

"My guitar?"

Last he remembered, it had been leaning against the brick wall at Northern Lights.

"Outside at the club."

She actually began to swing her legs off the bed. "I have to go get it."

"No, you're going to get back in the bed," he said, rising to his feet and looming over her.

She didn't listen and began to sit up, leaning on her elbows. Adam lightly pushed her shoulders back and she hardly had any fight in her. She squinted at him, but the light from the bathroom bothered her eyes.

"That guitar means more to me than that shitty van outside."

"You can get another one."

"No, I *can't*," she argued. A braid of hair slipped in front of her face and she knocked it away. "Ever had something that meant the world to you? That completed you in a way that nothing else did?"

Adam stepped back and rubbed the back of his neck.

"Well, that's my guitar. There are a million others out there that I could replace her with, but she's special. She's unique. She's irreplaceable and she's mine. Now give me my keys."

He snorted. "You're in no condition to drive. Stay in the bed and…" *Shit. Was he really going to do this?* "Stay in the bed and I'll go get it."

"Promise?"

His brow furrowed and he folded his arms. "You're a trusting woman. You don't have any questions about how you got here or who I am? All you want is for me to take off in the middle of the night, sneak around the back of a bar, and retrieve your beat-up guitar?"

She eased back onto the bed with her eyes closed, touching her face. "You got it."

"And how do I know you'll still be here when I get back?"

One eye popped open and even in the dim light, he could see the beautiful color that looked milky green. They were either hazel or green, and he wished he could flip on the light to find out.

"Because, Scratch, I am giving you my word and that's all I got in this world."

"I'll be right back," he said, swiping the keys from the table and smelling the leather from his coat as he slipped it on. "Don't wander downstairs. It's a cheap-ass motel and the blockheads who hang out in the parking lot are nothing but trouble. If you're thirsty, the bathroom is right there. I'll bring back something to eat."

He swung the door open, unable to believe he was stupidly trusting she wouldn't bail on him. Then again, what did it matter? Adam glanced over his shoulder as he went out the door, certain he'd never see her again. "And my name's Adam, not Scratch."

"If you say so," she murmured in the darkness.

"You come with a name?"

"Everyone knows me as Jasmine—it's what I put on the flyers

and I don't like people knowing my real name. That's for friends only, and I don't have any friends."

"I'm not a friend?" He leaned against the doorjamb.

"Maybe. I haven't decided yet," she said, her voice softening around the edges.

Adam's hand tightened on the handle and he lowered his eyes. "The guy on top of you almost didn't walk away alive. The other two have a few broken bones in their faces, and if you want to know the truth, they're not going to be so lucky if I run into them again. They seem to be regulars at that bar, and there's a chance you could see them again. If that happens, call me and I'll take care of it, you hear? I'll give you my number."

He turned around and gripped the keys tightly as he swung the door closed.

"Sadie."

He pushed the door open a crack. "What?"

"My name. It's Sadie."

When Adam returned to Northern Lights, he was surprised to find the guitar still propped against the wall. Maybe because it was next to a pile of trash near the dumpster no one had taken notice. He hoped by driving her van, she wouldn't decide to leave on foot. Plus he didn't think he could hold a guitar and drive a motorcycle at the same time. He didn't notice anything special about the instrument—it was just a simple Gibson six-string with a few dings on the face and a heart drawn on the back with a marker. Adam walked to the parking lot to check on his motorcycle before heading back to the motel.

He cut off the engine and sat quietly in the van, amused by her quirky lifestyle. From her cowboy boots and feminine dresses to the vintage van with the giant steering wheel—everything about Sadie fascinated him. He glanced at the guitar on the floorboard to his right. Why would anyone call something so cheap and beat up irreplaceable? Adam had sold all his cameras with the exception of two. They had dings and scratches, but he'd never put anyone's life at risk to retrieve one. You move on and you get one that's newer, better, and not so damaged.

Dirt and blood stained her turquoise dress, so Adam figured she'd want to change clothes. He got out and opened the side door, rummaging around until he found a duffle bag with some clean clothes neatly folded inside it. He grabbed the neck of the guitar in his right hand and headed up the stairs. The lights were off in the room, so he quietly opened the door and propped the guitar against the wall.

The beds were empty.

He tossed his keys on the table disparagingly with a swing of his arm and leaned against the closed door. Had he really expected a girl who'd been assaulted by three men the night before to be eager to hang out in a motel room with a stranger? The guitar had been a ruse to get rid of him.

The bathroom door clicked open and Sadie stood in the open doorway wearing a terrycloth robe, squeezing the ends of her damp hair. She switched off the light, but the outdoor lamppost filtered through the window and allowed him to see shapes.

"Did you bring something to eat?"

It caught him off guard to see her and he tripped over his words. "Shit. I knew I forgot something. Be right back."

"Don't sweat it. I'm not famished or anything. My lip is too sore for me to enjoy eating," she said, shuffling back to the bed. "I'm going to flip on the light so I can see who you are."

His heart stammered. She called him Scratch and he assumed it was because she could see his scars in the dim room.

"Uh, maybe that's not such a good…"

Click.

The light illuminated the room and she rubbed her eyes. Sadie had propped herself up against two oversized pillows stuffed behind her back. Adam didn't want to frighten her, so he spun around and gripped the doorknob.

"I'll pick up some burgers."

"Please don't leave me alone. I like having someone around to talk to for a change."

He stood motionless, facing the door.

"We can order a pizza if *you're* hungry, but don't put yourself out to feed a scrapper like me."

"I'd hardly call you a scrapper," he said to the door.

"Are you a smoker?"

He lifted his eyes, staring at the peephole. He hadn't expected her to be so random. "Yeah. Lately."

"You should quit. It's a sign of a weak man. You don't seem like a weak man to me."

"You judge a man's character by what he puts in his mouth?"

"Absolutely. Everything you consume feeds your soul. Food, alcohol, cigarettes, drugs, anger—all of it. Everything we ingest one way or the other either cleanses or pollutes who we are. I used to smoke and I quit about a year ago. It's tough, but maybe these are the things that test how strong we are. So… are you going to turn around? I want to see the hero who saved my life."

"What makes you so trusting?"

"Because I woke up safe. You cleaned my face and took off my boots to make me comfortable. I found a cup of water on the bedside table, and those men had torn the buttons off the top of my dress, but I found a safety pin holding the front together when I went into the shower. Maybe I don't know you, but I know enough to recognize a good guy when I see one. So, let me get a look at you."

Adam took a deep breath and stuffed his hands into his jean pockets, slowly turning around.

She was more than beautiful—Sadie was pure innocence. The lamp between the beds cast a subtle glow on her smooth complexion and sparkling eyes. You couldn't look at this woman and not feel desire, and it had more to do with the way she looked back at you— the way she seemed to be more alive and in the moment than most people. Despite how he'd found her bleeding in the dirt, this girl had an unbreakable spirit.

A smile pushed the apples of her cheeks up and she squeezed a few droplets of water from her hair. "Nice to meet you, Scratch."

A muscle twitched in his cheek. "My name's Adam. Maybe a girl who makes fun of a man's scars shouldn't judge someone for smoking a cigarette."

Her jaw went slack and the smile faded away. "Um, what?"

"Scratch. You keep calling me that."

She breathed out a soft laugh. "Of course I do. It's how we first met."

Adam peeled away his coat and slung it over the chair. "Is that so," he murmured.

"I never forget a voice. It's a thing I have—maybe a gift or maybe nothing at all. When you spoke to me earlier, I remembered you from the club a few months back. I bumped into you and dropped my guitar. It wasn't just an accident; I was chickening out and ready to leave. God, I was so nervous. It was my first time on that stage and if I hadn't crashed into you, then I wouldn't have found the courage to get up and sing. Sometimes you need a minute to just breathe and get your head together. I noticed a scratch on your boot. Probably the ones you're wearing right now," she said, peering over the bed.

Adam lowered his eyes to his motorcycle boots and glanced at the left one, which had a deep cut on the side.

"So you're the guy with the scratch on his boot who kept me from running away from my dreams."

What could he say to that? The girl left him damn near speechless. Adam stalked toward the bed nearest him and sat on the edge, dialing the phone. After ordering a supreme pizza, a two-liter bottle of soda, and an Italian salad, he brought Sadie her duffle bag.

"Thought you could use some clean clothes."

"Thanks," she said in a sullen voice, unwinding one of her thin braids. The lock of unbound hair held a strong wave.

"You sure you're okay? I could take you to a hospital. I should have taken you, but…"

"But you'd get in trouble," she finished. "No need to explain. I can tell you're a Mage."

If it weren't for the idiot singing next door, he could have heard a pin drop.

"Sorry, didn't catch that," he said.

She had almond-shaped eyes and perfectly arched brows, just as light as her hair. When Sadie looked up at him, he held her gaze.

"I'm no stranger to your world—I've been living in it for years. I can always sense a Mage when you're not holding in your energy.

It feels kind of like… I don't know… like the little hairs on my arms are charged up or something. I'm sensitive to it now. I used to think nothing of it whenever I got chills but I wasn't cold. Now I know it's one of you causing that reaction, but most people have no idea a Mage is in the room with them. They just get the shivers and brush it off. Vampires and Chitahs are easy to spot, but forget about Shifters. Those guys blend in, except for the dominant wolves. Half the time I just mistake them for assholes."

A laugh burst out of his mouth. He could hardly get it under control and turned his head to the side. "You're full of surprises, Kitten."

"Kitten? Since when do *I* have a nickname?"

"Since you started calling me Scratch?" He decided not to tell her it was because she made mewing noises in her sleep.

She unzipped the bag, sifting through a few garments. "Mind if I stay here tonight? I can head down to the van if—"

"You stay here."

It wasn't a request or an offer. If she'd even attempted to walk out the door, Adam would have thrown her over his shoulder and carried her back to the room.

"Thanks. Feels good to cozy up in a real bed, and it's been a harsh winter."

A knot formed in his stomach. "How long have you been homeless?"

She slid her legs off the bed to put on a pair of sweatpants and he turned away.

"Maybe three months. If you want to know the short and skinny, I had a relationship that went south and this guy took me under his wing. He was a Mage and said he'd help me find a job. The cost of living is high in Cognito, so I agreed. I didn't know about the Breed until he told me, and what a trip *that* was," she added. "He seemed really honest at first, but I found out he wanted something in exchange. It didn't take long before he began asking for sexual favors. I'm not that kind of girl, so I left him."

"And started living in your van?"

"Bingo. He's been following me ever since, and that's why I go by Jasmine in the clubs. He recently saw my picture up on a flyer and found out I was playing at Northern Lights."

Something didn't mesh. "Why would he care about helping you out? I don't mean it like that, but you're just a human."

"Uh-huh. He was um..."

She sat down and Adam heard the covers rustling around. When the bed creaked a little, he stole a glimpse and saw she had dressed herself in a white T-shirt.

"He was a juicer," she admitted. "I think he got his bigger doses elsewhere, but sometimes he just wanted a tiny hit off my energy, especially before he went out on business meetings. I let him because it just made me a little weak, but it didn't hurt. It's not like we were having sex."

Adam's fingers clenched into fists. Taking someone's light was an intimate act. It wasn't the same as sharing sexual energy, but you could feel that person's light within you. *Damn right* that asshole was taking advantage of a girl who didn't know better.

"Don't do that with anyone again," Adam said, rising from the bed. He kicked off his boots and dropped them in the corner of the room by the bathroom.

"Why not?"

"They get addicted to not just the high, but to *you*. Everyone's light tastes different. That explains why he's still looking for you."

"Oh, great. Why didn't anyone tell me this?"

He glanced over his left shoulder when she angrily pounded her elbows into her pillow. Then she hissed and rolled over, turning her back to him.

Adam walked across the room and knelt by her bed. "What's wrong?"

"My face hurts."

"Let me see."

She slowly rolled onto her back and swept her wavy hair away from her face. The cut on her lip had reopened and a bright bubble of blood smeared across her chin. Adam reached in the drawer where he kept a stack of napkins and folded one up, then held it in front of her mouth.

"Lick it."

Her eyes widened. "Are you serious?"

"Just lick it."

A laugh bubbled from her throat and she murmured, "That's uh, quite a pickup line you got there, Scratch." She poked out her tongue and dampened the end of the napkin.

Adam held it to her lip and leaned in, assessing the injuries on her face. All the while, her eyes explored the marks on *his* face. Then she lifted her hand and brazenly ran her finger along the jagged line that ran down his forehead on the left side.

He froze and his heart began to thump wildly in his chest.

No one had ever touched his scars.

Her finger felt calloused from playing the guitar. It wandered across his eyelid and then she trailed the path of another along his right jaw. Sadie finally retracted her hand.

"You're a handsome man."

Fire burned his cheeks. Adam rose to his feet and sat at the table, going through the money in his wallet.

"Just wanted to lay it out there that it doesn't bother me that you have marks on your body. It's a story, and maybe not one you want to talk about, but I just felt like telling you the truth so you wouldn't get the wrong idea about why I touched you just now. You're handsome. I've always loved men with brown eyes and thick hair. Never seem to end up with them," she said with a chuckle.

"I don't think I've ever met anyone as easygoing and upbeat as you," he finally said, struggling not to sound judgmental. "You were brutally attacked last night and almost raped, and you're sitting there trying to lift *my* spirits."

The air stilled and Adam abruptly looked up.

Sadie covered her face with one hand and wept.

He cursed under his breath and walked between the beds. "I'm sorry. I shouldn't have said it like that."

"I was stupid for not parking out front. I've always been safe, but I was running late when I got there and couldn't find a spot. They just rushed me out of nowhere."

"You okay?"

Sadie didn't answer. He sat on the edge of her bed and touched her chin, turning her head to face him. The bleeding in her lip had stopped. "Did they do anything to you before I got there?"

Sadie shook her head and sniffed.

"I shouldn't have let them walk away."

"I'm glad you did. It's what the better man does, and you're the better man."

Adam leaned back. "You don't know what I've done in my life to say something like that."

"I knew it the moment we met. You could have been a jerk and stepped over me, but you didn't. I can hear it in your voice beneath all the growling and attitude."

"I don't have an attitude."

"You *so* have an attitude."

His eyes fell to her lips and he hated seeing that cut because Sadie had bitable lips. The kind a man could kiss and suck on and then nibble just a little bit. The thought was extinguished when he realized she would probably have a scar to remind her of that night.

"That's the pot calling the kettle black, Kitten. Why don't you lie back and rest until the food comes. You don't have any family I can call?"

"Um, no. That's the one thing I don't have."

"No family?"

"Haven't you heard? It's a hard-knock life."

She yawned and after a few long blinks, Adam reached over to the wall and switched off the lamps. He left one turned on low, providing just enough light so he could see.

"Let me know when the pizza comes," she murmured. "I'll get up and help you clean off the table."

"How 'bout you stay right here in the bed and eat?"

Words he'd thought he'd never say. He was brought up to eat at the table and it's something he'd carried through most of his life. His mother used to say that anyone who resorted to eating in bed was no better than a pig, that despite your living conditions, you should rise above and show dignity.

"You ordered a supreme," she mumbled, falling asleep.

Adam liked the sound of her sleepy voice.

"So you're a pepperoni girl, is that what you're telling me?"

A smile ghosted her lips. "I don't like onions."

He reached over and switched off the light, his voice falling to a whisper. "I'll pick them off for you. Go to sleep."

CHAPTER 11

AFTER TWO HOURS OF SPARRING with Justus in the training room, I dragged myself into the shower. Justus hadn't liked discovering that I'd been withholding my powers. I knew my light was strong, but I still didn't have a full grasp of my abilities. And I sure hadn't liked being yanked away from the dinner table in front of our guests so I could hit the mat with a drill sergeant.

Logan remained upstairs, caring for Finn. It was surreal to imagine they would be temporarily living with us, although the offer sounded permanent. I had my doubts—Justus could barely tolerate living with me. I wanted to talk to Logan about his thoughts because he didn't seem like the type of guy who could live under another man's roof.

I stepped beneath the hot spray of water and opened my mouth, letting the rush of clean water beat against my face. My muscles ached from our session, but I'd walked away unscathed. Justus had tried showing me how to ball up my energy and concentrate it into a single burst of movement, a skill he had mastered but one I was too exhausted to learn after the fiasco at dinner with blasting him to the floor in front of company.

I lathered my hair with my favorite coconut conditioner and before I knew it, I was singing "What's New, Pussycat?" by Tom Jones. Usually I preferred Elton John, but sometimes I just sang the first thing that popped in my head. I couldn't carry a tune—my ex had made a point of telling me to *shut the fuck up* while beating on the bathroom door.

Justus might not have liked my singing, but he never mentioned it. Christian, on the other hand, never missed an opportunity to bring it up in conversation.

I had hit the chorus, singing *I love you*, when an unexpected noise in the room startled me. The opaque shower curtain revealed a silhouette of a man like a stalker in a horror movie. I covered my chest and stood motionless as he moved closer and stopped at the edge of the tub.

"I love you too, Little Raven," Logan said with an amused chuckle.

All I could make out was the shape of him. His fingertips touched the curtain, trailing down. I stepped as close as I could, knowing he couldn't see me and yet wishing he would rip it away and end this charade of modesty.

"How long have you been standing there?" I asked.

"Long enough to know I need a cold shower when you're done. I can *smell* you," he said in a lustful voice that implied he scented more than my shampoo.

His hands pressed harder against the curtain until they met with the soft curves of my breasts. His fingers outlined my nipples and his face came close enough that I could see the shape of it.

"Do you want to join me, Mr. Cross?"

I heard him take a deep breath and his hands moved away. "I'm afraid that wouldn't be a wise decision, as I would ravage you in ways that are not meant for your Ghuardian's ears."

I rinsed the conditioner out of my hair and shut off the water. "Well, if you're going to be living here on a permanent basis, then we need to talk about this."

Without warning, I ripped the curtain open and scowled. Logan had his eyes closed and a broad smile stretched across his face.

"Logan Cross, will you look at me?"

"No." He bent down and whispered seductively, "But I'll *taste* you."

I snatched the towel from the rack inside the shower, drying off my legs while he stood with his head tilted to one side.

"How's Finn?" I asked.

"His voracious appetite has returned. He polished off two plates of Levi's macaroni. After that, his wolf came out. I think by morning we can let him roam around the house. Little Wolf has adjustment problems with new places—we should give him some space."

"Maybe we should go back to your condo and gather up some of his blankets and pillows so he'll feel more at home. Oh my God..."

Logan frowned. "What's wrong?"

"I can't believe you two are living here. It's so weird, but so wonderful. How long do you think you'll stay?"

"Your Ghuardian has spoken with me privately and understands the Chitah ways. Family is important to us, and we often live in the same house or building with our siblings. Our family has been split apart for years and it's not healthy. Lucian has become more reclusive and Leo has expressed a desire to purchase some property to rectify our situation. I also respect your customs, and it would not benefit you to leave the care of your Ghuardian before you're ready just for the sake of becoming my mate."

I smiled and tossed the towel in the hamper to my left. He flared his nostrils when I stepped out of the tub and walked by him to slip into a thin robe.

"You can open your eyes; I'm dressed. So... my male wants to live with me?"

A deep purr, barely audible, rumbled from deep within his chest. The intensity of his emotions drew me nearer to him. From behind, he slipped his capable arms around my narrow waist and kissed my ear. Logan Cross was a tall and delicious man with defined muscles and a formidable presence.

"You are my mate and I do not sleep in any bed but yours."

"Please tell me you didn't say that to Justus."

"I will have this conversation with him. Justus is a male who understands needs. It is impossible for me to live under the same roof and not share the same bed. I will request that he either moves upstairs or we do."

I turned my mouth to the side, feeling his body press closer against my back. "Request all you want, but I have a funny feeling that Justus is not going to let you bunk with his Learner."

"I am not asking permission to have rapturous sex with my female; I am only giving him the courtesy of deciding which floor he prefers to sleep on."

"Rapturous sex?" I snorted.

"If we share the same bed, then I am going to *take* you in that bed and pleasure you in ways you've never imagined."

"But I like *my* room," I argued.

"Then it's settled. Justus will move upstairs." His mouth tickled the sensitive skin of my neck and his large hand cupped my breast, squeezing gently. "I might want to claim my female in the middle of the night and make her come. I don't care *who* hears, but I know you would have issues with it."

"Um, you got that right." I turned around and looked up at Logan. The black rims surrounding his golden irises swelled with desire and his upper fangs descended enough to suggest his arousal.

Logan curved his left arm around my waist and slid his right hand between my legs, moving beneath the fabric of my robe. I locked my arms around his neck and moaned softly. His finger slipped inside me and I gasped, heat flushing my cheeks. Logan's mouth brushed against mine. I greedily sucked on his lip and kissed him hard. His body stiffened as he shifted me against the sink and found a rhythm with his hand.

"Oh God," I whispered, feeling that biting sweetness of arousal.

A knock hammered at the door. "Learner, you're leaking," Justus bellowed.

He meant my energy, but I laughed against Logan's chest. Justus had no idea just *how much* I was leaking. Our bodies divorced and Logan watched me with predatory eyes.

"That's why Justus is moving upstairs," he said firmly. "As for how long this situation will last—that remains to be seen. I will respect him as your Ghuardian, but he will respect me as a man. I will not tolerate him crossing the line in how he speaks to me."

"Please try not to kill each other."

His eyes widened as he looked at my chest and whispered, "*Jiminy*."

"What?" I glanced down and saw my nipples were pressed like bullets against the silky fabric of my robe.

"Have I ever told you, Silver, that you have the loveliest bosom?"

"Yes, Mr. Cross. Right along with my spectacular gams that I'd love to wrap around your neck," I said with a tease in my voice.

"Mmm, now we're getting somewhere," he said, spreading his

hands around my back. His lips brushed along my neck and his breath warmed my skin.

"For now, sleep upstairs until we figure it out tomorrow. I'm not in the mood for verbal warfare."

He slid his mouth against my ear and whispered, "As you wish. Now hurry up and get ready for bed. I want my female draped across my naked body until she falls asleep."

"I thought we weren't sleeping together?" I protested a little.

Logan smiled seductively. "I want you to fall asleep in my arms, Little Raven. Then I'll slip out of your room and go upstairs, as we agreed."

"I don't know if I can sleep in the same bed with you if you're naked."

"Worry not, my sweet. You'll be naked too."

Before heading to bed, I checked on Finn. He was fast asleep—facedown with his feet hanging off the edge of the mattress. I tiptoed into the study and closed the door for privacy. Sunny was usually online at this hour and we often sent messages back and forth, but this time I started up the video chat.

"How's it going, girl?" she asked, finishing what looked like a cup of yogurt.

"Same old drama. I guess Novis filled you in on Nero's attacks?"

She lowered her eyes.

"I'm sorry about all this," I said with a disgusted sigh. "At least you're safe. Novis keeps his home heavily guarded and you couldn't be in better hands."

"Yeah," she said in a delicate voice, stirring the spoon slowly. "But what about everyone else?"

"Well, Logan and Finn are down here in the bunker with me." I smiled and twirled a pen around on the table. I thought about something she mentioned in our last conversation. "What made you decide to go to a Relic instead of a human ob-gyn?"

"Relics have more experience and availability. I don't know, I'm living in this world now and it seemed like the obvious choice.

Novis didn't like her and switched my doctor, so now I'm seeing someone new. Someone he trusts who comes with a truckload of qualifications. There's *no way* I'm going to be able to pay him back. I had a part-time job working at a nail salon before I got pregnant. Knox wanted to take care of me, but you know I can't just sit around. I love being where all the action is. I miss going out shopping and having dinner with friends. I miss my red Mustang."

I smiled wistfully, remembering how much she used to complain about her car. "What about Knox's Jeep?"

She turned her mouth to the side. "Too big. I'd love Adam to take it, but he's obsessed with his bike. I don't know how I'm going to manage to hold down a job after the babies are born. Have you seen the prices for daycare? Highway robbery. I wish someone could take care of them while I worked, and before you say a word, *no*. I love you, Silver, but I'm not leaving my twins in your care. You're a new Mage and you might accidentally—"

"I know, I get it. You're a mom and it's your nature to protect your babies. I'm a Mage and I can fry bacon with my hands, so maybe it's not a good idea to have Aunt Silver as the babysitter."

She leaned in and arched her brows. "Oh, you'll be babysitting. I wouldn't rob you of that wonderful experience while I get out and take a breather. But just not for long periods. Plus you have maniacs trying to kill you, which leads me to another concern. I'm scared Nero might try to come after my babies."

"He's not going to be after us forever, Sunshine. We'll get him."

Sunny rubbed her eye sleepily. "So Logan and Finn are there for good, huh? How's that going?"

"We'll see. It's only the first night, so no blood has been spilled. *Yet*."

She wound a curl of her blond hair around her index finger, the soft glow of a lamp illuminating one side of her face. Sunny had lovely features with expressive eyes, round cheeks, and plump lips. Between her and Knox's genes, their children would be beautiful, charismatic, and strong.

"I think I'm ready to let Knox go." Her eyes were distant and solemn.

I laced my fingers together as Justus often did and stared pensively at my friend.

Sunny continued. "What's in that urn isn't Knox—not the man I remember. He wouldn't have wanted me to be holding on to him like this. He would have said *Let me go, Baby Girl. I'm always with you.* Maybe it seems silly, but I feel like if I give his ashes to the ocean, the world will drink him up. That he'll live on because he'll become part of the world. Knox grew up on the coast near the Atlantic and used to tell me stories about how he'd stand near the cold waters in late winter while his father got drunk in a tavern near the shore. He lived in an abusive home and once told me that hearing the sound of the waves constantly moving forward gave him a sense of peace and calm. This is what he wanted. Holding on to Knox is keeping him from going home… where he belongs."

"When do you plan on doing this?"

"Soon. I can't wait around for this Nero thing to go away. I have a life to live and it's not as long as yours. Whenever I decide to go, Novis said I'll be heavily guarded. He hasn't mentioned anything about it being too dangerous, so I'm glad for that. Anyhow, I don't want to depress you before you start knockin' boots with your Chitah man, but I want to ask if you'll come with me. With everything going on, I'll understand if you can't make it."

"Firstly, I'm not knocking anyone's boots with my Ghuardian sleeping within earshot. What does that even mean? I sure as hell don't wear boots in bed."

A bright laugh filled the quiet room and she tossed her empty yogurt cup in the wastebasket.

"Secondly, you just say when and where and I'll be right beside you. It's going to be harder than you think, so I want you to know that despite all the drama going on around me, I'm always here for you. You're my Sunshine."

"Your *only* Sunshine?" she teased.

I wanted to sing the song but opted against it. Sunny would record the chat and use it against me as blackmail. I knew this girl too well.

Her eyes flashed up and I heard a voice.

"I'm just talking with Silver. ... No, not yet."

"Is that Novis? Tell him I'm sorry about dinner."

She narrowed her eyes at me playfully. "Now we're *really* going to have to do more catching up. I must have missed out on something good."

"Only me electrocuting my Ghuardian."

She looked up again. "Just a few more minutes. I'm not really tired."

Novis appeared behind her and leaned down, staring at me through the camera. "Silver, I'm afraid your friend will need to end this conversation. It's late and she needs rest."

"She doesn't look tired, Novis. By the way, do you have any jobs for me to do? I'm getting a little cabin fever."

"Silver," he said in a scolding tone. His messy hair obscured his eyes. "You can speak with Sunny tomorrow if there is a need. Her medical condition is of a delicate nature, and your thoughts should be on her well-being."

"She's pregnant, Novis. Sitting comfortably at a desk and talking on a computer is hardly comparable to making her run on a treadmill."

I got a little nervous when I saw the strict look on his face and a spark of light in his eyes. "Careful, young Mage, and be sure not to bite a feeding hand."

He slammed the laptop shut and I laughed at his screw-up of yet another idiom. Novis could be hardheaded—always thinking he's right. Wise, yes. But by no means a prophet. He was an honest employer, but sometimes the lines were blurred and he interfered in my personal affairs. Sunny might have been living with him, but that didn't give him permission to control her decisions. And why was he so restrictive all of a sudden? It made me think he might actually care about her condition, but that seemed unlikely. Novis believed emotions made you weak. He distanced himself from anything with an impermanent lifespan because loss was grievous and not good for the immortal soul.

That's where we disagreed—the fragility of life is what makes humanity so beautiful.

When I slipped into my bedroom, the lights were out and the cool air brushed against my skin. I stood anxiously by the door, waiting for Logan to pounce me in another practice attack.

"Come lay with me," I heard him say in the darkness.

God, if *that* didn't make a tingle run through my body.

"I just talked to Sunny for a little bit," I said, scooting beneath the covers and lying on my right side. I could feel his body heat in front of me and knew he was naked beneath the sheets. Logan not touching me was so erotic that it consumed my thoughts.

Logan sighed thoughtfully. "I worry for how a female will raise two young without a male to protect her. It is unfortunate that Knox had no brothers."

"It wouldn't be their job."

The sheets rustled as he moved up and I imagined him lying with his head propped in his hand. "Chitahs look out for family. If a male is taken before his time, either her brothers or his will care for that female. I'm assuming Sunny has no siblings if she's here in Cognito alone."

"No, she has an older brother."

Judgment clung to the edge of his words. "And where is he?"

"She doesn't know. They broke contact over a year ago and she wants to find him. Kane has always been a bit of a nomad and moved around a lot, but he always made an effort to keep in touch with her. Something must have happened to him—he's never missed her birthdays. I've met him a couple of times and he loves her to bits. I can't imagine Kane would just cut her off and not even call unless there was good reason."

"Perhaps he is dead."

I placed my hand over his mouth. "Don't say that. I don't even want to put that out there in the universe because of the hell she's already been through. I'm starting to see a glimmer of the old Sunny coming back—the one who'd take me to the bar and fill me up on nachos and drinks. The girl who loved making me buy ridiculous slingbacks I never wore."

"What are slingbacks?"

"Shoes. Never mind. Knox changed her in all the best ways, and

I pray that him dying doesn't undo all that. I'm starting to see that it hasn't, but I don't think she could take any more bad news at the moment—especially with the babies. God, I still can't believe she's going to be a mom," I said, my voice falling to a whisper.

In the darkness of the room, Logan slid his hand over my hip and kissed my forehead. I leaned in and nuzzled against his warm neck—our bodies still distanced by air.

"Stop thinking about it, Silver."

"I know, she'll be fine."

"That's not what I meant," he said, his voice tickling my ear. "You are whole to me, and yet you still doubt my love for you."

I leaned back, my head sliding onto the pillow. "I'm not following."

"I know your scent, Silver. When you think about children and us, it's a specific flavor on my tongue I'm quite familiar with. Words need not be said to confirm when your mind is plagued with doubts that I love you completely. A male wants family, yes. But as long as you are by my side, I will not have want. My mind will never change on this matter, so you can put it to rest."

"What about the chain? The metal will let us sleep together without all the problems of my energy spikes, Logan. I know you want to prove that you love me as I am, but God, you have the option of having *all* of me. Are you afraid that I won't live up to your expectations and—"

"Enough!" he roared, sitting up in the bed.

I swallowed thickly and pulled the sheet up to my neck.

"I will not allow you to degrade yourself in such a manner." His hand slowly brushed up my leg, reaching my thigh. "You are a beautiful female, and I will spill the blood of any male who lays a hand on you. I have vowed to change my ways and leave my violent past behind, but I will always protect my mate, and that is something you can depend on. We were born for each other and fit like pieces of a puzzle."

Logan eased back down beside me, much closer now, and the sheet had fallen between us. His breath warmed my left cheek as he spoke and he trailed his fingers up my hand, wrist, and the curve of my body.

"You try so hard to fit more pieces in our picture, but we are enough. You have accepted me as a Chitah, even knowing that when I flip my switch in bed, I become dangerous and unstoppable. You trust me, and I am honored by your devotion. Nothing about you is less than a woman, but *more than*. Do you think because you cannot touch me with your hands that you are not able to touch my heart? Your energy is unique to me and I love the thrill of feeling the electric current touching my skin when you're aroused."

He shifted my legs open, sliding his knee between them.

"My blood heats and I crave your taste when I see your eyes turn silver," he said in a dark voice against my lips.

Logan curved his right arm around my thigh, pulling it up higher, while his left arm slid beneath the pillow. We slowly came together, fitting in a way that felt effortless and divine.

He tasted my lips and I immediately forgot what we had been arguing about as my hands began to explore the contours and hard muscle of his arms and shoulders.

"Sleep, my female. I'll see you in your dreams."

CHAPTER 12

THE NEXT MORNING, ADAM WOKE up and wiped the sleep out of his eyes. He stretched his legs and threw the pillow away from his groggy head. The room seemed too quiet and he glanced at the bed on his left.

Sadie was gone.

So was her bag, guitar, and the entire box of pizza he had left on the table. It came as no surprise as she didn't seem like the kind of woman who would stick around for long. Free spirits never did.

He spotted a piece of paper on the table and threw his legs over the bed, then rubbed his face wearily. It had been a long night. Adam had hardly slept because he'd been concerned about the negative effects of Sadie having been unconscious for such a long time, so he'd kept a close eye on her.

He pulled open the heavy drapes and squinted at the bright sunlight that pierced the room like an invasive glare. Adam took a seat at the table, put a stale cigarette in his mouth, and flicked his lighter a few times until the flame lit up the end. The yellow note snagged his attention and he noticed how neatly she had folded the paper in half. After finishing a second drag, he set the cigarette in a groove on the ashtray and slowly unfolded the letter.

Dear Scratch,

I almost skipped out when you went to pick up my guitar, but I like you. Sounds strange, as we hardly know each other, but I'm sitting here watching you sleep and wondering why a guy like you is living in a motel. I don't know where you came from or who you are, but all that matters is you saved my life. That's a big deal in my book. Maybe I don't have much of a life to save, but someday I'm going to find my place in this world and I'll remember your kindness. I hope I can repay you if our paths cross again. Stay handsome, and quit smoking.

Kitten

Adam set the note down and patted out his cigarette with a wide grin on his face. Sadie reminded him in many ways of the women in his family—strong women who spoke freely and possessed a carefree heart.

He stared at the pack of smokes and thought about what she'd said. She was right about it being a weakness. It's not something he savored and enjoyed like Knox had, but rather used as a crutch when his mood altered. Life had hardened him as a man, but it had also withered his spirit. Smoking was only a symptom of his disease, so he dropped the pack into the wastebasket and decided he'd had enough. Not just enough of nicotine on his tongue, but all of it. The resentment, the anger, and especially the grief he felt for losing a good friend.

His twin sister's death had profoundly affected the direction of his life, and the mean streak he'd carried during that turbulent time had channeled into a career that made him do regretful things. But that's not who he was. Adam had been raised with character and integrity. He'd grown up in a Bohemian atmosphere and had worked hard to take care of his family as he entered his teens. His parents had died young and he'd dropped out of school to support his sister. Now he was putting his own needs first, and that didn't feel so good.

He folded up the note and carefully tucked it in his wallet. This wasn't the last time they'd see each other. Sadie performed at Northern Lights, and Adam had every intention of sitting in the back row to make sure no one messed with her. Just for a couple of weeks. He had a feeling those men in the alley would be back.

Adam scratched his stubbly jaw and wondered why he kept thinking about seeing Sadie again. He barely knew her, but as he stared out the window at a bird perched on the railing, he began to worry if she'd be safe on her own. What if she got hypothermia while sleeping in that piece of junk she called a van? Novis had taught him a Mage should stick to their own kind—it made things less complicated.

But damn, he couldn't stop thinking about her clever smile. She had a sweetness in her eyes and a purity to her face—one that wasn't marred by imperfections such as his own.

That made him shift in his chair as he wondered what she really thought about him. Humans had a tendency to say kind words for the sake of being polite, unlike Breed who would lay it out on the table without an introduction.

Not that it should have mattered how she really saw him, but suddenly... it kind of did.

He touched a groove in his jaw, wondering if things would have gone differently had he looked like his old self. Adam had never given his looks much thought in those days, but women had often said he had a charming smile. You could be the toughest man on earth who's been through hell, but acclimating back into society with defects or disabilities will test any man.

Adam texted a quick apology to Silver about dinner, explaining he had a lot on his mind. He thought about taking a long shower and going to a diner for breakfast.

Tires screeched outside and Adam launched out of his chair. He stepped outside into the corridor and leaned over the railing to have a look.

A smile crept up his face. Sadie had illegally parked her VW at an angle between two parking spaces. Adam straightened up and stretched his arms behind his back, waiting for her to come up. He still had on his weathered jeans from the night before, although he'd stripped out of his shirt. The cold air felt good against his skin, like a snap of life waking him up.

His brows furrowed when Sadie didn't get out of the van. Maybe she'd seen him and was having second thoughts about coming back up.

The concrete chilled the bottom of Adam's feet as he walked to the end of the balcony and descended the stairs. As he approached the van, he came to a hard stop. Energy circulated in his body and sent light flooding to his fingertips.

Sadie was slumped over, her forehead pressed against the glass.

He crossed the parking lot in seconds flat. As soon as he tugged on the door handle, she wilted into his arms. Her baggy jeans had a rip in the knee and she'd stolen his black sweater—the sleeves so long her arms disappeared inside them.

"Sadie," he said sharply, giving her a hard shake.

Adam reached over and pulled the keys out of the ignition. He gently lifted her out of the seat and charged toward the stairs, holding her tight in his grip.

"He found me," she whispered in a broken voice.

"Who found you?" he asked without looking down. Adam struggled to keep his emotions in check so he wouldn't inadvertently leak energy into her through his hands.

"Cedric."

Adam froze mid-step and looked down at her eyes, open just a sliver. That's the name Oliver had given him. "What did you say?"

"The Mage I lived with. I went to pick up my check at the club and he was there. He juiced me. I feel so weak; he's never taken this much."

"Motherfucker," Adam ground out as he hurried up the stairs.

"Am I going to die?"

He could barely look in her in the eye. "No, Kitten, you're going to be just fine."

Once inside the room, he kicked the door shut and placed her on the bed. Sadie lay helpless as he raked his fingers through his hair and paced in a circle.

Adam couldn't heal a human.

Without missing a beat, he called Silver and got the number of her Relic. If Silver trusted Page La Croix, that was good enough for him. Adam needed a specialist who would know how to treat a human juiced by a Mage. Because of the recent assassinations, asking Novis for help was out. He would never put his Creator's life in jeopardy, and aside from that, Novis would have no interest in saving a human.

Adam made an urgent call to Page. At first, she rejected his request. When he told her it was life or death, she said she'd be there in fifteen minutes.

Adam dragged a chair beside the bed and tilted Sadie's head back so nothing obstructed her breathing. She was fading in and out of consciousness, murmuring incoherently. He sent Silver a message and thanked her for the Relic's information. When she asked where he was, he assured her everything was fine and told her to stay put.

A knock sounded at the door and he rushed to answer it.

"I came as fast as I could," Page said, out of breath, pulling an oversized winter hat off her head. "Where is she?"

Adam stepped aside and Page walked in, placing her black bag on the chair and unzipping her coat.

"How long has she been this way?"

"Twenty minutes, maybe. I don't know how the hell she managed to drive here in that condition," he murmured, pacing to the end of the bed.

"She's got a strong spirit," Page said. "Sometimes that's enough to get us through the most difficult times. I don't have any of my equipment, so I want you to hold up a drip bag for her IV. I'm going to give her what her body needs to restore some of that depleted energy. Are you listening?"

Adam gawked at her round belly, speechless.

"Take a good long look, Mage. I'm pregnant. Lo and behold, the Relic is knocked up. Now get over here and help me set up my instruments."

After Page sterilized and prepped Sadie's arm, Adam watched her slide in the needle until the catheter was in place. She held a plunger at the opposite end, secured a clamp, and then taped up the site of the needle as if she'd done this a million times before.

"There. We'll give it thirty minutes and see how she's doing. Can you hold it for that long?"

"No sweat. What's in there?" He took the bag from her hand and held it up.

"All the nutrients a growing girl needs. I've treated patients in her condition before, but usually among Breed. I've administered this treatment to only three humans and one of them still died. Juicing is a serious problem on our streets, so that solution you're holding is widely distributed in the Relic community. Let's just hope she's a fighter."

After checking Sadie's blood pressure and pulse, Page walked around the bed and set her medical bag on the table. She eased herself into the chair, glancing out the window and stroking the impressive curve of her belly. Her clothes didn't look big enough, more like an oversized sweater stretched to the max.

"How long have you been pregnant?" he asked. "I don't remember you being that far along when I last saw you."

She reached in her purse and pulled out a pair of reading glasses, then wrote a few notes in a small book. Obviously, she wasn't there to answer personal questions.

The sunlight picked up a few highlights in her short brown hair. She smiled surreptitiously, her face glowing. The few times Adam had been around Page, he'd never seen her with makeup on. A woman like her didn't need it. Something about the richness in her brown eyes and hair made up for that. She was lovely, and he could see why men would take a shine to her.

Adam continually alternated the IV bag between hands as his upper arms became sore. Every so often, Page would put down her pen and look at Sadie with concern.

A burst of noise outside the door made Adam's heart kick into gear as shouts were drawing nearer. His eyes immediately noticed the unlocked door and he stepped forward, about to drop the bag and secure the deadbolt.

"Adam!"

His brows knitted. That sounded like...

The door swung open and Justus filled the space like a tyrannical storm. A cold draft blew in from behind him but immediately became an inferno of heat.

Justus lowered his eyes to the bed, but Adam obscured his view. All he could see were Sadie's legs and Adam holding a drip bag for the IV. Justus approached the bed and relief washed over him when he saw Sadie's face, which pissed Adam off.

"What the hell are you doing here?" Adam scowled.

"Silver told me there was an emergency with the Relic. That's all she said. I searched her phone and found this address."

"Nice of you to drop by," Adam said sarcastically.

"The Relic wasn't injured?"

"No, the Relic is just fine," Page said from her seat at the table. "Unlike the Mage who just stormed in here like a barbarian."

Justus looked to his left, not having seen Page tucked in the chair beside the window.

His eyes flicked between them. "What is your need for a Relic?" he asked Adam.

Page frowned. "What business is that of yours? This is a private consultation and you have no right to—"

"Keep quiet," Justus said, eyes still locked on Adam. "I asked you a question, *Learner*."

"You can cut that Learner shit out, because you're not my Creator. Mine treats me with a hell of a lot more respect than you do with—"

"Who are you telling to keep quiet?" Page interrupted in a dangerously sharp voice as she rose from her chair. "This is a medical emergency and my services were requested. How dare you barge in and breach their confidence. And then to have the nerve to stand there and tell me to shut up! Your presence is obtrusive and I have a patient to treat."

Justus dropped his keys on the floor, eyes wide on her pregnant belly. His face turned a blotchy red and Mage light flickered in his eyes like fireflies.

Page walked over and checked Sadie's pulse. "She's doing better; we can stop the drip now." After removing the tubes, Page taped a bandage over the entry site on Sadie's arm. "I'll stay here for a little while and keep you company. Once it looks like she's in the clear, then I'll leave you be. She needs to conserve her energy and rest," Page said in soft words. "Sleep does wonders. Why don't you close the drapes?"

Justus turned the corner in his new Mercedes and Page gripped his arm for balance. Maybe he was maneuvering around those corners sharper than he should have on purpose. She quickly placed her hands in her lap and gave him a cold stare.

"I don't see why you wouldn't let me call a cab," she said.

"Where is your car?"

She pinched the bridge of her nose and yawned. "It conked out on me and wasn't worth repairing. I get around just fine in the city. Trains are cheaper than cabs, although I never feel safe taking the train at night."

"Nor *should* you."

Page had never felt more uncomfortable sitting beside a man she had seen naked. Maybe that made it all the more worse. She periodically caught him looking at her belly from the corner of his eye.

"You could take a picture," she suggested. "Maybe hang it over the fireplace and stare at it all day."

His hand made a rough sound as it gripped the wheel tighter. The next ten minutes were met with silence and she felt sad about that. Remorseful. Breaking it off with Justus was so much harder than she'd thought it would be, but doing the right thing is never easy.

"Pull over here for a second," she said, pressing her finger against the glass.

He eased into the parking lot of a donut shop and put the car in park. "What do you need?"

She unbuckled her seatbelt and pushed open the door. "Donuts, silly. I'll be right back."

Page had been craving strange things, as to be expected with any pregnancy. But something she couldn't pass up was a donut shop. Without looking at the menu, she ordered a variety box.

It might have been freezing on the streets, but it felt toasty warm inside the bakery.

Or maybe it was just the Mage who had crept up behind her without saying a word. Page could sense Justus but, still angered by the way he had spoken to her, refused to acknowledge his presence.

"Here you are, miss," the baker said with a toothy smile. He was a thin, wiry man with cloudy eyes. "Would you like a hot cup of coffee?"

"No, she will not be having caffeinated beverages," Justus declared.

Her brows popped up and she turned around. Justus was holding her jacket, which she had refused to put on when she left the motel. The man infuriated her with his righteous attitude.

"Should you be eating those?" he asked.

Page lifted the box and took a bite of a jelly donut. "*Mmmhmm.* Definitely." The sugar awakened all those happy little endorphins in her body and she smiled, savoring another sweet bite. "Want one?"

He eyed her box of gluttony. "Rolls?"

"Oh my God. Please tell me you're joking."

But he wasn't. Justus was serious. He was a man who kept his mind and body conditioned—probably eating a high-protein diet and rarely indulging in sweets. But to have never tasted a donut?

"Take one," she insisted, holding the box between them. "My treat."

"Page…"

"Mr. De Gradi," she said in a clipped tone that appeared to irritate him.

His large hand hovered over the assortment, quickly avoiding the ones with pink and yellow sprinkles.

"Try that one," she suggested. "It's my absolute favorite."

His blue eyes traced her features and he tilted his head. "Then why did you not eat it first?"

She shrugged. "I always like saving the best for last."

A warm chuckle rocked his chest and he quickly suppressed it. "And you were going to eat all these *before* your favorite? That's a hearty appetite, Page."

She bit her lower lip and smiled. "Go on, fraidypants. Try one while they're still warm."

He pulled out the one she loved the most—the cinnamon apple-filled donut. He took a generous bite and made an appreciative moan.

"See? Yummy, isn't it?"

A few bits of the gooey filling fell on his shiny combat boot and he glanced down. "Perhaps we should sit."

It's a good thing he didn't get it on his nice button-up shirt, she thought.

"One large coffee," Page said to the clerk.

"She will *not* be having coffee," Justus insisted.

Well, Page was a little tickled by his behavior and leaned on the counter. "Coffee for my friend. I'll have a small orange juice. How much will this total up to?"

Justus fished out his wallet and laid a large bill on the counter, which made the man's eyes widen. "For your trouble."

Then he escorted her to a small table in the back, away from the doors and the window. Page stared at the narrow booth and frowned, attempting to scoot in the seat when he cupped his hand around her arm.

"We'll sit here," he said, pointing to a table on the other side with regular chairs. "Will this be suitable?"

"Yes. Sorry, I'm a whale, I know."

She set the box on the table and sat down while he held her chair. Justus quietly sat across from her and shoved the box against the wall before placing two small plates in front of them and a stack of napkins in the middle.

Page's taste buds rejoiced when she took another bite of the jelly donut and washed it down with juice. "This is what life is all about. When you can just sit down and enjoy the simple pleasure of a delicious pastry that melts away all your troubles. And all that time you used to say I didn't eat enough," she said with a giggle. "Bet you wish you could eat those words now that you've seen the good it's done for my body."

He leaned forward and softened the rough edges in his voice. "You are large because you are with child, not because you have kept yourself nourished."

Page laughed and covered her mouth. "I'll probably be mad at you later on for calling me large, but I'll let it slide for the time being."

"Would you mind telling me how this came to be?"

"Well," she began in a facetious voice, licking jelly from her thumb. "It all begins when the penis meets the vagina."

He slammed his hand down on the table and made her jump.

"What do you want me to say, Justus? That I'm having another man's baby? *Yes*."

"And how is it possible?"

She opened her mouth to speak, but he must have sensed sarcasm making a swift arrival.

"How could you not disclose your pregnancy all this time? Who fathers this child?"

"Well, now that my private sex life is being discussed in front of half the store, I'll tell you." She lowered her voice and her flaring temper. "Slater."

"I knew I should have killed him sooner," he ground out through his teeth before taking a long sip of coffee.

"Look, what's done is done. I can't go back in a time machine and fix this. You don't want to be mixed up with a woman who's pregnant. He did things to me in that lab I'll never know, and I'm afraid of what it could have done to this baby. I guess I'll find out soon enough. *Shoot*."

"What?"

Her face soured. "My donut got cold." She set it down on her plate and tears welled in her eyes. Here came the waterworks. It had nothing to do with the donut or Justus finding out she was pregnant. Page had learned that she no longer had control over her emotions and experienced frequent outbursts.

Justus reached across the table and cupped his hand over her plate. After a few seconds, he retracted his arm and began picking at his donut. "See if it's to your satisfaction."

When she touched the soft edges, the donut was toasty warm and the glaze melted against her fingertips. Page smiled. "I still think that's an amazing gift you have. I wish I could do something like that."

"Intelligence is your gift," he said with a short nod.

Page's cheeks stung with heat. She put her hands in her lap as they began to turn red and she glanced around. She had forgotten how good it felt to banter with Justus, how their petty quarrels always ended with compliments and humor.

"You're still sending me orchids," she said in a quiet voice. "But you can stop now."

"No," he said, eyeing the box of donuts. "That will continue."

Her eyes widened. "What for?"

"Are they not agreeable?"

"My bedroom looks like a botanical garden, as does the rest of my apartment. I've had to give away some to my neighbors and even nearby shopkeepers. In fact, sometimes I'll give them to a random stranger walking by on the street. Some of the flowers have died because, I hate to tell you this, but I have a black thumb. Those are fussy plants and require too much attention."

A smirk wound up his face. "That sounds like a flower I know."

She snatched his donut and took a bite, claiming back her favorite. "I hardly think you're one to talk."

He reached in the box and pulled out a chocolate-glazed, sending slivers of crumbs to his plate. When he took a large bite, his lips were smothered in dried glaze.

Page burst out laughing. "Here," she said, handing him a napkin.

Justus wiped his mouth and then cleaned off his fingers. "Is there anyone caring for you?"

"I went to a Relic a couple of times, but I don't know. The fetus is growing so fast and I don't want to draw any attention. It could be dangerous and um… I just want to fly under the radar and try to live a normal life."

His finger touched the edge of her glass and he pushed it toward her. She indulged him with a short sip and set the juice to the side.

"Do you plan to keep the child?" he asked, drinking his coffee and avoiding eye contact.

"Despite how I feel about Slater, the baby is half *mine*. Someday I'll have to tell him what his father did to me—to him. But I never thought I could have children, Justus. No matter how I try to see this as an abomination, I can't help but marvel at the life growing inside me. I mean, I'm having a baby. I'm bringing a life into this world and *that* is a miracle. This was never my future, and maybe that's the only thing Slater ever got right in his meaningless life. I'm not sure what will happen with the baby because of all the drug cocktails I received, but I can't deny him. No child is born evil, and no deformity erases the love a mother has for her baby. Whatever I'm about to bring into this world is going to be beautiful, because it's mine. I'm just scared."

He reached across the table and she drew comfort from his touch.

No words would have had a greater impact than the simple gesture of him holding her hand, because Justus was not a man who invited physical contact. That hadn't been the case during their intimate times together, but to be so bold as to show her *public* affection? Her heart constricted.

"Maybe Slater didn't think my body could carry it through, so he found a way to speed up the gestation. The fetus is developing rapidly and I'm afraid he might age too quickly. It could slow down… I don't know."

"He?"

Page tapped the side of her nose and watched a lady in a walker make her way to the side door.

"I don't know the sex, but I'm almost positive it's a boy. He's got a strong kick and I'm carrying high."

Page felt silly giving those reasons, because as a Relic, she knew better.

When Justus stared pointedly at her stomach, she slouched in her seat and cleared her throat.

"How will you care for the child and work?"

"Well, I don't plan to decide that over a box of donuts. I know you must have a ton of questions, but I don't know that I have all the answers. I'm just taking it one day at a time."

He lifted a sprinkled donut and placed it on her plate, briefly warming it. The chocolate began to melt down the sides and her mouth watered.

"I must admit that pregnancy becomes you. It pleases me to see you eat."

She smiled wide and picked off some of the chocolate icing. "You just like the big girls, don't ya?"

His neck turned fire-engine red. Justus had once admitted she didn't eat enough and had gone on about how larger women were once revered. It was true. Rubenesque women were found attractive during his time, until the last couple of centuries when women had begun squeezing into corsets. Page had been average, perhaps on the leaner side, before she had become pregnant. Of course, now she was the Pillsbury Doughboy, and watching his eyes widen as he looked at her full breasts sent a flurry of laughter to her throat.

Embarrassed or not by her brash remark, he liked what he saw. She couldn't help but feel embraced by his acceptance of her, no matter what size she was. He complimented her regardless and seemed more concerned that she was healthy and eating properly. In all fairness, he was never in the wrong. Page had several vitamin deficiencies that she'd ignored prior to the pregnancy, but all that was rectified now that she was taking the right pills and eating healthy.

She watched the way he blew the steam from his coffee before sipping it and how he'd lick his lip before setting the mug down. Page realized she didn't want to feel those residual feelings for Justus blossoming like a flower with each passing moment. There was something inexplicably magnetic about this Mage. It had nothing to do with the fact he was a Charmer, because that had no effect on Page. But there were brief moments when he held her gaze and a delicious warmth licked over her skin.

She felt guilty entertaining the idea of starting up something he didn't want.

"I think I'm done," she announced. "This was probably not a good idea."

"On the contrary, Page, I think it was an excellent idea. Finish your juice and I'll drive you home."

CHAPTER 13

"That's your third hamburger," I said, eyes wide with disbelief.

Finn took a monster bite and grease rolled down his wrist. "Hungry," he murmured with a full mouth.

I laughed and Logan eased up beside me in my living room. Justus didn't care for eating outside the kitchen or dining room, but Justus wasn't here. When I'd told him there was an emergency with Adam and Page, he'd checked my phone and stormed out the door.

"Do you want me to cook you up another plate of fries?" I offered.

"Got any onion rings?"

Logan cleared his throat. Chitahs didn't believe women should serve men, and Logan decided he'd had enough.

"If you want onion rings, Little Wolf, then you will go into the kitchen and make them yourself."

"Logan," I said, holding his arm.

"A male should not be coddled like a child. He is strong enough to move about and eat, so he is—"

"Still sitting in the room. So quit talking about me like I'm not here," Finn said, putting his burger down. After dusting off his fingers, he wiped them on his sweatshirt. "I asked because it seemed like the polite thing to do. I don't like digging through other people's drawers and using their appliances."

"This is your house," I said. "Dig all you want."

He looked at the plate on his lap and finally set it on the end table. Finn had difficulty maintaining eye contact. His years in captivity with Nero, when he'd been beaten and branded, had made him into a submissive wolf with aggressive tendencies. He was getting much better about his outbursts and learning to speak up, but I often wondered what kind of future he'd have in this world.

"It feels weird," he admitted.

I sat on the edge of the couch and Logan clasped his hands in front of him.

"You'll get used to it," I said. "It just takes a little time. Now I have someone to teach me about geography." His eyes lit up as I tapped into that curious mind of his.

"There are security alarms within the home," Logan pointed out. "We won't be giving you the access codes because you won't be leaving without one of us to accompany you. If you manage to open a door when the security is on high, you'll set off the silent alarms and it will alert Justus."

I snorted. "Trust me, he's got it hooked up to his phone somehow so he knows what's going on when he's not at home."

Finn stood up and stuffed his hands into his oversized jean pockets. "So I'm a prisoner again, is that how it is?"

"No," I quickly said, reducing the space between us and giving him a hug. "It's not safe for anyone right now, but especially you. Once we catch Nero, it won't be like this anymore." He stepped away from me and combed his hair with his fingers. "If your wolf needs to run, you hang up a sign in the bathroom that you're downstairs and we'll stay up here and no one will bother you."

He nodded. "Coolio."

"We're heading out," Logan said.

Leo had called earlier and wanted to meet with Logan. It had to do with Finn, so Logan had asked me to join him.

I pinched Finn's cheek and he grinned, plopping into a swivel chair.

"There are a few movies in the cabinet—just slide them in the computer over there and it'll come up on the screen."

"Which one?" he asked, staring at the wall full of monitors.

"All of them. It's better than the movie theater, and there's microwave popcorn in the pantry if you want to make some. We shouldn't be long. Just stay away from the ice cream."

Finn looked over his shoulder. "Why's that?"

"I've staked my claim on the dark chocolate. It's *mine*."

"Glad you came, brother." Leo greeted us, opening the door to his home.

It was the first time I'd been to his place and my eyes roamed around as I took off my jacket. Like Logan, he also lived in a condo, but it was tastefully decorated. The walls had rectangular panels with white trim, and the rooms were velvet red. It seemed like a bold color for a man, but it was a deep, masculine shade and was complemented by the black furniture. I felt like I had stepped into a magazine.

A crooked smirk accented my expression and Logan peered back at me with a smile in his eyes.

Leo took our coats and hung them up. "Join me in the living room; I have lunch."

Unlike Logan's barren apartment, Leo's was vibrant and lived in. The white couch had clean lines and faced a brick fireplace. The rest of the furniture was black leather. I never could figure out why men were obsessed with leather. I imagined their get-togethers must have involved lighting up cigars and doing manly things like discussing sports and whittling with a giant machete.

The glass coffee table had a tray of delicious-looking goodies to snack on.

"Are these pigs in a blanket?" I said excitedly.

Leo chuckled, sitting in a leather chair while Logan stole the one across from him. I nervously sat on the edge of the pristine sofa, certain I would spill something on it.

I waited and Leo leaned forward, holding out his hands. "Eat, female. I made those when Logan said you would be accompanying him."

Which was an honor—Chitah men cooked for women they respected. After I loaded up a small plate, Leo and Logan fixed their own. Apparently Leo didn't entertain guests in the afternoon with alcohol since he served lemon water.

"Mmm, these are good," I said, devouring my third one. They

were still warm with just a hint of spice.

"What is the importance of this meeting?" Logan sat with his legs wide apart and his arms on the armrest.

Leo dusted crumbs off his fingers and set his plate on a glass table to his left. He shared similar traits with Logan—especially his smile. The light from the window behind him picked up the highlights in his reddish hair, making him the kind of man that stood out in a crowd. His stout physique and refined characteristics made it feel as if I were in the room with a leader. A closely trimmed beard shadowed his face and what I loved about him were the laugh lines high on his cheeks near his almond-shaped eyes. I always felt I could trust a man with laugh lines.

"A man named Rupert Wade visited me last night."

My eyes darted toward Logan to catch his reaction, but he held a blank stare. He scratched his head and drew my attention to his choppy hair. After the night I'd cut it off, Logan had vowed never to wear it long again, saying that kind of devotion comes along once in a lifetime and it would dishonor me to grow it out.

"The name rings no bells," Logan replied, stroking his chin pensively. My eyes wandered down to his black shirt, which hitched up in the front and revealed a patch of skin above his cargo pants. I felt silly ogling him until his nose twitched and a smile played on his lips.

Leo cleared his throat and took a sip of water, the ice clinking in the silent room. "Rupert is Finnegan's father." He and Logan held each other's gazes as if a silent exchange was transpiring between the two.

"What did *he* want?" I asked tightly.

"Rupert wants us to return his son. He belongs to a pack now and has the Packmaster's support."

"He can't do that!" I exclaimed. "Did Finn ever tell you that his beloved father was the one who sold him into slavery?" I set my plate on the table and stood up. "I can't believe this. You're not going to do it, are you?"

Logan interrupted. "Finn is a man now. He's not a boy that a parent can tug around without his approval."

"Finnegan is also a Shifter," Leo reminded him. "They have different rules, and they're questioning his ability to make sound decisions. He's chosen to live in a house with Chitahs and that has insulted the Packmasters in the territory. They think we're feeding him lies and brainwashing him."

"What does Rupert want with him?" I asked. "You can't let this happen. Finn has a home here and that man… I can't believe this."

Leo's nostrils flared as he drew in a deep breath and shifted in his chair. The leather creaked beneath him. "I'm afraid there may be nothing we can do. This is out of our territory and our elders will not defend us on this matter because Finnegan is not a Chitah."

"No. Absolutely not. I'm sorry, but this rings like déjà vu. My Creator had full rights to me and do you want to know what he did when my Ghuardian handed me over to him? He beat me."

Logan's canines punched out and his lips peeled back. "I will not give my brother to a man who threw away his child."

"If he gains support from more Packmasters, it's going to happen," Leo said. "My hope is we can bribe him. He's clearly a man that responds to money, given his past. Once Finnegan is living on his own, this should no longer be an issue. But as it stands, he is within our care and that is an insult to Mr. Wade."

"Let him be insulted," I said. "I'm pretty insulted he sold his child. I don't even want to think about why he wants him back. Did he ask for money?"

"No, and that is what concerns me. He may not care about his son, but his pride has been pricked. Word somehow got out—you know how Breed talk—that we took in a Shifter as one of our own. That kind of thing does not go unnoticed."

I sat down and put my head in my hands, my hair falling in front of my face.

"Pay him," Logan said in a flat voice.

"It won't end once it begins," Leo said. "Men like him don't take a one-time withdrawal if they know the bank is always open. He might discover a way to blackmail us and this will never end."

"We're not giving Finn up," I said. "He's living under my roof now and I forbid it. Over my dead body will I hand him over…"

My finger was pointing in anger but tears began to well in my eyes.

Logan rose from his seat and sat back down to my right, then rubbed the back of my neck. I leaned against him, feeding off his strength. Logan always managed to keep a level head where I would lose my emotional cool.

"We have other options," Logan suggested in a dark voice.

Leo's eyes sharpened. "I will not be a part of that. Murder is not an option."

"I didn't say you had to be a part of it."

Leo leaned forward and his expression gave me goose bumps. "I'm a member of HALO, in case you've forgotten. If you suggest you're going to carry out murder, then I'll have no choice but to take you down. You're my brother, but I have an obligation to uphold the laws."

Logan sighed and lowered his head, studying his strong hands. "What else did he say?"

"That we had a few days to talk it over and get Finn's belongings packed. That's why I think Rupert's giving us time—hoping we might care enough that we'll pay him off. I don't think he's certain of our feelings for Finn as a brother. He knows Chitahs are loyal to family, but even Shifters rarely take in outsiders. I'm willing to bet he assumes we have an ulterior motive. Perhaps he thinks Finn has somehow acquired money and we're using him, or grooming him to work as a spy."

"That's preposterous," Logan snapped. "The boy doesn't even know how to operate a vehicle, let alone work as a mole."

"Shifters are prideful men. Rupert won't back down; of this I'm certain."

I lifted my eyes to Leo. "What if we lie and tell him Finn ran away? We live underground and I doubt Rupert knows where he lives. He'd have no proof."

"It's not advisable. He'll eventually find out we lied and then his Packmaster will be out for blood. This is more than just a father staking claim on his son; if the pack gets involved, then we're at a disadvantage. This is a tug-of-war, and Finnegan is the rope. The question is: who will let go?"

"His father," I said through clenched teeth.

"This could turn political."

"Why doesn't anyone ask Finn's permission?" I said, raising my voice. "I'm sure he could talk with those Packmasters and tell him where he wants to live."

"Again," Leo said in a rational tone, "they deem him incapable of making sound decisions since he's living with us. If they question him, that could do more harm. They will discover how socially inept he is, not to mention that he's suppressing his alpha instincts. That will offend them more than anything."

"It's because of the slavery Finn is like that, not us."

"But their contention will be that we're a hindrance—that living among Shifters is the only way he'll overcome those issues and be whole again."

"Maybe they're right," Logan conceded.

I turned a sharp glare his way. "Explain."

His pensive gaze softened. "It's the very reason I insist you live with Justus; you will never grow as a Mage if you don't learn what you can from him. If I removed you from that environment, it would be detrimental to your growth. He's teaching you what you're capable of, educating you on your history and immersing you in his world so you know how to engage and interact with others of your kind. If I denied you this opportunity, it would make you a weak Mage. That would be a selfish act on my part."

Leo rose from his chair and paused in front of the fireplace, watching the embers glowing in the soot. "It's not unlike the story of King Solomon, who settled a dispute between two mothers, each claiming the same child was theirs. When the king offered to cut the child in half, the real mother gave up her claim so he would live. Love comes with sacrifice. Sometimes we must do what feels wrong because we know in our heart it's the right thing to do."

That hit home for me. But this felt so different, and I couldn't let Finn go. Not to a man I knew nothing about, aside from the fact he didn't love his son.

"Finn won't want to go," I pointed out.

"We'll talk to him and see how he feels about this," Logan

said. "He has a right to know what's going on and should make the decision himself. We'll have to stand behind that choice, no matter what it is."

Leo shook his head and folded his arms. "Finnegan is a cunning young man and I hope he might offer some insight. This is so unfortunate." Leo excused himself and left the room.

Logan ran the pad of his thumb across my brow where a line deepened from my frown. "We'll figure this out."

"If we send him back and something happens to him, Logan, I'll never forgive myself. If his father beats him, sells him, or murders him, that'll stain your conscience for the rest of your life."

His eyes slowly closed.

"I don't care if this starts a political war," I continued. "I'm not letting him go. Maybe you and Leo are more willing because that's how the Breed world works, but family is family. If I send him back to the man he despises, it would be like erasing every time I told him I loved him. Like it never happened. Don't let this be the deal breaker with us, Logan. I love you more than life, but if you send Finn to a man who will destroy his beautiful spirit, I will never forgive you."

His eyes opened and he touched the sides of my cheeks, rubbing his nose against mine. "Talking about the options does not mean doing. But we must consider the consequences of every possible action. If he doesn't want to return to his father, then I will stand by his side and fight to the death to protect him. Finn is a Cross now."

I kissed Logan tenderly on the mouth. My fingers grazed across his smooth chin and I felt him grin against my lips.

"What's so funny, Mr. Cross?"

"Someday I'll tell you, Little Raven. Now give me your tongue."

CHAPTER 14

On the drive home from Leo's, I asked Logan to swing by Simon's apartment. Logan volunteered to wait in the car and I didn't blame him. Simon could run his mouth and loved to play mind games. He was a button pusher, and Logan was a man who didn't like to be pushed.

After a long elevator ride up, I walked down a hallway and knocked on Simon's door several times. Since I had a spare key because of game nights, I unlocked the door and eased it open.

"Simon?"

I heard laughter, chatter, and techno music at a low volume coming from the living room area. When I didn't see anyone on the sofa or chairs, I glanced to the left toward his computer desk and my mouth swung wide open.

Spread across the floor was a giant plastic mat with colored circles. A girl with the straightest black hair I'd ever seen had her hands on the mat behind her and her legs spread wide. She looked like she was crab walking without a stitch of clothing on except a black G-string.

Simon had on his leather pants, no shirt, and was in such a precarious position that it led me to believe he was going to lose this game.

I cleared my throat loudly and irritably. Not because he was playing naked sex games with a girl behind closed doors—what Simon did on his own time was his business. But I had called him not ten minutes prior to announce I was on my way over. He'd made it sound like he was just hanging around watching TV.

"Hey, love. There's room for one more."

"Um, no," I said, folding my arms. "Is this a bad time?"

He peered at me from beneath his armpit and grinned wickedly.

"It's a bloody fantastic time. You can keep your knickers on if you want."

"Simon, I'm leaving."

"Wait," he said, hopping up and standing astride the woman whose legs muscles began to quiver. "How important is this?"

"Important enough I can't discuss it in front of random, naked women?"

He offered his hand to the woman on the floor, who proceeded to lick her upper lip seductively. "Rain check."

"But we're not naked yet," she protested in a breathy voice.

The dimple pressed deep in his cheek as his eyes slid down to her bare breasts. "Swing by tonight and I'll rectify that."

"I have to work tonight," she complained, still positioned with her foot on green and hand on red.

Simon had the look of an impatient man. Women like her didn't challenge his intellect—they were merely a recreational pastime.

"Then come by tomorrow in those lovely garters with the red bows."

Her thin brows arched and she spoke like a viper hissing. "It's my mother's birthday."

His face tightened and he pulled her up by force. "Then you can bugger off and have birthday cake with your mum instead of having me lick icing off your knockers." He tossed a thin dress and a small red clutch at her. "Off you go."

She flipped her hair over her shoulder, showing him her breasts. "You said we were going to screw, and I've wasted all this time playing your stupid games. What kind of man seduces a woman like this? You're a royal asshole."

"Maybe so. But I'm an asshole with a large cock and a hungry appetite, so put on your dress and piss off."

"Simon," I said, cautioning him in a low voice.

She slapped him in the face and he barely flinched. In fact, Simon tucked his thumbs in the belt of his leathers and tapped his bare foot, his cheek turning red.

"I want my money," she demanded, slipping into her black dress and holding out her hand.

"Is she a hooker?" I asked in surprise.

The woman whipped around and carved me up with her beady little eyes. "You need to shut the hell up, skank."

My jaw tensed and I saw Simon's lips twitch.

"Maybe you need to just go home quietly," I suggested in a cool voice, fighting back the urge to swing her around by her hair. Simon deserved better than a woman like her.

Her eyes scraped me up and down before turning back to Simon. "I'm telling my manager about you."

He cocked his head to the side. "Go ahead and tell your pimp all about me. This was *never* agreed to as a business arrangement."

"You missed out on a once-in-a-lifetime opportunity. I'm the best for a reason. Enjoy your classless *whorebag* over there."

Light flickered in his eyes and his face tensed. Simon cupped his hand around her arm and rushed her to the door. "Piss off, you nasty little strumpet. Insult my friend again with your crass assumptions and I'll be sure to pass the word along to your pimp that you're overcharging for your minky and stashing the profits. And don't think I don't know about it, because I do my background checks on the women I bring home. I thought you were a little more sophisticated than this. Now stop your mewling and bugger off!"

He shoved her into the hall and dramatically slammed the door. She yelled out a few nasty words, but Simon indifferently rubbed the back of his neck and lazily walked toward me as if this were an ordinary occurrence.

He widened his mouth in a yawn, stretching all the anger out of his face. "Someday I'll play that game with someone I can truly enjoy it with. Now what's this all about?"

"Novis told me you saved his life."

His shoulders sagged. "I confirmed that the men who robbed the documents from his truck belonged to Nero, so I went to share the news. Whoever was running the experiments kept the documents and key employees separated to make it difficult to piece it all together. Right hand didn't know what the left was doing and all that."

Simon walked across the plastic mat to his computer desk,

unscrewed the cap from a bottle of water, and took a long sip. Some of it dribbled down his chin and trailed across his chest. When half the bottle was gone, he sauntered across the apartment and led me to the kitchen.

"One of the men who hijacked the truck was captured and questioned. This buffoon didn't know diddly outside of the heist. Well, I take that back. He knew of two homes where Nero resides, but I checked them out and they're abandoned."

Simon pulled out a blue container from the fridge and grabbed a fork, eating cold pasta right out of the bowl.

Few men could pull off leathers as sexily as he could. Simon was a few inches taller than me with a leaner build than Logan. Brown hair, caramel eyes, and lush lips were his trademark. Not many men had a mouth like his, and I already knew firsthand that he knew how to use that God-given instrument. Those lips were meant to be on a woman's body. However, he suffered from irritable mouth syndrome, which inevitably put a damper on anything I'd felt for him sexually.

"Nero is an idiot," I grumbled. "He's wasting his time coming after me."

"Maybe this is his form of recreation."

"Maybe someone should buy him a hobby."

Simon tossed his fork in the sink and shoved the bowl back in the fridge. "I received a peculiar call from your Ghuardian a little while ago." The cold air made his nipples harden and he smirked when he caught me looking at the silver ring he had in one of them. "Care to show me yours?"

"What did Justus want?" I put my elbows on the counter behind me and leaned back.

"Something about Page being pregnant. Well, isn't that a juicy bit of gossip I hadn't heard about? And full term. Which means she was shagging Justus with a bun in the oven."

"So the man playing naked Twister with a prostitute is one to judge?"

He stretched out his arms and made a growling kind of a sound. "I don't judge people by their profession. She seemed like a nice girl when we talked last night, but games are no fun with those women because they don't even try to win. I think it's time for another game night. Bring your cat if you want."

"Don't call Logan my cat."

"Would you rather I call him your pussy?"

I rolled my eyes and a hyena laugh pealed out of Simon. He moved across the floor to a small table in his kitchen, shuffling his feet the whole way. Simon lived simply, and half his décor looked like it was from the 1970s.

"Did Novis hire you to work on this case?"

He slipped into the chair and tapped his fingers on the table. "I can't talk about *who* employs me and *why*, but you can be privy to information regarding Nero, as it is not confidential to those who already know."

"I hope whoever hired you is also paying you to track Nero down and find out where he's hiding."

"We found two of his homes. The Enforcers have taken over and are fumbling about with their incompetent methods."

"I'm surprised he didn't torch the houses."

"Not sure Nero is one to keep that many personal items which would link back to him," Simon said. He began waving his hand as he spoke. "The thing about a man like Nero is he's always got his lackeys doing his dirty work. He's like the wizard behind the curtain, pulling all the strings, and he pays his men good money so they don't mind if they're caught. Of course, he also doesn't like blabbers, which is why Ray ended up sleeping with the fishes."

"And Ray seemed like a nice guy from what I remember."

"Everyone has a price," Simon said with a dramatic sigh.

"Finn's real father is trying to claim him back."

His eyes lit with interest. "That so? Bloody hell, what a mess. Shifters get territorial, and not just with property but with people. Pay him off."

"What if he keeps coming back for more?"

"Then blackmail him. I'm sure I can help you dig something up. Piece of cake."

"Will you? It would mean a lot to me, Simon. Everyone has

their hands full with Nero and I haven't lived among the Breed long enough to know how to fight something like this." I paced toward the kitchen table and twisted some of his tangled hair between my fingers. "I'll pay you if it's a lot of work."

He winked and kissed my arm. "Haven't you heard? When it comes to my friends, I do it for free."

"That's what she said."

Simon's building had a walkway that led to an indoor garage. It required an access code to get in, one I'd given to Logan so he could park and take a nap.

The garage had six levels of parking, so I sent a text message to Logan to come find me. As I walked toward the ramp, one of my sneakers squeaked on the smooth concrete.

Winter had started with a bang, but spring was waging war against the frigid temperatures and slowly winning. I stuffed my cold hands into the warm pockets of my bomber jacket. My jeans offered little protection from the cold, but they were warmer than a skirt would be. My mind began drifting to Logan. I sometimes wondered if he wanted me to dress more feminine, like some of the Chitah women who exemplified grace. He'd never mentioned a word about my style, and I never said anything about his. I preferred when he dressed up in slacks and a casual jacket, which wasn't often because Logan enjoyed wearing cotton shirts and jeans. But man, did he look *delicious* in a blazer.

Even in his sneakers.

Perhaps it was his swagger and confident gaze, but I melted a little when I saw him decked out just for me. His eyes would glimmer if I wore a pretty dress or pinned my hair up. As I approached the ramp, I decided I was going to make an effort to look nice for Logan more often. I didn't want to get too comfortable with him, and besides that, the wave of sexual energy that rolled over my body when he admired my low-cut blouse was totally worth it.

I chuckled softly and glanced up.

A lick of energy snapped at my skin as I felt the spark of another Mage.

"Who's there?" I called out.

When no one answered, I sharpened my light and prepared to flash.

In the garage full of cars, cylindrical pillars went down each row of parking. There were no openings on the outer walls, so the only light came from caged bulbs affixed to the concrete pillars.

Energy continued to prickle my skin and my hands were out of my pockets as I turned in a slow circle, scanning the room.

With impossible speed, a figure flashed from the right and I ducked, avoiding a punch to my face. I flashed to the right toward a line of cars and turned to look at the Mage.

He had a full beard and dark eyes, like you would imagine any villain to look. Maybe it was his thick brows and chalky skin, but a chill went up my spine.

"Did Nero send you?" I asked.

A grin hooked the corner of his chapped lips. "I've always hated the chatty ones. Let's just get down to business, shall we?"

"Why don't you kiss my ass," I replied.

He belted out a laugh and stroked his beard. I couldn't take my eyes off him to look around and see if he had any friends.

"You're a mouthy little bitch. Not like that blond human who pleaded for her worthless life."

Snap.

Whatever thread of reason I possessed, vanished. *This* was the Mage who'd juiced Sunny and almost killed her. This was the man who'd fired bullets at two people I loved, murdering one of them. Images flashed in my head of what those last moments must have been like for Knox, and I barely noticed blue light bleeding from my fingertips.

The Mage noticed. In fact, he was quite confused by it. A Mage often leaked visible light during the healing process or when pushing out a burst of energy, but not while standing still. His eyes flicked up to mine—the silvering must have been noticeable. It only occurred in my pupils, but against my bright green eyes, it looked bizarre.

"What the fuck are you?" he breathed.

A malicious smile appeared on my face. "The last thing you'll ever see."

I rushed at him with impeccable speed and punched his collarbone. I felt it crack and thrust my elbow into his side when he hunched over.

The Mage reached for my ankle and almost got a hold, so I flipped him off-balance and kicked him in the stomach.

Tires screeched around the corner and Logan's car appeared, grinding to a halt. When I turned to look, the Mage yanked my feet out from under me.

The hard concrete slammed against my back and knocked the wind out me. Pain radiated across my shoulder blades and I expected him to jump on me, but he didn't. A dagger appeared from his pocket and he directed his attention to Logan, who had flung open the car door and stepped out.

Logan's eyes were obsidian black, and his fangs glimmered like weapons. He walked with a heavy gait—spotted patterns rippling across the skin on his neck but hidden beneath his white sweater and tan slacks. If this turned bloody, Logan was going to look like a hot mess.

I sprang to my feet and the Mage flashed toward Logan.

"No!" I screamed.

It was too late. Logan's moves were raw as he took on a brazen Mage who thought he could best a Chitah of Logan's caliber.

The Mage swung his fist a few times before Logan caught his arm and held it. Every attempt the Mage made to touch Logan with his other hand was thwarted with a block or a strike. Logan flung the Mage on the hood of the car, causing a clamor. Logan had lunged forward to bite when the Mage kicked him in the gut with brutal force, thrusting him back five feet, and he fell to his side.

The bearded man rolled off the hood and we flashed at each other simultaneously. A rapid pulse fired off in my chest as I spun out of his way, but he gripped my hair and yanked me back. Justus knew hair was a weakness and maybe that's why he kept his head shaved.

Gritting my teeth against the pain, I punched him in the stomach with several blows before he threw me to the ground and landed on top of me.

By this time, Logan had risen to his feet, and the Mage whirled around and threw his dagger with precision. It sank into Logan's chest and he began to fall.

Without hesitation, I reached out with my hand and used my energy to pull the blade before Logan had even dropped to his knees. I manipulated my energy to flip the blade around, and the handle came into my hand.

Startled, the Mage's eyes widened when I stabbed him in the back. The stunner paralyzed him and his dead weight pinned me to the floor.

"Logan?"

"I'm fine," I heard him grunt. "Did you get him?"

"Yeah, he's out like a light. Are you sure you're okay?"

When Logan fell silent, I reached in my pocket and turned on my phone to text Simon a brief message. I wasn't sure if he'd flashed down the stairs or caught the express elevator, but he was in the garage within moments.

I glanced up, trying to see through the Mage's beard. He was still on top of me and half my face was covered. Simon was wearing a T-shirt that said *Dirty and Flirty*.

He glanced at Logan and then back at me.

"Is he all right?"

Not being able to see, I couldn't answer. "How does he look?"

"Well, the white sweater was a mistake, but I suspect he'll live. Judging by the bloodstains, it looks like he took it in the shoulder. Hope it didn't sever an artery; that hurts like buggery."

"Simon, a little help would be appreciated." I grunted.

He glanced down at the heavy body lying on top of me. "You took him out yourself?"

"No," I replied. "I just felt like making out with a total stranger in front of my boyfriend in the garage."

He winked. "Atta girl."

"Simon?"

His eyes still surveyed the scene with amusement. "Yeah?"

"This is the Mage that killed Knox."

All color bled from Simon's face, leaving a cold and stoic expression I'd never seen before. He wasn't even looking at me when I broke the news, but his eyes remained fixed on a caged bulb. "You sure?"

"Positive. He's the guy who pulled the trigger."

Simon's gaze nailed me to the floor and sparks of light flickered in his eyes. His lips mashed tightly together and he lifted the man off me by his hair. As I scooted back and caught my breath, I noticed Logan was making a call and removing his sweater at the same time. His eyes searched the garage—we were in the open and couldn't risk having a human call the police.

"Logan, where's Christian?"

He hung up the phone and lifted his eyes to mine, walking with a compelling stride in my direction. Blood trickled from the stab wound and he looked pale. "Are you hurt?"

"No, I'm fine. He just knocked the wind out of me."

Logan scanned my body, brushing my hair away from my face and then glancing at my arms. "Novis called before you came down. He said your phone was off and he couldn't get through. There was an emergency and he had to summon Christian for help."

"What kind of help?" I asked, twisting my arm around and noticing I had a skinned elbow.

"Perhaps he needed him to charm someone for information, or there was another attack. I don't know. I assured him we were heading straight home and you would be under my protection."

Simon dragged the Mage to a dark corner behind a large van. I winced when I heard what sounded like Simon beating and kicking him relentlessly.

"Novis left me without a guard?"

Logan helped me to my feet and I placed the palm of my hand over the puncture wound in his shoulder to stop the bleeding.

"Novis knows a million Vampires, so if he asked for Christian, it must be related to Nero. Or maybe they're trying to locate another lab. He said he was sending a replacement, but maybe he hasn't made it yet."

"Maybe the Mage took him out before I walked in."

Logan shook his head. "I couldn't scent anything in the car with the windows rolled up. I felt the spike of energy and only when I cracked the window did I scent your emotions."

"I wonder if I should call Novis. Maybe there's another attack underway. Sunny's in the house," I began, my voice becoming panicked.

The first thing I did was call Page to let her know we were on our way over because Logan needed immediate medical attention.

Then I called Novis.

"Is everything all right?" I asked.

"Fine, Silver. I'm sorry I had to remove Christian temporarily as your guard, but his services were required. There's a delicate matter and I need his skills to question the despicable man who attempted to assassinate Hannah."

"Hannah?"

"Yes. You made a valid point about sparing lives in order to obtain information that could prove invaluable to our efforts. We can't afford to miss an opportunity that would lead to Nero's capture or the shutdown of these labs. My fear is they are more widespread than we realize."

"Is Hannah okay?"

Not that I liked the woman, with her wolfish eyebrows and all those damn pins in her hair—she had a frosty personality and we didn't mix. But Hannah was one of two Councilwomen in our territory, and I respected a woman in a position of leadership.

"She was injured but has since healed. Christian will return to his watch shortly—this evening at the latest. I trust no other Vampire and can't risk bringing in someone new. I would advise you to go straight home."

"Your competent man hasn't arrived and I've already been attacked."

His voice lowered. "*What?*"

"The man who killed Knox and shot Sunny is being taken care of," I said, glancing to where Simon had gone. I couldn't see anything but heard noises that made my skin crawl.

"Bring him to me," Novis insisted in a textured voice, ripe with malice.

"Simon has a hold of him and the odds aren't in his favor. He's not walking out of here alive—we're going to need some cleaners to tidy things up."

He answered with silence.

"Novis," I began, lowering my eyes to the ground. "Tell Sunny. Let her know that she'll never have to worry about that Mage again. Tell her the man who killed her lover is dead."

CHAPTER 15

"We're here," I said into the intercom. Thanks to Cognito traffic, it had taken forty-five minutes to get to Page's apartment, and Logan had begun to get drowsy from the blood loss.

Page buzzed us inside her building and I helped Logan down the hall as he used my shoulder as a crutch. A Chitah wouldn't die from those wounds—in fact, they healed much quicker than a human. The bleeding had slowed down and Logan looked to be in pain, so I wondered if the knife had severed a nerve or cut a bone. We needed a doctor to check him over and stitch him up. I joked in the car he could lick his chest, but he just gave me a bemused look. Clearly, he didn't get the joke about his long tongue.

He held his sweater against the wound, concealing most of the blood. But it didn't stop people from gawking at the six-and-a-half-foot man with firm muscles, walking shirtless in broad daylight on the wintry streets of Cognito.

Page swung open the door and we hurried inside.

"Not in the living room," she said. "Come into the kitchen."

Page had a small kitchen with a round table in the middle. Logan pulled back a chair and sank into it, eyeing the equipment she had laid out on the table. I peered around the corner into the living room.

"Ghuardian?"

Justus stood in the center of the room, looking at his phone. He slipped it into his pocket and closed the distance between us.

Then his large hands grasped my arms. "You were attacked?"

"I'm not hurt, but he stabbed Logan and Page is taking a look."

He searched my eyes. "Simon took care of the problem." He hesitated for a second before an intangible emotion glittered in his eyes. Was that pride I saw when he looked down at me? "Simon mentioned you single-handedly took down the Mage."

"Guilty as charged."

"You should have been armed."

With Christian around, I'd been doing that less lately. Mage or not, I was still a woman, and going out with a knife strapped to my chest was all kinds of uncomfortable.

"I didn't know Christian would be summoned away. Novis said he wouldn't need him much longer."

Justus uncharacteristically slid his hand around the nape of my neck. I felt a warmth rising to my cheeks. It *was* pride in his eyes, after all. I'd held my own, although Logan had fought by my side.

And wasn't that a wonderful feeling? To know the man I loved had transformed from the Chitah who once covered me like a shield and took a beating to protect my life. Now he respected me as a Mage, and even in his primal state, he hadn't pinned me to the ground as if I were some damsel in distress. Logan would die for me, but he would also fight by my side—as equals.

"Why are you here?" I finally asked Justus.

"Miss La Croix was without transportation."

A smile touched my lips by the way he pronounced her name in perfect French. "So now it's *Miss* La Croix? What happened to Page?"

"Learner," he began.

"How's Adam? I hope everything's okay with him, but he didn't give me any details. Why did he need a Relic?"

"He is caring for a woman—a human attacked by a juicer."

I sighed, knowing the grave reality of juicers among the human population. "Did she die?"

"She has received treatment and her recovery is uncertain. Not many humans survive a juicer stealing beyond the limit of what their body will restore."

I wanted to ask what he thought about Page being pregnant but decided it would be a major faux pas given their past relationship. So I let it become the elephant in the room.

Logan roared and I dashed into the kitchen. He gripped the seat of his chair while Page sprayed a solution on his wound. The ends of her hair were wet and it looked like she must have taken a quick shower before we had arrived. I guess after two emergencies in one day, she was squeezing in personal time wherever she could.

"He's lost quite a bit of blood, but he's lucky it didn't pierce his lung or it would have taken much longer to heal. This formula will help the internal injuries mend faster."

"Maybe we should call Adam to come heal him."

When I saw the scornful look in Logan's eyes, I took that as a no. *Male pride.* Chances are it had more to do with the fact that Adam had once carried a torch for me and had already saved Logan from death.

"Fine, sit there and bleed," I said, tightening my expression.

Logan relaxed and the Cross smile made a guest appearance. "Female, you know how I love that fire."

The way he said it was smooth like brandy and wildly seductive—enough that I got a few butterflies and smiled against my shoulder. *Damn, how was it possible for that man to still make me nervous after all this time?*

"You need to rest," Page ordered. "Once I stitch you up, I want you to lie down for at least an hour. I'll give you a mild sedative, but your body's natural healing abilities need to do their thing and I'd rather you stay motionless."

"I'm familiar with the drill," he murmured in a dispassionate tone.

"I also want to give you some electrolytes—you need plenty of fluids so you can replenish the blood you've lost."

Page sat across from him and leaned forward to clean the wound. Her fastidious demeanor was admirable as she prepared him for stitches. Logan studied her attentively. "You are a fearless female." Then he placed his hand on her stomach and she looked up at him. "I wish good health for your young. I hope that one day a male of worth sees your noble qualities and cares for you and your child."

Page's voice softened and she looked at him, her eyes benevolent. "Thank you, Logan."

I glanced to my left and Justus watched with a distant expression, his gaze centered on Logan's hand.

I kissed Logan on the mouth and he stirred a little in Page's bed. He'd been asleep for a while after she'd given him fluids and a sedative. The drapes in her bedroom were closed and I glanced around, noticing she hadn't bought anything for the baby. I guess with work, she hadn't had time to think about it. I indulged myself in another kiss, feeling how pliant and soft Logan's mouth was. It made me want to curl up beside him and tuck my body against his. My fingers traced the features of his face—his strong nose and cheekbones, the tiny lines at the corners of his mouth, and his brow, which seemed more relaxed and less menacing. His hair was a couple of inches long and looked sexy the way he styled it. He was undeniably attractive now that I could see all of him without the long strands of hair falling in the way.

Page and Justus were in the kitchen, talking in low voices. When I joined them, Justus had set a bowl of fruit in front of her and she was giving him a funny look.

"I think the donuts will tide me over until next millennium," she said with a private smirk.

"Eat," he insisted, taking a seat to her right.

I sat across from her and admired the kitchen. It was a step up from her last place. The fridge was stainless steel and all the cabinetry was painted white. It complemented the wallpaper, which had tiny yellow flowers. Then there was another feature about her apartment that didn't go unnoticed.

The orchids.

I hadn't said anything, but *my God*, they filled every room. Several were dead, while the rest held the most gorgeous blooms of lavender and pink. They lined the windowsill in the living room and all along the walls—I couldn't imagine how much money that totaled up to.

"Do you like flowers?" I stupidly asked, breaking the silence.

Her chest flushed with scarlet and Page pulled an orange from the bowl, holding it in front of her nose and smelling it.

Part of me was curious if Page had decided to give the baby up. "Um, I noticed there aren't any baby things around here. You're due pretty soon."

She set the orange down. "I haven't had time. I'm a little worried because I still don't have a partner and I won't be able to make all my appointments. It's becoming more difficult to keep up the pace—especially without a car."

"You shouldn't be driving in your condition," Justus chided in a deep voice.

Page tapped her finger on the table. "I'm not sure how you think I'm going to earn money to pay for a baby unless I work. Hopefully I won't lose any clients."

"Do you at least have diapers and clothes?"

Page rose from her chair, arching her back and struggling to stand. She walked out of the room and Justus held an enigmatic expression on his face I couldn't read, but it looked like uncertainty, judging by the vertical crease in his forehead and the slight downturn of his brows. His strong features were amplified by his neatly groomed hair shaved close to his head and his warrior's jaw. He had the presence of a man who had battled with heavy swords and armor and yet possessed the honor and nobility of a decent man.

"I've been busy," Page said with a proud smile. She set a small cardboard box on the table and I peered in.

"Oh my God, did you make these? They're adorable!"

I pulled out different sizes of knitted booties, a hat, and mittens. I placed them on the table and she picked up a tiny hat and said, "This one is my absolute favorite. I used a multicolored yarn of green, purple, and pink because it's pretty gender neutral."

"Well, the rest sure isn't," I observed, sifting through all the different shades of blue and green.

She tossed the hat back in the pile. "It's kept me busy at night when the baby is kicking and I can't sleep. I'm getting better at it—my grandmother would be proud."

Justus touched the knitted hat she'd declared as her favorite. He turned it in his hands and Page sat back down. Simple tasks like getting up and down required effort and she always looked uncomfortable.

"I'm glad you're turning this into a positive thing, Page. Especially after what Slater did to you."

"He's dead now and I refuse to let him control my future and happiness." She put a few of the booties back in the box. "I can't regret having had sex with him. After all, it brought me this miracle I never thought possible."

Justus blanched and slowly turned his head toward her. "Say again?"

She scooped up the baby clothes and I helped her put them back into the box. "I don't even know what came over me to have slept with Slater, but I guess we all make mistakes."

My brows knitted. "I thought he inseminated you during the kidnapping?"

Justus pulled his collar away from his neck so abruptly that a button popped off and rolled across the floor.

She blew a strand of hair away from her eyes and slid the box to the side. "No, that couldn't be possible. If this were an insemination, I'd be terrified to know what he put in me—some kind of Breed concoction. We had sex before the kidnapping and that's why we had a big falling out. I became pregnant and he wanted to use me as his lab rat."

"Impossible," Justus interrupted.

She smiled softly. "Sex is *quite* possible."

"You didn't have sex with Slater."

"I think I can assess who I have and haven't had sex with; it's a pretty unforgettable experience. Don't be ridiculous."

"You didn't have sex with Slater," he repeated, "because…"

"Because?"

I felt an eruption coming on and leaned back in my chair. The ambiguous look on his face made me uneasy.

He leaned toward her, his voice falling to a whisper. "You couldn't have had sex with Slater because you were a virgin."

"Yes, I *was*. Not that it's any business of yours who I lost my virginity to."

He stood up and raised his voice. "It's *absolutely* my business because I am the one who *took* your virginity! You insult me with a lie such as that. A man knows the feel of a virgin and the loss of innocence, and do not ask me to physically describe an act so intimate as it would dishonor you."

A confused look crossed her expression. "I'm sorry, but you're wrong, Justus. I should know when I lost my virginity."

A knock sounded at the door and that was my cue to get the hell out of Dodge. This conversation was derailing and quickly approaching a steep cliff.

I looked through the peephole and swung open the front door. "It's about time you came."

Christian breezed by me. "I get that a lot," he said darkly.

The voices in the kitchen quieted and Christian pursed his lips. "I heard you were in a bit of a scuffle."

"Yeah, no big deal," I said, slamming the door. "Just some Mage trying to kill me. The usual. How's life with you?"

"Grand."

He removed his trench coat and hung it on a hook by the door. Christian had on dark jeans and a chocolate-brown shirt with a V-neck. He actually looked nice with a belt on, but he still wore his black lace-up boots.

Arguing ensued from the kitchen and Christian backed up. "I should wait outside."

"No, you need to stay here and tell me what's going on with Novis."

"Personal business, lass," he said, reaching for his coat.

I yanked it off the rack and flung it into the kitchen.

"What the feck? That's my favorite jacket."

"Go get it," I hissed through my teeth. "You're not taking off; Mount Justus is about to erupt."

Christian lowered his dark brows over his black eyes. "And you think I want to be around to watch a domestic quarrel? I have better things to do than hear someone rabbit on about popping a cherry."

"Why do you look guilty?" I asked, suddenly noticing how peculiar Christian was acting.

"Men with big cocks always look guilty."

I narrowed my eyes and gripped his sleeve. "Get in there." I dragged him into the kitchen and gave him an accusatory glance. "Do you know anything about this?"

Justus turned his head so slowly it was felt more than noticed. His blue eyes burned into Christian's conscience.

The Vampire immediately threw his hands up and took a

wide step back. "I've been knowing you many years, Justus. I don't appreciate that look you're giving me."

"You scrubbed her, didn't you?"

"What?" I gasped, looking up at Christian in shock. "Is that true?"

His shoulders lifted in a shrug and his mouth turned down. "Seemed for the best."

Page's mouth dropped open. "Did I ask you to scrub me?"

"With a loofah?"

Justus lunged and grabbed him by the throat, shoving him against the wall.

Christian was strong enough that he could have easily knocked him away, but a mutual respect existed between them. Years ago, Christian had worked closely with Justus as his guard.

"Talk," Justus demanded, squeezing his throat tighter.

Christian flashed a white smile beneath all those whiskers on his face and held up his hands. "Seemed for the best, given the circumstances of her traumatic kidnapping. I was just helping her out."

"By making her think she had sex with a man she despised?"

"Justus, let him go," Page said, still sitting in her chair. "Vampire, come over here and return my memory. I want every scrap of it. If you were trying to protect me from thinking my baby is a monster created in a lab, then you're not doing me any service. I'm a Relic, and part of my job is to pass knowledge down to my children. I will love this child no matter where it came from, but you could have erased other facts that I need to know that could answer questions."

Justus slipped his hand behind Christian's neck and shoved him forward. At some point, Christian decided he'd had enough and stood straight and immobile.

"Hands off me, Mage. I'll give the Relic what she wants."

Christian angrily spun a chair around and folded his arms over the back of it, staring intensely into her eyes. It didn't take long before Page fell under his charm and he leaned in so close I didn't hear what he whispered to her.

Page blinked a few times and went into a fog. It seemed like minutes passed, but when she finally snapped out of it, her face turned to stone.

"Get. Out."

"Pleasure is all mine," Christian spat out, kicking the chair aside and stalking out the door.

She studied the table as if she were reading something.

"Page," I said. "It doesn't matter what Slater did to you. All that's in the past."

"All of you. Out. I want to be alone. I'm sure you don't want to upset me right now in my condition. When Logan wakes up, I'll tell him you two went home. His car is outside, so it shouldn't be a problem for him to drive. Don't make me say it again. Please, get out."

I silently turned around and glanced up at Justus. His jaw clenched as she covered her face.

"Come on, Ghuardian. She needs time to think and we need to get home and check on Finn." I glanced at Page with sympathetic eyes. "Please have Logan call me when he's on his way home, and thank you for everything. I'm so sorry about all this."

She nodded at the box of baby apparel and sadness washed over her face. Now her worst fear was realized about the insemination, and I hoped it didn't influence her decision to keep the baby. Maybe she would see me as an example of how something positive could come out of all this genetic experimentation. Maybe Christian's intentions were in the right place when he'd made Page think the baby was nothing but a Relic, but what good can come from living a lie? I was a child of genetic testing myself, and while I struggled with feeling disconnected after learning my origins, knowing who I was made it easier to become the best version of myself.

When the door closed and the room quieted, Page pressed her palms against her forehead and wept. The pain of knowing the truth gutted her. Christian had not only made her believe she'd slept with Slater, but he'd erased the significant detail of Justus having been her first lover. The Vampire had inserted an alternate version of the facts. One where she would have raised that baby thinking he was nothing but a Relic. In truth, the drugs Slater had given her might have already done their damage.

Injections she would never know the contents of since the secret would remain buried with Slater.

She pushed the box tenderly away and wiped the tears from her face. The baby was kicking against her belly, so she placed her hand over it and whispered an apology. None of this was his fault, and yet he would be the one to suffer. She worried for his future, wondering if he would ever find acceptance among the Breed and what his place would be.

After Christian had returned her memories, everything became vividly clear. And yet now she was torn in a way that she couldn't have imagined.

Her life had changed on the night she'd fallen ill and Justus had called a Relic to the house. That Relic had revealed an unexpected surprise—Page was pregnant. Shock overwhelmed her as a man she had worked next to for years had betrayed her, impregnating her with God knows what as part of his science experiment.

With her memory restored, Page now remembered the night she'd gone to the park to confront Slater. Christian had accompanied her so that he could release the false memories implanted in Slater's mind and allow her to question him one last time. Page had found out the facts—more than she could have imagined. The following day, Christian had shown up at her doorstep and offered to erase the truth from her mind. When she resisted, he'd gripped her arms firmly and said, "Sorry, I can't watch a man be destroyed by all this foolishness." Then he'd scrubbed her, taking it all away.

Page closed her eyes and allowed the memories to come flooding back. She could almost feel the cold snap of winter air against her skin that had made her wish she'd worn a hat. She remembered with clarity when Slater impaled Christian, leaving him incapacitated beside the park bench.

They had argued, and suddenly her small kitchen vanished as her mind traveled back in time to that fateful night. There she was—standing before Slater as he seized her arms and she struggled against him.

"Stupid Vampire—taking someone to a park with trees," Slater said, snatching her coat when she tried to turn away. "No, no, honey. You're not going anywhere. It's too late for that."

He yanked her against him and puckered his lips for a mocking kiss. Page screamed.

"Shut up, I'm not going to kill you. As much as you disgust me, I have other plans."

"Let me go!" she yelled.

"Are you kidding me? We're going to make a baby together, Page. That'll make us practically married. You'll have an obligation to that child by allowing me to be his father. I've been chasing you since we were teens and I think it's time that you grow the fuck up and take the offer."

She squirmed, struggling to break free from his grasp. "You disgust me. You're a disgrace to all Relics, Slater. Nothing you could say or do will justify your selfish need to pass your genes on. By God, if I can help it, this baby will never know anything about you," she growled, clawing at his face.

Slater grabbed a fistful of her short hair and yanked her head back. "What the fuck do you mean by that?"

"Let go of me—get your hands off me, you sick maniac!" She thrashed as he continued to pull her hair and shake her.

"What did you just say, Page? What do you mean by this *baby?" he shouted, spitting in her face by the near proximity.*

She looked at him defiantly, unable to admit his baby-making experiments on her had worked in his favor. Page felt a fierce instinct to protect her unborn child. He must have read the look on her face and figured out the truth.

"You little fucking whore," he breathed through his bared teeth. "That's not my baby in there, you stupid slut. I didn't inseminate you—I only primed you for conception. Who the fuck's baby is in there?"

Violence erupted in a flash. She heard a crack of bone and lost her breath when someone pulled her out of Slater's grasp in a protective move. Justus moved in like a Titan and she shuddered as he squared off with Slater.

Page recoiled when Slater swung at her and Justus snatched his neck with lightning speed, gripping tightly.

Slater reached down and pulled a dagger from beneath Justus's shirt. Her heart raced when he swiped his arm and sliced Justus across the chest. Crimson soaked through the fabric of his shirt, but Justus maintained his stony expression.

When the fight ended, it ended in bloodshed. They fell to the ground and the knife found a home in Slater's heart.

If Slater had only *primed* her for conception, that left one unbelievable answer.

Justus was the father of her child.

By some miracle, her body had accepted his Mage sperm. The Relic who uncovered her pregnancy had given her inaccurate facts on how far along she was. But that had to do with how her pregnancy had sped up and it explained why her morning sickness occurred immediately. It seemed impossible that Justus could have fathered this child. He was a Mage, and they were infertile! Upon creation, a shift takes place within their bodies that no longer allows them to reproduce. Perhaps the energy coursing through them causes a woman's body to reject their sperm. Maybe an egg wouldn't survive the highly charged sperm of a Mage, even in the body of another Mage. She didn't specialize in Mage genetics like some Relics did.

Their sterility was a well-known fact without exceptions.

Until now.

Page thought about the necklace he had put on and wondered if that could have aided in his ability to impregnate her. She doubted the metal could have been solely responsible. No one creates that kind of technology without exploring *all* the possibilities.

It must have had to do with the injections, because Page was barren. Slater had found a way to strengthen and heal her ovaries so a Mage could fertilize her egg. Maybe his formula neutralized the energy within Justus's sperm to allow it to survive.

All kinds of questions arose in her mind. Would this child continue growing at an increased rate? Would it be deformed? Would the other injections she'd been given affect its DNA?

Would it look like Justus?

Then there was *that*—the glaring truth amid all the drama. Humans who chose the life of a Mage forfeited their desire for children. Justus had been alive for centuries, and a man who's lived that long without family was used to doing things his own way. It explained his abrasive behavior and sanctimonious attitude.

Page couldn't bear the thought of Justus rejecting this baby, nor did she want to put her child through the kind of pain that abandonment brings. It was a silly notion to think Justus could ever love a Relic—a mortal.

Then her mind really began to absorb the gravity of the situation. If by some small chance he did take her in, he would be subjected to watching his woman and child grow old and die. Most immortals never had a human family. They severed ties with the past and gave up on loving mortals they couldn't hold on to.

And he couldn't hold on to this child. As a Mage, Justus could kill the baby inadvertently.

"Oh my God," she whispered. "Slater, what did you do?" Tears spilled down her cheeks.

And yet, a tender thought filled her heart.

The secret of knowing that this baby belonged to Justus, that she'd always have a small piece of something meaningful—a reality that could never be between an immortal and a Relic. This wasn't a novel where love conquers all; this was complicated and messy. The romantic in her wanted Justus to sweep her off her feet and say that he would love her for the rest of her life, but the cynic reminded her it would never last.

Then she thought about how he'd feel when she reached menopause and had to start taking calcium supplements. How would he react if she got into an accident and became paralyzed, or suffered from dementia as a senior? The thought of Justus changing her diapers made her cry all over again.

"Female," a voice rumbled.

Logan gently moved her arms away from her face and she turned to the right where he was kneeling beside her. Concern brimmed in his warm, golden eyes.

"Why is there so much sorrow? It woke me from my sleep."

Page shook her head, unable to answer.

His nostrils flared and he pulled in several puffs of air, allowing the taste of her emotions to settle on his palate.

"Anguish, regret, fear... I don't enjoy these emotions when they come from a female. Whatever you're suffering through will pass. Among Chitahs, the greatest gift a female can give us is her love and respect. The second greatest gift is a child. I came close to becoming a father once, long ago. It was not my young, but that of my enemy. The love I felt for this female was immense, making me long for those days of holding that infant in my arms. I wanted to surrender to the life of a father and instill my values into that baby. You are more than a mother, but a teacher." He placed his hands on her belly and sighed remorsefully. "I sometimes wish the child had lived, even if Katrina did not. Don't trouble yourself with the woes of life, for they will only prevent you from giving all of yourself to others. A child needs his mother's love, not her tears."

Page touched his cheek appreciatively. His sincerity and compassion gave her renewed courage. "I hope you and Silver find a way."

Logan cocked his head to the side. "I will not hope for something she is unable to give me. It wouldn't be fair to Silver. Without stars, there is still the moon to light up the night sky, and Silver is my moon. Why wish for the stars when I have all the light I need?"

Logan rose to his feet and reached in her cabinets.

Page pulled herself together and wiped her nose. "Silver and Justus had to leave. She wants you to call her on your way home."

He set a mug on the cabinet and tore open a package of cocoa. "Once you have settled down with a warm drink and I have prepared you a meal to reheat later, I will leave."

"That's not really necessary, Mr. Cross."

"I am in your debt for assisting me. Aside from that, you know that as a male Chitah, I cannot abandon a woman in distress. It goes against my very nature. Factor in the young you are carrying, and I will make sure you are well fed and smiling. Do you like pasta?"

CHAPTER 16

AFTER PAGE AND JUSTUS LEFT the motel room, Adam kept a close watch on Sadie. She'd slept through the morning and at around two in the afternoon, he dozed off beside her with his fingers laced together across his stomach. An old black-and-white cowboy movie on the TV had lulled him into a nap.

He awoke with a gasp and a hand pinching his nose. With wide eyes, Adam glanced to his right and looked at Sadie, who was lying on her side.

"You snore," she said in a soft voice, retracting her hand.

"I don't snore."

A broad smile brightened her hazel eyes. He hadn't noticed before, but up close, she had dark blond lashes. "Either you've never slept with a woman, which I doubt, or all your previous lovers have been liars."

Adam rubbed his hands against his face until he felt more awake. He turned to his right and propped up on his elbow. "You feeling okay?"

Sadie yawned a little and rubbed her eye. "Like I ran a marathon. Sorry I had to skip out on you, but I don't like to impose on people."

"You want to tell me what happened with Cedric?"

She licked her lips and Adam reached for the glass of water across from her and placed it in her hand. After she took a short sip, he set it aside and gave her his undivided attention.

"Well, I went back to the club to pick up my paycheck. I didn't know Cedric would be there, but he found out I hadn't gotten paid and figured I'd eventually show up. He wanted me to come live with him again and I told him to kiss my ass."

Adam wanted to smile at her confidence, but he was too pissed off.

"I guess no isn't an answer he likes to hear very much. He followed me out to the van and then we really got into it. I managed to get away and thought he'd let it go, but when I stopped at the red light around the corner from the motel, he opened the door and tried to pull me out. Then he juiced me. He thought if he could get me weak enough, he'd be able to haul me out of there. I guess Cedric didn't plan on the wrench I keep tucked between the seats."

"What made you come back here?"

"I had no other place to hide out. I figured you might get a little heroic and protect me if he came snooping around. He just took so much that time. Usually it was controlled and I never needed more than a short nap, but he got greedy."

"Tell me more about this guy. What does he do?"

She shrugged with her right shoulder and turned onto her back. "Not sure, but I think it's illegal. Most of his business dealings were either on the phone or outside the house. He'd get in a mood sometimes and start rambling, but I couldn't make any sense of it. I think he had anger issues because of his looks."

"Handsome?"

Sadie snorted and shook her head. "He's albino. I'm sure there are some handsome albinos in this world, but Cedric isn't one of them. He uses that self-tanning lotion and sometimes looks like a carrot, which doesn't go with his hair. It's short and almost white, just like his eyebrows. I never looked close enough to see if he had lashes. He's older; I think he was probably forty-five when he was made. That's my guess. One of his front teeth is capped in silver. Don't ask me why I hooked up with him, but I don't judge people on their looks. He came across as a cheery kind of guy when we met. I guess that makes me a terrible judge of character. Maybe I'm just too young to have figured people out."

"How old are you?"

"Twenty-four. My birthday is coming up, but I only keep track so I can get a free meal. Some places have free dinners if it's your birthday."

Adam couldn't figure this girl out. He'd never met anyone that could get over a traumatic event as quickly as she could. If Sadie was her first name, resilience was her last. Maybe when you have nothing to lose, you just learn how to endure life's beatings better than everyone else. He knew a little about that kind of life, but it also felt like she had built up an impenetrable wall around herself. The kind of wall that she didn't use to keep people out, but to keep her emotions in. The emotions that might weaken her and make her lose hope. He got up and grabbed a bottle of water, taking a seat at the table and putting distance between them.

"Why do you keep sitting across the room from me?" she asked. "Am I too ugly to look at?"

"Is that how you fish for compliments, or are you trying to make a point?"

"Not everything is about you, Adam."

He fumbled with the cap from his water bottle. It wasn't that she had indirectly brought up a sore topic, it was the fact she had just called him Adam. He wondered if it was intentional or a slip, but he didn't make mention of it. Hearing his name roll off her tongue was a lovely sound.

"Do you have Cedric's information?"

She propped a pillow behind her back and pushed herself up. "I know where he lives, but I'm not telling you."

"And why not?" he asked, drumming his fingers on the table.

"Because you've got that macho look in your eyes. You're a good guy, and I don't want to be responsible for you getting hurt."

"You should give me a little more credit than that," he said, casually stretching out his legs.

She swept her hair back and an unruly strand snapped back in front of her face. "You haven't been around long, which means you're probably still a Learner."

"What makes you think that?"

She held up her hands and glanced around the room. "Immortals don't live like this. They amass a fortune in their lifetimes. Money always runs out, so they become skilled at something and buy land and homes for security. Immortals don't live in a rundown motel on the seedy side of town and hang out in human bars."

She had a point. Novis had given Adam lectures about the

importance of finding his worth in this world. Once a Mage learned what he was skilled at, he could make money. Homes are important; no one respects a Mage who doesn't live well because the immediate assumption is that they are without skills.

She slid her legs over the edge of the bed and picked at the hole in her jeans. "Sorry I stole your sweater."

He glanced at the oversized black sweater falling off her shoulder. "Keep it. Do you need help standing up?" Adam rose to his feet and held out his hand.

Sadie gripped it and tried to stand on her own, but her stance became shaky. Adam hooked his left arm around her waist and pulled her up. She melted against him, standing closer than what made him feel comfortable.

Her hazel eyes felt invasive as they looked upon him. When she pressed her body against his, he scraped his teeth against his bottom lip and his heart began to speed up. He'd never felt so damn nervous with a woman before.

Jesus. Sadie was the kind of woman every man would throw away his life for. She had the heart of a poet, the soul of a saint, and the body of a sinner. But she also had modesty, something he found attractive. Adam liked a woman who could make a loose pair of jeans sexy.

He also liked the way she kept staring into his eyes, and a fire began to kindle within him—one that made him wet his lips with desire. She pulled on his neck as if trying to stand taller and suddenly... kissed him.

Her lips were lush and soft, tenderly brushing against his. He froze in a panic as if he'd never been kissed before. Hell, it felt like his first kiss all over again.

Sadie leaned away and he blinked in surprise. "Why did you do that, Kitten?"

"Someday, Adam, you're going to want to kiss me back. But I'm not at a place in my life where I'm ready for a relationship. So don't worry, it all started and ended right here. I have dreams I want to chase before I get caught up in love. In the meantime, I'd like to make you smile more often because you're a debonair guy and that's what they do. *Smile.* Cut loose the anchor that's weighing down your conscience and let go once in a while. You also look like you aren't used to hearing a girl speak her mind. So that's the deal between us, and I wanted to lay all my cards out on the table. Maybe someday, maybe never. But right now, I need you to help me to the ladies' room."

Justus and I sparred for an hour in the training room after leaving Page's apartment. He no longer tolerated my complaints after experiencing my power firsthand. The fighting techniques were one thing, but Justus began to focus on other Mage abilities. The flashing I had down pat, but he wanted to show me how to ball up my energy and use it in a burst—to move faster than visible to the eye.

Finn sat on the sidelines watching, and I got a little nervous about that. He'd never seen me sparring and as protective as he was, Finn handled it with class. In fact, a few times when I knocked Justus down, I had my own cheering section in the corner.

Our session came to a halt when Justus received a call. He turned around and I stared at the tattoo of a sun between his shoulder blades. His voice fell to a low murmur and I sucked on a bottle of water, noticing Finn was carving a piece of wood in his spot in the corner. Finn had a God-given talent with whittling little animals out of wood.

"What's that one going to be?" I asked, out of breath.

"You like games, so I was going to make you a chess set."

"Are you kidding me? I'd love that."

Logan swaggered in from the hall, looking rested after a long nap. He'd spent some time with Page before heading back and was beginning to look better with each passing minute. Even his injury was showing early signs of healing. I couldn't help but smile every time I saw him, and it felt like such a silly reaction. Maybe it was the fact he was still shirtless. He had a bandage taped across his right shoulder. His healthy color had returned and so had that predatory look in his eyes that told me I was about to become dessert.

He leaned down and spoke against my mouth. "I should be the

one making my female sweat." As punishment, he pulled back and withheld my kiss.

I adored it.

Logan had a way of drawing out the tension between us until the desire to feel his body against mine became an unbearable ache in my soul. He was skilled at working me into such a frenzied state that I could scarcely look at him without getting aroused. A brush of his lips against mine, a graze of his finger across my nipple, sexy words spoken softly against my ear, and especially the way his eyes would roam across my body like a man with caged passion.

When his nose twitched, I knew he'd caught my scent. He strutted through the room, a smug look crossing his face.

"Adam is on his way over," Justus announced, setting his phone on a bench. "I'll be in the shower."

"Wait a second. What's going on?"

He lifted his tank top from the bench and wiped his red face. "Go upstairs and use the shower."

"I think not," I argued. "Since we have guests down here, I have no intention of someone tapping their foot on that damn lift button and lowering me down here in the middle of my shower. Can Simon design an elevator? That is the most ridiculous—"

"Then get a towel and wipe yourself down. Novis will also be coming."

He disappeared down the hall and I glanced at Finn.

"I think you smell just fine," he said with a shrug.

I flounced down the hall. "What ever happened to ladies first?" I yelled at the bathroom, slamming my bedroom door.

Thirty minutes later, I hopped in the shower after Justus was through. There wasn't time to wash my hair, so I pulled it back and slipped into a pair of black sweats and a pink shirt. Justus wasn't impressed with my attire, but this was an impromptu meeting, so he was going to have to live with it. He was lucky I hadn't put on my *Slacker* shirt.

Logan remained in bed, following the Relic's orders. Finn decided to hang out in the training room and carve his pieces of wood.

I wandered upstairs and waited until the silent alarms went off.

After checking the monitors, Justus went to let Novis inside the house. I watched the monitors as Adam turned up the driveway on his motorcycle. He was sans helmet, wearing jeans and a long-sleeve shirt. No jacket. Apparently, real men didn't need clothes in winter. Justus was the exception because as a Thermal, he could regulate his body temperature. But he always made sure *I* was dressed for the weather. He looked upon me as a sort of daughter, so he meant well. He'd once asked me to call him *father* when I'd accepted Logan's claim, but I never did. Justus was my Ghuardian and always would be.

"Let me take your coat," Justus offered as Novis entered the house.

I joined them and gave them worried look.

Novis bit the tips of his gloves and pulled them off. He looked casual in a pair of denims and a white button-up shirt with an ashen sweater pulled over it. The V-neck was stylishly wide and the fabric tight. Novis reminded me of Justus in how his version of casual was always trendy and put together. He'd gelled his black hair as usual and spiked it in different directions.

I stared into his clear blue eyes and waited for him to smile.

When he didn't, I looked to Justus.

"I feel Adam is near," Novis said.

My Ghuardian stepped into the hall and disappeared.

"Can I get you a drink?" I offered.

"No. Are we alone?"

I nodded. "Logan and Finn are downstairs. Let's sit in the dining room."

I lit a few candles on the table and then the sconces on the wall. The room basked in a warm glow that made the painting behind Justus's chair come to life. The wine bottles glistened from the rack on a narrow table by the wall. The dining room had an inviting appeal with its quiet ambiance. Our table was hammered wood and a long bench ran along the right side. Novis took a seat in the chair by the entrance, clasping his hands together and somberly looking at the painting on the wall.

A few murmurs filled the hall before Adam and Justus entered the room. I listened to the sound of their clothes rustling as they took a seat at the table—Adam across from me. He glanced my way, but his thoughts were elsewhere.

Adam smoothed the palms of his hands across the wood and flicked his eyes between the two men. "I know the name of the man who's buying the metal and selling it to Nero. I made a silent vow to finish what Knox had started, and I didn't think I'd get very far with it. I met up with his old partner and he gave me some information, including a name. Cedric."

Justus drew in a sharp breath and pushed back his chair. He gripped the edge of the table as if he might stand up.

"Say again?" Justus said. "Is he a human?"

"No," Adam replied. "All I had at first was a name. Then I found a girl in trouble and by some random coincidence, she had an albino Mage on her tail. Guess what his name was?"

"Cedric," Novis answered. "I would have never expected him to get heavily involved in the black market. He's progressively gotten in more trouble with his taste for human girls. One unfortunate victim didn't survive his juicing habit and he served time. That was eighty years ago. Since then, he's flown under the radar. I had a few files that detailed how the girls had voluntarily lived with him, so there was nothing we could do because it was consensual."

Adam pressed his finger against the scar that ran across his left eye. His facial hair was the usual five-o'clock shadow. He carried a dark expression that marred his good looks more than any scar.

Adam rubbed his face, but his voice remained smooth and confident. "I got his license plate, and I shouldn't have any trouble getting his address. We need to move fast before he catches wind we're onto him."

Justus met eyes with Novis. "Cedric might know the whereabouts of Nero if he's dealing directly to him. This is a strong lead."

Novis pinched his bottom lip and stared vacantly across the room. "We'll need Christian. The last man we caught had limited information; no one seems to know where Nero hides."

"Can we not find another Vampire to do the job?" Justus spoke with guarded resentment.

Novis sat up straight and tipped his head to the side. "Why

would we do that when we have entrusted him this far?"

"Because he scrubbed a Relic without good reason."

Novis touched his chin pensively and never took his eyes off Justus. "Christian does nothing without good reason. I've known him longer than you, Justus. Perhaps not by much, but we have worked closely together over the years. Let not your personal feelings get in the way. We have no time to find a trustworthy Vampire when we already have one. A bird in the bush is a handful of two."

I belted out a laugh and covered my face. I couldn't help it; Novis had really botched that saying, and I felt Adam's foot lightly kick my leg underneath the table. I made a terrible snorting sound and sighed. When I looked up, Justus paid no attention.

"Who is this girl that knows Cedric?" Novis inquired.

"She's a human. A couple of thugs beat her down and I've been taking care of her."

Novis nodded, clearly impressed. "That's a noble gesture, Adam. We must question her immediately."

Adam stroked his jaw. "She's at a motel."

Novis took a moment to think. "Justus, I'll need you and a couple of your HALO brothers on standby. Drive into the city and wait for my call. I want everyone to move fast when we find out his location—we don't have time for you to coordinate the raid and rush him at once. I'll go with Adam to the motel to talk with the woman, but I don't want you anywhere in proximity. If Cedric is around, he'll grow suspicious since you work for HALO. While I may be a Councilman, it's also public knowledge that Adam is my progeny. If he sees us together, he is less likely to panic. Everyone will conceal their light."

"We should be safe," Adam assured Novis. "Cedric doesn't know where she's staying. He attacked her around the corner and she knocked him out cold. I moved her van down the street behind a building and out of sight."

"Smart move," Justus said.

"I keep all my bases covered. Feel me?"

"So where are you going to question him if you capture the guy?" I asked. "Nero might have someone watching him and if word gets back…"

"Good point," Novis murmured, folding his arms and staring down his straight nose. "Logan will accompany Justus during the capture. He'll be able to scent anything out of the ordinary that would tell us if Cedric is expecting our visit. If Nero has placed a Vampire on guard, then Christian's ears will alert us."

"Wait a second, Logan's hurt. He was stabbed and needs time to recover."

"I'm not asking him to fight or get involved, Silver. I only need his assistance to assess the scene using his keen sense of smell."

"Not necessary," Justus said, staring at his phone. "Leo will go in first. He's positioned himself in the center of the city and is ready to move."

Relief washed over me and I played with the saltshaker.

Novis smoothed his finger across his bottom lip. "Once Cedric is captured, bring him to Adam's motel. I'd rather not have Cedric in any of our homes; it's too much of a security risk."

"Can I come?"

"Learner," Justus said, rubbing his hands over his bristly scalp. Whenever he lifted his arms above his head it made his biceps look twice their usual size.

"I'm not asking to tag along for fun, Ghuardian. If something happens, Adam might need an extra hand to protect the life of our Councilman."

Justus shared a look with Novis while keeping his hands locked behind his head. "Will your guards be on duty?"

"I have four men on me at all times," Novis replied.

For a split second, I was thankful Simon wasn't in the room to give his "that's what she said" line.

"Sounds great, Ghuardian. I'll stay home and cook popcorn instead of protecting my *boss*."

Novis's wide smile lit up the room. "I see no need to keep her confined, Justus. Silver is a Learner who must learn through experience, not fighting predictable attacks in the safety of a training room. Let's not waste time," he said, rising to his feet.

The men followed his cue and I clutched my heart when I saw

Logan standing in the doorway. Very still. Menace dripped from his eyes and my heart raced with uncertainty.

Novis turned around and greeted him with a nod. "I hope you are on the mend."

Logan ignored him. His eyes were locked on Adam like a target and blackness swirled in them.

I stood up, my palms sweating as Logan cut through the room and gripped Adam by the throat, shoving him against the wall.

He ran his nose along Adam's collar and face in a purposeful motion. "Take me to her." His voice held quiet venom, the threat clear.

Tension crackled in the air and everyone watched with alert eyes.

"Logan, what's the matter with you? Let him go," I said, attempting to move around the table when Justus gripped my arm in caution.

Logan squeezed his fingers around Adam's neck, causing his face to turn a deep shade of red. "*Where is she?*" he asked, his voice lowering an octave. The hairs on my arms stood up when Logan's poisonous fangs grazed across Adam's cheek. By the look of Adam's fingertips, I was willing to bet he had sharpened his light.

"Chitah, back away from my Learner," Novis said, widening his stance.

"Where?" Logan repeated.

"Who?" Adam growled back, unable to get air in his lungs.

With measured restraint, Logan leaned in so close that their eyes almost touched. Logan peeled back his lips and lowered his voice.

"*My sister.*"

CHAPTER 17

I RODE WITH LOGAN, TRAILING BEHIND Novis's motorcade with Adam leading the way on his bike. Justus had gone ahead of us in his new car to wait for further instructions. Because Novis's expensive car would stick out like a sore thumb at the motel, he planned to change cars and ride with us.

I tried to question Logan, but he gripped the steering wheel and refused to speak. I couldn't read his emotions like he could mine, and his anger caught me off guard.

After picking up Novis in front of a gas station, we parked inconspicuously beneath a shady tree and hurried up the motel stairs. Adam pulled out his key and led the way.

As he unlocked the door, Logan stood behind him and Adam bristled, appearing unnerved by the bomb Logan had dropped. Adam had somehow crossed paths with Logan's human sister.

The one who'd been given up at birth, as is the custom among Chitahs when a human child is born into the family. Mortals face risks with the perils of our world, and Chitah parents cannot endure the loss of a human child aging and dying before their eyes. Logan's mother hadn't survived Sadie's birth. Logan had witnessed the end of one life and the beginning of another. He'd told me he held his baby sister in his arms and owned her scent—meaning he claimed it to memory, like an imprint.

I never could have imagined that by a strange twist of fate, Adam would save her life. Logan hadn't heard that part of the story because he'd come into the room after our conversation had ended.

The door creaked open and we stepped inside. I peered into the dark and musty room. Novis casually walked around me and opened the drapes, letting in a shower of sunlight. Particles of dust floated around the room and created a thin haze.

"Where is she?" Logan swung the bathroom door open, only to find it empty.

"She must have bailed again," Adam replied, looking at a sock on the floor. "I should have known she'd never stick around."

Which didn't sate Logan. He threw his arm forward and pointed an angry finger. "I want you to tell me where she stays. I own her scent and if I have to track her from this room, then I will. But if you know—"

"Adam?"

A girl with wavy blond hair stepped into the room. She held a can of red soda in her left hand and was wearing Adam's black sweater, which looked five sizes too big. I recognized it because of the long thread hanging in the back that he'd never cut off.

Logan examined her bruised face and he roared, "What did you *do* to her!"

Adam lifted his chin defiantly. "If you think I would harm a woman, then you and I are done with friendly terms."

"A couple of idiots jumped me," she interrupted. "Leave Adam alone."

Sadie glanced apprehensively at Novis and I noticed some discoloration on her cheek and a cut on her lip. Nothing dramatic, but against her light skin, you couldn't help but notice it. Her beautiful hair stretched down her back in natural waves, and two narrow braids from each side joined in the back. I looked at her closely and could see a slight resemblance to Logan. It sure wasn't in her hazel eyes. She had full lips and only wore lip balm, but possessed a natural beauty that didn't require makeup to enhance.

"Did you go out there barefoot?" Adam scolded, staring down at her bare feet.

"I wasn't aware you were throwing me a party," she retorted, setting the can on the dresser.

Logan and Adam were in the center of the room beside the farthest bed. I took a few steps toward the table, watching with avid interest.

"What's your name?" Logan asked softly, apprehensively.

"Jasmine."

His nose twitched. "You're lying; that's not your real name."

She smirked. "Can't ever put one past a Chitah. My name is Sadie."

His cheeks flushed and he stumbled over his words. "How did you get that name?"

"There was a note pinned on my baby blanket when I was dumped off like a piece of trash."

Logan flinched as if she'd slapped him. He bowed his head. "Did you have a good home as a child?"

"I was adopted at birth, but when I was six, my mom died. Her nearest kin wouldn't take me in, so they threw me back into the system. I bounced around in foster care for a while. But hey, it made me stronger. Mind telling me who you all are that I'm being asked such personal questions?"

Logan approached Sadie and knelt before her. He gently touched her hand and placed his forehead against it, visibly distraught. I was so moved by his grace that I covered my mouth, tears hovering at my lashes.

Sadie looked at Adam, who offered her no explanation. Logan's tears wet her hand and she asked in a delicate voice, "Who are you?"

I knew Logan couldn't say it. For whatever reason, he was unable to move. So I spoke in his stead.

"That's Logan Cross. He's your brother."

Her eyes went wide and she glanced down at him again. "Can't be. He's a Chitah."

Clearly she knew about our world—if she'd lived with Cedric, of course she did. "You're the human baby his family gave up."

Then it hit me. Logan felt guilt. He held that baby in his arms all those years ago and let them take her away. What he was asking for on his knees was not acceptance, but forgiveness.

Sadie's eyes searched for the truth. None of us wavered in our respect for the moment, and perhaps the looks on our faces cemented the feeling that this was no hoax.

"On his word as a Chitah, Logan is your brother," I said.

She looked down and touched the very tips of his blond hair. It seemed like decades had passed as her expression changed to that of wonder. When she finally spoke, the melody of words must have filled his heart like a song. "Where you been all my life?"

I wiped the tears from my eyes, watching Logan rise to his feet. He wrapped his powerful arms around Sadie and lifted her off the ground. My heart soared for him.

She held his neck and looked down at him with a close-lipped smile. "How do you know it's me?"

"My sister," he said in a broken voice. "I know your scent. I have carried it with me my whole life and never thought I would hold you in my arms again. You were so small…"

Her fingers grazed the slope of his tearstained jaw and then she pulled his lips into a smile. "Yeah, I kind of see myself in you. A little in the mouth, and we have the same ears." Her hands finally settled on his broad shoulders.

"I'm sorry for your life—that we let you go. I was led to believe you had a family, and it angers me there was no one to protect you. This will never happen again. You have family now."

"Wow," she said, half-laughing and looking at him. "I have a family?"

His face grew sullen. "Our mother died in childbirth, which is why I was the one to give you a name. The Cross brothers will look out for you, and I can promise the male who put his fist to your flesh will pay."

"You named me?" Sadie's arms slipped around his neck and she nuzzled against him in a tight hug. She was so much more trusting than I would have been in that situation, but some people are just wired that way.

Logan lightly turned and the joy exuded from his face as he closed his eyes. "*My sister*," he whispered.

I sat down in a chair and Novis stepped forward. "Logan, I recognize the importance of this moment, but we do have urgent matters. Can we question the young woman before you resume your reunion?"

She peered over her shoulder and Logan bent forward until her feet touched the floor. "Question me about what?"

Novis shut the door and leaned against the wooden table. "You are familiar with a Mage named Cedric, is this correct?"

She nodded. "Yes, I know Cedric."

"Did he do that to your face?" Logan interrupted.

"No, Cedric only juiced me."

Wrong choice of words. For a split second, I thought Logan was about to flip his switch right in front of her.

Sadie twisted around and addressed Adam. "What's this all about?"

Adam came away from his position by the wall and stood between the two beds. "The man you know as Cedric is involved with a dangerous outlaw. He's wanted for questioning by the Mageri. This is important, Sadie. Where does he live?"

"Are you going to kill him?"

Logan's lower canines punched out.

"No," Novis replied tightly. "Our plan is to detain him."

"I would like time alone with him," Logan stated in a voice that invited no argument.

"We're not killing him." Novis said, folding his arms.

"You have my word I won't kill him, but I want retribution for him laying a hand on my flesh and blood. It is within my right as a Chitah to protect my family." Then he turned to Adam. "I would also like to know why my sister's scent was so heavy on your *mouth*," he growled.

"Logan," I interrupted. "Not now. Please, Sadie. We're trying to capture a dangerous man and Cedric knows how to get to him. Your help could save a lot of people."

She looked away and stuffed her hands in the pockets of her baggy jeans. "He stays in an old house off Deacon Street. I don't know the address because I never paid bills and it wasn't written on the mailbox. It's on the same side of the street as a pawnshop—you can't miss it. The house is brown with tacky blue trim. Baby blue. He also has a thing about birdfeeders; they're *all over* the yard."

Novis made a quick call and relayed the information to Justus.

Sadie noticed me again and Logan took his place by my side. "Sadie, this is my kindred spirit, Silver."

Her mouth opened a little. "I know a little about Chitahs, but she doesn't look like a Chitah."

"Silver is a Mage," he said proudly, curving his arm around my lower back.

A clever smile appeared on Sadie's face and she nodded. "Good to see things are changing. People can be so uptight about interbreeding, but love is love, right?"

I smiled at Logan. "I think I like her already."

After Sadie disclosed everything she knew about Cedric, Adam walked Novis outside and waited for the guards to bring his car around. What I admired about Novis was that despite the looming threat on his life, he didn't stop *living* his life.

I relaxed on the lumpy bed, giving Logan and Sadie a chance to play a little catch-up at the table. She believed Logan's story. Maybe it was the sincerity in his voice or the fact he had given her his word, but Sadie never accused him of lying. She didn't freak out, she didn't roll her eyes or do all the things I might have done in her shoes.

She hadn't changed clothes, but Logan had insisted she put on a pair of socks. When she suggested borrowing some from Adam, Logan had removed the pair from his own feet and asked her to put them on. She dangled them in front of her nose and I could tell Logan wanted to horse around with her, but he was being more reserved than usual. Sadie held nothing back and few people could say that about themselves.

"Do your siblings know about me?" she asked.

Logan leaned on his forearms, unable to keep his eyes off her. "They don't know you're here, but yes, they know of their sister. I was the only one of them present during your birth. Our mother thought by welcoming a new child into our family it would turn my life around."

Sadie crossed her legs and her voice became humored. "You were a bad boy, huh?"

"I had not lived an honorable life."

She sipped her red soda and flipped at the tab. "So, did I change your life?"

He lowered his gaze. "I was too far gone a man. Had we kept you, I'm certain you would have. Our mother was a smart female and knew I'd become fiercely protective of a little sister."

"What's my father like?"

"Serious. Distant. Absent. He travels and occasionally we get together. Chitah siblings are much closer with one another than with our parents. He's stuck in his old ways of thinking. Leo is now the patriarch of the family and works for HALO. Are you familiar with them?"

"I've heard it mentioned," she said with a shrug. "I learned a lot living with Cedric, but not everything."

"Did he... ever hurt you before?" Logan swallowed back his anger, but it edged his voice.

She shook her head. "No. It was all about juicing my light. He'd take just enough, but never hurt me. In return for letting him do that, I got a place to stay and food to eat. It helped me save enough money to buy my van. It's been tough, but life gives me writing material for my music."

His brows drew together. "You're a singer?"

She flashed a smile and that's when I saw the resemblance to Logan. "Musician. I sing and play guitar, but I also write my own music. You should come check me out sometime. I'm a regular at a couple of bars around here, and sometimes I perform at the coffee shops on Sunday... when they let me."

"I would very much enjoy hearing you sing."

"How did Adam help you?" I asked, curious to hear the whole story.

She grimaced a little and pried the tab off her can, flipping it between her fingers. "Well, you see my face. Some guys jumped me and Adam happened to be close by. If it weren't for him showing up at the right time, I can only imagine where I'd be now. There were three of them. I tried to scream but the big guy knocked me out cold."

Logan began rubbing his eyes with his fingertips as he joined me in imagining how that scene had almost played out.

"You shouldn't be so hard on Adam," she said protectively. "He's a decent guy."

"I agree." I watched Logan lean back in his chair, but he didn't acknowledge our compliments. Apparently, *big brother syndrome* had kicked in and he didn't like the idea of his baby sister shacking up in a motel with a man.

"Do you have somewhere we can take you?" he asked.

"Nah. I live in my van."

Logan vaulted to his feet. "Unacceptable," he said tersely.

"I'm sorry you feel that way, but it's my life."

"And you are my sister. No sister of mine lives in a van."

"Which is kind of why I'm staying here for a little while." She raised her palm, motioning toward the room.

That didn't go over well either. "You will not sleep in this room with that Mage."

"That Mage saved my life," she reminded him.

Despite the disagreement, I felt her patience with Logan.

"And I am in his debt," Logan confessed.

"What if you moved in with Levi?" I suggested. "He's one of your older brothers. You'd really like him and Levi's the kind of guy who will stay out of your business. It'll give you a chance to put some money away and get an apartment."

She flipped the tab around on the table, tucking her fist against her cheek. "Sounds great, but I've never met him. You're hitting me with a lot of news all at once and I'm still not sure how I feel about it. Part of me wants to be angry that you gave me up, but what's done is done. It's made me the person I am today. I couldn't move in with someone I don't know."

I shifted on the bed. "Sadie, you moved in with Adam."

"Yes, but I trust the kind of man he is because of how we met. That's all I need to know."

"Please consider it," I urged. "It's too cold to be sleeping in your van and you could get hypothermia. Just until summer and then you can make up your mind."

Logan took a seat and held a fist in front of his mouth.

"Maybe. I'd feel better meeting him first, so I'll stick with Adam until then," she said, swinging her eyes up to Logan. "Big brother or not, I still make my own choices. He's helped me twice and I feel like I can trust him to look after me. Maybe it was fate he found me, but fate only meets you halfway and it's your job to do the rest."

Logan's eyes flicked up and he spoke with the utmost seriousness. "You believe in fate?"

She took another sip of her soda and then pushed the can away. "I've had too many strange coincidences leading me from one thing to the next to believe it's not all connected. Maybe I'm a free spirit and that's how I see the world, but I think skepticism is negative energy. There's enough of that in this life and then some. If Adam hadn't been there at that precise moment, I would have been raped—maybe killed. He could have left me there and walked away. But out of everyone on this planet to show up, it turned out to be a man who would lead me to my brother. When I left the motel earlier, I didn't intend to come back. Apparently, the universe wasn't on board with that plan. Fate doesn't always give us what we want, but it gives us what we need."

Sadie was undoubtedly a unique young woman. She lived a life free of rules and responsibility, an artistic soul who interpreted the world in a poetic way. It helped to nurture her music, no doubt, but it would be interesting to see how she got along with her new family. I just hoped she wouldn't disappear after we left. Logan would track her down, but it would crush him.

"I trust Adam," I said. "He's the kind of guy you can turn to when you're in trouble, so you're safe to stay here a couple of days. I'll have a talk with him."

This girl needed to know she could trust the people around her, and I didn't want her to get spooked before she got a chance to know her family. While overwhelmed, she must have felt some sense of elation. If I were in her shoes and found out I had a family after years of living alone, I'd want to know *everything* about them.

Logan's belief was that human children who were given up were sent to good homes. If he'd known she was being thrown around in foster care, he might have taken her away from that life.

In fact, I'm certain of it.

"I will agree to you staying with Adam temporarily," Logan finally said. "But under the condition there is no physical contact between you two. If he is a man of honor, then he'll keep his hands off my sister. I'll arrange a meeting with the family."

"Just so it's out there," she began, "I've already kissed him. Sorry if that deflates anyone's balloon. You're right. Nothing will happen between us. I've already laid down the rules that I'm not going anywhere with him. I'm too young to start up a relationship—especially with a Mage. That seems like a dead-end street what with me being human. I have a career I want to focus on. I've seen girls go down the wrong road by latching onto a man before they figured out what they wanted for themselves in this world. Anyway, Adam isn't the kind of man I'd have a one-night stand with, so you have a deal on the no-hanky-panky rule."

Logan's jaw slackened. I privately smiled and he sliced me with a glare.

"Maybe we can all have dinner at our place," I offered.

"They'll all be there?" Sadie wrung her hands and nibbled on her lip. "I'm nervous. This is hitting me really fast."

Logan reached across the table for her hand and a quiet moment passed between them. I noticed how similar their hair color was, except Sadie's was a little darker. Human children of Chitahs didn't have the same telltale features in regards to eye color and height, but the resemblance was there.

"It pleases me you kept your name," Logan said, giving an imperceptible smile. "The midwife must have overheard—she's the one who took you away."

Sadie frowned and pulled her hand free from his grasp. "How did my mother die? I thought you guys lived a long time."

Logan cleared his throat and eased back in the chair. "A pregnant Chitah doesn't have the ability to heal during pregnancy. She's vulnerable. In order to carry the child, the magic within her shuts off. Her body does not rejuvenate during those nine months, and she is susceptible to all the dangers of childbirth that a human is. It's why males are fiercely protective of our women. They give life knowing they could lose their own in the process. The midwife said the labor was daunting and Susannah, our mother, suffered a hemorrhage. Her death altered our father."

"I can imagine. Maybe it's best I never meet him."

His brows knitted. "Why would you say that?"

She stroked her hair and gazed pensively out the window. "She'd be alive if it weren't for me. He probably blames me for her death, and maybe it's worse that she died for a human and not one of you."

Logan stood up and knelt beside her. I could see fire in his eyes, but not anger. "Our mother would have laid down her life for you, Sadie *Cross*. This I know. She took risks with each child, and she might have kept you had she lived, although it's unheard of. Our mother had different opinions on certain matters. She would have been proud to know you are a musician. She had an enchanting voice and often sang to you during her pregnancy. Our father called her a canary, but I see that's where you got some of your talent. *Jiminy*," he breathed. "You remind me so much of her."

A content smile touched her lips. "Logan, Leo, Levi, and... Luca."

"Lucian," he corrected. "He's the youngest with the dark hair and personality."

"Ah," she said with a smile. "Then he's the one who needs the most love."

"And of course Finn."

"You didn't mention a Finn," she said.

"He's a Shifter we took in as one of our own. He's family now."

"So I have five brothers."

It's as if stereotypes meant nothing to her—something Logan had grown accustomed to in his world. After meeting me, he'd begun to see how irrelevant some of those old beliefs and laws were. Judging by his expression, her acceptance moved him deeply.

"How long have you two been dating?" She pointed between us and I smirked at the word *dating* to describe our relationship.

Logan sat beside me on the bed. He placed his hand on my knee and squeezed it a little. "This is my kindred spirit, Sadie. She is the one I was born to love."

I expected laughter—being that she was human—but received no such outburst. I also selfishly wanted her to leave the room so I could climb on top of my male and kiss his neck endlessly for the compliments I'd indirectly been receiving.

"We're not the obvious match, but he's the best man I know," I said with a gentle smile. "Logan's the kind of man who will protect what he loves, but he's also given me the freedom to figure out who I am and what I want in life without smothering me. You couldn't have asked for a better family. He talked about you when we first met—several times. You've always been important to him. When I asked him about his family, he didn't exclude you. He assumed you had been given a better life. It's too dangerous for human children to grow up in our world."

"It's kind of dangerous out there in ours," she said absently.

Adam walked in and looked between all of us.

Before he could speak, Logan stood up and gripped his arm. "I need to speak with you outside, Mage."

That was the serious talk coming, and out they went.

Once alone, I sat across from Sadie at the table and lowered my voice. "Please don't abandon Logan. Maybe it won't work out—and that's fine—but don't just walk out of his life. Give him the chance to get to know who you are. It would devastate him if he lost you again. After we leave, your head is probably going to hurt thinking about all this. I know what you're going through, but if you can trust anyone, trust Logan. I'm not sure how his brothers will react to you, but if you ever need to talk, my door is open."

"Thanks, is it… Silver?"

"Yes," I said with a soft chuckle. "I've heard all the jokes. Seems like every time we go to a bar, someone has to make a wisecrack."

"Are you two getting hitched?"

Sore subject. "Not legally. They don't accept marriages between different Breeds. We can have the ceremony, but I'm not afforded all the rights by law as a mate. It may not seem like such a big deal now, but I don't know enough about Chitah laws to understand what that could mean down the road."

"Will you be there at dinner?"

I snorted. "I'll probably be the one cooking it, so I hope you have an iron stomach."

CHAPTER 18

WE REMAINED AT THE MOTEL until Adam returned with groceries. Logan refused to leave until he knew Sadie would be taken care of and fed. Adam had even bought a small microwave and set it on the dresser.

I kept an eye on my phone, hoping for an update from Justus on how things were going with Cedric. We stopped by a Mexican restaurant for tacos and Christian grabbed a booth in the back, keeping his distance. I thought about him tampering with Page's head and remembered how he'd done the same to me many months ago. Now I knew why Simon wore sunglasses around Vampires. It wasn't just having a Vampire *steal* information, but the threat of one *erasing* important memories.

Justus finally sent confirmation that they'd captured Cedric and were heading to the motel to question him. Adam decided he didn't want Cedric anywhere near Sadie, so he called the office and rented out a separate room for the interrogation. Justus wasn't sure when it would all be over, but he said he'd be back the following morning at the very latest.

Logan parked his car outside our rural home. The sun had just set after a long, unbelievable day. I opened the garage and we dragged ourselves inside.

"There's a lot of room in here to rollerblade if you want to have some fun," I said dryly.

Logan tugged at the back of my hair and spoke in a scolding voice. "I do not enjoy walking on wheels."

I let out a snort as we rode down in the elevator. "I don't think I'd call what you were doing... *walking*. But the Wright brothers would have commended you for your attempts at flight."

Once downstairs, I locked the door behind us and removed my coat. "Finn?"

Toenails clicked against the wood floor and a large red wolf paced toward me. The hairs on his face were tinged with grey, and his ears were larger than the average wolf. He didn't seem like his usual self, but these surroundings weren't familiar to him yet.

"Hey, Finn," I greeted, stroking the soft tuft of fur behind his ear.

Logan bent down and offered him the palm of his hand, which Finn's wolf sniffed. "He's going to need some time to adjust."

"How long does he stay like this?"

"Usually by breakfast he switches back."

I went into the control room saw Christian moving on the security monitor, but he quickly disappeared behind a tree. Sometimes I wondered if he really liked his job; he'd once mentioned an interest in doing something different. Christian had deterred attacks against me on more occasions than could be counted. He never bragged about it either. In fact, Novis was the one who had told me about a number of encounters. But Christian took his failures seriously, and perhaps I should have taken his successes more to heart.

While Logan prepared leftovers for Finn, I journeyed downstairs. Max was lounging comfortably on Justus's pillow, sprinkling his little black hairs all over the bed.

After washing my hair, I slipped into a pair of loose shorts and a soft black T-shirt. It was the one Justus couldn't stand that said *Fucking Classy*.

Logan loved seeing me in that shirt and it always roused a smile on his face.

"Anything good on?" I asked, staring up at the sea of monitors in the dark living room. Logan stretched out on the sofa, lying on his back. He tucked his right arm behind his head, dragging his eyes up the length of my body.

"There was nothing good on until you walked in the room."

I strolled up to the sofa and blocked his view. "We don't get many channels and I have to rent movies. Justus doesn't allow downloads to his computer because he's afraid of hackers and viruses. He barely lets me use the Internet unless I'm talking to Sunny; I guess he's afraid I'm going to jack up his computer by downloading a Trojan."

"Come lay with me, female."

Logan stretched out his impressive body. He had on a pair of grey sweats and no shirt, his left leg bent at the knee. What a magnificent body he had. Svelte, conditioned—the perfect specimen of a man with hard muscle and smooth skin. I got tingles just looking at him and his eyes became hooded as he picked up my scent.

"Female," he said in a rough voice, "I want your body spread over mine."

"If you keep talking to me like that, Mr. Cross, I'm going to need another shower."

I saw a thickening in his sweats and his lips parted. Logan slipped his right hand between my thighs, slowly caressing in subtle strokes as he worked his way up. I sighed and shut my eyes as he ventured even higher, teasing the skin just above the hem of my shorts.

"Female, you are a test of my willpower."

"And how's it holding out?" I asked in a breathy voice.

His upper fangs slowly descended. "Not very well."

When a flash of warm colors and distinct patterns rippled across his skin, I could no longer deny him. I crawled over Logan with the sofa against my back and my left leg bent at the knee, resting over his legs. I plastered my body against his warm chest and nestled my face on his shoulder. Because of his height, our bodies didn't line up, but that's what I found so attractive about him. Logan seemed larger than life—like a god. I stroked my finger against the tip of his chin and every so often, he'd kiss or suck on it.

I needed to feel his warm chest against mine. When Logan turned his attention back to the movie, I reached down and lifted my shirt, pressing my bare chest against his.

His reaction was immediate. His fingers bit into my skin where he held my back and his muscles stiffened.

But it wasn't just his body that stiffened.

Logan kissed me salaciously, pulling my body upward so he could reach me better. Nothing was more erotic than a buildup of sexual tension over a period of days that ended with a penetrating kiss. Not the kisses that were slow and simmering, but the immediate slide of his tongue against mine as it stroked deep. Feeling his desire for me became a rush.

His hands roamed down the back of my shorts and gripped my ass, rocking my hips while he groaned. I wanted him to strip off my shorts, but instead, he worked his hands around to my hips, rubbing and giving me hope that he'd pull them down.

But he didn't, and it set me on fire.

My body sank into his as if we were made to be together. Logan's lower canines slid out as I continued kissing him. Chitah venom had no effect on me, and regardless, I would never hold back from giving myself to Logan. He was the one man I trusted completely with my heart and my life.

When his chest began to vibrate from a deep, contented purr, it drew out a natural reaction in me to press my cheek against his. I had inherent Chitah instincts—just as I did human ones—and I didn't try to fight them anymore. My ex-lovers had thought they were simply peculiar bedroom habits, but Logan didn't object when I nuzzled or lightly bit his shoulder.

My mouth traveled down to his neck and the vibration tickled my lips.

"Would Justus ever purchase an apartment?" he asked.

I lifted my head, panting and wiping a swath of hair away from my face. "Why do you ask that?"

"I want to take you on *my* couch, in *my* bed, and on *my* floor."

"The floor, huh?" I kissed his chin and he kissed my nose.

"We could secure an entire building. Levi knows some people who can renovate small buildings into apartments."

I lightly drew in my bottom lip and studied him. "You're serious, aren't you?"

He shifted beneath me and I pulled down my shirt as we both sat up. Logan dropped his right foot on the floor and faced me.

It was a thought-provoking idea. I'd never been a fan of the underground bunkers—Leo sure didn't live in one, and he was also a member of HALO. Justus loved his cars, but surely he could secure an oversized garage somewhere in the city.

"I don't know, Logan. He's so set in his ways."

Logan threaded his fingers through my damp hair. "Imagine it,

Silver. We could renovate spacious living quarters—large enough that my brothers could raise a family of their own. Chitah siblings live in the same building, if possible. When families become too large, we move to the suburbs in the Breed district and purchase a street. Justus could have his own place and we could have ours. But you would still be close enough to train with him and live under his guidance."

"Justus won't listen to me. I've asked him a thousand times to move into the city."

Logan smirked and it crinkled the outer edge of his golden eyes. He draped his left arm over the back of the sofa and stroked my knee with his other hand. "He could still live in the Stone Age if he chooses. We don't have to run electricity into his apartment."

I belted out a laugh and curled up beside him. "Maybe Simon could talk him into it."

"Perhaps Leo is in a better position to convince him. Leo could give him peace of mind in the security that kind of living situation will offer a Mage. Not just with alarms and owning the entire building, but living with Chitahs. Most HALO members in the past have been attacked by one of their own, not other Breeds. A Mage would be foolish to attack a dwelling where Chitahs live."

"Sadie could have her own place. And Finn." The idea was growing on me with each passing second.

Logan kissed the palm of my hand. "Then it's decided. I'll speak to Leo and we'll begin scouting for locations. I know you come from the human world, Silver, but family should not be separated by miles. You can only build something great by putting smaller pieces together."

"I love you, Logan Cross."

He cupped my neck and planted a sweet kiss at the corner of my mouth. "My heart beats only for you, Little Raven."

"Forever?"

He paused for a moment and disappeared into my eyes. "I will love you until the stars burn out and we are nothing more than cosmic dust."

The next morning, I woke up on the rug with Finn's wolf lying on top of my legs. We had stayed up half the night talking about the idea of moving in together. Logan had pressed his lips to my forehead while I curled up beside him, listening to his heartbeat. But Finn's wolf kept nipping at Logan's arm and trying to wedge between us. When the growls became savage, I made popcorn and sat on the rug with Finn before he started pissing on the overpriced leather. I couldn't figure out why he kept trying to separate us, but I'd never understood much about animal behavior.

Finn was very much an alpha wolf when he wanted to be. Logan said many alphas remembered the time during their shift, but not all. Finn didn't seem to have much control over his animal. I don't think I'd want to see everything from a wolf's eyes. *Knock me out.*

A deep growl snagged my attention and when I opened my eyes, flashing lights were going off.

"Logan?" My adrenaline spiked.

I sat up and Logan leapt to his feet—alert and ready to attack. Finn's wolf trotted toward the door and when it opened, Justus wedged in.

"Learner, come take away this animal," he said gruffly.

"That's Finn, not an animal."

I joined Logan's side while Justus hung his new car keys on a small hook in the hall, murmuring about how the retinal scanner needed to be looked at.

Suddenly, Finn shifted to human form and before I could say anything, Logan slapped his hand around my eyes.

"Finn, go downstairs and put on some clothes," Logan shouted.

"No sweat," Finn replied. I listened to his bare feet smacking across the floor.

When he left the room, Logan uncovered my eyes and murmured, "We need to tell him about his father."

"Now?"

"Learner, I want you dressed appropriately."

I wasn't sure if Justus was more offended by my shorts or the

T-shirt with writing on it. "Ghuardian, no offense, but this is my house too and I'll wear what I want."

Which didn't go over well. Justus folded his muscled arms and presented me with a stern face. "That is not appropriate attire for me to look at."

Logan took a step forward. "But the skimpy outfit you make her put on in the training room *is*?"

"The clothes I provide for training give her the ability to move around freely," Justus said, eyes still on me.

"Perhaps you should dress her in what she would be wearing in a real fight so she can feel the limitations that clothing can bring."

When I saw a muscle twitch in Justus's cheek, I knew this was going to turn into an unnecessary quarrel. They each played an important role in my life and they were vying for the position of top dog.

I wrapped my hand around Logan's arm and lightly squeezed. "I'll go change. It's too cold around here to be in a pair of shorts anyhow. I think that's why Finn's wolf was lying on my legs last night," I said with a chuckle.

It only took me a few minutes to slide into a pair of comfy jeans and combat-style boots. My sense of humor was running amok as I headed upstairs. Justus glared at me briefly while sipping his gourmet coffee in the living room chair, looking sleepy and in need of a shave. He preferred me in feminine clothing, but dressing up is something I only did for fun when I went to a club or a party.

Logan's hungry eyes watched me strut into the room. He sat on the sofa, his legs widening and his eyes sliding down to the heavy treads on my boots. He sexily wet his lower lip with a sweep of his tongue. The heated energy from his gaze rippled through the room as he devoured me in a glance, and damn if it didn't turn me on that he got aroused no matter what I was wearing.

Finn ambled in the room with a plate in one hand and a piece of bacon in the other. He stopped in front of me and faced Logan. I peered around him to see what was going on. Logan slid his eyes up to Finn's and narrowed them. Finn widened his stance and continued munching on his bacon.

What was going on with all this male posturing?

"Finn, we need to talk to you about something serious," Logan began. "Sit down."

A flokati rug covered a space in front of the fireplace and Finn sat Indian style with his plate on his lap.

"So, what's up?" he asked, biting into a buttermilk biscuit.

I sat in the chair beside Justus and crossed my legs. Logan leaned forward with his elbows on his knees and hesitated before dropping the bomb on Finn.

"Your father paid Leo a visit."

Finn swallowed hard and wiped his hand against his jeans. The sleeves on his shirt were short enough that it showed the deep scar on his right arm. The one Nero had put there with a branding iron in the shape of the letter *N*. He had a habit of covering it with his hand whenever something was bothering him. His fingers briefly wandered there and then he put the plate to the side and stretched out his legs, crossing them at the ankle.

"And?"

"He wants you back." Logan maintained eye contact and rubbed his chin pensively. "I don't know what your home life was like before he sold you, but this is not our decision to make. It's yours. We want to know what your thoughts are so we know how to handle him."

"Why don't you tell that feebleminded asshole to go to hell where he belongs?"

"Because under the circumstances, he might gain support of the Packmasters and forcibly remove you from our home. We want you to stay, but there's no guarantee he won't find a way to take you from us. I don't know his motive—"

"Money," Finn confirmed with a despondent look in his eyes. "That's all he's ever been about. Filling his pockets with dead presidents."

"What's his line of work?" Justus asked, propping his chin against his fist.

"He used to own a few bars but was never a good businessman—just an extortionist. He sold me to pay a debt and I never saw him again. I was just a kid, and the last thing he ever said to me was 'Quit crying, you big pussy.' I don't know what he's been up to since, but he's sure not on easy street if he's trying to hustle money from you guys. That man didn't give a crap about me. Maybe it would have been different if we had lived in a pack." Finn's shaggy hair covered his eyes as he lowered his head.

"Your father was testing us to see what our motive was for keeping you," Logan said. "Word gets around, but everyone knows Chitahs are loyal to those we take in. Little Wolf, I'm going to ask a question and I want you to think carefully before you answer. If you need time, then I'll give you that. But honesty is what I want, and remember—I can scent a lie."

Finn's cheeks were mottled, his lashes wet. "Yeah?"

"Do you want to go back to your father?"

Without hesitation, Finn replied. "No."

"Then it's settled." Logan sat back and crossed an ankle over his knee.

Finn resumed eating the biscuit he had stuffed with bacon.

Simon had promised me he would help dig up something on Finn's dad, just in case he tried to blackmail us. I hoped Simon would pull through. Finn didn't need to know what we were up to—it was a precautionary measure, and I didn't want him to get the wrong idea. Especially if he harbored any kind feelings toward the man despite what he told us.

Max sauntered in the room and flicked his black tail in serpentine motions. He had an aristocratic expression—as much as a cat could—and lifted his regal chin as he stepped across Finn's legs. Finn snatched his tail and Max swatted him, scratching him on the wrist.

Finn snapped his arm back and tiny bubbles of blood pooled on his skin.

"I'm *not* a cat person," he muttered.

Max growled and leapt onto Logan's lap, rubbing his face against Logan's stubbly chin. Logan made a peculiar chirping sound that was so low it could scarcely be heard. Max responded and grew less agitated, curling up beside him.

I looked at Justus and couldn't help but notice he seemed

a million miles away. A vertical line etched between his eyes and his mouth formed a grim line. The floor lamp accented the blond highlights in the short hairs across his scalp. He was a man who didn't talk just to fill the silence; when Justus De Gradi had something to say, people listened. I'd come to realize Justus had a side to him that was thoughtful and gentle, and it often made me wonder if those were the pieces of the human I was seeing—the man he was *before* he became a Mage.

"What did you find out from Cedric?" I asked.

"Nero is a resourceful man. They've been working together exclusively for years, and he paid Cedric well for keeping it that way. Do you recall the bomb attack at Novis's home?"

"Yes." *How could I forget?*

Justus rubbed his chin as he spoke. "No one has ever managed to get liquid fire into an aerosol form. It has unique properties and often breaks apart when tampered with. Cedric's inside man in the Special Forces is a scientist. He received a large sum in exchange for the canisters used in the attack but wasn't given the details on how he achieved such a feat. Now that Nero has seen the magnitude of destruction, he wants to acquire the knowledge for himself. He's been using the metal to chain his captives, but these trinkets are not enough. Cedric was given orders to find out the identity of his insider, but he's not skilled enough to complete such a task. Nero wants war—he wants our world to be the way it was before Councils and Breed laws. It's not just the Mageri he's after."

"Does Cedric know where Nero lives?"

"He has a phone number which Simon is researching, and he also gave us a location. This is not my concern."

"What is?"

Justus slowly turned his head and leveled me with his blue eyes. "That Nero will remain elusive until he coordinates an attack."

"He already did that," I pointed out. "He's attacking the Council."

"No," Justus interrupted. "Something on a grander scale. He's testing our weaknesses and creating a stir of panic. He doesn't want anyone to feel safe. People want to feel protected by their leaders, and he's trying to shake the very foundation we stand on. During their last communication, Nero asked Cedric to speak to his contact about artificial venom."

Logan's eyes flashed up. "That would be cruel."

"Indeed," Justus said in a rough voice.

"What would be cruel?" I looked between the two, not understanding.

Logan stood up and crossed the room, pensively looking at the floor. "If he found a way to extract Chitah venom or have it artificially engineered, it would become a weapon. Depending on the quantity, it can do everything from paralyze to kill a Mage. But one Chitah can only provide so much—it works a lot like adrenaline where our bodies only produce it as needed. Imagine tainting the wine at a Mageri gathering with every elected official present."

I gasped and sprang to my feet. "We have to stop him, Justus. He'll do it. Are you going to raid his home?"

"Nero has many homes," Justus reminded me. "Christian scrubbed Cedric's memory and we supervised, making sure that in conversation, Nero will never suspect he's been tampered with. One of the homes is upstate and in a rural location. With luck, we might even find the stolen boxes from the lab. They could reveal the locations of other labs or even names of those involved. I'm willing to bet there are facilities on the property that would allow him to house his captives."

His captives being the other humans who had been given their first spark by Samil. The ones Nero had kept chained in a cell. The unique metal suppressed the light of a Mage so they couldn't use their powers, but it didn't prevent Nero from extracting their energy.

"It's important this plays out so innocent blood is not spilled."

"We can't waste time sitting on it," I pointed out. "He'll find out we're onto him. How are you going to do this?"

"We're not initiating a raid without knowing the lay of the land; it would be foolish and impulsive. Leo knows someone who can provide blueprints of the property. He works in construction, among other things. We'll have an idea how many men Nero has guarding the property. We'll have to present this to the Mageri to obtain a warrant and utilize their Enforcers. But it's too risky to go to them now; our plan could leak. We'll wait until the last minute to approach them. We don't know what we're up against and I won't have our men going in blind. This is something HALO does with those we hunt down, and patience holds value. If a man runs into a river to catch a fish, he will scare them away and create ripples that reach far and wide. If he eases in slowly and stands very still, the water will remain clear. He'll see the depth, know where they congregate, and with skill, he'll reach in and catch one with his bare hands."

"I didn't know you liked to fish," I said absently.

Humor accented his expression. "How do you think I survived before takeout?"

CHAPTER 19

FINN PLAYED VIDEO GAMES FOR the remainder of the day until he discovered Justus owned an extensive collection of literature. Finn lit up with excitement and disappeared into the study.

Tonight was the dinner party and Logan believed it was his obligation to prepare the meal for his sister, so he refused to let me help in the kitchen. Leo couldn't attend due to work, but Lucian swung by and hung out in the garage, admiring Justus's extravagant cars. Justus was proud to give him the tour and the last time I'd checked the monitors, they had the hood open on the Mercedes and were deep in conversation. Lucian was an introvert by nature, but they'd found a common interest and it just so happened to be the one thing Justus obsessed about.

Cars.

I selected an elegant dress for our gathering. It had an empire waist with a V-neck that showed off a little cleavage without going overboard. I loved the thin fabric, so delicate and not sheer at all. Justus had given it to me few months ago, despite the fact I made my own money and his purchases were excessive and unnecessary. I'd occasionally find a white box on my bed with something special inside—it was just his way of showing affection. The dull green dress made my dark hair and bright eyes stand out. Justus believed a woman should wear a dress that complemented her eyes without outshining them.

I was nervous about making a good impression. I would be seeing a lot more of Sadie and wanted to make a positive connection with her.

As I walked into the kitchen, Logan burned his hand on a hot pan and slammed the cookware against the stove. A curse flew past his lips and he licked his wound, immediately healing the raw skin.

"Need help?" I offered.

"It's under control." He leaned on the counter with straight arms, staring at the pan.

I stayed close to the door and noticed how tense he was. "Smells good. Look, why don't you relax for a little while and let me take over? You're wound up like a ball of yarn."

"Because it has to be perfect," he murmured, sampling the fresh-cut potato chips he'd baked.

I leaned on the counter and listened to the men pour in through the front door. I turned to look when I heard the boisterous sound of Levi's voice.

"Hot damn, someone is cooking in here. And I don't mean you, Lo. Have you checked out your female over here?" He looked approvingly at my dress and I beamed a little, giving him a hug. "Not a fan of the perfume," he said, sniffing my neck, "but I guess it's a chick thing."

Logan turned around and admired me with apologetic eyes. "Silver, you're stunning, as always. I don't mean to ignore you; there's much to do."

"Well, let me help," Levi said with a chuckle, strutting through the room in denims and a T-shirt that hugged his body in unimaginable ways. He was the Cross brother who owned his swagger to the nth degree.

"There's nothing to do," Logan said, eyeing him as he approached the fridge.

"Bullshit. You know I'm the best damn cook in this family, and if we're meeting my sister, I'm not about stand around and let you take all the credit. Step aside. What's on the fire?"

"I'm making our mother's favorite."

Levi glanced at him and lowered his voice to one of nostalgia. "Chicken casserole, peas, and cucumber salad. Are those her chips?"

Logan knocked his arm away when he reached out to grab one. "They're for later."

"Did you make the dip?"

Logan straightened out a wrinkle in his black shirt. He wore a pair of dark trousers with a leather belt. But he stayed true with his trademark sneakers. These were black with black laces.

"Move it, brother." Levi reached in the cabinet for a bowl. "You better have all the ingredients here or I'm going to the store. If we're doing this, we're doing it right. Mom would have loved it."

Tears touched my eyes unexpectedly as I thought about Logan's family in a different way. These hardened men had once been boys who had a mother they'd cherished and lost. Who never knew their sister, but loved her anyway.

Logan cut across the room and cupped his hand behind my neck. "No tears," he whispered. "You look elegant. Thank you."

"For what?"

"I don't believe in coincidence. If not for Adam rescuing you on the night you were attacked, I would not have met my kindred spirit. If not for you, I would not know Adam, who found my sister."

"So, does this mean you two are going to bury the hatchet?"

He laughed darkly and offered a handsome smile that deepened the laugh lines on his cheeks. I loved falling into those dangerous, bright eyes with inky rims. He'd styled his hair neatly tonight—still fistably long, but not haphazard.

"I wouldn't go that far, but we'll see," he said.

Logan stood at a proud six and a half feet, so I stretched up on my tiptoes and kissed his chin.

"Smooth," I said, landing another small kiss on his shaved face so as not to smear my lipstick on him.

"Just as my female likes."

"Can you two take that somewhere else? You're throwing off my sense of taste," Levi said, crunching on one of the chips.

When Adam sent me a text that they were getting close, I slipped on a thin jacket and hurried up to the garage to let them in.

"Party?" an Irish voice said from behind.

I spun on my heel and caught Christian leaning on the hood of the black Porsche.

"What are you doing in here?"

"Came in while the Chitah and Mage were tinkering about with their toy cars. Justus still isn't speaking to me. Knowing him, I suppose that won't change."

"Do you blame him? You scrubbed a Relic so she'd forget she was artificially inseminated in a lab. Why would you do that?"

"Aye, the silly whims of a Vampire," he rattled on, stalking toward the garage doors.

"Have you ever done that to me, Christian? I mean, aside from the hotel thing when I walked in on you and that slut?" I hugged my arms.

He threw a glance over his shoulder and watched me with liquid black eyes. "No. Care to explain why a woman who seeks my companionship must wear such a colorful title?"

"I don't think it's your companionship she was seeking."

A crooked smirk touched his lips. "To be sure." Then his eyes slid down and noticed my dress. "You look fetching tonight," he said in a dark voice. Not just dark, but possessive, and it made me shudder.

"I'd ask you to join us, but it's a family thing and you have too much fun stirring the pot."

"You have a tongue that could clip a hedge."

"This isn't the night for a cauldron of wicked Christian. Logan's human sister is coming over to meet the family for the first time."

Christian pinched his chin, eyes locked on my dress. "Is she now?"

I could hear Adam's motorcycle thundering up the road and an awkward moment passed between us.

"They're here."

"Who?" Christian suddenly blinked as if snapping out of a haze. "Ah, here comes Adam on his mechanical horse. Have a sublime evening," he said, ducking beneath the garage door as it opened.

He gave me a backward glance and I knitted my brow, soon forgetting the oddness that is Christian and waving at Adam and his female passenger. She had on Adam's helmet and leather jacket, but her poor legs had been exposed to the frigid temperatures and were pale against her white dress.

Then I noticed her cowboy boots. Brown, soft leather that looked good on a girl, but it made her stand out in a city like Cognito.

Adam pulled into the garage and threw open the kickstand. He looked pissed as she held on to his shoulders and got off the bike, shivering. "You could have put on the sweats and changed when we got here."

Sadie pulled off her helmet and a blanket of hair spilled down her shoulders in beautiful waves of soft blond. "I may be casual, Scratch, but I'm not country."

"Could have fooled me." Subtle humor edged his voice as he stared at her boots.

"Hey, this is stylish," she said, tossing him the helmet. "Showing up in a pair of sweatpants or ripped jeans is not."

I grimaced. "Your hands are red. Come inside. Justus cranked on the heat and you can sit with a blanket in the living room while we set the table."

"Thanks, Silver."

But she didn't move. Her eyes roamed around the spacious garage from floor to ceiling.

"Hey, you nervous? We can go," Adam said quietly.

Sadie took a cleansing breath and gripped the sides of her dress. "Show me the way."

I pointed toward the open elevator and she went ahead of us.

"Should I be upset she's calling you Scratch?" I whispered to Adam with concern. I didn't care for the word, given the implied meaning behind it.

He chuckled and rubbed at his whiskers. "It's not what you think. It's how we first met. Don't say anything to her about it. I… I kind of like it."

"Well, Razor, I see how it is," I said, swirling around and flouncing toward the elevators. I threw him a smile over my shoulder and he put the helmet on the bike and joined us.

I couldn't help but notice Adam's body language. They didn't walk together, but when we passed through a set of doors, he held his hand behind her back without touching it. His hand sure didn't fly around *my* back, but other than that, the banter between them seemed casual, as if they'd known each other for years. In a strange way, Sadie reminded me of Adam. He'd always seemed like an old soul.

We reached the main door to the house and when it opened, Logan and Levi hung back in the hall. Levi rushed forward and without a word, gave her a bear hug that startled Sadie so severely she let out a squeak.

"That's enough," Adam said, closing the door behind him. "Give her some space."

"Space?" Levi said in a bewildered voice. "This is my sister, Mage." Levi backed away and studied her overwhelmed expression. "You're right, Lo. She looks a lot like Mother… only shorter."

Sadie cleared her throat. "I'm guessing we're related, but I don't think you've managed to spit out your name."

He snorted and winked at me. "She's a Cross, all right." Levi bowed and locked eyes with her. It made her blink and she looked away. There was a pregnant pause before he spoke again. "I'm Levi Cross, the best-looking male in this family."

"I'm Sadie Howell, the best-looking female in this family."

He rocked with laughter. "Girl, you're the *only* female in this family."

She slapped him on the arm and walked toward Logan. "Exactly."

Sadie's face sweetened as she looked upon Logan. An intangible connection seemed to exist between them—a familiarity in the way they looked at each other. Perhaps from those moments when he'd held her as a baby and whispered her name, she somehow remembered him. It seemed impossible, but I wondered if she had any Chitah instincts as I did.

Sadie didn't speak but slyly looked up at Logan and tilted her head. A single braid hung from her right temple and beaded bracelets the color of Justus's eyes adorned her wrist.

"You look lovely," he said, bowing as gentle as a breeze.

A graceful smile touched her lips as she looked down. "Love your shoes."

Logan's cheeks reddened and he flicked a worried glance my way. He must have thought she found them absurd until he stopped and pulled in a scent. His shoulders relaxed and he held out his arm.

"Come sit and warm yourself." He shot a hostile glare at Adam who threw his hands up in defeat, conveying he'd tried, but she wouldn't listen.

After she settled on the sofa with a blanket, I brought in a few cups of coffee and Levi proudly set his cheese dip on a table with the homemade chips. Everyone dug in and Logan disappeared into the kitchen.

Lucian emerged from the study and lingered in the doorway behind the sofa.

"These taste amazing," Sadie gushed, dusting off her fingers and looking between us. Then she caught the direction of our stare.

When she turned around, Lucian took a step back.

"Lucian, come meet your sister." Levi stalked toward him, swinging his heavy arms at his sides. I got up from the chair and walked close enough to hear their low murmurs.

Levi leaned in tight. "You need to let that shit go, brother. Come say hello."

Lucian's lips curled angrily and he flicked a glance at Sadie. "She killed our mother."

Sadie continued munching on the chips, oblivious to the friction that pulsed in the room like a rapid heartbeat. Their energy spiked enough that it bristled me, and even Justus leaned forward in his chair with concern brimming in his eyes.

"You are *not* going to blame an infant for the death of our mother. She's a grown woman and part of this family, now get your sorry ass in there and show her you're a Cross," Levi demanded.

Levi made no attempt to physically force him, but fire blazed in his eyes until Lucian conceded defeat and stalked into the room, stopping short of the sofa.

"I'm Lucian Cross."

Sadie moved the blanket away to stand up, but the apprehension on her face was evident. This wasn't a guy who was going to give her a Levi bear hug.

"So... you're my youngest big brother."

Lucian tucked his hands in his pockets and lowered his bright eyes. The angled line of his cheekbones sharpened as he clenched his jaw.

She stood up and gently touched his onyx hair. He didn't have the height of a Chitah and was just shy of six foot. Among Chitahs, his traits were undesirable.

Finally, Sadie spoke. "You have the most distinguished features. I've seen a few Chitahs before, but they're all blond, like me. But your dark hair paired with those brilliant eyes—it's stunning. I guess you get that a lot. Sorry, I didn't mean it to sound cheesy, but you're a striking young man."

Lucian drew in short puffs of air as Logan often did when tasting an emotion. Confusion spread across his face and he threw a brief glance at Levi, who simply shook his head in disbelief.

Sadie didn't seem like the kind of girl who bullshitted, so Lucian was taken off guard by an unexpected truth.

His sister thought he was a handsome man.

After an intimate pause, he stiffly bowed his head and moved across the room, looking about as comfortable as a balloon in a porcupine pit.

Levi scratched his chin and noticed Sadie's outfit. "Adam, we're going to have some words later on," he promised. "I don't want my sister going anywhere on a bike if the temperature is below eighty."

"Gotcha," Adam said from the chair beside Justus. The two of them faced the fireplace with everyone standing to their right. "I may take up Sunny's offer on the Jeep Commander to drive Sadie around."

"That sounds a little long-term for my taste." Levi wrinkled his nose and it made me smile.

Sadie sat on the arm of the sofa. "I own a van."

Levi's brow arched. "If no male looks after you, how do you survive?"

Her face brightened. "I sing. I would have brought my guitar over, but we had the bike. You should come hear me perform sometime. I still get stage fright when it's a new club, but all those fears melt away the moment I'm in front of a microphone."

"No shit. I've never seen you."

"I don't sing in Breed clubs. I've had too much trouble getting in because I'm human."

Levi's neck reddened and his lips drew tight. "You let me know where you want to play and I'll make it happen. That's bullshit. You can make some serious cash in Breed clubs."

She shrugged and nodded all at once. "I know. I found that out from the Mage I lived with. I guess you guys have centuries' worth of money stuffed in those deep pockets." Her gaze floated about the room and I could only imagine what this place seemed like to her, especially with all the monitors plastered on the wall.

Justus kept staring at the floor with a vacant look in his eyes. He could often be a quiet man, but he wasn't as engaged as he normally was. I began to worry something was going on with Nero's case.

Logan returned and his face glistened from the heat in the kitchen. "Ten more minutes," he announced. Levi began talking about a sweet red sports car he saw on the way over.

I sat beside Sadie and she spoke privately. "So you let Logan do all the cooking? Nice work."

"It's a Chitah thing," I whispered back. "It's an honor to have a male prepare a meal for you—it's their custom."

"What about your custom? Do you like to cook?"

"No, I prefer eating, so it kind of works out."

She snickered and touched one of her bracelets. "I'm right there with you. I've never been able to find a man who would cook for me though. Do you like being a Mage? I haven't seen many women like you."

"It's not easy, but I'm proud of who I am. I can't imagine being any other Breed. It's a challenge because I have to learn how to use my energy, so it takes time."

"You don't... juice others, do you?" she asked warily.

"Sadie, we're not all like Cedric. It's not just rogues you have to worry about. Light is addictive, and a good Ghuardian or Creator will train his progeny not to become dependent on healing light. I think they're afraid because when we're young, sampling it more frequently will form an addiction. Besides, I'd never resort to juicing. I've gone through a few bad experiences and I know what it's like to be used."

"I'm sorry to hear that."

I looked up at Logan and his eyes were fixed on mine as he continued talking to Levi. It reminded me of the night I ran into my ex at a bar and how in tune Logan was with emotions—how he always kept watch over me.

"Don't ever let a Mage take light from you, Sadie. Consensual doesn't make what they're doing right."

The silent alarms suddenly flashed and Justus vaulted out of his chair. He rushed into the security room—a tiny space with a few monitors and a computer station, all hidden behind a secret panel in the hallway.

The lights didn't seem to alarm Logan and Levi as much as Justus's scent did. Logan blocked the hall and looked over his shoulder. "Stay where you are. If we need you to move downstairs, then I want you to do it fast."

I approached the hall where the lift was, Sadie close to my side. Adam took a position several feet in front of us, keeping his eyes on the entrance that led to the front door. His fingers were splayed, ready to fight.

A cell phone rang in the living room and Justus picked it up. "Yes, I see them, Christian. Did you ask their business?"

"What's going on?" Sadie asked in a worried voice.

I shook my head.

Justus tucked his phone in his pocket and walked toward the front door. "Regulators are on the property," he bellowed. "Stay here and be on your best behavior."

Regulators were similar to Enforcers, only they served as officers for the higher authority. Technically, there was no organized form of government comprised of all Breeds, but Regulators were connected with operations within the Breed jail.

Logan crossed the room to stand in front of us and I scarcely breathed. Lucian remained seated in a swivel chair near one of the monitors to my left, gripping the armrests. The men were strategically positioning themselves in different areas.

"What's going on?" Finn said from the hall behind me.

"Finn, go back downstairs," I said, glancing over my shoulder.

His hair looked a mess—all scrambled and covering his eyes a little.

"I fell asleep reading and the lights woke me up. Why are they blinking?"

"It's the alarm that lets us know someone's on the property."

Murmurs sounded from the hall and Christian floated in, his black trench coat flapping behind him. He slanted his eyes to locate my position and when he reached the center of the room, he pivoted on his heel and folded his arms. His expression was grim and I nervously gripped Logan's arm.

"Under what premise?" Justus barked out.

"By order of the higher authorities of the court," a crisp, loud voice replied.

"I am a member of HALO and you have—"

"Yes, Mage. I'm well aware."

A tall blond with sharp cheekbones and blistering yellow eyes entered the room, the heels of his dress shoes clicking on the floor. He wore black slacks and a tight-fitting jacket of the same color. Another man walked in holding papers in his right hand. But what caught my attention was that each of them was armed with a katana—a gently curved steel blade that looked over two feet long. On their other hip was a dagger, both weapons prominently displayed outside their attire.

"What the hell are *you* doing here?" Levi said with a familiar tone, walking toward the Chitah in black.

The man lifted his hand. "Stay back, Levi. This is official business."

Justus sent a quick text on his phone and stood beside Christian. "The Mageri knows nothing of your visit."

The Chitah pursed his lips and rolled his eyes. "Of *course* they don't, Mage. As you're well aware, Regulators carry out orders given by any Breed member of the higher authority once a warrant for arrest is issued. We are here on orders of the Chitah Overlord."

With a flick of the wrist, the second man handed the papers to Justus. I clutched Logan even tighter as my Ghuardian meticulously reviewed them.

"This is ludicrous," he muttered.

Ignoring him, the Chitah moved toward me. Logan's posture rapidly changed to an aggressive one.

"By order of the higher authority, the Regulators of the Security Force have been summoned to serve a warrant and place Logan Cross under arrest for the murder of Tarek Thorn, Lord of the

Youngblood Pride. The investigation is complete and the family of the victim seeks justice for your deliberate actions. They feel your baneful influence poses a threat to their good name and is a danger to our society." He coolly stepped in front of Logan as they locked eyes. "You will be held in the Breed facilities until such time that the Council has determined your fate."

"You can't do this!" I shouted. "Call the Overlord. Logan is my kindred and—"

"The Overlord is the one who issued the warrant. Law is law, young Mage. You break a rule and you pay the hefty price."

The second man lifted his eyes to meet mine and I felt the distinct flare of a Mage. He began increasing his energy to prepare for a confrontation. Attacking a Regulator was a criminal offense.

Logan peered over his shoulder with a look of defeat. The rims of his eyes pulsed—this was one battle he couldn't win. It's something he'd tried to prepare me for in conversation, reminding me that the investigation was still ongoing and until the case closed and the family settled, it was a looming threat. The orders had been issued by the Overlord, but the decision for the arrest had to be unanimous among the leaders within the higher authority.

My fingertips buzzed as the tension in the air thickened.

The Regulator arched his brow. "Well, then. If this is your refusal, Cross, perhaps you'd rather us take your female."

When the man reached out to touch my arm, Logan blocked him and Finn shifted into his wolf, causing Sadie to scream.

"Finn, no!" Logan roared.

The wolf paced forward, canines bared, crouched low. Levi swiftly corralled Finn in the hallway.

"You have two choices, Cross. Easy or… not so easy," the Chitah continued, squeezing the hilt of his katana. "A warrant is not debatable; you can plead your case with the Council of elders, but think twice about resisting arrest. It will go on your record and may sever any sliver of hope you have of overturning their decision."

"Logan, no," I pleaded. "They can't do this. You saved my life…"

I grimaced at the emotional turmoil ravaging my heart. The sharpest ache I'd ever known constricted my chest. I looked to Justus whose eyes briefly darted to mine while he spoke in a low voice to the other Regulator. The man continued shaking his head and pointing at certain passages in his papers. Everything began moving in slow motion.

Logan placed a heavy hand on Levi's shoulder. "Take care of my female. Protect her as if she were your mate."

Levi lifted his dimpled chin. "I will guard her with my life, brother."

This isn't happening, I thought. *It's a nightmare and I'm going to wake up at any moment.*

Logan turned around and cupped my neck, tenderly kissing away the tears that spilled down my cheeks.

"My female," he whispered softly against my cheek. "Bars will not cage my love for you. Distance will not keep me out of your dreams. Death will not stop my heart from beating for you, Little Raven. You knew this might happen."

"I know, but I don't want to lose you," I said through sobs, holding on to his neck. "Please don't leave me here alone."

He gripped me tight and I felt him slipping away, so I squeezed my eyes shut and tried to imagine this moment wasn't happening.

"I'll never leave you," he whispered against my hair.

"Promise?"

"Let's go," the Chitah barked out, gripping Logan's arm and pulling him away.

Logan lunged toward me and held my face, giving me a desperate and soulful kiss as he spoke against my lips.

"You're the reason I exist."

"Come on, Chitah," the Regulator said, tugging him away. "Time to face the man."

"Watch over my sister," Logan demanded of Adam as the men cuffed him.

All I could think about was how handsome Logan looked tonight. He'd gone out of his way to put on something that would impress Sadie so it would be a night to remember. One she would remember for years to come.

And it was.

CHAPTER 20

I WAS INCONSOLABLE AND ENRAGED. How could Logan's leaders allow so many months to elapse before deciding to incarcerate him? Sadie was visibly shaken and Adam drove her back to the motel after I loaned her a pair of my jeans to wear beneath her dress. Because Levi wouldn't leave my side, Justus volunteered to drive Lucian home. Finn remained in wolf form—agitated—so I walked him down to the lower level.

Levi didn't like the scent of my distress and looked close to flipping his switch a few times. I could trust Logan in that primal state, but I had no idea how volatile a man like Levi might be.

Still wearing my green dress, I slipped into a leather jacket and zipped up the front.

"Going somewhere, female?" Levi folded his thick arms and tilted his head empathetically.

"To see the Overlord," I replied, retrieving my car keys from a bowl in the living room. "He's the only one who can stop this. We're not going to argue about it, Levi. You can come or you can stay here. You decide. Logan asked you to look out for me, but he didn't ask you to control my decisions."

"Damn, girl. I wasn't going to say anything. I guess you must be used to that shit from Logan."

I grabbed my phone and tucked it in my coat pocket. "This isn't the day to get on my bad side, Levi. Don't joke about Logan when he's given me more freedom than any man I've ever known."

I put the alarms on the highest setting, and since Finn was downstairs, I placed the chicken casserole by the lift with a note, telling him not to go upstairs under any circumstance until I came to get him. Finn had everything he needed down there from books to workout equipment. Superman couldn't break into that house, but if for some reason he did, he wouldn't find Finn as long as he remained hidden downstairs.

"And where do you think you're going?" Christian asked in his Irish lilt, leaning against the garage door with his hands stuffed in his pant pockets. He pulled out a small peppermint and began to twist the wrapper off.

"To see the Overlord."

He popped the candy in his mouth and tucked the wrapper in his pocket. "I don't think that's such a grand idea," he said, walking toward my car and blocking the driver's side door.

"Move out of my way, Christian. You aren't the boss of me and this is none of your business."

"Protecting you is my business, and you're about to walk into a lion's pit." His black eyes swallowed me up and I dodged his glare, noticing he'd trimmed up his beard a little.

Christian touched my chin and stepped forward, lifting my head. "Don't look away from me, lass. I've already promised I wouldn't charm you." His eyes floated to my mouth and I jumped when Levi slammed his fist on top of the car.

"How 'bout you take your hands off her and do your job? I know a few guards, and they shut their trap and don't get involved."

"Maybe *my* brawn comes with a brain," Christian suggested. "Clearly yours doesn't if you're allowing her to walk into danger. I have no patience for ineptitude."

Levi's fingers tapped on the hood angrily. "I don't allow anyone shit. You *allow* children, and Silver is a woman who makes her own choices. She's also my brother's mate, and you had better put your hands back in your pockets. I'm going to take this shit up with Novis. When guards get too involved with who they're protecting, they don't concentrate as hard as they should. They become easily distracted. They make mistakes. Their emotions compromise the safety of their client. So back the fuck off, Vampire."

Christian's stoic expression fell on me once more and he turned around and hit the button to the garage door, stalking outside with his black coat flapping in the wind. He sat on his bike, the headlamp off despite that it was a moonless night.

"Silver, there's just one thing," Levi said.

"What's that?"

"I know where the Overlord lives, but you're not getting on the property."

"I'm sure there's a call button or a guard; he'll have to let me in. This is important."

"It is," he said. "But to a man like him? Business as usual. I don't think he's ever let a Mage on the premises. I'll call Leo and see what he says. Get in the car and turn on the heater before you freeze."

I did just that. A forgettable song played on the radio and I watched Levi in the mirror talking to Leo on the phone. He paced and had a habit of holding a fist to his head when upset.

Justus sent me a message not to leave the house. I grew irritated, knowing Christian had ratted me out. My facetious reply suggested that he order Christian to charm me. Justus didn't respond.

The car bounced when Levi sat in the passenger seat and slammed the door. "Well, this is unprecedented. The Overlord is giving you a golden ticket. Leo said he spoke with the Overlord and he owed you a favor. Damn, girl, you know how to work your connections." He buckled up his seatbelt and pushed the seat back for more legroom.

Not long ago, Novis had sent me on a job to give the Overlord inside information about the experiments, but not in explicit detail. It made sense to involve him after we found Chitah venom in the lab. Not to mention my surrogate and biological mothers were both Chitahs. Perhaps Quaid, the Overlord, owed Novis more than he did me, but I worked for Novis and I knew he was extending the courtesy.

"Here goes nothing," I said.

Levi tested my sanity during the drive with his rendition of a Red Hot Chili Peppers song. When we arrived at the Overlord's mansion, he had a couple of security checkpoints on the property, just as Novis did. The Overlord's Chitah guards scared the hell out of me. Luckily, we didn't have to get out of the car. They questioned us and leaned in, taking in our scent. After determining we had no weapons or intent to inflict harm upon the Overlord, we were permitted entry.

"I feel violated," I said, rolling up my window after I'd been sniffed over by the guards.

"So do I, but in a different way," Levi replied. "That last guy wasn't a fan of deodorant."

After we parked in a designated area to the left of the ostentatious residence, a guard escorted us inside the mansion and we waited in a spacious room. It was definitely a house designed for entertaining a large number of people. Before I could soak in the grandeur of it all, we were hustled into an office where the Overlord was sitting behind a mahogany desk. Bookcases filled the wall behind him, and a window on the right had the champagne-colored drapes closed.

Levi bowed and I followed his example.

Quaid, the Overlord, extended his arm and offered us a seat in the burgundy chairs in front of his desk. They were plush and certainly expensive.

When I removed my coat, he looked at my dress and frowned. "I do apologize it had to occur during a festive occasion. However, when the order is made, I have no knowledge of the locations of those arrested. The Regulators are sent forth to serve the warrant and take them to jail."

Breed jail. Each major city had a building that served as a prison for all Breeds. Perhaps they were concerned it would raise red flags to have a number of different facilities for each Breed. One per city didn't raise suspicion among humans and was easier to conceal. Prisoners were detained until the higher authority determined their punishment. Usually it was decided prior to the arrest.

"Why after all this time?" I began. "Why give us false hope?"

He laced his fingers together on the desk, looking between us with crisp, citrine eyes. The Overlord had a remarkable appearance because his coal-black hair was a rare trait among Chitahs, although it was turning salt-and-pepper. His regal features set him apart—Quaid was born to lead. Logan said the man had a strong genetic line and his father had once been the Overlord, even though it wasn't a title passed down to their children. The position had to be challenged for, but only by a Lord, and only during the period that allowed for a shift in power.

Quaid drew in a deep breath and held it for a moment. "We have been unsuccessful in proving facts that would release Logan Cross of his guilt. You state you are his kindred spirit, but there is no written evidence to prove what you claim. I may be able to scent the truth from you, but I am bound by the law. As it stands, a Chitah cannot become a Mage and I can only assume you are being led to believe a lie. We have eyewitnesses that Tarek killed the human, and the autopsy confirmed this when traces of venom were found in his throat that linked to Tarek."

"Isn't that enough to discredit Tarek as a Lord?"

"Perhaps. But we do not know what transpired between him and the cop that made him react violently. Both victim and assailant are deceased. The elders have been in a longstanding debate as to whether this should weigh in on the case. While you state your life was in danger, you openly accepted Tarek's claim in public, so a few have been skeptical as to how *forced* the situation was, as you claim. Our Sensors picked up strong traces of emotions within the cop's house that lead us to believe there is some truth to your story, although they cannot detect who the emotions came from. Keep in mind our decision must be *unanimous*."

"If you are Logan's leader, why is your decision not the final call?"

"It must fall within the allowances of our laws. I have the authority to overrule the elders to some degree, especially when a human is involved."

I leaned forward. "I'm his kindred spirit. Your law states that it is within a man's right to protect his soul mate by any means necessary if her life is in danger."

"Then prove your claim in writing. We cannot bend the law on word alone."

"Nero stole the papers that could contain that proof! The scientists we questioned admitted it, but most of the documents were stolen. Somewhere out there is evidence that my biological and surrogate mothers were Chitahs."

"What?" Levi exclaimed. "What did you just say?"

"Chitah, you may leave the room," the Overlord commanded.

Levi's eyes widened—he'd never been part of our investigations.

He only knew I was Logan's kindred on word alone, and perhaps he accepted it as an anomaly. I nodded and he left with a look of disbelief.

"I don't care who knows anymore," I said matter-of-factly to Quaid. "It's time I come out of the genetic closet and stop hiding what I am."

His black brows angled and he reached for a glass of water, taking his time to respond. The glass clicked on the wood surface when he set it down. "That is your decision to make, but err on the side of caution when you consider the ramifications of exposing these experiments without supporting evidence. People will fall into a panic at just the idea. I have spoken privately with Tarek Thorn's family on several occasions and offered them a settlement for their loss. They've had a difficult time, as I don't believe they respected Tarek. I approached them a final time this week and they adamantly declined, stating they wanted justice for the death. Their family name has been shamed by gossip and the brothers have no hope of claiming the title of Lord. An open challenge was set and a new leader was selected within their territory. If they had accepted the settlement, the investigation would have ceased."

"How can they do this? They disowned Tarek because he raped Logan's mate years ago, and now they suddenly respect their brother and want revenge?"

"Perhaps not for Tarek," Quaid pointed out. "A man's good name is not easily reclaimed once it has been soiled with scandal and controversy. Pride comes at a hefty price."

"An innocent man," I said.

"Young Mage, provide me with written evidence and I can grant him a pardon," he said, tapping his hand impatiently on the desk. "You are fortunate that your Mageri fought to protect you."

This took me by surprise. "What do you mean?"

"You were accused of acting as an accomplice, but the charges were dropped. Your leaders expressed you did nothing to violate their laws, and it is out of my jurisdiction to punish a Mage if the Mageri is not willing to pursue. Aside from that, it couldn't be proven."

I shivered and leaned back, feeling my life spinning out of

control like a top on a sloped surface. The faint smell of aging books and a trace of fresh paint filled the room. I noticed how white the baseboards were and imagined they must have touched up the room weeks ago. *What kind of room was my love in?*

Quaid drew in a deep breath and licked his lips. "Despite all that has befallen you, I can sense your love for him. Despite public opinion, I admire the fortitude you both possess in following your hearts. You each have made sacrifices to stay together, and I don't often see interbreeding work out. I hope you are able to provide us with evidence, and soon. I won't sit before you and evade answers or lead you to believe there is hope. Logan Cross will be put to death. There are still discussions going on in regards to his fate, but it will inevitably lead in that direction. Tarek's family wants retribution. The murder of a Lord is treason—one of the highest crimes a Chitah can commit. You are no longer in the human world, nor do Mage rules apply. You might not agree with our laws, but they serve a purpose that is beyond your comprehension. You have not lived enough years to appreciate their value."

I fought hard not to lose it when he confirmed my belief that Logan could die. I wrung my hands and stared at the glass of water, wondering why we hadn't run away together. The threat had never seemed imminent to me, but Logan had understood the serious nature of the investigation more than I had.

"Can I see him?"

Quaid stood up. "Breed jail is not operated in the same manner as human prisons. I can grant you visitation rights and a stay in his cell if you choose. Keep in mind that I do not know which prisoners may be on his floor, and you could be subjected to verbal assaults or otherwise. This might agitate Cross...," he said, as if having second thoughts.

"Do you mean I can go into the cell?"

"Typically visitations are held at the door to their cell, but you have shown your devotion to this male and I see no reason to keep you separated when his life is on the line. The Thorn family wants an eye for an eye, so there is no need to go beyond that to punish the prisoner. I would feel peace of mind in knowing that he came to terms with his decision and wrapped up any loose ends."

I gasped and turned my head away, pulling back the tears. "Is that all I am? A loose end?" I threw my head back and stared at the ceiling, tears trailing down my face and behind my ears. I'd spent so much time trying to find evidence to prove I was a Chitah and kept hitting wall after wall. I had to make a choice. "Can I only stay with him one night?"

"You would want to remain in a Breed jail longer than that?"

I finally looked down and reached for my jacket. "I want to stay there until the end," I said in an unwavering voice.

His lips parted in disbelief. "Female, you must consider what that means. You are subjecting yourself to confinement and will be expected to follow the same rules—"

"I know. But if you're going to send the man I love to his death, then every second with him is all I have left." I stood up, sliding my hands through the sleeves of my coat. "I'll go tonight."

"And if Logan does not want this?"

I laughed and zipped up my jacket. "Logan knows by now that he can't argue with me. I'm a stubborn woman who doesn't back down," I said, pulling my hair away from the collar.

"An admirable female is hard to come by. So many have disingenuous traits, and I have never heard of an instance where a female made a similar request. If this is what you wish, then I will notify the facility of your arrival and the circumstance. Should you change your mind, alert the warden. I'll leave instructions that this is a conditional stay and that you are not under investigation. But as I stated before, you will be subject to the same rules that prisoners are held to, including meals, showers, and sleeping arrangements."

"I can assure you I've been in much worse living conditions," I said, remembering my time in Samil's basement. While Nero's compound wasn't the Hilton, he at least fed me sometimes and I had hay to sleep on. My own Creator had given me nothing more than a concrete floor and an empty plate.

Quaid's eye twitched and he lowered his gaze. "It is regretful to hear when a female has been mistreated," he said, taking in a subtle breath of air. "I will have someone stop in to check on your condition. While there are rules, I will forbid any punishment of you that would restrict food and sanitary privileges. If this happens, notify my guy and I'll be sure that is rectified."

I had to stop and think for a minute, as this was a spur-of-the-moment decision. "Someone needs to bring me undergarments. I don't know if they house women and what's available, so please talk to the guards and make sure those get delivered to my cell."

God, what was I going to tell Justus? I dreaded the call because I planned to go directly to jail. He might really disown me this time, thinking I'd officially gone batshit-crazy. But I gave it further consideration. If this were in reverse, I had no doubt that Logan would do the same. Did he deserve any less from me?

Quaid walked around his desk and sat on the edge. "They issue uniforms within the prison, although I doubt they will fit your slim size. I can't seem to recall a time when a female has been arrested, so I will provide you with attire in the event that their uniforms are not suitable. They will have to be nothing more than sweats and a cotton shirt. They provide shoes only upon request, and they do not have laces. Most prisoners are barefoot, so I assume the cells are kept warm."

Made sense. Where was I walking *to*?

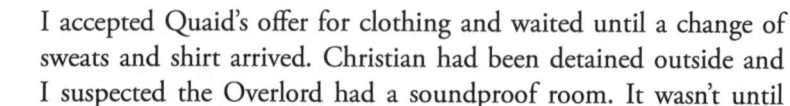

I accepted Quaid's offer for clothing and waited until a change of sweats and shirt arrived. Christian had been detained outside and I suspected the Overlord had a soundproof room. It wasn't until I walked outside and told Levi where I was going that all hell broke loose.

Christian flew at me from out of nowhere—gripping my arm and curling in his lips angrily. "Are you *daft*? Do you know what kind of filthy men are housed in that facility?"

"Get your hands off her!" Levi growled before Christian could finish. He threw out a right hook and Christian barely flinched when it struck him in the jaw, but he let it slide.

Levi wedged between us and stared him down. He was fearless.

"You know better than anyone what she's about to walk into,

and you're going to stand there and give her a push?" Christian argued. "You're a fecking imbecile."

"Are you done?" Levi said. "I don't have to pick up your scent to know what's going through that bloodsucking head of yours. She's *not* your youngling. I know a little about Vamps and how possessive they get to those they've given their blood to, but you don't own Silver. She's not a Vampire."

Christian rolled his eyes and huffed out a sigh. "You think all guards stand quietly in the shadows and don't build a relationship with their clients? I've worked for some plonkers in my time, but I've also made connections. I'm still a living, breathing, being. You can't expect a man to dwell in the shadows and not have social contact with the lives he is working to protect."

Levi stepped forward and his shoe crunched on the concrete sidewalk. "If you decide you feel like having contact with Silver again that requires touching, you're done."

When I saw Christian's gaze tear away, I stepped around Levi.

"Wait. Christian is only looking out for me. While it's none of his business, I appreciate that he cares. If he were just doing his job, he wouldn't have said a thing."

Christian's black eyes softened and he tilted his head, watching me observantly. I couldn't read his expression.

"Think about it, lass. Try to imagine the vilest of men watching you, leering at you, saying vulgar things to you from a nearby cell. Do you think your cat is going to remain calm? How is this helping him? It's selfish."

"No, Christian," I said in low words. "Selfish would be leaving Logan to rot while I enjoy a hamburger, deciding his problems aren't mine. I've committed myself to this man and he's not going to sit in that cell alone. He's not going to have one second to doubt my loyalty and love for him, because I'm going to be there..." I paused and drew in a deep breath. "I'll be there for every second that could be his last. It's not official, but Logan is to be executed for his crime. His crime, Christian, was loving me! How can I abandon a man who was willing to give up freedom and life for me? *How?* Maybe you don't understand why I got the tattoos because you think love is irrelevant, but what I feel for him is infinite." I felt Levi's arm come around my shoulder and a vibration from his chest mellowed me out. "You can go home until they release me, Christian. Go have a hamburger, on me."

With my lids heavy and my body weary from sorrow, Levi held me close and walked me to the car.

"I'll have a talk with the guys in there and I'll make sure you're treated right," Levi promised. "Fuck Christian and his black heart. What you're doing is noble. If my brother is going to die—as unrighteous as that is—I'll sleep better knowing his mate comforted him in his final hours."

Levi's voice broke and without looking up, I knew tears stained his cheeks. The love he must have felt… I simply couldn't fathom how he didn't blame me for all this.

But he didn't, because Levi had taken an oath to protect my life. Not because Logan had asked him to, but because he had already taken on the role of my brother.

CHAPTER 21

Justus was beside himself after he'd dropped Lucian off and Silver had called to say she was on the way to Breed jail. He'd tried talking her out of it, but she had always been an obstinate Mage. Justus had even drove to the building to pull her out by force, but the guards—seeing his aggressive state—had refused to let him on the premises.

He was livid, heating up the interior of the new car she had bought him as he sped aimlessly through the dark city. He called Novis and waited for an hour before the call was returned. Novis had reached out to the Mageri and their hands were tied as long as she was there of her own volition.

Essentially, the Mageri didn't care. Novis agreed to look into the matter, but felt it would be in vain. Simon wasn't answering his phone.

It was twenty minutes after nine on a chilly evening in Cognito. Justus knew the time without looking at his Rolex. He had dressed casual for the dinner, wearing tan slacks and a matching jacket with a white undershirt tucked in. But after leaving the jail, he'd swapped out the blazer for his black hoodie.

It sickened him to think she would be kept in a vile cell with no privacy. The guards were to treat her fairly, but that didn't bring him comfort. Justus had a bond with Silver that went beyond Ghuardian and Learner.

Maybe he denied it, but that feeling was love.

He felt love for her as a parent would a child, and that's why he was so demanding. Justus wondered why his own Creator had never developed that kind of personal bond with him. He'd once held an immense amount of respect for Marco, his Creator, up until

Marco showed him how low his morals were. He had offered Justus his entire fortune in exchange for Silver. He'd wanted someone to barter with and hadn't realized he couldn't clean his conscience with a bloody rag. Marco had wanted to free one of the women held in captivity by Nero, but in the wake of good intentions, he had ruined a number of lives all for the sake of one.

Justus vowed never to become that kind of example for his Learner. Despite their differences, he would never turn his back on Silver.

If he couldn't get her out of that damn prison, then he would make calls and see that she had what she needed.

They were at a standstill with Nero until Leo obtained the blueprints for the property. Their goal was to free his captives—no Mage should be shackled and kept prisoner. According to Finn and Silver, Nero brainwashed them. In all likelihood, he was planning to find a way to fuse their light onto his own. Adam confirmed Nero had an Infuser on hand. All he needed was to locate a Mage with Merc's ability to pull core light—and who knows, maybe he had.

Justus couldn't expend energy thinking about possibilities. He'd seen enough in his career to know that wealthy men were capable of the most heinous and unimaginable crimes. HALO's job was to bring them in, and sometimes it took decades.

When he pulled the car to the side of the road, his surroundings were familiar and he realized he had driven to the Relic's apartment. The lights in Page's window were on.

Maybe Christian had the right idea in making her forget the painful truth of what Slater had done, but he'd crossed the line when he made her believe she had willingly slept with a deplorable man who had abused her emotionally as well as physically. Justus squeezed the steering wheel and shut his eyes. That false memory offended him because it erased the truth of Page giving Justus a precious gift. There were only a few moments in his life that shone like a brilliant diamond. Of all the women he'd slept with, he had never known how honorable it was to be entrusted with something so pure that a woman gave it away only once. Not only that, but it was given by a woman who had the power to deny him.

It shouldn't have mattered to him that she carried another man's child, that this Relic had been victimized by her own kind and was living alone.

But it did.

He shouldn't have been fixated on a mortal who would perish in the blink of an eye.

But he was.

Justus couldn't get her out of his head. Her skin—like the finest silk beneath his touch. Otherworldly brown eyes that even behind her reading glasses snagged his attention when she fanned her long eyelashes. She had regal features on her heart-shaped face—the kind of woman who projected sophistication and intelligence. He enjoyed the way she'd tilt her head to the side when he threaded his fingers through her short hair, the soft texture and how it carried a subtle scent of vanilla. How smooth the skin on her neck was against the press of his lips. He remembered her breasts molded against his chest in the heat of passion and the taste of her sweet skin. Justus could recall every subtle change in her expression when he'd moved on top of her and she'd writhed beneath him, locking her legs around his, her fingers biting into his shoulders. He'd handled her gently, doing everything to gratify Page so she wouldn't feel pain or embarrassment during the act.

Page La Croix was the first woman he had brought to his bed. The first woman he'd allowed to sleep beside him after pleasuring her for hours. The first woman he'd caressed and touched as he made love to her. The first woman who listened when he spoke and who responded with her opinion, even if she didn't agree. The first woman who'd challenged him and never let a remark slide, as Silver sometimes did.

The first woman he wanted to see again.

She affected him in a way that was wholly unfamiliar. Her laugh, her banter, and the devotion she had to her job. He knew about that kind of devotion because HALO had become his life.

Justus flinched when a knock rapped against the glass of his car window. He'd been so consumed by his thoughts that he hadn't even felt the increase of energy. When he rolled down the window, a lovely face greeted him—one with pink cheeks from the biting cold.

"Well, Mr. De Gradi, are you going to sit outside in your car all night or come in for a cup of hot cider?" Page asked, holding her bare arms.

Justus pulled the hood away from his face and quickly rolled up the window. Page stepped to the side as the car door lifted.

"It's thirty degrees out here. Where is your coat?" He shut the door and stripped out of his jacket, wrapping it around her as they walked toward the door.

"Wait, you're walking too fast," she complained.

He slowed his gait and looked down, having forgotten she was full term and not able to keep up with his pace. What did he know of pregnant women? Justus helped her up each step as she struggled to climb.

"Sorry, I'm still not used to the extra weight," she said in an embarrassed voice, opening the main door.

Page had a slight waddle to her walk, like a duck, and he suppressed a grin. The sleeveless black dress she wore fell to her knees and her legs were covered with some kind of thick stocking he'd seen women wearing.

This time when he entered her apartment, he saw how she really lived when she wasn't expecting a visitor. The stereo played a soothing melody by an old blueswoman he remembered from the early nineteen hundreds. A small table lamp cast a mellow glow near the window, which was covered by a sheer curtain. She draped his coat over the armrest of the sofa and sat in a beige upholstered chair in the left corner. While the new neighborhood was decent, this apartment was unacceptably smaller than her last. He glanced at the sofa on the right side of the room and then turned his attention to his left. She had several piles of books stacked on the floor along the wall, but something was noticeably missing.

"Where are the flowers?" he asked.

"I had to get rid of them. I saved a few in the bedroom, but it was too much watering and it's not easy for me to bend over. Please don't send any more. I have a baby coming and I need all the room I can get." She pulled a blue afghan onto her lap. "The built-in bookshelves at my last apartment were great, but I may have to buy some shelves for this place. I got rid of a few things to make extra room. Oh..." Page leaned forward to get up. "I forgot your cider."

Justus stood in front of her and touched her shoulders. "Stay where you are. I am not thirsty."

He took a seat on the sofa, feeling the distance between them.

"I also got rid of the leather chair. I never did like sitting on leather. It was only for my clients and was too heavy to move. The baby is going to sleep in my bedroom, but I need to set up a playpen or something in here. So tell me why you're parked outside on my street. Is something bothering you?"

"Logan has been arrested for the murder of a Lord and Silver has chosen to remain with him until he is sentenced."

"Oh my God," she said in a hushed breath.

"I came here to ask for your help. Is there any documented evidence you can provide that will prove she is of Chitah descent? Our files were stolen and the ones Simon kept are of no value to Silver. We're at a loss, but any proof might free him. I would rather her conceal what she is, but if it could mean saving his life, she'll do whatever it takes. Is there a blood test that will show her genetics with certainty?"

"I'm afraid not." Page brushed her bangs away from her face. She kept her hair short to the nape of her neck, but her long bangs touched the tip of her nose. "It's not as simple as that. The only way to prove she's part Chitah is if we performed a DNA test on her and compared it to her Chitah mother. I can guarantee you they would discredit her surrogate human mother, but the Chitah egg that was used to inseminate her—that is who you would need to find."

The likelihood of that Chitah still being alive was slim to none. They'd have to locate another lab with file copies or a scientist who was part of the experiments on Silver's mother. They'd shut one down a month ago, but none of those men had any knowledge of the original test subjects. Grady, the Mage who'd led Silver's mother to the labs in the first place, knew nothing of what was used in the insemination and where it derived from. His only part was infusing his energy within the fetus to strengthen it so she could carry to term.

Page rose from her chair and went to the bathroom down the hall. When she returned, she was holding a stack of folded clothes.

"I want you to take these. They're the clothes you sent me."

Gifts he had specially selected that would suit her frame, complexion, and eyes. "Keep them," he insisted.

Her expression soured. "Keep them? Aside from the fact they're too expensive, just look at me—I'm a house! I can't wear these," she said, holding one of the slender button-up shirts over her swollen belly. Her lip pouted and Justus crossed the room and lifted her chin.

"You'll need suitable clothes for work after the baby comes. Keep them."

"I'm never going to have my old figure back. I ate a gallon of ice cream in two days."

Her eyes welled with tears and Justus began to laugh. In fact, he couldn't stop. He rocked with laughter and folded his arms, shaking his head at her belly.

Page glanced down and wrapped her arms around the lovely curve. She smiled and began to giggle. "Be careful what you wish for, Justus. You said you wanted a woman with curves and I think this is about as curvy as it gets."

His laughter cut off.

He analyzed every word she had just said. Did she mean she wanted him back? Or was it a flippant comment? It was time to clear the air.

"Page, allow me to stay the night."

Her face paled as she looked up at him. "What for?"

"To resolve what has not been resolved. You have drawn the conclusion that I have no interest in pursuing you because you are mortal and with child. I'm a man of honor, Page. What happened to you was against your will."

He could no longer continue when he felt his chest tightening. Justus had her undivided attention and was about to say things he'd never said to a woman. His palms began to sweat and his pulse sped up.

Justus was about to open his heart.

He stepped closer and his fingers grazed the slope of her cheek. Her skin flushed scarlet, warming his fingertips.

"I won't forsake you, Page. Now I know why we quarreled on night you left my home. The Relic discovered you were pregnant, didn't she? I couldn't have known—I thought you were sick again from the injections or a human virus. I apologize if I said anything harsh before you left. I'm a fool for having let you walk out so easily."

He took her hand and placed it over his heart. "I am an immortal. This heart will continue to beat for longer than I deserve. Can you feel it beating?"

She nodded and he swallowed his fear.

"I have never allowed a woman to touch my heart, until you. I'm not a man of many words, and I have no knowledge of how to love a woman. This is something I've stumbled at doing and… I've no doubt made a fool of myself."

"Justus, it's not your money I want. You've gone over the top trying to win me back with things I don't care about: expensive clothes, jewelry, and flowers. That isn't who I am." She placed her other hand on his chest and soaked him in with her eyes. "You know money has always made me uncomfortable. Do you want to know what I'd love? For you to warm a handful of peanuts for me using your gift. Or to make me a cup of cocoa when I'm too tired to get up. I'd like to take a quiet walk down the street and talk about anything but work. I need a man who can make me smile and remember that life shouldn't be so serious. I'd like to show you how to blow a bubble, because I'm willing to bet you don't know how."

His brow quirked. "That is hardly a challenge."

Page reached down and picked up a package of gum, then peeled away the wrapper. "Oh, really? I'm not asking you to march into battle and win me a crown, Justus." She held the pink gum to his lips and smiled. "Maybe you can win my heart with a bubble."

With a stern face, he bit into the gum and began chewing. She smirked and tilted her head, biting her lower lip as she watched him. "I just want to see the real you, Justus. Not the person you allowed someone else to shape you into."

The gum became soft and pliable, like his heart. Her words rang true. The man he was as a human was not the man Marco had made him into. Marco was an artist himself and had sculpted Justus into a Mage who defined the quality of life by surrounding himself with extravagant things.

"I need to sit down," she decided, moving toward the sofa and settling in the middle.

Justus walked around and sat on her right.

"Well, let's see it," she said.

"And what do I get for accomplishing this foolish challenge?"

"You get to stay the night."

Energy shot through his body like a reflex and he reeled it in, concentrating on the task at hand. He had no idea how this was done.

"I'll give you a brief lesson." Page turned as much as she could to face him and pointed at her mouth. "Flatten the gum inside your mouth just a little with your tongue and push it against your teeth." She started chewing and looked up at the ceiling as if trying to remember how it was done. "Then part your teeth with your lips still closed and begin to push your tongue through."

Justus began to realize this sounded a hell of lot more complicated than he'd first thought, but he said absolutely nothing because it would have meant Page putting her tongue back in her mouth. He very much enjoyed watching her move it around in slow motions.

In fact, he was getting aroused by it.

"After you push it past your lips just a little bit, retract your tongue and blow. The air has to get through. It's harder to explain than I thought." Page tapped the side of her nose, looking upward. When she swung her eyes back down, Justus began pressing the sweet strawberry gum against the front of his mouth.

He did as instructed and the when he blew, a hole punched through and it made an embarrassing sound. A flurry of laughter burst from her mouth and his cheeks heated.

"This is foolish," he murmured.

"No, no. Don't give up. Just because you aren't good at something doesn't mean you can't master it with a little practice. Your lips are too stiff, Justus." She lightly held his jaw with her delicate fingers. No woman had ever had this effect on him—it's as if he could feel her sincerity every time she touched him. "Loosen up a little. That's it. Now slowly push your tongue out."

Her breath hitched when he locked eyes with her. Something was developing between them—a memory of the intimacy they had shared. Her pupils became engorged and she lowered her hands. Justus placed his gum on a piece of paper on the end table and looked upon her with reverence.

"I want to kiss you, Page." He cupped her cheek and scarcely breathed. He needed his mouth on her, and he knew she felt the same. It was the way she parted her lips and how she couldn't take her eyes off his mouth.

"You can't mean that. Just look at me."

"I've never seen you more beautiful," he said truthfully, moving his mouth closer to hers. "Your full breasts, the way you wet your lips when you look at my mouth, the life that grows within you, the radiant glow of your skin—we hold Creators in high regard because they have the ability to make another Mage. You, Page, are a creator of life. We may have the ability to extend life, but you are making one." He allowed his hand to slide over her belly.

"And that turns you on?"

"You turn me on, Page. What you can do with your body fills me with admiration."

His lips brushed against hers and the nearness of her set him ablaze. He reeled his energy back in and placed his hands on the sofa behind her.

"Yes or no, Page." He swept his tongue across her lower lip and stared at her with hooded eyes.

"*Yes.*"

His body tensed when he kissed her ravenously. He felt the slide of her tongue against his and she gripped the back of his neck, a strangled moan escaping. God, how he missed her taste. She sweetened on his tongue like ambrosia.

"Ahh." Page made a sound of discomfort and he broke the kiss.

"What's wrong?"

She blew out a breath and touched her stomach. "The baby's karate lesson just started. Do you want to feel?"

Justus pushed back the sexual energy that coursed through his fingertips, nervous about the idea of touching her.

"I don't know if that's a good idea," he admitted.

"Is your energy in check?"

"Yes, but—"

She took his wrist and splayed his hand across her belly. Justus tried to pull away the moment he felt a kick, but she held his hand firmly against her. His eyes widened when he felt the baby move. He marveled at the sensation of a living human inside her, kicking and alive.

"Isn't he strong? I've been looking at baby books for a name, but I just haven't figured it out. I'm not good with that kind of thing; I've never even had a pet. It seems strange to name someone without meeting them first, you know? I feel like we at least need to introduce ourselves beforehand."

Justus watched her long lashes fan down and she smiled elfishly. He planted a soft kiss on her mouth and eased back on the sofa, tucking Page against him so her head rested on his shoulder and he could feel her baby.

"I've been working day and night for months and no case has been serious enough get you off my mind. What kind of man do you want me to be?"

"That's not what I'm asking for, Justus. Be yourself. You've been De Gradi for so long that you forgot about *Justus*. Be the man that you were born to be, not the one that life made you. I'm not perfect either, and I'll try not to be curt with you, but I can't promise that through the end of my pregnancy. My hormones are having a Mardi Gras and I have no control over what I feel and say from one minute to the next. Stay with me tonight and we'll talk. I just don't want to get my hopes up when you're going to eventually realize the truth."

"What truth is that?"

"The one you're denying. The truth that I'll die someday. I'm not sure I've ever seen an immortal in a relationship with a human or Relic. In the blink of an eye, I'm going to be sixty, and you're not going to want to share your bed with someone who looks like your mother. Be fair to yourself, Justus. I have a child on the way and you could accidentally hurt it with your energy."

"Never. On my word, I will never harm your child, or you. I have spent centuries learning to control my energy. That's something you need not worry about," he said, brushing her hair away from her forehead.

"Let's not plan our lives together tonight. I'm willing to give us a chance, and maybe now that you've seen me pregnant, it's pretty obvious it's not just a sexual infatuation anymore," she said with a quiet laugh. "Why don't we just do one day at a time and see what happens?"

He didn't like the skepticism in her voice. "I will agree to that."

Internally, his mind did not agree. Justus wanted more. All the fear and anxiety of what he'd carried over the last few months melted away. Now Justus had something he didn't have before: hope. He wasn't blind to the realities they faced, but he couldn't ignore what he felt for this mortal.

She shifted in her seat and grimaced. "My back hurts."

He lifted her chin, stroking her soft skin with the pad of his thumb. "I'll take you to bed and see that you have all the comforts you require."

"Will you read me Shakespeare?"

Did she know he owned the entire collection? "I will read whatever you desire, *Mon Ange*."

"Do you need clothes to change into?" she suddenly asked, staring at his tank top and trousers.

His lips brushed across her mouth. "I will not require sleeping attire. The greatest honor you can give me is to allow me to guard you with my life."

"My life is not in danger," she reminded him.

"Perhaps, but I will not sleep this evening. I will read to you and give you food and water as you need. Once you are asleep, I will pull up a chair beside your bed and watch over you. That is the best way I know how to honor you, Page. Allow me to do that."

Maybe she thought it a strange request, but Justus felt an inexplicable need to protect her. He came from a different time when women were vulnerable to the cruel nature of men. It's why he'd driven to her apartment on many nights and slept in the car, just to make sure no harm came to her. Maybe it had to do with the century he grew up in, or maybe it was the fear that she could be taken from him like a woman he'd once admired from afar.

"I'll agree to that," she said. "But only on the condition that when

I wake up at four in the morning—because that's when the baby wakes up—that you'll go to sleep and let me cook you breakfast."

He turned his mouth to the side and she quirked her brow, waiting for him to argue with her.

"Agreed. On the condition that you will not open your door for anyone. If I am asleep and someone is at the door or calls, you will wake me up."

She smiled with closed lips and patted her stomach. "This is the strangest arrangement I've ever made, but I can tell that nothing with you will ever be predictable. You have a deal. Can you search the pile over there for one of his books?"

"Which do you want me to read?"

"*The Tempest.*"

Justus didn't think he was up for reading a play. Knowing Page, she would want him to put more exaggeration in the dialogue, and that was more up Simon's alley. "Do you have a collection of poetry?"

Page moved to stand up and he gave her support. "Yes. I think it's in that stack," she said, pointing her finger.

He rose to his feet and held the sides of her belly, looking gently into her eyes. "Then I will begin with a sonnet."

CHAPTER 22

I HAD A NEBULOUS RECOLLECTION OF entering the jail. Levi had kissed my forehead and spoken words of comfort while Christian flayed me with a look of disdain. Two Regulators then escorted me inside by order of the Overlord.

The lady at the front desk had barely looked up when she handed me a few papers to sign. "We'll need to search you for illegal contraband."

That had been a blur as well.

A guard had walked me into a room and performed the search. He'd confiscated my shoes but allowed me to keep my socks and mood ring. The clothes Quaid had given me were deemed acceptable. Afterward, he stalked over to the woman's desk and they engaged in a heated argument. I must have been the talk around there; none of them looked pleased to see me.

"Come with me," he said, gripping my arm and ushering me down a hall. The jail was a sterile-looking environment with polished white floors and blank walls. "We're in the middle of construction. They're going to erect a second building and connect the two with a skywalk, but they haven't begun. I don't see the need—some years the floors are almost empty. Unless they're about to crack down with adding more laws."

"Does Logan know I'm coming?"

"No. We try to avoid engaging in conversation with the prisoners. Is he your... mate?" His eyes judged me with a single scrape, concluding I wasn't a Chitah.

"Yes," I said firmly. "Logan Cross is my mate."

We stepped into an elevator with steel walls. "Inmates are usually separated by Breed, but there's an overflow on the Chitah ward this year. Cross was housed with other high-profile cases. Your visitation threw a wrench in things and we had to move him upstairs with the Sensors."

"Why?"

"We don't get women in here, so we had to put him in a cell where he wouldn't have neighbors across the hall. You'll have most of the floor to yourselves. Sensors aren't known for committing serious crimes and half the time they end up busted by the human police."

"Why not put all the prisoners together? You separate them even in jail?"

He chuckled and pushed the elevator button. "We used to mix everyone up when the jail first opened, but it became a riotous atmosphere. They're more placated with one of their own. Less agitation, less bickering."

The elevator rocked and the doors opened on a floor that looked identical to the last. The hallway spanned from left to right and several steel doors lined the walls in front—presumably each being a room of cells. An older man sitting at a desk to the right buzzed us through one of the doors.

This room was not as bright and cheery. I began shaking as the grey slate floor and walls suffocated me with the reality of where I was. I took a deep breath of stale air and followed behind the guard.

"What is this trickery!" Logan roared from up ahead.

I froze where I stood, noticing the cells we passed were empty.

"I can scent my female," he said, disheartened. "You are cruel to torture me with the scent from her clothes." His voice drifted to silence and the Chitah gripped my elbow, leading me farther down the hall. We stopped at a cell to the left and the guard unlocked the door.

Butterflies formed in my stomach. What if he didn't want to see me?

"I suppose he'll fill you in on the deets," the Chitah said, nodding his head toward Logan. "The next meal is in nine hours." The door slid open and he stretched out his arm. "I have no time to wait."

I hurried forward and the moment I stepped into the cell, the door slammed behind me.

It was the most basic confinement imaginable. A mattress lay on the floor to the right, a metal sink straight ahead with a bar of soap, and a toilet to the left.

Logan had his back to me, standing between the mattress and the sink, his forearm against the concrete wall. He wore a pair of dark blue pants, a loose cotton shirt, and no shoes. It reminded me of the uniforms that technicians and assistants in hospitals were required to wear.

It reminded me of the night we met.

"Logan?"

He slowly turned around—eyes wide and unbelieving. Then without warning, he lunged at the cell door and gripped the bars. "What is this? I demand to speak to the Overlord; she is innocent!" he yelled vehemently.

"Yes, of course she is, Cross. It is by her request she's here, and the Overlord has granted permission. We've had the occasional overnight stay, but I'm not comfortable with this arrangement any more than you. It's allowable within our facilities, as long as you have approval from the highest authority on your Council. You know the hours we walk the floor, but you'll have privacy otherwise." The guard's eyes skimmed over to mine and he lowered his chin. "If you need anything or decide you want to leave, let me know."

I backed up until I felt the cold sink press against my back. *What if he blamed me for all this? What if being here would cause him more grief?* The guard slammed the main door and Logan peered over his shoulder, his anger palpable. He spun around and stalked forward with molten eyes.

"Why would you do this, Silver? *Why* would you allow yourself to be treated as a prisoner? You of all people!" He placed his hands on either side of the basin and I winced. "Why!"

"Because I love you," I said through clenched teeth. "Because I'm not going to sit at home and watch television while you're in a place you don't deserve to be. You're here because of me, Logan. And I'm here because of you." I slipped my arms around his neck and nuzzled against his cheek. "*Please* don't. This is so unimaginably difficult for me; please don't yell. I'm not leaving your side, no matter what happens."

I felt his head drop against my shoulder and the warm press of his hand on my lower back, pulling me closer. "Silver," he whispered. "This is retribution for *my* sins, not yours."

I placed my cheek against his. "I'm not letting anyone keep me away from my male. Don't even try to force me out because I'll tie myself to this sink."

He laughed and put his lips against mine. I felt the sorrow in his kiss and I wanted to savor every moment.

"Have you been fed?" he asked.

"I'm not hungry."

Logan leaned back and noticed my outfit. "These aren't the clothes they issue."

"Quaid didn't think they'd have anything that would fit me properly, so one of his men bought me these sexy sweats. You like?" I asked with a naughty smile.

"I am grateful to him," he muttered in a conflicted voice.

"Are we alone on this floor? The cells looked empty."

"No. There are two men to our left. The one nearest me has gone for his shower. The man farthest down the hall never speaks; he only whistles."

I smirked and straightened the ends of his shirt. "Sounds like a real party you've got going on here."

"Are you being a wise guy?"

"Just a wiseass."

Logan brushed his fingers gently across my cheeks. "This is better than where they kept me before. I wouldn't have allowed you to stay if they'd kept me on *that* floor."

"I heard. The guard said something about the cells being filled to capacity and because I'm a woman, they couldn't allow anyone directly across from your cell." I glanced at the toilet and realized why.

Logan cupped his hand around the back of my neck and drew in a long breath.

I'd never felt more alive than in that moment, never more aware of how warm his skin felt and how taut his muscles were beneath my fingertips. The way his scent changed so subtly in my presence. A Chitah marking a female exuded a powerful and inviting scent that staked their claim. He kept it contained, but sometimes it sifted from his pores like a heady fragrance caught in the summer wind.

There was no reason for him to mark me—I was already his. But he smelled indescribably wonderful, like a mixture of spring storms and something familiar. I loved the way he reverently stroked my right arm with his knuckles—I hadn't even noticed he'd been doing it because of how gentle his touch was. I loved the way he'd end some of his sentences with a soft growl. And I especially loved hearing his purr, the one at such a low decibel that it was only audible when he held me in a lover's embrace.

"Who's that?" a man said from the hall as someone walked by. I couldn't see around Logan but heard a cell door slam and lock.

"Keep your nose in your own business," the guard ordered in a flat voice. "Your time is almost up, so don't go stirring up trouble. Unless you *like* it in here."

A clatter made me jump and we both turned to look at the guard. He tapped his baton against the bars and gave us a friendly smirk. "I'll bring in a bag of cookies. It's against regulations, but I don't know when the last time you ate was. You're a female, and despite what Cross has done to ruin his life, I won't have you going to sleep hungry."

"My gratitude," Logan replied with sincerity.

The Chitah's eyes locked on Logan and I could tell he harbored no goodwill toward him. Logan was incarcerated for assassinating a Lord, not a minor infraction of the law. It made me realize that Logan's family name would forever be tied to this crime.

"If you eat one of her cookies, I'll put you on food restriction," he said.

Logan stalked forward and I grabbed the back of his shirt. "If you continue to stand there and accuse me of taking food from my female—"

"Logan, please," I urged. "What he thinks about us doesn't matter."

The guard looked between us and shook his head, making his way out.

Exhausted, I collapsed on the firm mattress. It was clean with a dark sheet tucked around it and a thin blanket on top, folded neatly at the bottom.

Logan knelt on the mattress and turned over on his back, his feet hanging off the end of the bed. "Lay with me, female. Are you warm?"

With the wall behind me, I curled against his side and rested my head on his left shoulder. Logan slid my hand beneath his shirt and held it over his heart.

"I want you to promise me that we're not going to argue about why I'm here," I said. "If I had alternatives, I would have stayed on the outside to help you. Just accept that I'm your stubborn female and I'm not letting you sit in here alone."

He kissed the top of my head and his deep voice rumbled. "I cannot deny the pleasure it brings to feel you in my arms. This beats dreamwalking any day."

"I tried to talk to the Overlord, but it was useless. He said the only thing that would exonerate you was written evidence of what I am. When I found out they allow one-night stays, I didn't see why they couldn't extend it. I don't mind. This isn't so bad compared to my last house," I said with a warm chuckle. "Justus doesn't know the concept of central heating."

He splayed his fingers across my hip and pulled me tight against him. "It was worth it," he whispered.

"What?" I looked up and his eyes were fixed on the ceiling.

His jaw flexed and I admired the strong contours of his face.

"Accepting the job from Nero. Hunting you down. Taking you to my cave. I had a choice that night, Silver. I could have handed you over to those men and called it a day like I'd done a number of times before. I knew from the moment we met that you were my kindred spirit, but you were also a Mage—my enemy. I was conflicted."

"Is that why you asked for a kiss?" I softly laughed. "You wanted to make sure I was worth it?"

He pursed his lips as if in deep thought. "Male curiosity. I'd never felt anything but animosity toward a Mage. And there I was, having impulsive feelings to protect you. I was stalling, but it wasn't until the Mage leered at you in those woods that I made up my mind."

"Are you still carrying the debt for Nero?"

He quieted for a moment. "The debt is null and void. My instructions were precise and he deviated from our arrangement."

"Why were you in his debt?"

"He's a man who collects favors. I was in a bind years ago after a job and his money bailed me out. Little did I know… I don't regret the decisions I've made, Silver. No matter what happens to me, I want you to know that."

My lip quivered and I felt his embrace tighten.

"No tears, female." Logan touched my cheek, calming me in a way that only he could. I'd never felt more protected than when he touched me, and I began to dread the absence of his touch and all the things I'd taken for granted. "Save those for the years ahead when you look back on this moment, but don't spoil what we have now. If you want to know the truth, I always saw this fate for myself. I've slaughtered men in cold blood, tortured people, and handed over lives to those who fattened my pocket. It was only a matter of time before justice caught up with me."

"But those you killed were criminals," I protested. "You told me they were guilty."

"And you're correct. They were the vilest men imaginable. But perhaps a higher power agrees with your views that a life should not be taken."

I sat up and brushed my hair away from my face. "That's not what I meant. I've never judged you, Logan. But what I saw at Club Hell that night was you making a choice to end two lives instead of turning them over to the authorities. I'll defend your actions with killing Tarek, because there was no other choice. That's the only point I've ever tried to get across. Maybe I haven't been an immortal long enough to think of a life as disposable, but I didn't want to love a man who did."

"Our laws would not have punished those men because they did not commit a crime in the eyes of our leaders. In mine, all they had to do was slap you one time." Logan rubbed his face and his arms flexed. Every muscle beneath his thin shirt was defined and perfectly proportioned for his svelte physique. Logan had the body of an athlete, and yet all that power couldn't help him out of this situation.

"I'm sorry," I said, sitting on my knees. "I don't want to sound judgmental. That's where my head was and it's not easy for someone like me to understand. You have to remember I used to be human, and I didn't see this kind of violence on a daily basis. I had a regular job and—"

Logan propped up on his left elbow. "Perhaps you did not know immortals were a reality, but you were not naïve to the violent nature of men. That is not unique within the Breed."

Logan touched the rib my ex-boyfriend had broken as a reminder.

"You didn't change me, Silver. I changed the way I saw the world because I began to see it through your eyes. I have no desire to toughen your disposition—it is the very thing that has altered my course. I've always known the life I led wasn't a moral one. I wasn't always a violent man but once led an ordinary life. I've dishonored my family. I can scent a guilty man, so the blood on my hands was not innocent. But perhaps you are right in that I played God for too many years, and regardless, my hands are stained."

"I never said that, Logan."

I realized he had been sitting in this cell, thinking about his life to determine what led him here. He didn't blame me. He blamed himself. Logan felt he hadn't atoned for his past sins, so the universe was giving him a hard shove.

"Cookies," I heard the guard say and then a loud smack as something hit the floor. Seconds later, the door at the end of the hall slammed shut and I peered at Logan.

An intense, magnetic pull began to thread between us.

I lifted his hand and brought it to my shirt, sliding it beneath the loose fabric. The moment his fingers touched my bare breasts, his body went rigid.

Without a word, I curved my left leg over his hip and straddled him, never breaking eye contact.

His hand massaged my breast, and when I felt the pad of his thumb roll over my nipple in circular motions, I released a ragged breath and rocked my hips.

"Silver," he whispered in protest as if he didn't deserve my affections. *The hell he didn't.*

I gripped the ends of my shirt and pulled it off. It was the first time Logan had seen my naked body, and this time he didn't shut his eyes.

Sorrow had never felt so sweet, knowing this could be the last time we would be together.

His fingers circled the contours of my nipples, and every nerve ending in my body fired off from the complexity of his experienced touch. His eyes drank me in and the sound of desire rumbled in his chest. Awareness burned in his smoldering eyes as his hands trailed down the flat of my stomach and rested on my thighs. God, the feel of his touch. I decided that Logan's hands were the sexiest thing about him because he knew just what to do.

When his thumbs circled over my sex, I let out a whimpering moan and my entire body ignited.

Sexual energy flooded to my fingertips and I found myself moving my hands over my head to keep him safe.

Logan hissed between his teeth as I did this and rubbed the palm of his hands over my breasts, the contact of skin becoming torturous. His eyes hooded. Every brush of his finger across my nipple, every pinch, and every maddening stroke made me respond with a gasp, a whimper, or a rock of my hips.

In a motion too fast to track, Logan sat up and flipped me onto my back. His mouth laved at my breast and the familiar stroke of his tongue was everything my body craved as it dragged across my flesh.

Logan sat up and hooked his fingers around the hem of my sweats, pulling them all the way off. While he took off his own pants, I closed my knees. I was bared to him and feeling a little bit shy all of a sudden.

Darkness swirled in his eyes but the amber constricted it as he kept his animal in check. His heated gaze fell upon me and I'd never felt more aroused than when he centered his eyes on mine in that moment. His tongue swept across his bottom lip.

"Spread your legs for me, female."

My heart raced as I parted my knees and opened myself to him. Logan's fangs punched out. All four of them. His possessive eyes rolled to black as he battled the inner animal with him—the gold finally won.

His lustful eyes drank in every inch, every curve, and every secret place of my body he'd never seen but only felt. Now I belonged to all his senses—I was truly *his*. Logan had never been a shy man, so I'd seen him in all his glory, including once when I had tried to join him in the shower and he'd shut his eyes. But fully aroused, Logan was an impressive man. So much so, I wondered how I'd been able to take him.

When he caught the direction of my stare, a ripple of spotted patterns flashed across his skin. The main breakers suddenly switched off and plunged us into darkness. Dim, yellow bulbs in the hall provided subtle illumination, but all I could make out was his silhouette.

"Sorry," I whispered, thinking they would have kept them on all night.

His hands were not gentle as they firmly ran up my inner thighs, forcing my legs apart even more. "I can see better in the dark than you," he growled, stroking my core with a brush of his fingers.

I gasped and bucked all at once, but Logan's hands firmly pinned down my hips.

"Be still, female," he said in a caged voice, awakening every nerve in my body as he draped himself on top of me. I immediately pulled away his shirt, careful not to touch him with my hands. But oh God, the heat from his chest against my skin had me unwound.

I put my hands behind my head as my sexual energy spiraled out of control.

The weight of his body settling on mine had me tasting his neck greedily. Logan groaned when I locked my legs around his and lifted my hips.

He chuckled darkly and murmured against my ear. "You are a greedy lover, Little Raven."

"Don't wait," I said in a desperate breath. "I want you inside me *now*."

"You don't know what that does to me," he said, his voice rough and sexy. "Don't speak that way or I'll take you hard."

Logan savored a slow seduction, but my body writhed and trembled beneath his, unable to control the craving. My stomach tightened and tingles roared through me as I gently stroked his hips with my calves, sliding them up and down the length of his legs.

My mouth was against his ear as he kissed my shoulder. "I want my male to take me."

A deep roar filled his chest and Logan thrust himself inside me with one penetrating stroke.

I gasped but had no time to catch my breath as he pounded his hips against mine in the most animalistic, turbulent way. Logan had given in to instinct, no longer holding back, no longer teasing or seducing me with words.

He pushed himself up with his hands so he could look down the length of my body, and I lifted my hips as he rocked faster and harder.

I knew we were on a floor with Sensors, but I didn't give a damn.

I gripped the sheet behind me, wishing I could touch him. I was beginning to adjust to the dark and I could see his nostrils flare. My eyes roamed leisurely over the outline of his body and I released a soft, guttural moan.

He suddenly slipped his hands behind my back and pulled me up on his lap. I threw my arms over his shoulders, keeping my hands at a distance as I kissed his neck and stroked my tongue across his Adam's apple.

Logan responded with a vibration in his chest that tickled my tongue and sent an erotic spike of desire through me. As we stared into each other's eyes, I began rocking my hips against him. He placed his hands on my backside, coaching me on how to move. A man's touch shouldn't feel so wicked, but no one's hands lit a fire in me like Logan's.

"Where do you want my mouth?"

My thighs clenched at the animalistic lust that clung to his words. "On every conceivable inch of my body."

I arched my back and he leaned forward, sucking on my nipples. His tongue worked a frenzied magic as he enveloped me with his heat. Logan lazily dragged his tongue across my breast and pulled me upright once more.

"I want you to look in my eyes when you come," he said in a thick, dominant voice. It wasn't a request.

As he said this, Logan eased me onto my back and propped himself on his elbows, melting me with his molten gaze.

I released a whimpering moan as he worked his hips, analyzing my facial expression and reading my body like a book. He noticed the way my body writhed beneath him, and he scented the peaks in my desire. Logan was learning me. This man had the capability to become the ultimate lover who memorized the intensity of every thrust, touch, and kiss to determine what pushed my buttons.

And holy hell, he wasn't just pushing my buttons—he was slamming them hard.

Heat licked over me as he increased the speed of his thrusts, shortening them so that I wanted more of him. Then he changed tempo and buried himself deep, rocking his body with mine.

I wanted to turn my head, but Logan touched my cheek with his hand so I would face him.

His eyes. My God, the intensity behind his eyes as they watched me nearing climax.

His words became an erotic whisper against my mouth. "Come for me, Little Raven."

"I can't," I said, suddenly aware of our surroundings.

"Look in my eyes. Nothing else exists—only you and me." As I looked up and licked my lips, his mouth pressed against mine with a crushing kiss. He tasted like velvety wine with every stroke of his inviting tongue and I craved more. "I can scent you, female. You're almost there."

When he quickened his thrusts and my body tensed, I instinctively leaned up and bit his shoulder.

He suppressed a roar, trembling as he pushed back to look into my eyes again. They were wild and wide—the action of biting him was supposed to incite him to climax, but he refrained with every shred of willpower he possessed.

"Oh God, Logan." My legs shook and I felt the swell of power between them as he drove harder.

"Do I sate you, my female?"

"Yes."

"Are you my kindred spirit?"

"*Yes,* Logan."

"Am I the only male you desire?"

"*Yes.*" I threw my head back and gasped, holding my breath as he tilted my neck and forced me to look in his eyes. "Are you going to come for me?"

"Yes!"

He pounded so hard I began to see brilliant flashes of light. I'd never felt anything more intense in my life. When I came, it was seismic and aftershocks followed. My knees weakened and legs widened, but Logan hadn't stopped his rhythm. As I reached the end, releasing a satisfied moan, Logan came off his elbows and fell over me.

"Bite me!" he growled. "Do it *now!*"

I leaned up and bit his neck, sucking on his salty skin as I did so. Not hard enough to draw blood, but his reaction was instantaneous.

Logan's entire body stiffened and quaked as his rhythm slowed. Before he finished, he delivered a salacious kiss, his tongue like heaven against mine.

"I have always loved you, female," he said firmly, tapering off his kisses and cupping my face in his hands. "I regret nothing. Maybe forever was too much to ask."

I closed my eyes, curving my arms around him as he heavily fell to my side. I felt no concern if a guard walked in on us. I was in the arms of a man who had taken my heart captive.

I offered a smile as we struggled to pace our heavy breathing. "Have you ever slept naked in a prison with your lover?"

He chuckled wistfully and brushed a few strands of loose hair away from my face. "Tell me something you've never had and I will give it to you."

Tears filled my eyes. "Marriage."

"Silver," he whispered.

I sat up and snatched the blanket, draping it over us. "Sorry, Logan, but you asked." I smiled as I fell beside him. "I'm setting the challenge and you're just going to have to figure out a way. That means you aren't allowed to go anywhere until you fulfill my wish."

His lips tightened and he clasped my hand. "I can't stop it if they choose to execute me. Your wish can't stop inevitability."

I snuggled against him and splayed my fingers across his heart. "Maybe it can. Maybe if I love you hard enough, the rest of the world will disappear."

"Little Raven, I would not want the world to disappear. You are my world, so stay right where you are."

CHAPTER 23

LOGAN SLEPT FOR WHAT SEEMED like hours. It was uncharacteristic, and so was the fact I could hardly sleep at all. I finally needed to get up and use the toilet. We take privacy for granted until it's revoked, but the payoff far exceeded the sacrifice. As I washed my hands in cold water, I smiled at Logan and gave myself a small pat on the back for wearing him out the second time we made love; prison bars had proved a useful thing to grab.

He didn't even rouse when I dropped the soap in the sink and it clattered about. The main lights still hadn't come on, so I took a seat in front of the bars and tore open the package of cookies the guard had left.

"That's not going to go on every night, is it?" I heard a deep voice say from a cell down the hall.

"The cookies?"

"The nookie," he replied with a soft chuckle. "I ran the sink to drown out some of the noise."

I nibbled the vanilla cookie and sighed. I'd promised to visit Justus in the Grey Veil during my stay, but I needed to speak to him in person. Hopefully the Overlord would grant me visitation rights. Technically, I wasn't a prisoner, so I didn't see any issues.

"Did the guard really bring you cookies?" he whispered.

"Yeah, you want one?"

"Not seeing that happening."

I pressed my forehead against the bars, trying to peer down the hall. "Where are you?"

"Two cells to your left."

I reached through the bars and set the cookie on the floor. "I used to be good at air hockey," I said. "Get ready, because here it comes."

I stretched my arm farther out so it wouldn't bounce against the wall and end up on the other side. With a hard swing, I sent the cookie sliding across the concrete and then heard a grunt.

"Got it. Thanks!"

"No problem."

"They used to let my girl bring me food, but that stopped when a guard complained. You seem a little happy to be in here," he said in a hushed voice.

I nibbled on the filling and frowned. "What makes you say that?"

"I'm a Sensor. I touched your cookie."

Oops. It was a good thing I didn't have other things on my mind.

"What are you so resolved about?" he asked, still munching. "You've reached some kind of decision, but I don't like the way it feels."

"Stop messing with my head," I scolded. I decided I'd never let a Sensor touch my cookie again.

His voice softened. "Shit, I didn't mean to nose into your business. I'm hypersensitive. I've been learning to control it more, but I can't shut it off."

Curiosity got the best of me. "What are you in here for?" I whispered.

"Murder."

A gripping chill ran up my spine. While my mind wanted to give them the benefit of the doubt, I knew these were hardened criminals. They had to be.

Then I glanced at the man asleep behind me. Yes, he'd spilled blood. But with that act, he'd saved countless lives.

"I'll be out of here tomorrow," he whispered back. "Been here a year."

"A year?"

"Damn right." He attempted to lower his voice and I could hear the excitement in his words. "It's not so bad. It gave me a lot of time to think about what I want to do with my life. I got a girl waiting for me—a good girl. One I'm going to do right by."

"Good for you."

"Thanks. The guy who whistles has been here forever. You don't have to worry about him; he minds his own business."

I turned my mouth to the side and rubbed my thumb on the bars. "You say that like we're going to be making a bunch of noise or something."

He chuckled and spoke with a mouthful. "First night in here and you've already set a record. I don't think I had that much action when I was on the outside."

I did a facepalm. "Sorry."

"Don't be. You love him. That's a hell of a thing for a man to feel—the love of a good woman, I mean. That was a damn good cookie. What's your name?"

"Silver."

There was a brief pause as I heard him shifting around. "That's an odd name. Are you also a Chitah?"

"No, I'm a Mage."

"Holy shit. You're serious?"

"What's your name?"

The main door clicked open and heavy footsteps approached from the right. I scrambled back to the mattress and wedged myself between Logan and the wall. This was a different guard, and he lingered at the door, looking in. He carried a small flashlight and shone it on the bed. I remained silent with my hands curled against my chest, my heart galloping. While not a prisoner, I had a niggling fear they might eventually treat me as one and start giving me punishments. I didn't want to risk being sent home or moved to another cell. I was also thankful I had gotten dressed, because he kept leering.

Logan's voice rose with each word spoken. "If you do not remove that flashlight from my female, I will sever your hand."

The words lingered in the room as if they held power. The Chitah drew in a few breaths before moving on.

Logan covered me with the blanket and turned on his side to face me. "Stay by my side at night, Silver. I can't protect you if I'm sleeping and you're not beside me." His large hand stroked the back of my head and he peered over his shoulder toward the doors.

"The Overlord said he might have news by tomorrow," I whispered.

The door shut after the guard finished his rounds. "I can break you out of here. The guards are mostly Chitahs and their venom won't hurt me."

"Silver, don't speak nonsense," he said dismissively. "You would only find yourself in your own cell. Don't even consider retaliation."

"Why not?" I said, talking out my fantasy and nestling against him. "We could run out of here like a couple of outlaws and head up to the mountains in Canada."

"You don't like nature."

"We could stay in your cave and hide out."

He kissed my forehead. "Without electricity?"

"Sure. I could cook our meals over the fire."

Logan chuckled warmly. "You don't like to cook, female."

I touched his face, feeling the bristle of whiskers beneath my fingertips. "But I'd do it, Logan. If it meant we could stay together."

He pressed his forehead against mine and traced the line of my jaw with his finger. "You must prepare yourself for the worst. Make peace with it because if they deliver a death sentence, you will need to find the strength to go on alone. I want you to become a great Mage, and that will take time and experience. Learn what you can from Justus, but take something from my brothers—*your* brothers. Courage, family, heart, strength, and all the things you need to arm yourself with in our world."

I shook my head, trying to turn away. "Don't say those things to me. Don't speak to me like you're leaving."

Logan pulled me tightly against him. "I will never let you go if you keep me in your heart, Little Raven. I will never leave you as long as you hear my voice whispering in your ear. No one lives forever. It's not what you take from this life—it's what you give. When it's my time—whenever that may be—I want to know that I left you with hope. You gave me that gift on the night we met, when I watched you hum a song in the kitchen while heating up enchiladas for a stranger at your table. Pass it on someday to someone who needs it more than you."

While tears stained the pillow, I pulled his hand up to my mouth and kissed his palm. *My beautiful Chitah.*

"Don't let death harden you as it did me, Silver. That is the inevitability of becoming immortal. I allowed the death of my mate to consume me, and it festered into something dark and venomous. I'll always have that darkness in my soul. But now there's light. There's you, my little battery charger."

I rocked with laughter. "Are you sure you don't want to bust out of here?"

"And spend the rest of our lives being hunted by your Ghuardian?"

Whimsical idea—the two of us outlaws—but I could never do that to Justus.

The next morning, I woke up alone on the mattress with the sheet twisted around my right leg. I stretched my stiff body and sore back, noticing an unfamiliar smell.

The smell of prison.

Logan hovered over the sink, brushing his teeth, and I suddenly got an ugly dose of reality. We weren't walking out of here and there were no chairs, sofas, nor a kitchen to cook up a meal. I sat up and leaned against the concrete wall with my legs outstretched.

"I'll rub your back when I'm done," he mumbled, continuing with his vigorous strokes. His pants were slung low on his waist and I admired the V-cut below his abdomen.

Using my Mage ability, I could sense it was just after seven in the morning. I got up and dragged myself to the bars, gripping the cold metal and staring at an empty cell across from us.

The water shut off and Logan's arms slipped around my waist. "Ready to go home? I'll call the guard."

"No. I'm staying, Logan. But I need to talk to Justus."

He pressed his lips to the back of my head. "The guards will be here soon. It's almost breakfast."

As if on cue, the outside door opened with a creak and I listened to the heels of someone's shoes tapping in our direction. I didn't recognize the guard who appeared before me.

"I need to speak to my Ghuardian. I'm here as a guest and the Overlord has—"

"I know who you are," he snapped, appraising me with a look of contempt. He rapped his baton against the bars. "Get back, Chitah."

Logan backed up until he touched the sink, his eyes predatory. When he drew in a breath, two canines descended. "Touch her and your blood will wash my floor."

"Don't worry, Cross, I like my girls clean." He unlocked the door with a jangle of his keys.

I hadn't even brushed my hair—it was a scrambled mess on my head. I hugged my body as the guard led me downstairs to call Justus. He didn't tarry and promised to be there in ten minutes. I had my doubts since we lived so far out.

He made it in seven.

Justus was a force to be reckoned with as he torpedoed down the hall, removing his hooded jacket. His blue eyes centered on mine and he looked prepared to assail any man who got in his way as he approached my room. It was a confinement tank with two chairs, a table, and a scenic window of the front office. The guards had made a point to inform me the windows were shatterproof. Justus placed his fingertips on the receptionist's desk just outside my door. She began fumbling with her hair and smiled dumbly when he leaned forward. I watched as she took off her thick glasses and mashed her burgundy lips together.

Justus was dressed in the same clothes he'd worn the day before—tan slacks and a white tank top, minus the blazer. If his Charmer ability wasn't enough to make her drool, then his thick biceps and tattoo would seal the deal. You could almost see his washboard abs beneath the snug fabric of his thin undershirt. He draped his jacket over her desk and I backed away from the door, preparing for him to come inside.

He sailed through the door and I braced for a tongue-lashing.

Justus cradled my head in his hands and pressed his forehead against mine. "Learner, I will take you home," he said, the door closing behind him.

"I can't go. Did you find anything? Please tell me you did."

I sat down and Justus dragged his chair beside mine. He leaned forward with his forearms on his knees.

"I have nothing that would satisfy the demands of the higher authority. Page is not able to prove conclusively you have Chitah in you from a blood test. Not without parental DNA."

I smiled. "Is that where you've been? With Page? I thought you looked a little scruffy this morning."

He sat up and drummed his fingers on the table, shifting his gaze to the door.

"Go home and check on Finn," I said. "Levi went back to our house after he dropped me off, but he can't get in without the codes. He said he was going to sit in the car because he didn't feel right leaving Finn by himself, and neither do I."

"Learner, there is no need for you to stay here," he said in a rough voice.

"When you love someone, there's nothing you wouldn't do for them. Sleeping in a cell isn't so bad because at least we're together, and I don't know how much time we have left. I'm still hoping for a reprieve and that all this will go away, but I don't know," I said, shaking my head doubtfully. "If Tarek's family has some leverage… What if I paid them? Maybe the Overlord didn't offer them enough. Maybe if I spoke to them, they'd have a change of heart."

"I'll make some calls," he said, rubbing his bristly jaw. "I can help with money, but I don't have swing in the Chitah community and they will resent the offer if it comes from a Mage."

"See if Simon has any ideas, but make sure he doesn't stop working on Finn."

Justus frowned and his eyes looked darker somehow. "What's he doing for Finnegan?"

I bit my lip. "I asked Simon to dig up something on Rupert, just in case he gets any ideas about extorting Leo for money. Reverse blackmail."

"Silver…"

"Don't quibble with me," I said in a humored tone. "Just tell Simon I still want that on his priority list. I also need to borrow some light."

That snagged his attention. "For?"

"If I need to speak with you, I don't want anything preventing me from it," I said with an honest shrug. Simon had a knack for going to the Grey Veil, but he was an older Mage and more in tune with his energy.

Justus set his hand on the table and turned it over, palm up. Retaining eye contact, I ran my left hand across his palm, hearing the hiss of skin as it made contact. Within seconds, tiny threads of blue light leaked from his fingertips and absorbed into mine. I felt a wonderful rush moving through me like a drink of water, and I felt Justus. His energy weaved with mine. I'd never just taken light from him without healing and it felt amazing.

His expression remained melancholy during the exchange and when I had enough, I gracefully placed my hands in my lap, twirling the mood ring in a circle.

"Your time's up," the guard said, poking his head in the room.

"I have to go. I just wanted to see if you found anything—if something else could be done." I was exhausted from tears, but emotion took hold of me as I looked into his blue eyes. I remembered how swept away I'd been by them when we first met, how secretly flattered I'd felt that a man like him had approached me. I touched his palm and placed my ring in his hand, closing his fingers around it. "Keep this. I'm so sorry I failed you."

I stood up and Justus rose to his feet, slipping the ring in his pocket. He placed his hands on my shoulders and I looked down.

"Always hold your head up high. I don't see a failure before me—I see a woman who respects the law and believes in someone enough that she'll stand by his side. What do you think HALO brotherhood is all about? You honor me, Learner. You teach me."

The Regulator yanked me back by the shirt and I stumbled toward the door. Justus raised his hands and I could see the energy accumulating.

"No, Ghuardian! Please…"

He lowered his hand and made a tight fist as the guard escorted me back to my cell.

I'd never be the same after this and Justus knew he would lose me if I walked out alone. I would be lost to myself.

I'd become the puzzle missing the last piece that makes me whole.

It meant everything that he didn't coddle me by offering words of reassurance—that there'd be other men in my life and I'd get over this and move on, as he had done. His compassion meant the world and I hoped one day he'd experience love this real, this passionate, this immeasurable.

One that's everlasting.

CHAPTER 24

"You are a big fat cheater!"

Logan arched his brow. "How does one cheat at Rock, Paper, Scissors?"

"I don't know. Maybe you can scent what I'm about to do."

"Are you suggesting I'm using my nose illegally?"

He smiled and leaned back on his hands. With my back against the concrete wall, I challenged his amused expression. Logan had watched me work out that morning. There wasn't much room in the cell to move about, so he'd pushed the mattress up against the wall. After my workout, I'd showed him a few moves until I stumbled against the sink. Afterward, I'd called Novis to see if he had any pull with the Overlord. Novis had little to say over the phone and it left me with an unsettled feeling.

Maybe he was tired of the drama I'd brought into his world.

Breakfast was better than expected. They served us sausage patties, tomato slices, and scrambled eggs on a tray. The kind of trays that have little grooves for each side item like the ones they use in elementary schools.

I took the quickest shower in the history of prison showers. The guards normally supervised, but I raised hell until he left me alone. Still paranoid he might walk in at any moment, I washed up in less than five minutes. Maybe three. I didn't have a band to tie back my wet hair, so it hung over my shoulders, dampening the white cotton shirt.

I didn't like the feel of the gritty floor beneath my feet, so I kept my socks on. Logan chose to be barefoot and spent most of his time shirtless. I enjoyed the casualness between us and sure didn't complain about the scenic view.

Now that Logan was familiar with my body, he stole every

opportunity to abuse his newfound privileges. While I was brushing my teeth at the sink, he slipped up from behind and fell to his knees, running his hands over my backside. He slid my pants down and I squeaked, about to turn around and give him a playful smack when he firmly held my hips so I couldn't escape.

"What is this?" he asked, rubbing his finger along the crease of my thigh.

"My Creator's mark."

He angrily yanked my sweats back up. "I don't like that another male has marked you."

I rinsed my mouth and spit in the sink. "That can hardly be helped."

"No, but I'll be reminded of that worthless Mage who beat my female each time I have to look upon that mark."

I spun around and tugged my sweats down in the front just a little bit. "And each time you look at *these* marks, Mr. Cross, you'll be reminded of how much this female adores your sexy self."

"Mmm," he murmured, planting his warm lips against my skin and kissing the tattoo that marked my lower belly with cheetah paw prints. His tongue traced the pattern and I gripped the sink, losing my breath.

Those were moments I cherished. Despite our confinement, we continued to learn new things about each other. Logan told me stories about his family and I showed him how I could wiggle my ears. I didn't know many games outside the ones Simon had taught me, but a few came to mind and we played for kisses. Although some of those kisses got a little steamy and out of control.

The main door clicked open and we both rose to our feet anxiously. This time, more than one person was approaching based on the number of footsteps we heard. One was softer than the other—more like sneakers.

Novis came into view with his arms folded and chin down. He wore a black zip-up jacket and denims. It was his pissed-off look, and thankfully, I didn't see it too often. The guard set a chair down in front of the bars and lingered a moment.

"You may leave us," Novis ordered the guard. "Silver, stand

before me. Logan, I will ask you to remain seated and absent from this conversation."

I gave Logan "the look" and walked toward the bars. Novis's clear blue eyes shredded me to ribbons.

"Have a seat," he said curtly, motioning toward the floor.

I sat down Indian style and Novis took a seat in the chair, placing his hands on his knees. He looked like royalty, and in a strange way, I could visualize him as a king.

"Silver, I have been summoned to the courts."

"For me?"

His stiff jaw gave a rigid appearance to his expression and some of his black hair swept over his eyes. "Representatives from every Breed are summoned on a weekly or biweekly basis to make a public ruling and determine sentencing. It rotates and it's my turn. While reviewing the paperwork, I was intrigued when I came across the name of a Mage I wasn't expecting to see in this facility."

I bit my lip and prepared to be reprimanded.

He leaned forward on his arms, pushing his shoulders up. "Simon."

"What?" I breathed. "Tell me you're kidding. What did he do?"

"Kidnapping."

I shot up to my feet. "Who?"

Novis leaned back in his chair and folded his arms. "A Shifter."

Oh shit. I pressed my lips tightly together and spun around. *I could scream.* He was supposed to surreptitiously sniff out some blackmail on Finn's father, not haul him off and do God knows what to him.

"Do you know anything about it, Silver?"

"No."

"Hmm."

I turned around and gripped the bars. "Can I see him? I'm not a prisoner here. Well, not technically."

"That would be another issue I'd like to discuss, but it would be a waste of valuable breath, I'm sure."

"You're right," I agreed. "I think we both know where I stand. Did you talk to Simon?"

"He's not talking."

"I want to see him. What kind of punishment will he get?"

"This is where I get involved," Novis said, standing up. "When a crime is committed against another Breed, both leaders come together and review the facts. We do not always see eye to eye. Personally, I do not feel this warrants punishment, as technically, we have no laws against kidnapping unless it results in death or torture. The victim has no desire to press charges."

"Let me see him. I'll get Simon to talk if I have to squeeze it out of him by twisting that nipple ring of his."

Logan chuckled and I speared him with my gaze.

"Please, Novis. If it's too crowded in his wing, then maybe we can talk privately in one of those locked rooms downstairs."

"As your employer, I value honesty and expect you to provide me the details. I am displeased to have a respected Mage locked up for something as frivolous and random as this."

"Well, if there's one thing Simon is, it's random."

"The Overlord should be in touch soon, Logan. There is a possibility your case will be presented this evening, so be prepared. The both of you," he said, offering me a chilling glance.

Novis arranged for a private room so I could speak privately with Simon. The guard swiped a card key to open the door and gave me a shove, locking me inside.

Simon teetered on the back legs of the metal chair—shirtless—with his ankles propped on the table. The harsh lights bounced off the spotless tile below my feet.

"Did you miss me that much?" I asked, taking a hard seat in front of him. I couldn't see around his big feet, so I tickled the bottoms.

He jerked his legs back so hard he almost lost his balance and fell out of his chair. "Bloody hell, woman. You're a regular riot, you know that?"

"Where's your nipple ring?"

His brown eyes told the story as they rolled upward. "Wouldn't let me keep it because the metal wasn't bound. I suppose they thought I'd hatch a scheme to impale one of the guards in his pinky toe while I made my great escape."

"Simon, what are you doing in here?"

"Freezing my arse off. I see the uniforms haven't changed much since my last stay," he said, snapping a thread off his loose pants and holding it in front of his face. He began flossing his teeth with it.

I narrowed my eyes. "Is this some elaborate scheme to get us out? Because I could have done that on my own."

He snorted and leaned on the table, waggling a brow mischievously. "Love, I'm not *that* fond of your boyfriend. I'm here because of a favor I promised you."

"I don't seem to recall kidnapping or incarceration on my favor list."

"No, but one thing leads to another."

I sighed at his evasive answers. "Why won't you tell me? They could lock you up for years. What did you do to him?"

He shivered and sat back in his chair. "They might have caught me in the act, but they technically cannot serve me with a sentence unless Rupert was found dead at the scene—which he wasn't, or if he chooses to press charges—which he won't."

"What makes you think he won't?"

A crescent smile showed off his dimple.

"You got it, didn't you?" I said with contained excitement.

Whatever Simon had found on Rupert would not only win us custody of Finn, but keep Simon from years of bondage. Not that Simon would have minded a little bondage, just not within the confines of Breed jail.

"I promise I won't tell anyone."

"Don't be obtuse," he muttered, rising to his feet. "They could order a Vampire to question you if they wanted."

"And they *can't* with you?"

"Not legally. I had someone pay me a favor a long time ago, so I'm fortunate in that regard. I've worked high-profile cases for the Mageri; they don't want their dirty little secrets accidentally leaked due to a bumbling Vamp."

"Well, so long as you're getting out of here. Why didn't you tell Novis the truth?"

Simon walked around the table and began giving me a shoulder massage. "Novis doesn't care if I get out or not. He's a nosy fellow and wants to know what I'm up to, that's all."

"He's a Councilman," I reminded him.

"Correct. But he's also a bleeding stickler when it comes to keeping things hush. There's one more thing I need to do, and I don't want his exalted opinion on the matter. I'm a little insulted he assumed I would blab all my secrets to you, but you're going to have to trust me on this one, love."

"So you're telling me that you're untouchable and… Stop *doing* that!" I said, slapping his hands away from my shoulders. "I'm not in the mood for a massage while Logan is up for sentencing and my best friend is behind bars for kidnapping."

"For pity's sake, it wasn't kidnapping. It was… coercion," he said, strolling around the room and adjusting his balls. "There's no law against that."

I stood up and gave him the once-over. Simon's nipples were like miniature bullets in the chilly room and I finally had to ask. "Where is your shirt?"

He pursed his lips and held out his hand. "You could always lend me yours. Be a dear, will you?"

Simon winked as I walked past him to the door and gripped the handle.

"Silver…"

I glanced back and caught a look on his face I couldn't peg. "Yeah?"

"I'm sorry for Logan."

I left the room without a response because the weight of his words sank in my heart like an anchor. Simon was never sorry for anyone. The way he'd delivered that line was like something you say to a friend at a funeral. A thought crossed my mind that Logan could be sentenced to serve over a hundred years in Breed jail. Was I willing to stay that long? My heart told me to go where he goes, but in the end, Logan wouldn't want me to waste my life.

He would want me to wait for him, like he had waited for me.

CHAPTER 25

Novis had become agitated when I told him Simon wouldn't talk. He feared another attack might be imminent and likened it to being in the eye of a hurricane. Novis also disclosed a few facts I wasn't aware of, like some of the Chitah Lords had been attacked, as well as members of the Shifter Council. Someone was trying to put a scare into everyone, and that someone was Nero. He despised humans and felt threatened by the gradual alliance developing between all the Breeds.

The guards walked Logan to the shower while I waited alone in the cell. I paced restlessly, pushing off the wall as the confinement began to make me feel caged. The door opened and I heard unfamiliar voices murmuring.

A young woman strolled past my cell and I stepped back as she peered at me. Her perfume drifted in and smelled like wildflowers in a sunny field.

The guard left and she slowed down, examining me closely. I would have killed for silky brown hair like hers. She wore it pulled back into a neat ponytail and it made a small scar on her hairline visible. She must have left her jacket downstairs as she wasn't dressed for cold weather, wearing only a dark green cardigan sweater and black jeans.

"Are you a prisoner? I didn't know they held women here."

"I'm here of my own free will. They arrested the man I love and I go where he goes."

Her face saddened. "Mind if I ask how long the sentence is?"

"I don't know yet. They're still deliberating."

"I would say I hope it's not a long sentence, but I don't know his crime. I hope the punishment is just. I'm so sorry for your situation."

"Thanks," I replied, taking a seat on the mattress. When I looked up, she was gone.

I hugged my knees and leaned against the wall. My mind returned to the idea of running away with Logan and becoming outlaws. What would be so wrong with that?

Then I thought about Justus sitting alone in his dining room and what my betrayal would do to a man like him. He'd devoted his time to shaping me into a Mage he could be proud of—one who would become independent someday and perhaps be a valuable contributor within our world. It was an opportunity for him to influence a life in a way he never had with HALO.

All this because of Marco, Justus's Creator. The one who'd decided my strong human energy might be a good offering for Nero's little harem. My mind drifted back to the night I'd gone out with Sunny before my attack and how I'd felt a strange sensation in the bar we were in. It was Samil. He had been given my information by Marco and was stalking me, following me home and waiting for the opportune time to put his spark in me.

After cutting my throat.

I wondered about the method to his madness. Regardless, I would have still been born a Unique. It was already in my blood because of the electrical storm during my birth. But weakening me to a state of near death—either that was his perverted way of getting off, or he really did have a formula. Simon speculated his process might elicit extremely rare abilities that would make a Mage more valuable to Nero. But Samil was also a sadistic man who'd enjoyed beating me; I'm sure he found pleasure in strangling his victims prior to creating them. He resented being in Nero's debt, unable to satisfy him enough to clear it.

Simon had told me not to dwell on the past—that dead men always take secrets to the grave and sometimes they're not worth learning. I was still alive, and that's all that mattered.

I hated to waste my time thinking about it, but that's what confinement will do. It forces you to analyze every detail of your life, and I realized I would never have all the answers to everything. No one does.

And should we?

I wanted to stop looking in the past and start looking ahead. But it was hard when all I saw were steel prison bars. I began to get butterflies, and not the good kind. Having Logan absent from the cell became indescribably difficult because it reminded me that we could be separated.

I glanced up expectantly from my spot on the mattress when someone approached. The guard looked fully charged by the way he held up his hands. Logan kept his arms at his sides and stood compliantly, waiting for the Mage to open the door.

Logan drew in a deep breath and stepped in the cell. "Female, come."

The door slammed and I listened to click of the guard's heels as he left us alone.

"Your anguish smells worse than the soap," he said with a straight face.

I sniffed out a laugh. "Then you might want to ask them for some air freshener, because it's not going away."

He slowly walked in front of me and knelt down, placing his hands on my knees. "I do not want you to become hardened and indifferent to the loss of life. Draw strength from the courageous woman who fought against me the night we met; who escaped, despite my warning; who endured the beatings of her captors, never allowing them to take her spirit. The *fire*, Silver. I don't want to see you put it out with tears."

"Then *you* tell me what to feel!" I said, rising to my feet on the mattress. "I'm more than willing to get us out of here because… what alternative do we have? I spoke to the Overlord and he won't budge, and he's the only person who can grant you a pardon. We have no evidence of what I am to prove you're my kindred, and Nero is the only one who could possibly hold that key. Do you want me to go to him and trade my freedom for yours?"

His canines punched out as he stood up to face me.

"I didn't think so. But I would, just so you know. I hope to God he never figures out what to do with all that evidence. I hope he doesn't find those labs or who is funding them. If he figures out how to make a powerful Mage and seal their core light to his, he'll be all-powerful! What am I supposed to feel when I'm incapable of helping the one person I want to live the rest of my life with? I'm running in quicksand, Logan. I'm trying to save you without a clue how to do it. I promised someday I'd save your life—"

"Silver," he said. "And I told you that you already did."

"Not metaphorically speaking. For real. You've put your neck on the line for me so many times and proved your worth, proved your love for me."

"Is that what this is about? Proving your love?"

"No, Logan," I said softly, touching his smooth chin and looking into his eyes. "It's about *saving* my love."

He lowered his head and leaned into my touch.

"Can Leo talk to Tarek's family?" I asked. "Can they be convinced? Justus is willing to help with the money."

"Pride is not easily bought. If they are salvaging their good name, or what's left of it, we could offer nothing of value. Tarek wasn't the only one who paid for his crime—his brothers will carry the weight of that shame. It matters not if they disowned him or supported him; the damage is done. Regardless of their stance on past affairs, they have been dragged down in the mud by his malevolent deeds."

"Maybe I could talk to them."

"They won't listen to a Mage," he said, cupping his hands around my neck. "If the Overlord found no success in offering them a settlement, then we have nothing."

Logan slipped his arms around my lower back, holding me close.

"Does your father know you're here?"

He sighed heavily and shook his head. "I have an estranged relationship with my father—we all do. He comes into town and we have dinner for the sake of appearances. He's still family and we will always respect and fight for family, but this is something he expected from me. I have shamed him."

"Your father is a jackass."

Logan smirked. "So is yours."

"Justus isn't all bad. I've learned a lot from him, but I also hope he's been able to learn something from me. Sometimes rules have to be broken; sometimes you have to follow your heart. Sometimes doing what you're told isn't always the right thing to do. I'm sure we wouldn't have all these great inventions and philosophies if people always just did what they were told."

Logan's broad smile stretched across his face and he leaned forward and kissed my nose. "There's that fire."

I jumped when the outside door opened and heavy footsteps rapidly approached. Logan snaked his arm around my waist and moved in front of me. When the guard walked past us, I breathed a sigh of relief.

"I've come to release you. I hope during your imprisonment you've had time to reflect on your actions and turn away from a life of crime," the guard said from down the hall. "Stand aside."

The sound of keys jingled and a door opened. Then I heard the frantic sound of kissing and an excited squeal.

We quietly watched as the prisoner and his woman came into our line of vision.

My heart dropped and I gasped.

I shoved past Logan and lunged toward the bars. I gripped them tightly and pressed my face through the cracks to get a better view. As he moved out of sight, I couldn't remain silent a moment longer.

"Kane?"

The movement stopped.

"Be right back. Just one minute, guard."

A man walked into sight with beautiful eyes—the kind of hazel eyes that made women swoon. His brown hair was in disarray and I looked him up and down. He seemed to have lost weight.

"Thanks for the cookie. Hope it all works out for you."

"Kane, I know you," I said urgently.

His brows knitted and he shook his head. "Sorry, I don't know you."

"Yes, you do. I'm Zoë Merrick. I don't have time to explain why I don't look the same, but I know your sister."

Now I had his attention, but the guard cleared his throat and time was ticking.

"Please, Kane. We've met a few times. You sent me money to give to her. Sunny needs you, Kane. She's here in Cognito."

"How do you know my sister?" he said, stepping forward.

"She called you Snoopy because you used to rifle through her things. Please believe me—even if you don't think I'm Zoë. She's been looking for you for the past year. Why are you here? I don't understand." I paused for a few beats. "You said you were a Sensor, but *how* is that possible?"

He drew in a breath and blinked, looking at me with a confounded expression. "How do you know about my sister?"

The guard appeared and grabbed his arm. "I have orders. If you choose to act out, I'll have to report it and they'll toss you right back in for another year."

"Kane, no," the woman urged. "Please, let's just go home."

I walked to the edge of my cell as the guard coaxed him away.

"Look for Justus De Gradi! He's a Mage. Tell him I sent you," I yelled as he moved out of sight. I wanted to tell him she was pregnant, but he might snap and get in trouble with the guard. I bit my tongue and prayed he'd listen.

"Justus De Gradi!" I yelled once more. "He works for HALO."

The door slammed.

"What was that?" Logan asked. "You know him?"

I clutched my heart and turned around with my back to the bars. "Oh my God. I can't believe it. Kane didn't seem like the kind of person who would end up in jail. And a Sensor?" I said, throwing my hands up. "What is going on? I wonder if Sunny knew he was adopted and never told me. Or what if she was the one adopted? He probably thinks I'm criminally insane. Jesus, this is…"

"Your hands are shaking," he said, grasping them. "Calm down. He's free now; it shouldn't be difficult for them to find each other if they choose to. If he cares for his sister, he will search for her. There is a possibility he is ashamed of his crime and does not want to explain to her where he's been. She is also a human and he is not—perhaps he wants to sever the relationship for that reason alone."

Grief touched his expression and I held his hand. "You would have gone after Sadie eventually. Maybe fate gave you a nudge for a reason. Sometimes Logan Cross needs a good kick in the pants," I said with a burst of laughter.

He popped me on the behind playfully and nipped my ear.

"You smell nice, Mr. Cross," I said, touching the ends of his wet hair.

"My shower only lacked one thing."

"Hot water?"

He kissed my neck and ran his nose along my jaw until our lips met. "No. You."

CHAPTER 26

THAT AFTERNOON, I SLIPPED INTO the Grey Veil and spoke with Justus. Leo had received the blueprints for the property and they were reviewing satellite imagery. It confirmed their suspicions: a separate building on the property housed Nero's captives. While they wanted to take down Nero, they didn't want to endanger innocent lives. Justus wanted to secure their safety even though he was uncertain if Nero had brainwashed his captives. Especially after what had happened with Cheri and Ray betraying the Mageri. After their release, they'd supported Nero's reign of terror.

Justus mentioned Christian had been temporarily relieved of his duties until my release. Christian deserved a vacation, but I could see that Justus was still upset with him. I hadn't thought it would be a big deal to a man like Justus that a woman remembered he was her first lover. When it came to women, Justus had always been a player. But he also didn't talk about his emotions, so I never knew what was really going on in that head of his.

Perhaps Christian had injured his pride.

I had bigger issues at hand. One of which was the sentencing. We'd received word that shortly after dinner they would escort us to what was referred to as "the court." Most sentences are decided before an individual is incarcerated. But the higher authority had not come to a unanimous decision in our case, which centered around the murder of a human, the kidnapping of a Mage, and the death of a Chitah.

I stretched out on the mattress and Logan sat beside me with one knee bent, his expression tranquil as he ate his meal. I had no appetite for hamburger patties and mashed potatoes, so I wrinkled my nose.

"Eat," he urged, holding out a piece of meat.

"I'm not hungry." I rolled to my side with the wall behind me and picked at the fibers on the blanket.

Logan suddenly leaned over and caged me with his arms, lowering his gaze. "I will not sit idly by as my female hungers. You may not have an appetite, but your body needs nourishment." He held the meat between his fingers in front of my mouth. "Eat from my hand, Little Raven."

I cracked a smile and took a small nibble. It was disgustingly bland and dry. After three bites, I waved him off. "That tastes like Justus's socks after a workout."

"And how do you know this?"

"It smells the same."

"Then let's try the bread," he suggested, taking a bite. It crunched and tiny crumbs sprinkled on his lap. "Mmm. Reminds me of my homemade baguette with seasonings."

"Don't be ridiculous," I said with a snort.

A magnificent smile tugged at the corner of his mouth. "Try it."

I capitulated and ate what he offered, reminded how nice it was to share a meal with Logan. I thought about our night in the cave—how unpredictable and animalistic he'd seemed to me. I'd grown accustomed to his nature, even if he did stare at people harder than he should have. He simply didn't comprehend the power behind his body language.

"Logan?"

"Yes."

"I think Finn's going to be all right. Simon is working on it. I don't have any details, but I have faith in him. Despite being in jail, he seemed in good spirits. Normally I'd expect to see his grumpy side, but the guard told me they released him this morning. Justus filled me in when we met in the Grey Veil and said he's at home, looking after Finn."

"Good," Logan said in a resolved voice. "And Levi?"

I laughed and sat up. "He's probably lounging on the sofa with a bag of chips, watching movies with Finn. Justus doesn't like people eating on his trillion-dollar furniture, and I'm sure he won't have nice things to say about the condition Levi leaves our bathroom in."

"Yes, that's a problem." Logan slid the tray toward the bars and it made a *whoosh* sound. "Levi has a disability."

My heart skipped a beat. "What do you mean?"

He stretched his back and stood up. "It's a type of vision impairment. Since childhood, Levi has never been able to see a hamper."

I laughed and fell back on the bed. "Sounds like the bachelor pad is going to be interesting. I don't think it will take long for Justus to warm up to Finn. He's a little quiet and likes to read. Justus appreciates people who self-educate. I just hope he doesn't try to get him to start training in the gym. Poor Finny."

"Might do him some good," Logan said, stepping up to the bars and lifting his nose. "Little Wolf must learn to protect himself so others won't have to do it for him."

"The pen is mightier than the—"

I launched to my feet when the outside door opened. Logan backed up and widened his arms, shielding me from the guard.

"Logan Cross, I've been summoned by the court to escort you to your sentencing. Put your hands behind your back and turn around. Walk in my direction and stop when I say."

Logan did as the guard asked and the man reached through the bars, cuffing his wrists. I immediately ran to his side as the guard opened the door.

"Step back, Mage," he said, holding up his baton in a threatening manner.

Logan turned around and stood between us. "Raise that weapon to my female again and I'll inflict hell upon you," he said darkly.

"I have permission from the Overlord," I insisted. "Where Logan goes, I go. I was a witness to the events, so if they question him, then they'll need to question me too. Go ahead and handcuff me, but you have my word I won't try to escape. I'm not technically under arrest, so…"

"Fine. I want you to walk ahead of us and keep your distance. Whenever we reach a door, you stand to the opposite side of the prisoner. That would be to my left."

This was the same idiot who had taken me to the shower. I

did as he asked and we rode the elevators to the ground floor. Two additional guards escorted us down a flight of stairs until we reached an underground tunnel.

"Where are we going?" I asked nervously, feeling the chill against my skin.

"Adjacent building. We built this tunnel years ago to prevent anyone from escaping during transport. If you choose to run, the only place you have to go is back to jail or straight ahead."

I swallowed thickly. "What's straight ahead?"

The guard smiled mechanically. "Your fate. That's what always lies ahead."

We approached a door and the two guards in front of us unlocked it with a swipe of a card. The concrete stairs led up to a tiny room with a second door. I wanted to clutch Logan's arm but was forced to keep my distance.

When the heavy door slowly swung open, the hinges creaked loudly. My heart galloped and fear gripped my spine as we entered a spacious room that resembled a gymnasium in size. The people within paid no attention to us over the chattering. A wide aisle divided the seated audience, which all looked to be prisoners by their uniforms. The guard led us to a row of empty chairs on the right side. Up ahead was a low stage with several rows of ascending tables, each with men and women seated behind them.

The higher authority.

The chairs went halfway to the stage, and at the front of the room was a large congregation of people standing on either side of the aisle. My eyes immediately settled on a built man with a shaved head, searching the crowd. Seeing Justus should have filled me with relief, but I took an unsteady breath, attempting to regulate my erratic heart rate.

The Overlord was seated in the center of the panel, wearing a dark suit and a red tie. Novis was on the front row to his left. *So this is where all the official rulings are made.*

Flashes of lightning pulled my attention to the windows high up toward the ceiling. A heavy roll of thunder followed, simulating the bone-deep feeling of dread in me. A guard sat to my right, separating

Logan and me. Logan leaned back and nodded to let me know it was all right.

But it wasn't all right.

I wrung my hands while the panel reviewed papers and made decisions on individuals who were not present. I had never seen so many officials in one place, and there were several from each Breed represented. A Vampire and Chitah bickered and the Overlord impatiently said, "Enough!"

Cascading down the wall behind the leaders were long red curtains with gold embroidery. At the front on the extreme left and right were doors, each guarded by two Regulators. Not the prison guards, but higher-ranking, uniformed men armed with katanas.

My eyes roamed around the room that was otherwise plain with concrete floors and slate-grey walls. The lights above weren't bright and the ceiling was high—like it might have once been used as a warehouse. Obviously renovations had been done to reinforce the walls and seal up all windows, except those that were out of reach.

The guard on my left smacked the back of my head, forcing me to pay attention.

Logan shot to his feet. It caught the attention of a few people up front before the guard who had cuffed him yanked him back in his chair. Logan had no concern of the consequences. If someone laid a hand on me once more, I was certain he would attack.

Another prisoner shuffled through the back door and sat in the chairs across the aisle to our left. He had a beard down to his navel and looked wild in the eyes, like some kind of mountain man. I couldn't help but notice he had only one guard with him as did most of the men seated, while Logan had the entourage. His was a high-profile crime against a Lord, and noticing that small detail reminded me of the severity of his crime.

I touched my chest, feeling a tightening that made it difficult to catch my breath.

"Giotto Antoni, please step forward," a voice from the panel called out.

A brittle-looking man two rows in front of me stood up and approached the stage, moving past the bystanders at a slow gait.

It looked like a Vampire who was speaking, but it was hard to tell from the back of the room—I could only see his luminous skin and a hint of dark in his eyes. He whispered to someone on his left.

"You have been arrested and found guilty of charming a member of the Mageri for sensitive information. Your recommended sentence is two years."

"Outrageous," Novis interjected. "A crime against the Mageri is not a minor offense. We hold to our recommendation of a ten-year sentence."

The Vampire laughed and coughed into his fist. His hair was as black as midnight and wavy, hanging to the length of his chin. "Ten years? Truly, what was the cost? Giotto's memory has been scrubbed and he sold nothing."

"Do you have evidence?" Novis kept his fingers laced together and stared coolly at the prisoner. He was speaking to the Vampire to his left but avoided direct eye contact. I didn't think a Vampire official would try to charm him in front of the crowd, so perhaps it was to make a point that he didn't trust him.

"We captured him leaving the scene," the Vampire countered, straightening the cuff of his sleeve.

I leaned to the left for a better view. Novis brought his clasped hands up to his chin and raised his index fingers, touching his mouth. "And did you confiscate a phone from the prisoner's belongings?"

The Vampire stretched back. "We did."

"And did you check the history to see when the last outgoing call was made?"

"This is ridiculous!" the Vampire said, rising to his feet. "I will not concede to a term of ten years for an unproven claim."

"Stefan," Novis said coolly, relaxing his arms on the table. "What will prevent others from attempting the same offense if their sentencing will be but a blink of an eye?"

"We do not hand out sentences to teach lessons to others. They are punishments for—"

"Agreed," Novis said tersely, writing something down. "The Mageri is requesting that the phone and records be turned over for our review. If we discover a call was made between the time he entered the home and when he left, I will bring charges against you, Stefan."

"For?"

"Obstruction of justice with intent to conceal evidence from the Mageri. I'm giving you the benefit of the doubt that your men have carefully checked the records and you have been made aware of their findings, as that is how all investigations are conducted. I make no accusation before the court at present. My assumption is you simply do not find our recommendation fair and, therefore, are lowering the sentencing to meet your standards. We hold to ten years. What say you?"

The Vampire blinked and angrily scribbled on a document, handing it to a guard. "Ten years agreed."

A gavel slammed against a wooden surface and the guard escorted the bearded prisoner away. I noticed the guard held a sharp stake against the prisoner's back instead of a baton. It was narrow and looked like it could easily impale someone with a simple shove. I eyed the prisoner closely as he walked to the back of the room and spit over his shoulder.

The manner of sentencing was arbitrary and at the whim of each leader on the panel.

"Logan Cross, please step forward."

My stomach dropped and I sprang to my feet.

"Sit down," the guard ordered. "You don't go anywhere unless summoned."

I held my breath as Logan walked by me and quickly kissed my mouth before the guard shoved him into the aisle. I touched my lips, still feeling the warmth of his kiss.

He walked with a confident stride, hands still cuffed behind his back. My eyes skated over to Justus, who stood near the wall on the far right. He glanced back at me with critical eyes—a warning to remain still.

My stomach twisted into tight knots as Logan stood at the front of the room. The stage was set up so each row was higher the farther back it went. All eyes were on Logan. Despite their harsh stares, Logan's broad shoulders and straight posture indicated he was a man without shame.

I gripped the metal chair in front of me and sat as tall as I could, only able to see the back of his head. My throat became dry and a flush of heat touched my forehead.

The Overlord smoothed a hand over his neatly combed hair. "Logan Cross, you have been found guilty of the murder of Tarek Thorn, Lord of the Youngblood Pride. The crime occurred on the property of a human police officer, who was slain at the hands of Tarek. His guards have testified they were ordered to stand down, and by order, watched him engage in an open challenge against you which resulted in his death. Your plea?"

"Guilty," Logan replied.

I gasped, wanting to yell out, but bit my tongue when Justus slid his eyes over to mine and shook his head.

Quaid, the Overlord, turned one of his papers over. "We have written testimony that Silver, the young Mage engaged to Tarek, was a witness. We have also collected statements that confirm she had escaped from his house the night prior. Tarek sent two guards to find her and one of them was found drained of all his blood. We hired an investigator to visit a local grocer, where surveillance footage shows her stealing a number of items and resisting arrest. Our Vampire also performed an investigation at the jail where she was briefly brought in by an Officer Stone—the human victim. The reason behind her shoplifting is speculative and will not be discussed. Based on the information our Vampire charmed from witnesses at the police station, Officer Stone was under the assumption Silver was an abused woman in need of protection. The testimony has gone into our records to confirm the intent behind Stone's actions, but keep in mind we have no documented proof any abuse took place. While murder against a human is a crime, Tarek would have been within his rights to challenge the male if he felt his female was in mortal danger."

My mouth opened and the guard yanked me back before I could say anything. I sat on my foot so I could sit higher, and as the crowd up front moved about, I caught a glimpse of Adam and Sadie. Eyes wide, I scanned the room and saw Levi and Leo to the left. Logan's brothers were all present, although I couldn't see Lucian through the crowd. Why would everyone show up for a sentencing?

The Overlord took a slow drink of water and set his glass down before proceeding. "The female Mage made a public acceptance of Tarek's claim, although she later recanted and stated it was by blackmail. We simply do not have enough evidence to support a justified reason for taking the life of a Lord. Tarek's brothers are present," he said, waving a hand to his left.

I weaved my head around but couldn't decipher in the crowd where they could be.

"They seek retribution and justice for the loss of their brother. The Pride seeks justice for the loss of their Lord. Logan Cross, do you have any supporting evidence that will give us a lawful reason behind your actions?" His eyes flicked to mine and I knew what he was asking for.

Something I didn't have.

Then he addressed the Thorn family. "Are you willing to reconsider the final offer I have made for a settlement?" Quaid's brow arched. "Very well."

He paused a beat before drawing in a deep breath. "Without evidence, it is by order of the court that you are hereby sentenced to death."

Logan's brothers were visibly distraught and I involuntarily rose to my feet as the guard struggled to pull me back down.

"You will be executed by manner of beheading before this court on this day. Regulators, please take your positions."

Everything moved in slow motion and the sounds in the room grew muffled and dull. My eyes went wide as several guards lined themselves between the crowd and Logan. A Regulator in black formal attire appeared, brandishing his katana.

"No!" I wailed. "*No, no, no!*"

Logan turned to look and the guard placed his hand on Logan's shoulder, urging him to his knees.

The crowd moved back as if not wanting to be near what was about to take place. Logan knelt with his hands still cuffed behind his back.

Thunder rolled outside and my bones ached.

The sound of shoes tapped on the floor.

Someone whispered, "*Traitor.*"

I fought, climbing over a guard, and when he grabbed my hips, I threw a blast of energy into him, knocking him on his back. As I ran forward, a strong hand seized my arm and yanked me back. I could feel his power and knew he was a Mage, so I was unable to use my power against him.

Energy buzzed through my body, stronger than ever before. A man on the left wall stood with a mop in one hand and a bucket in the other while the Regulator took a position to Logan's right, placing the flat side of the blade on the back of his shoulders.

"Bend forward, Chitah," he commanded in a low voice.

Instinct kicked in. Using moves only Justus had shown me, I turned to the guard restraining me and shoved my palm into his nose. Blood poured out and I knocked his arm away and kicked him to the ground. A Chitah ran at me with his fangs bared and I slammed my power into him as he attempted to bite my arm. His fang scraped my flesh but I didn't react. Suddenly, realizing I was a threat, several guards began to move on me.

A gasp went through the crowd. "Impossible!" someone chanted at my immunity to Chitah venom.

"Let him go! Release Logan Cross, that man is innocent!"

Novis shot to his feet and stepped around until he reached the Overlord. They spoke in low whispers and the Overlord adamantly continued shaking his head.

But all I could see was the glint of the blade. Logan would never resist his punishment because he'd always believed he needed to atone for the sins of his past. Dignity was all he had left, and he was holding fast to it. This was the "end game" Simon had forewarned me about, and there was only one way out of this stalemate that would save my king. I had run out of options.

I marched forward, Regulators rushing at me from all directions as the guards watched their prisoners with alert eyes.

"Sire, you said that Chitahs held sacrifice in high regard. I am offering my life in exchange for Logan's freedom."

Novis stopped talking and the Overlord rose to his feet.

"Repeat what you just said," Quaid demanded. "You would die for this Chitah?"

"Yes."

"A Mage?"

"Yes, I am a Mage and Logan is a Chitah. My life for his," I said, panting and feeling as if my lungs were constricting.

"Silver," a voice hissed. I didn't know who it came from—Logan, maybe Justus. My eyes were locked on the Overlord. No one else in that room existed.

"Sire, this is not a just sentence. I won't stand aside and allow you to take the most precious thing in this world to me. He would do the same—he has done the same—and this is the only thing I have to offer you. I freely take his place," I said, holding out my arms. The guards seized the opportunity to roughly grab my wrists and restrain me.

"Release her," Quaid said, pensively stroking his chin.

Novis blanched and slowly shook his head at me. I couldn't look at him. He didn't understand what it meant to love someone so much you would sacrifice yourself for them.

Knox had.

Logan also did, because he'd done it every step of the way in our relationship. He had so much to live for that I couldn't allow this. His brothers needed him, and Finn needed him. Sadie had just come into his life and she needed the protection and love of her big brother. She was also in the crowd, and I couldn't stomach the idea of his family watching this senseless execution.

Senseless.

That's what it was. All of it. I loved Justus and knew it would hurt him; maybe he felt betrayed. I didn't have time to think over the possibilities. I hadn't come into this world willingly, and perhaps my existence as a Mage was just an accident and was never meant to be. Or, maybe it was meant to be for this one purpose. I'd always known I was willing to lay down my life for Logan, I'd just never imagined it would happen so soon.

The Regulator turned his katana, bright blood wetting the edge of the blade as it pierced a sliver of flesh on Logan's neck. He lifted it up and I realized just how sharp the blade was.

"A life for a life," I begged. "If Tarek's brothers are here, then they should know that everything that led up to their brother's death was because of me," I said in a clear voice. "What better justice could be served? I beg the Thorn family to reconsider and spare our lives. What more can I offer? I would give you everything I own, but that wouldn't be enough, would it?" I looked at the crowd on my right. "If animosity is still felt toward Logan, then know by taking *my* life, he will receive a just punishment."

It killed me to say that because I knew it was true. Logan wouldn't want this, but it wasn't about what he wanted. I would rather him suffer a broken heart than be buried six feet under. Maybe we were never meant to be.

The Overlord leaned forward on the table where he stood, pressing his weight down on his fingers, which were splayed on the surface. "Release her," he said. "Come forward, Mage."

"Silver, no!" Logan growled. His eyes rolled black and he struggled to remain in control.

The Regulator lowered his sword and looked to the Overlord for direction. I glanced at Justus, expecting to see his back turned. But to my astonishment, he lifted his chin and proudly nodded once—pain never more evident in his face. I didn't understand the pride in his expression. It didn't register why he wasn't yelling at me and knocking down guards, but Justus was a man who held to different values than me. He respected the law, even if he disagreed with it.

"I'm immune to Chitah venom. Will you accept *that* as proof?"

There were a few murmurs. "It could be a fluke and won't prove your claim," the Vampire on the panel said dismissively.

"If the court will not allow my testimony of the events to hold any value, then all I can offer you is my life. Logan Cross has claimed me as his kindred spirit, and your law will not acknowledge his claim because we have no written proof. I cannot prove what's in our hearts. So let my blood be my proof."

I dropped to my knees, hoping someone would have mercy.

"You cannot listen to her," Logan shouted as a guard held him still. "She is not the one who took Tarek's life from this earth. I confessed, and I am ready for you to carry out the sentencing. Do not listen to the whims of a female who suffers a broken heart. This is not sufficient compensation for Tarek's family."

The Overlord remained motionless, moving his eyes between all of us. The crowd was silent, cemented in place. The Vampire on the stage, however, began to chuckle darkly, tapping the palm of his hand on the table.

"There is no greater honor you could bestow a Chitah than sacrifice," Quaid finally said. "If this Mage offers her life, it would be a fair payment for the Thorn family because she was directly involved with the events that led to Tarek's death. Her sacrifice would restore your good name, Cross. I accept this offering. Guards, you may remove his handcuffs; Logan Cross is a free man."

The Overlord took a seat as the handcuffs were unlocked, and without warning, Logan roared, lashing against the guards in a violent outburst. His canines punched out and the black circumference around his eyes warned he was close to flipping his switch. They gripped his arms, trying to contain him.

"Hold him steady!" someone shouted.

A guard with silver hair stepped forward and clasped his hand around Logan's. He was a Mage and subdued the prisoner by draining his power.

Logan swayed, still thrashing—fighting against the men and his own animal.

The Regulator's shoes clicked in my direction and I gave Logan one last pleading look. "I love you," I mouthed to him, and lowered my head, trying to summon whatever bravery I could to get through this.

I felt the swirl of energy in the air, thick as molasses. All the things I wanted to say. Logan was on his knees when I peered through my fallen hair. His energy drained, he still fought with all his heart, but the guards held him still.

Please God, don't let him watch, I thought to myself. *Look away, Logan.*

The footsteps of the Regulator approached and he swept my hair away from my neck. Every sound was amplified, from the steel blade scraping against the floor to the sound of sharp whispers. I felt the cool press of the katana against the back of my neck and released a shiver. My breathing was shallow and quick; beads of sweat trickled down my brow. I heard crying, Adam shouting, and all of a sudden through the midst of chaos, a comforting wave of energy swept through me.

It was Justus.

Somehow, he was flaring his energy in such a way that it felt like a father holding his child. I closed my eyes, tears falling to the floor. I had expected Justus to speak up, but doing so would remove my honor. The only peace I had was knowing Logan's family would remain whole and untouched by all this. I hoped one day they would find Nero and cut out his black heart. I hoped Logan would find a mate and raise a family. Maybe it should have ended the night Samil attacked me, but then I thought of the lives that had changed because of that incident. Sadie was home, Sunny was blessed with twins, and Logan had been redeemed. *Please don't let this tip him the wrong way.*

"Wait! Stop this," I heard an insistent British accent bellow from the front of the room.

I lifted my head and Simon hurried past the guard on the door to the right, holding up a white sheet of paper.

"I have permission to speak on behalf of the accused."

"On whose authority?" the Overlord inquired.

Simon's eyes locked on mine. "The Mageri."

Finn burst through the door behind him and when he saw me on my knees, I expected him to shift. But he coolly approached me while Simon climbed the steps to speak to the panel.

Logan was still on his knees fifteen feet ahead, surrounded by guards.

Murmurs surfaced through the crowd and I sat back, befuddled by the interruption.

"We have written evidence that will clear these charges," Simon declared.

Dear God, did Simon have no shame? He strutted in front of

the panel wearing a snug pair of leather pants, biker boots, and a black sleeveless shirt with a white skull on the front. I wanted to do a facepalm when he adjusted himself in front of the audience with a lecherous grin.

The Overlord leaned back in his chair and angled to his left as Simon approached.

"You have *written* evidence?" he pressed.

Simon slapped some papers in front of the Overlord and sat on the table, facing the crowd.

"Logan Cross was within his legal rights to take the life of Tarek Thorn." He twirled a skull ring he wore often on his finger. "Also known as the sodding bastard who attempted to blackmail a Mage for inside information, being that she worked for a member of the Council. Also known as the wanker who tried to sexually force himself on this female against her will," he said, using an accusation that would provoke the protective instincts of the Chitahs present. "Also known as the vapid gobshite who had close connections with one of the most hunted outlaws in Cognito."

Novis cleared his throat as a warning. Simon grinned and winked at me.

I stood up took a few short paces forward, just a few feet ahead of Finn. The audience was riveted by the unexpected turn of events.

"Those accusations are not enough to justify the murder of a Lord." Quaid pushed the papers forward.

Simon shoved them back in front of the Overlord, who threw him an irritated glare. "They are if Logan and Silver are kindred spirits."

The crowd reacted with disbelief, heads shaking, and one of the members of the higher authority slammed down a gavel several times to silence them.

"You see," Simon began, "I've spent *all bloody day* tracking down one of the labs involved in illegal activities. See my friend over there?" He pointed to Finn. "It started with his father extorting the Cross family for money. As a favor, I decided to track him down and have a little chat, and that's when I came across an unexpected nugget of information. Had Finn's father not been the greedy bastard he is, I wouldn't be here today. He's the reason I've spent my afternoon searching for a lab instead of eating macaroni salad and watching porn."

Logan wavered as he stood up and turned to watch Simon. The guards stepped aside as the Overlord crooked his finger in a gesture for me to come forward. I took a few paces toward the panel but stopped short.

"Proceed," Quaid said, his citrine eyes watching Simon like a hawk.

Simon sighed dramatically and hopped off the table, walking with his hands clasped behind his back. "It's time the truth came out. The public should know about the illegal activities going on that we can no longer conceal." He turned his attention to the crowd. "There are scandalous men who for decades have been working on genetic experimentation. Their goals have changed over the years, but the experiments have not stopped. I'm sure we all realize the repercussions of this kind of activity, as it benefits no one. We are not only in danger of humans discovering what we are, but the initial objective was to find a way to create a Breed who could infect the human population and turn them all into one of us. Imagine! Do you really want a whole bleeding planet full of Breed? I don't know about you, but I can barely tolerate most of you as it is."

Someone snorted and I shook my head.

"Simon, please reach your point," Novis said, standing on his feet with his arms folded.

Simon held an expression he often did before making a chess move that took out my king. I wanted to hurl one of the chairs at him for dragging it out, but quietly watched instead.

"What most of you don't know… Silver, with permission?"

I took a deep breath and nodded. This was it. The moment of truth when my identity—my origin—would be revealed to all.

"Silver was hatched in a lab."

I wanted to kill him. *Could he be less eloquent?*

The Overlord rubbed his chin and I could sense his intolerance.

Simon smirked and waggled his brow. "She was raised in the human world but bred in a lab. Something she hadn't discovered until after she'd become a Mage. And her creation was not by accident.

Her Creator, Samil, had worked in the labs many years prior. He had discovered that putting the first spark into these humans who were discarded as children for being perfectly normal yielded an unusual result. It seemed they had stronger light and extremely rare abilities, as we found out by talking with a couple of them."

The leaders nervously looked between one another; this was either going to be an epic failure or a turning point. There must have been at least fifty representatives on the panel, and none of them looked disinterested.

A few looked horrified.

"I won't go into the deets of how all this was done, but we have acquired written evidence as to Silver's origins. This is something that eluded us for a long time until I stumbled upon the files during today's raid on the lab. Silver is a Mage, but she was born with Chitah blood. Those papers collecting dust beneath your nose prove her birth mother's origins as a human child born of a Chitah, and we've managed to not only gain the testimony from her birth mother," Simon said, tapping his finger on the paper, "but a Relic performed DNA sampling to compare Abigail's blood with her Chitah mother. We all know tests won't show what Breed we are, but this proves Silver is of Breed origin. Now while you may turn up your nose at a human Chitah having any kind of genetic influence, here's the second half. Silver's birth mother was not her real mum, but a surrogate. According to the records, that egg came from a full-blooded Chitah female, and according to the records, she was murdered and her body disposed of."

The Chitahs in the crowd became outraged. Loud murmurs and headshaking were going on.

Simon licked his bottom lip and nodded. "There was a nice storage room full of frozen eggs, sperm, and all kinds of goodies that were neatly labeled and organized. We located the donor's frozen eggs and they were indubitably linked to Silver. The Relic had samples of Silver's blood and performed a test to come to a conclusive answer. God bless Relics and their advanced knowledge. These papers prove without a doubt that Silver is half Chitah."

I felt the sting of judgment from crowd's stare and caught

a glimpse of Lucian on the left, whispering to Leo. Justus had a resolved look on his face; he'd known the day would inevitably come when all this would air out in the open. I don't think he cared as long as it meant saving my life.

The Overlord reviewed the papers in detail and passed them over to another Chitah representative. A few others rose from their seats to look over his shoulder at the document.

Please God... Please God, let it be enough.

Simon scratched his ear and lowered his chin. "Nero is an outlaw who is not only privy to this information, but he is seeking war. He wants to dismantle the entire hierarchy system and go back to a lawless society. Nero was once all-powerful figure in his time. He wants to turn us against one another so that only the Mage Breed remains. He has formed false alliances with figures in power, some of whom are in this very room."

The murmurs in the crowd escalated to curses, and a few members of the panel looked at each other as the gavel banged down.

Simon chuckled and shrugged his shoulders, the dimple pressing hard in his cheek. "I'm sure it will all come out in time. As you can see, that is enough evidence to release these two from the charges. We'll have the full testimony from the scientists in the labs within a day. So you see, Logan was within his rights as a Chitah to protect his kindred spirit. And now... I'll hand the floor over to Finn."

My eyes widened as Finn spoke in a clear and audible voice. Unlike Simon, he'd dressed nicer than I'd ever seen him in khaki pants and a white shirt with short sleeves, which displayed the brand on his right arm. His shaggy hair was away from his eyes, and despite his youthful appearance, I saw a man emerging before me.

"Members of the higher authority, my name is Finnegan Cross of the Cross family."

Chills ran up my arms.

"I am a Shifter and a former slave of Nero. I was sold on the black market as a child and the only life I've known is one of submission and seclusion. No more." He stepped forward until he was a foot ahead of me and on my right. I felt a protective instinct to pull him back, uncertain of what could erupt in this unstable atmosphere. Especially with the Regulator so close, still holding his polished sword.

"I was born Finnegan Wade, son of Rupert Wade. A man who recently tried to put claim on me by means of extortion. This dubious man sold his own child into bondage so that he might turn a profit and pay off a debt. He is a wolf who cared *nothing* for his child. And now I stand before the higher authority as a man seeking a respectable path in life, one which I hope places me in a position where I can help others. Maybe one day I might be sitting up there beside you. I have a great respect for law, but your laws are contradictory. Improvements could be made to enhance relationships among the Breed and create a more uniform and just law. What kind of society allows an innocent woman to kneel before you and sacrifice her life? What kind of law turns a blind eye to corruption among its higher-ranked officials? I have a firm belief that we can work together to change, but I know it will take time."

"Shifter, please reach your point," the Overlord said impatiently but with respect.

Finn clenched his jaw and gazed earnestly at me. "I am here to plead for the life of my sister."

I felt love for this kid who saw me as family and who'd taken Logan's surname as his own.

Finn shifted his stance and allowed his eyes to roam across the crowd. "Simon's investigation turned up additional evidence. After questioning and further testing, Rupert Wade was the sperm donor for Silver."

I felt my heart skip a beat. *What? What did he just say?*

"I am pleading for the life of my true sister," Finn said, giving me a loaded glance. "We share the same father. Simon suspected it after finding out Rupert had been involved with the experiments. His hair is red, the same color Silver was born with. We believe the Shifter blood was the reason she shifted during her first spark— something unheard of when creating a Mage. She transformed physically into a new person, acquiring some of the characteristics of her Creator, Samil. Her unique genetic makeup can be attributed to this transformation. The Relic believes it was her one and only true shift."

I'd never heard Finn speak so formally. I loved him. A bond existed between us I couldn't explain, one that made me feel protective of him and he of me. What kind of person endures the punishment Nero inflicted upon him and would still lay down his life for a Mage he barely knew? His wolf had always been willing to fight for me. For what reason?

Instinct to protect family. His wolf had known all along.

I wanted to reach out and touch him—kiss his cheek.

"Silver is my sister," he said in a soft voice, looking at me with an elfin smile. "I have a family, and I will not allow you take something from me I've never known."

Hinges squealed when the door behind us flew open. "We're under attack!"

A flood of men surged through the door and there were chaotic shouts and screams as one Mage after the next flashed at the guards and cut their throats. The guards wielded their batons and stakes—weapons powerless against a Mage. The Regulators brandished their katanas and screams erupted.

Chaos.

The Regulators pushed against the front doors, but they didn't budge.

Finn turned to look at me and I furrowed my brow when he reached out and held my hand. His contorted expression alarmed me. Then my eyes dragged down and saw a wooden arrow protruding from his back that had sailed through his chest, the metal tip piercing through the front.

With tears glittering in his eyes, he let go and dropped to his knees, then collapsed on his side.

Blood pooled around my brother as I held my outstretched arm in suspended animation.

"Ladies and gentlemen," a familiar voice announced from the back. His words were crisp and commanding. "Welcome to the beginning of a new era."

Nero walked through the open door as more of his men and

women flashed in behind him and attacked the crowd. A full battle was underway. The panel stood up—some moved toward the doors while others tossed away their formal jackets and prepared to fight. Someone flipped a long table forward to cower behind it.

I fell to my knees, placed my hands on my brother's shoulder, and screamed.

CHAPTER 27

Logan's energy weakened as the Mage drained him to the point where he fell to his knees.

The predator in him gnashed and thirsted for blood to protect his female who was kneeling before the higher authority, offering her life. Yet her bravery filled him with gratitude and Logan knew he had found his chosen one. It was one of the greatest honors among Chitahs to sacrifice your life for another. Few males could ever hope for that kind of devotion to be reciprocated, as females did not feel the same connection the males did with their kindred spirits.

She would not die and walk into the darkness alone. Silver was the most fetching woman he'd ever beheld. Her emerald eyes glittered like saddened jewels, and he'd made the decision to rise to his feet and kneel beside his beautiful kindred spirit.

Her sacrifice would bring his family honor, but it would ruin him. She thought him a stronger man who could love again.

She was wrong.

Silver was his life, his breath, his love, his salvation. Without her, the heart drawn on his bedroom window would fade, time would cease to be relevant, and the stars would only remind him of the shining light he'd once held and lost. He would revert to the man who killed many, allowing darkness to swallow him whole and blood to be spilled in her name. Rivers of blood.

Oceans of blood.

The most powerful scent in that room was her resolve. The Regulator lifted his katana and Logan had moved to get up when a commotion sounded from the front of the room.

Simon burst in.

Logan watched in disbelief as Simon approached the higher

authority and provided the evidence needed to release them. He scarcely breathed as the facts were revealed in front of stunned witnesses who were hearing for the first time about the genetic experimentations. He stood up and listened with avid interest.

Justus had surreptitiously moved toward the front, his stony eyes alert and watchful.

Finn gave a speech that made Logan's chest swell with pride. Logan glanced at his brothers, who held the same expression. Despite his submissive ways, Finn was a born alpha. A leader. A man who was destined to do more than just lead a pack, but use his intelligence to implement changes within their archaic system.

What happened next was too fast to track. A guard flew in through the back door. "We're under attack!"

One Mage after the next flashed into the room and began cutting the throats of prisoners and guards alike. The innocent bystanders began to panic and flee, obscuring his view.

"Protect the women!" Logan shouted to his brothers.

Levi ushered women toward the stage. Many in the crowd were family members of the prisoners and not equipped to fight a single Mage, let alone an army of them.

Despite having had his energy juiced, adrenaline surged through Logan's body. He rushed toward Silver and then suddenly came to a hard stop. His eyes went wide and his breath caught.

An arrow had plunged through Finn's chest and the young Shifter fell to his knees.

Brother.

A Mage lunged and Logan bared his venomous canines, tearing at the Mage's throat and sending him to an agonizing death.

Logan pushed through the crowd of people who were rushing at him, trying to escape through the front doors. Silver had fallen to Finn's side, and then it happened.

"*Christ*," he breathed.

Her electric-green eyes lifted up, her stoic face eerily void of expression. Like something had switched off.

Or on.

Logan had seen this happen before and it was unmistakable.

Silver's eyes rolled black like a Chitah's. Her skin color didn't change, nor did she display the trademark canines of a Chitah. Only the unmistakable onyx coloring of a Chitah's eyes going primal in a Mage with mixed heritage.

She had flipped her switch. Silver stood absolutely still as chaos erupted from every direction.

Nero made a speech and walked forward at a sedate pace. Justus flashed toward him and three of his men became a shield as Justus engaged in a valiant battle. As one man went down, Justus pulled out his infused dagger with incredible speed and agility, taking out a second Mage. His skills were flawless.

"You have all brought this unto yourselves," Nero announced over the cacophony of shouts, screams, and bodies hitting the floor.

And *what* a puny man he was. Short, thin, and insignificant. His dusty brown hair didn't have the luster of a youthful man, and round glasses framed his soulless eyes. He didn't possess the presence of a tyrant or leader, but rather that of a conniving little malignancy that fed off fear and hid behind wealth.

"Nero, you will not win," Novis said from his position on the stage. "Call off your men and you might live."

A tall Mage hurled a woman to the ground by her hair and slammed his energy into her back. Leo tackled him and ripped open his throat.

Nero continued pacing forward with his hands clasped in front. "You call *this* civilized? You call *this* government? Do you believe we are unworthy of owning the power that is our birthright, that we should cower in the shadows of mankind?" His voice grew louder and more lethal with each word. "Are you so foolish to believe we can all come together and live in peace after centuries of bloodshed? Chitahs slaughtered my family and now you want me to call them *brothers*? The time has come for your reign to end. The Breed must rise up against mankind... and each other. May the best Breed win," he said, a smile ghosting his lips. "I have my army." He spread his arms wide to point out the voracity with which his men fought. "I have also acquired what I need to extract gifts from my powerful progeny. I have hand selected those with the rarest gifts and sealed them to my own core light. The rest serve me, because I. Am. Their. God."

He held his hands together and a concentrated ball of light began to swell between his fingers, the size of a grapefruit. Nero swept his arm back and then hurled the light toward the stage. Logan dodged as it burned through the air like a meteor, followed by a dull hum. People screamed and pushed to get out of the way when it slammed into a Vampire, breaking him to pieces.

Novis's face hardened and Logan turned his attention back to Silver, rushing to her side.

"Silver, are you hurt?"

She was unresponsive. Logan knelt before Finn, rage consuming him like an inferno. Adam appeared and dropped to his knees, placing his hands on Finn's chest around the wound.

"Pull out the arrow," Adam demanded. "Do it!"

Without hesitation, Logan broke off the sharp point that protruded from the front of his chest and then pulled it out from the back.

Adam straddled him with his hands on his chest. White light emanated from his fingertips and his face strained.

"Goddammit! I don't know if I can do this," he gasped.

"Adam! We have to get out," Sadie cried, reaching for him.

"Woman, get back!" he shouted.

Logan stood up and gripped Sadie's arm. "Stay close, female."

With everything going on, Logan didn't know who to turn his attention to. He couldn't protect them all.

"Leo! Lucian!" he called out.

Lucian appeared and wrapped his arms around Sadie, tucking her against his side. "I've got her. Come with me, sister," he said, pulling her to the wall and away from the stage, which had become a target. He made her sit in a tight ball and stood before her as a shield.

Logan spun around and reached for Silver. She was facing Nero, who had created another ball of light and cast it into the crowd, killing at least three. By some inexplicable logic, the energy broke their bodies into fleshy pieces.

A Mage flashed at Silver and Logan tackled him to the floor, biting his neck and taking a blast of energy to the chest. Logan moaned, turning to his side, feeling as if a truck had hit him.

Silver lifted her arms into the air and thunder rolled. A loud crack of lightning made someone scream and two windows shattered overhead. Shards of glass clinked to the floor and lightning flashed outside like strobe lights.

Logan stood by her side, fighting off every male who came within proximity. When a Mage had pinned Logan to the floor, Justus appeared and put him in a vise with his muscular bicep. He reached around and drove a stunner into the man's chest. The Mage crumpled to the side and Justus reached out to offer Logan his hand.

It was unfathomable how men continued pouring in through the back doors. The panel cowered, but a handful had gone into the crowd to fight alongside the prisoners and Regulators.

"Oy! Piss off, you pervy little wanker," Simon shouted from the floor. An overweight Mage straddled him and Simon stretched out his arm, reaching for a dagger that was just past his fingertips. He gave Logan a frosty gaze as the Mage juiced energy from his other hand. "How's the weather up there, Stretch? Give us a little help?"

Logan kicked the knife toward him and Simon went into action.

"Stop this senselessness, Nero." Novis stood on the edge of the stage with his arms by his sides, hands clenched into fists.

The swell of Mage energy in the room was palpable and felt like static against Logan's skin. It strangled his senses and he briefly became disoriented.

Nero locked eyes on Silver and flashed a heartless smile. "Well, there is the *star* of the hour. Are you raising your hands to give praise to your new leader?" He lifted his pointy chin and continued to close the distance between them, generating another orb of blue and white flickering light between his hands.

"I'm warning you, Nero. Call off your men," Novis said in a thundering voice.

Nero rolled a toothpick around in his mouth, glaring at him with insidious eyes. "I'm afraid I can't do that. We've released the prisoners and have managed to undo in minutes what you have spent decades building. I have more money than you, more power than you, more men than you. What makes you think I should *bow* to you?"

"Because I. Am. The. Law!" Novis leapt off the stage and stalked down the center of the aisle with a fierce stride. His pale eyes sparked with light and his mouth tightened. When he stopped a few feet ahead of Silver, he rooted himself in place.

"You are but a *boy*," Nero said dismissively.

"And you are a failed leader who desperately clings to a time when you had all the spoils of war and the luxury of power. These are not those times. Men do not wish to be ruled, they wish to be led by example. Your reign will only bring bloodshed to all."

"So says the man who was about to sit and remove the head from a Unique."

Logan stilled, his eyes carefully watching anyone who might have overheard. Fighting ensued from all angles and the only ones listening were Novis and Justus.

"A noble one, at that," Novis said with a growing smile. "Fear not, Nero. Silver is not the *only* Unique."

Nero's eyes widened at Novis, who was a man older than Stonehenge and who stood with absolute confidence and an enigmatic expression.

Thunder crashed outside and Silver's fingers reached higher.

"Snap out of it, Silver!" Logan hissed. Her eyes remained black and bottomless as threads of blue light leaked from her fingertips. She was primal and running on instinct, but whether that was the instinct of a Chitah or a Mage, Logan couldn't tell.

"You're bluffing," Nero spat.

"Do you think your little ball of light frightens me?" Novis asked coolly. "Go on and give me your best shot."

Without hesitation, Nero launched his weapon toward Novis, who threw out his hand and blocked it as if he had an invisible shield. The light melted to the floor and dissipated.

Novis raised his voice and it made the room tremble. "I want everyone in the middle and keep the attackers at bay on the outside. Now!"

People heeded his orders as the Regulators pushed Nero's men toward the walls. The members of the higher authority scrambled off the stage and rushed toward the center of the room. As all this was happening, Silver's hair began to stand on end. When a dagger sailed toward her, she altered its direction with a flick of her wrist.

"What's she doing?" Nero wondered aloud, collecting more light within his palms. As he watched her, he struggled to build more energy, and faster.

The ball of light grew larger and more terrifying. Nero looked as if he'd never created one as massive as this—his hands shook as he struggled to contain it.

"What's your plan?" Logan asked Novis, his eyes scanning the crowd.

Novis glanced at him over his left shoulder. "Trust your woman and stand at her side."

Logan nodded. As if he could do anything *but* trust this female.

A quick glance to his left and he saw Lucian had led Sadie closer. He tucked her behind his back and Leo stood guard on the other side. Adam and Finn's body were no longer in sight and Justus had disappeared.

Logan shuddered as he felt a lick of energy slide across his skin like a sharp tongue. He readied himself for whatever was going to happen, but all three were in some kind of energy standoff.

"I hope you've made peace with your maker," Novis said. "You'll be meeting him shortly for judgment."

Nero kept his eyes on Silver as he replied. "I am aware of the genetic tinkerings—do you *see* the result of what you have allowed to live? *Look* at her—she's revolting. A professed Mage with black eyes? If you had any respect for what we are, you would have put her down like a sick dog. The only thing I want from her is that sweet power she knows nothing of how to wield."

Despite Silver's impassive expression, something was beginning to happen. Silver light punched through the dark swell of her eyes, growing larger until the color completely took over.

"Ready yourselves!" Novis shouted, crouching down to one knee, arms spread wide.

Screams could be heard, chairs knocked over, and bodies hit the floor as the battle to keep the men on the outside continued.

"Don't touch her," Novis said quietly to Logan. "No matter what happens."

A bolt of lightning blinded Logan as it speared through the windows and connected with her right hand. A window smashed out as another bolt connected with her left. Silver began to shake as if she were trying to hold the reins of a wild horse that was out of control.

Nero increased the size of his light, which had now grown two feet wide. He positioned his body in a way that sent alarm up Logan's spine. Nero was going to attack his female. Logan moved around Silver and stood between them.

"Sentimental fools only get themselves killed," Nero said playfully.

"Get down," Novis said in an authoritative voice.

The snapping of electricity could be heard and a few people had stopped fighting to watch the show, distracted enough that their attackers gained the upper hand.

"Now!" Novis shouted.

Logan dropped to his knees and Nero launched the energy ball at her. Silver threw her hands forward and caught it with the current of lightning, sending it back. Nero held his hands out as if he were pushing against an unstoppable force. His face strained, turning a deep shade of red. But he couldn't fight the immense power of the lightning she wielded and he began to stumble backward.

The ground began to shake and Novis lifted his hands, his blue eyes snapping with light as he swept his arms around in a circle. Logan covered his ears from the low-decibel hum that became so loud it shattered pieces of glass and cracked the floor.

All around them, a shield of energy formed. The dome surrounded all the innocents within, and only Nero and his men remained on the outside. It was impenetrable as the attackers kicked at it and stabbed at it with their knives, only to be knocked away as if receiving a powerful electric shock.

The only thing it hadn't managed to do was break the connection between Nero and Silver. Some of Nero's men had run toward the back doors to escape when Silver moved her right hand and the doors suddenly slammed and locked.

"Can she hear us?" Logan yelled out to Novis over the hum of turbulent energy.

Novis remained focused with his arms stretched wide and his fingers splayed on the ground. "I can't hold the shield for long. Silver, you need to end this!"

A tear slid down her cheek and her raven-black hair settled on her broad shoulders. Silver's eyes bored into Nero as he weakened, even as he was still struggling to push his energy ball past her lightning. Only energy could penetrate through the protective shield Novis had created. Logan readied himself for the possibility that once Novis lost control and the shield went down, a full attack would be imminent.

The energy increased and the flash of light became blinding. Logan threw his arm over his eyes and shouted, as did everyone else. A final clap of thunder sounded within the room, so shockingly loud it knocked Logan to his side.

Movement ceased and a blanket of silence fell over the room.

Novis was hunched over, beads of sweat across his brow.

Logan surged to his feet and caught Silver before she collapsed. He wrapped his arms around her body and she blinked, revealing green eyes. Logan knelt down with her in his arms and felt the raw power of silence within the room.

The shield had collapsed and Nero was sprawled on his back—charred. Smoke rose from the remains of his lifeless corpse and those of his followers. The Regulators began to move all the cuffed prisoners who were still alive against the side wall. A gruesome display of bodies littered various places in the room, pools of blood surrounding some.

"Silver," Logan whispered hoarsely, brushing tangled hair away from her face. "You did it, my brave female. Open your eyes," he begged, feeling the lack of movement in her weakened body. He brushed his lips across hers. "Come back to me, Little Raven. I'm here, and I'm not letting you go. Do you understand?" He ran his fingers down her cheek and felt her chilled skin.

"Let me have her," Justus demanded, sliding in and pulling her away. Logan resisted at first but let go of any selfish need if it meant saving her life.

Justus laid her on the ground and opened her hands, lacing their fingers together. Her Ghuardian gave her his healing light.

Silver gasped, drawing in air, but still did not open her eyes. Justus began to breathe more heavily and his body grew lax as his energy drained.

"It's not enough, Justus." Novis reached out and took her right hand, clasping his other on top. "She needs the healing light of a Unique when it's gone this far."

He closed his eyes and looked down, a smile tugging at the corners of his mouth. The color in Silver's cheeks became rosy and she moaned.

"She'll be fine," Novis said, letting go of her hand. "Have Simon give her more light when you get home since Justus will not have enough. She needs rest. She'll be weak for a day or two as her core light readjusts."

Justus sat up and rubbed his face, then dropped his hands to his lap.

"You're a Unique, like Silver?" Logan whispered.

Novis crouched as they spoke privately, but oddly, he didn't seem concerned if anyone heard them. "Speak of this to no one," he said, turning his attention toward Justus. "I recognized her as a Unique a long time ago, although I've never seen one quite like her. I've always sensed there was something *else* unique about Silver. I couldn't have imagined she'd had Breed DNA in her since birth, and that must have been the dark shadow surrounding her light. Under extreme conditions, you see what she is capable of doing with her power. But she won't understand how to channel that herself for a long time. The Mageri wanted Adam as my apprentice, but truth be told, I'm the one who insisted it be Silver when Adam declined. I wanted an opportunity to help her understand her gifts so she will continue on the right path. She needs to feel purpose. We cannot afford to lose someone so powerful early on because we chose to blanket her from the dangers of our world. I must call the Mageri and find out how extensive the attack was and if the prisoners within the jail were set free. With hope, Nero didn't get that far."

Justus rose to his feet and bowed to Novis. "You have my gratitude."

Novis bowed back and a broad smile stretched across his face. "As you do mine, Justus De Gradi. You have been an enormous influence in this Learner's life, and I am quite impressed you chose this path. It is rare for one who is not a Creator to take in another Mage." Novis then turned his attention to Logan. "I think it's safe to say you will both be granted a pardon. Perhaps a legal mating ceremony may also be in your future." He patted Logan once on the shoulder and made his way toward the exit doors at the front of the room.

Logan cradled Silver's head in his lap, stroking her cheeks with gentle compassion. "Time to wake up, my female. Time to open your eyes."

CHAPTER 28

VOICES MURMURED AND AN INTENSE heat scorched my hands, yet my body felt chilled all the way to the marrow. I could smell Logan and feel his words whispered against my mouth, but didn't understand why I was lying down.

My eyes slowly opened and I found myself cradled in his arms. His amber eyes looked weary and confusion swept through me. *What happened?* The last thing I remembered was kneeling before the higher authority.

No wait, it was Nero coming in.

A flutter of memories skidded back into my mind and I remembered Simon's speech and then...

Oh God.

"Finn!" I cried.

And cried. Tears trailed down my cheeks uncontrollably and Logan pulled me to a sitting position.

"Nero is dead," Logan whispered. "You're free. We're free. There's nothing you could have done to save Finn. We'll go home so you can rest. Put all this out of your mind and focus on healing."

"No, Logan." I choked and covered my face with my hand as I sobbed. "You don't understand. Finn was my brother... my *brother*. All this time I didn't know and he held my hand..."

"Do you remember what happened? The lightning and shield?"

I shook my head, having no recollection of anything he mentioned. Nor did I understand why everyone around us moved leisurely, as if we were in no danger. I only remembered Finn bleeding on the floor with an arrow in his chest. A young man who'd once kept me company during a dark time, who'd made me laugh, who'd comforted and protected me. A kid who carved magnificent pieces of art, whose laugh could always make me smile.

My brother.

All this time we shared the same father. Rupert's greed for money had led him down a dark path in selling his sperm for illegal experiments, but I could have *never* imagined my roots would lead to Finn. A sharp pain speared my heart so intensely that I began to lash out and push Logan away.

He turned his head and held me tightly.

"Please, let me go," I said in a cracked voice.

He firmly cupped my cheeks and leaned in close. "I promised I would *never* let you go." Logan softly rubbed his nose against mine. "But I will let you up."

I took his hand and he pulled me to my feet. My fingers felt like they were on fire while the rest of my body was cool to the touch. Justus approached from my left and cradled my head in his hands, pressing his forehead against mine. No words were spoken, but I could feel his love.

My mind kept replaying that shining moment when Finn had spoken before the panel and looked at me not as a friend, but as family. I'd never known the joy of having a sibling, and now he was gone. And the horror of how he'd been murdered! Nero had robbed Knox of fatherhood and marriage, and who knows what great things that man could have accomplished with HALO. Now I'd never know if Finn would pursue a career in law. I had promised to take him to an amusement park in the summer, something he'd never experienced.

I covered my anguished face as Logan led me forward.

"Is she okay?"

I lowered my hand and glanced up. Standing before me was a man in a pair of khakis. His white shirt had a large stain of blood on the front around a tear in the fabric. His ears poked out from beneath tangled waves of hair.

I threw myself at him and clutched him as tightly as I could. "Finn, *Finn.*" I wept against his shoulder. "Oh God, how is this possible? Are we dead?"

He snorted. "I sure as hell hope I'm not dead. I don't want to wear dress shoes in the afterlife. They're killing my feet."

I squeezed him even harder and felt his hands wrap around my back. I held on to him as if he might disappear. Finn's grip tightened and the sorrow left my heart—I could breathe again.

"My sis kicked some serious Mage ass," he finally said.

This kid was too much. I leaned back and pinched his cheek as he turned his head shyly away.

"Guess this means you can treat me like a brother now, huh?"

"Finn, I love that we're related, but it wouldn't have mattered if we weren't. I loved you already."

"You won't have to worry about that piehole dad of yours," Simon chimed in, wiping blood from his leathers with someone's shirt. "If the cells are empty in the Breed jail, he'll be one of the first to fill them. The Mageri is contacting the local Packmasters to discuss his sperm meddling. Well done with the speech, Finn. For a minute there, I thought you were going to throw up all over those swank shoes." Simon patted him on the back and followed the crowd out the doors.

"*How* is it you're still alive?" I asked Finn again.

He averted his eyes and looked at the broken windows above. "It was Adam and that gift of his. That's pretty coolio what he can do—I thought I was toast."

My eyes scanned the crowd and I stood on my tiptoes. Logan towered over everyone and pointed. "He's there, by Leo."

Before he said Leo's name, I was running. "Adam!"

He swung around and looked smashingly handsome with his unruly hair and brown eyes. I no longer noticed the scars because all I saw was Adam. That's what happens when you love someone—you see only the good in them and none of the rest matters.

I skidded to a halt and clasped his hands in mine. He looked weak, his energy low from healing Finn with his rare gift as a Healer. I smiled and touched his scruffy face and leaned in for a fierce hug.

"You need a shave," I whispered.

He tucked his face against my neck and I felt the warm press of his lips against my skin. I moved my head away and kissed his cheek.

"Thank you, Adam."

He cupped his hands around my head and gave me his warm,

signature look. It melted me as I thought about how far we'd come from when we first met. "He's your brother. I wanted you to two to be able to walk out that door together. I know what it's like to lose a sibling, and I wouldn't wish that kind of pain on anyone."

Maybe Adam's salvation wasn't finding his sister's killer, but bringing my brother back to life.

"Go on, woman. Get some rest."

He patted my cheek, smiled, and turned away into the crowd.

Logan appeared beside me and hooked his arm around my waist.

"I'm fine," I assured him.

"You're two steps away from falling flat on your face. Now let me carry you, female."

"I'm going to walk out that door, Logan, on my own two feet. Then you're going to fill me in on what happened over a plate of Chinese food." I yawned and leaned against him. "Then I want my slipper socks on and Max curled up…"

My voice trailed off in a low murmur and Logan lifted me into his arms. "As you wish, Little Raven. But you can forget the socks. Your feet are all mine to warm, as is the rest of your luscious body."

I had fallen asleep in Logan's arms on the drive home.

Home.

We were free. The Overlord had granted Logan a pardon and asked to speak privately with us at a later time. When Logan told me what had happened, I was beside myself. I had no memory of Nero's death and Logan suggested I might have given myself up completely to instinct in that moment of grief. My inner animal, or *whatever*, had taken complete control.

Discovering Novis was a Unique was an unexpected revelation, but pieces began to fit together. In a crowd full of Breed, including Vampires, he'd told Logan not to reveal his secret. I remembered conversations I'd had with Novis in public. Ones I felt should have been private between us, but he had assured me no one would be able to hear. Novis possessed the ability to use his energy shield to block sound without significantly depleting his core light. While he could have used this gift without our knowledge in a Breed club, he never did. Looking back, it would have attracted attention if someone had spotted our table but couldn't hear our conversation when walking by. In a human establishment, few paid attention. As an ancient Mage, Novis had spent his entire life understanding his gift and learning how to use it. While we were both Uniques, he was not a Shiner like me and couldn't harness lightning. Novis was one of the other three types of Uniques that Page knew of, although I don't know what name he went by, or if one even existed.

Page had once revealed that Uniques often inherited the gifts of their Creators, which explained why many were *also* Creators. I hadn't inherited that gift, but I didn't care. I already had my hands full with being a Unique Mage with Chitah and Shifter blood. I'd shifted once during my creation as a Mage, and if that was the only time I'd experienced my Shifter abilities, I wondered if flipping my switch would ever happen again. I guess only time would tell what I was and was not capable of doing.

Maybe none of it mattered. Maybe all that really mattered was lying in bed with Logan tangled around me.

He didn't seem as surprised as I thought he'd be about my relation to Finn. Logan hinted that he'd had his suspicions from a similar scent we shared, but it was so muted he couldn't be one hundred percent certain.

I slept for eight hours straight before Logan woke me up because of an urgent phone call. Sunny said if she couldn't speak with me, she was going to hobble her pregnant fanny all the way over to the house. Logan left me alone so I could talk with her privately. She seemed at peace knowing that Nero and his men were gone and said Knox would have been proud of what we had accomplished. According to Sunny, he would have said, "*You did a good fucking job.*" I chuckled, because that was exactly the kind of thing Knox would have said. I wanted to tell her about Kane, but I was mentally exhausted. Being pregnant with twins and having already gone through enough emotional distress, I was afraid of slamming Sunny with even more things to worry about. Kane could wait until after the babies were born.

Simon wandered into the room and sat on the bed beside me. He brushed my hair back and kissed my forehead, right before licking my eyelid and making me push him away.

"Scared the piss out of me, love. I thought you were going to kill us all."

I turned on my side and smiled. "If you'd been wearing the leather collar, I would have just killed *you*," I replied in a husky voice, clearing my throat.

"Nah. The leather collar would have been too formal. Give me your hands."

I lifted my arms and put my hands on the pillow beside my head. Simon placed our palms together and began lending me his healing light. Tiny threads of blue light transferred between our fingers and palms as I began to feel the energy move through me and replenish the power within my own core light. Borrowed energy would always leave your body eventually, but in such a weakened state, it was needed to speed up a slow recovery.

As Simon fed me his light, I clasped my fingers over his hands and gave him a warm look. "You have impeccable timing," I said, remembering how close the Regulator had been to beginning the execution.

"First of all, if I ever see you on your knees again, it better be with someone's jolly in your mouth and not a blade at your neck. Justus sent me a message that the sentencing was scheduled and I had to haul ass. We'll talk about this later, but no one is worth dying for."

"We'll have to agree to disagree," I said, understanding his anger as much as I did his skepticism about love. "I didn't think you'd find anything that would help Logan and me, but I was hoping you'd dig up something on Finn's father… my father."

"Wouldn't call him that, love. Donors don't count. A father is someone who raises you with integrity and wipes your bum."

"That would be Justus, minus the bum wiping."

"The Mageri should have their plates full with taking the case off our hands."

My voice softened. "Do you think they'll ever find out who's behind it all?"

He blinked and I noticed how Simon had nice lashes. "The labs might be more widespread than we thought and could span countries. We'll keep shutting them down one at a time until they have no place left to go. You can't expect to catch all the crooks. Otherwise, we'd have nothing to do but sit around and watch Godzilla."

I admired the walls in my room, painted like a forest of narrow trees. Behind the bed was a wall of beautiful stones. Track lighting perfectly illuminated the room, making it seem as if I were really in the forest. The only thing that stood out was my red chaise, which sat against the wall by the door. Justus had done such a wonderful job at making my room a special place—a retreat.

I had no desire to meet Rupert, the man who shared my DNA. Justus was the only father I'd ever need in my life.

"Simon, I'm sorry for being a bitch."

He laughed like a hyena and scooted so he could raise his left knee on the bed. "That's what makes you so appallingly desirable."

"I'm serious. I should have never walked in on you like that. If you want to play naked Twister in your house with some hussy, then that's your business."

His mouth turned to the side. "Hussy that one was for mouthing off to you. Just think of sex as a recreational pastime and you won't get your head stuck in all the muck of relationships and worthiness. I have no need for all that."

"You don't think you'll fall in love someday?"

He scrunched his face and looked toward the ceiling. "I don't think I'm capable of love, to be honest. I just don't have it in me like you do. No woman has ever made me feel more than a hard-on. I care for you and all that, but not the way *you* see love. Sometimes a person is too damaged to work like everyone else."

"You're not damaged, Simon."

He winked. "Perhaps one day I'll meet a lady who can best me at chess, then we'll see if I have a challenge on my hands."

I had opened my mouth to say something when the door flew open and Christian came barging in.

"Get the feck out."

Simon glared over his shoulder. "Bugger off."

The look on Christian's face made me shudder. It was stony and pale—mixed with his black eyes and dark hair, it made him impossible to ignore.

I touched Simon's arm and tried to drag his attention away. "Simon, I think you've given me enough light. Can you check on Logan and make sure he's not burning down the kitchen? I need to be alone with Christian."

An irritated look flashed in his eyes and he let go of my hand and hopped off the bed. As he passed by Christian, Simon paused and slimmed down his eyes. Simon was fairly tall, so he had a slight advantage in height, but not by much. "If you upset her, I'll tether you and stake your naked body to the ass of an elephant."

Christian smirked. "That anxious to see me nude?"

I laughed and moved to sit up, propping the pillows behind me. Simon could be so random. After he slammed the door, Christian held his spot for an uncomfortably long time. My Mage energy was all out of whack, so I couldn't tell the time. I guessed it was daytime judging by the dark shades poking out from the pocket of his trench coat. Vampires had no trouble walking around in daylight; Christian said it only pierced their eyes. He didn't wear sunglasses in all instances. I suppose he felt it would impede his ability to see what was going on, so he endured the discomfort.

"The self-sacrifice of staying behind bars for your dearest love I could stomach, but when I heard you had knelt before the higher authority and offered your head, I wanted to take it myself."

"Christian…"

His hand flew up. "Silence. If it's one thing you learn in this life, it's that we only get one. Don't get swept up in the romantic notion of giving your life up for another. This isn't the picture show."

"You do it all the time," I pointed out.

"I put my life on the line for a paycheck. There's honor in what I do because my purpose is to thwart the wicked intentions of others to do harm."

"And you don't think that's what I was doing?" I objected, folding my arms.

Christian walked forward with a steady gait. "Foolish woman. Do you honestly think your death would have restored honor to that family?"

"No, but it would have saved his life," I bit out, taking a belligerent stand against his tone.

His Irish accent became thick with anger. "And what of yours? Jaysus wept, you offered your head on a plate. Do you think I do that for a living? I fight for the life of the one I'm hired to guard, but I also fight for my own life. I don't give it up freely. I don't hand it over like a parting gift so that another might live," he said, fluttering his lashes before rolling his eyes.

"Maybe if you loved someone, you would."

He drew closer. "Love is nothing but a festering wound. If you were my youngling, I would teach you that the greatest men in history died for naught. It's what humans write about in fairytales to remove the pain and truth of what love really is. Love destroys men. It robs them of sound decisions. It takes away their power and weakens their spirit for all the times it must be tested."

I scooted up in the bed and gripped the covers. "Is that what this is all about? I'm *not* your youngling, Christian. That's someone you've turned. I took a lot of blood from you, maybe more than you've ever given to anyone, but I'm not a Vampire. *Let go* of that sense of entitlement you have on me. You spend too much time meddling in my personal affairs for someone who doesn't give a shit about love or friendship."

He blinked and I could almost hear faint whispers coursing through my veins. His lips slightly parted and his eyes lowered.

"Aye, you are not a Vampire," he said in a gruff voice. "But part of me will forever course through your veins. Do you not... feel me?"

He stepped closer and brushed his fingers across my bare leg. My blood warmed and I felt a faint connection to Christian I couldn't articulate.

"I've tasted your blood, Silver," he said in a soft whisper. "I know a part of me is still within you. Vampires don't share our blood like you've seen in the movies. I've never given so much of myself to anyone."

His fangs descended when he sat on the bed beside me. Christian pressed the tips of two fingers against my neck, feeling my pulse—even though I was sure he could hear it.

"I'm a Mage, Christian. You could never turn me into a Vampire. I may have your blood, but I'm not your youngling. You have no control over my life. You're my guard, and you've clearly gotten your feelings mixed up because of something you've never experienced."

He leaned so close he was only a breath away from my mouth, but his voice was dark and rapturous. "What does the Chitah have that I do not?"

I looked into his bottomless eyes and my blood ran cold like ice. "My heart."

Christian sat back, regaining his usual tone. "Your fireworks show is the most talked about in town. That's some trick with the lightning." His jaw set and he stood up, turning his back to me. "Clearly it's a waste of time to try to knock any sense into you."

"Or you," I suggested. "Thanks for coming to see me. I know you care in your own demented way, but I need to outline what does and does *not* exist between us. I don't want you looking at me as if you own me."

Christian walked across the room and gripped the doorjamb, glancing over his shoulder with brooding eyes. "That's not the look I was giving you, lass."

CHAPTER 29

PAGE WARILY LOOKED UP FROM her spot in the back seat of the car. The Chitah in the driver's seat winked at her in the rearview mirror. Two days had passed since the attack on the representatives of the higher authority. Word had spread fast and she'd learned of it through a phone call from Justus, but he didn't divulge the details. She got those from her neighbor down the hall. Maybe Justus didn't want to worry her with the gruesome facts, but she was horrified to discover Silver had almost been executed and that Finn had nearly died.

Almost, if not for Adam.

Her neighbor's friend had witnessed the attack and narrowly escaped with his life. It was known among the Mage community that Adam was a Healer, but it wasn't widespread that he could heal all Breeds. People were talking about it as much as they were marveling over what Silver had done with the lightning.

Butterflies tickled Page's stomach as the car pulled in the driveway of Justus's home. His ostentatious garage was nestled amid a canopy of beautiful trees, the branches glowing orange from the setting sun. She noticed some of the trees near the building had been cut down and thought it was a shame he lived underground and couldn't enjoy the natural beauty of the forest.

"Do you need help getting out?" the Chitah asked. He hadn't revealed his name since showing up at her door with a message from Justus.

She peered through the windshield and watched the garage door open as Justus ducked underneath.

"No, I'm good. You don't know what this is about—why Justus has summoned me?"

He turned around and winked. "Just doing a favor for a brother."

Page unbuckled her seatbelt and opened the door. Justus reached in and gripped her arm, helping her out of the car. The blustering wind made her squeal as it whipped her hair to the side. She leaned against him when he cranked up his Thermal abilities. Justus tapped on the hood of the car and it backed out.

"What's this about?" she said, teeth chattering. "Is someone hurt?"

"Allow me to escort you inside where it's warm," he said, guiding her toward the garage. "I want to offer you my gratitude for assisting with the tests that freed my Learner."

Page smiled as the garage door closed behind them. "It's hard to say no to Simon. He can be quite persistent. Luckily our equipment is more advanced than what the humans have, but if I'd known the sentencing was on that same evening, I'd have worked faster."

"You did an excellent job uncovering the truth about Finnegan's father, as well as the additional testing from the Chitah eggs."

The elevator descended and when the doors opened, Page looked down a dark hallway she'd always found creepy. She loved windows and light—being able to look at the world instead of hiding from it. After going through a retinal scan, they reached the front door.

"So why am I here? I'm not exactly in the best condition to be driving all over Cognito. I could pop at any time."

Justus didn't reply and she didn't argue. It felt good to lean against him. To feel his heavy arm curled around her as he steadied her walk and made sure she was warm. They had agreed to take things slow, even though she wanted to fling herself into his arms like a silly romantic. Page had a child to think about now. Her baby was her number one priority, and having a man that might tire of his mortal family and abandon her wouldn't be fair to her child.

He took her coat and hung it on a hook in the front hallway. The lights were off, except for a dim lamp in the living room.

"Where's Silver? Can I see her?"

"She's sleeping," he said. "She's had a slow recovery. Her light is so different. If her body requires more time, then that's what she'll have."

Page snorted. "So you're confining Silver to her room? Maybe she needs some vitamins and a little exercise."

"I think I know what is best for my Learner."

Justus walked around her and she drew in a breath of his cologne. She liked this one above the others he wore, although she didn't know the name. He was wearing a tight-fitted shirt that hugged every inch of his chest and biceps. The deep blue color matched his eyes and the fabric was stretched thin. Page had only dated men with dark hair. Justus barely had any because he kept it shaved, but the bristles that grew out were sandy blond, making her think he had a beautiful head of hair. The bold tattoo that snaked around his right arm looked tribal, but the design held meaning to him in each line.

Something looked different about the tattoo and she leaned in for a closer look.

"Come with me," he said, leading her across the house with his hand on the small of her back.

They walked toward the bathroom where he had installed an expensive lift that could be activated when the bathroom door closed and the shower was turned on. Page felt vertigo as the floor lowered and she suddenly grabbed on to him.

"Don't let me fall. I don't have good balance like I used to."

He chuckled warmly and spread his large hands across her back. She could feel the heat radiating off them and he pulled her a little tighter to him. Page regretted not having brought her medical bag. Silver must have been in bad condition for Justus to call.

They crossed the training room and she was walking toward Silver's door when Justus suddenly tugged her by the wrist.

"This way."

"But Silver—"

"Are we arguing?" he asked, his brow drawing into a frown. "There is something I must show you."

Page was in no condition to fight, so she stood by the door to the study. "I'd like to do a few blood samples and make sure Silver's not lacking any nutrients. I think if you're giving her any Mage light, then you probably need to—"

The door swung open and Page gasped, feeling as if someone

had knocked the wind out of her. Justus walked toward the center of the room, rubbing his tattoo. The soft light from a white lamp cast the room in a heavenly glow.

She was speechless. No, speechless wasn't even the correct word. Stunned.

The walls were pale blue with puffy white clouds painted on them that looked so real she wanted to touch one. Straight in front of her was a white baby crib with a canopy of lace draped elegantly over the top. The right wall had a changing table and beside it was a white dresser with pale images of wild animals painted on the drawers. She stepped inside and turned around, looking at a tall wooden shelf filled with diapers, pacifiers, precious little outfits, baby hats, teethers, and stuffed animals.

No expense spared on the necessities and luxuries.

She clutched a pale green bunny and held it tight to her chest.

"What is all this?" she said, her lower lip quivering.

"I cannot sit here knowing you are alone in that apartment, ready to bring a life into this world. There are too many dangers I cannot protect you from."

"But we went over this, Justus."

"Page, listen to reason. The knowledge about the experiments is out. There is the potential someone could discover the truth about your child. I am a man who lives by a moral and ethical code. I will not have your death on my hands if someone were to retaliate."

Page sagged with the realization that Justus was only doing what he perceived to be the right thing. "This is lovely, Justus. It's beautiful but—"

"But nothing," he interrupted, placing his hands on the crib behind him. "Here you will be able to rest, knowing your child is safe. I can arrange for a nanny to care for the child if you do not trust me holding him. I understand you must continue working so you don't lose your clients, and I want to offer my assistance."

"That's all?"

She smelled the fresh paint in the room and began to cry. It was the most extraordinary thing anyone had ever done for her.

His jaw set and he lifted his eyes to hers. "I want to be in your life." He squeezed the railing on the crib until his knuckles turned white.

Maybe it was hormones, but her cheeks flushed and when she looked down, she was blushing all over. Her hands, wrists, and probably her neck. She snuggled the bunny close to her chin and looked at the marvelous touches throughout the room.

"This must have cost you a fortune."

He blew out a breath and looked at the dresser. "I painted this myself." He raised his eyes toward the ceiling, which had more soft clouds and a few birds flying around them. It wasn't cartoonish, but so lifelike. "I bought the furniture on the night I found out you were pregnant and kept it in another room. They were bare, so I painted them. I haven't painted in a long time," he said, his voice trailing off. "I finished the walls this morning, so it needs to air out."

"You bought and painted furniture when you found out I was pregnant?" She held her breath, unable to comprehend it all. "Even knowing this baby is Slater's? That it could be born with disabilities because of all the drugs I was given?"

A vein in his forehead protruded and he clenched his jaw. Justus turned his back to her and looked in the empty crib, speaking in soft words. "Are you saying that now you don't want this baby?"

"Of course I do! It's *our* baby."

She covered her mouth and her eyes widened.

Justus spun around so fast he could have created a vortex of energy to consume him. Her soft brown hair tapered down her neck, his most favorite part of her. He could get lost in the curves and angles of her body. She looked up at him with anxious, loving brown eyes.

"Say that again, Page." His heart pounded against his chest with a feeling he'd never known before.

She gripped the floppy bunny and held his gaze. "This is our baby, Justus. Slater never inseminated me. His injection prepared my body so I would have viable eggs, and it's likely he used some ancient DNA or blood from an extinct Breed. That was his specialty—he studied the history of ancient Breeds and helped collect and store many of the artifacts that remained. I have no doubt he could have figured out a way to use the magic within their genes to temporarily heal my body. He never inseminated me, Justus. That makes you the father of this baby because there has been no other man."

Her hands dropped to her sides and she balled one up into a fist, staring at him with glittering brown eyes.

Justus was silenced by a woman.

Silenced by the graceful way she spoke and the regal beauty of her gaze. His mind became focused and clear. The night he'd followed her to the park with Slater, Justus had felt an undeniable pull that was like *gravity*. Something he'd never felt with anyone else, especially one who wasn't a Mage because their energy was weaker. He'd felt that way around Page ever since, and now he knew it had to do with the life growing inside her that was also a piece of him. His body reacted to that energy, instinctively wanting to become a shield and protect it.

Justus knelt on one knee and spread his large hands across her round stomach, experiencing awe for the first time in his immortal life. He pressed his forehead against her belly, feeling the life that moved within her. The stuffed rabbit tumbled to the floor when Page cradled his face in her hands. A smile played on her lips as she touched him.

"How is this possible?" he whispered in disbelief.

She ran her fingers across his bristly head and squeezed his ears playfully.

"Magic?" she suggested. "Please don't hate me for keeping this a secret, but you have to realize I'm a package deal now. When Christian released my memories, I was afraid to tell you and my reasons may seem petty, but I didn't want you turning away from your baby. I'd rather him grow up without a father than with a father who rejected him. He'll be unique to any other child that's ever been created."

"This will be *my* child," Justus stated firmly, dragging his eyes up to hers. He rose to his feet and touched her cheek. "I can sense your energy and I'm drawn to it from a distance. It's one I can no longer be separated from. I will protect you and watch over this child. This isn't about wealth or power; this isn't about pity or obligation. You will never be more adored," he said softly, stroking her cheek with his thumb. "You have interrupted my life and I won't let you go."

That was as close as Justus could come to telling Page he loved her. One miracle at a time. His heart was already on his sleeve and he'd never felt more exposed.

She leaned into his touch and closed her eyes. "You can't say things like that to me. I'm a whale. My feet and nose are swollen, my back hurts…"

He wrapped his arms around her and planted his lips on her forehead. "Children are not possible for a Mage. You have given me such gifts," he said quietly, breathing in her soft scent. Her eyes watered and he brushed away her tears with the pad of his thumb. "I will never leave your side, for whatever time we have together, *Mon Ange.*"

She kissed him back and a piece of his soul locked into place. This choice would not be an easy road, but it was his chosen path to take. The hard journey leads to a greater destiny. Those are words he had once told Silver. Now he finally understood the truth in their meaning as he touched the ends of Page's silky hair.

"I've sent for your things," he said. "If you do not wish to sleep in my bed…"

"Where else should I sleep? The crib?"

He laughed haughtily. "Quit your stubbornness and let me take care of you."

"I want this to last, Justus. As long as it can. I wish I could be one of you," she said, holding him tight.

Justus gave it consideration. Novis was a Creator and perhaps he could ask him for a favor. All things to be considered in time. Justus had a baby to think about first. His smile never waned as he could no longer disguise the pride he felt looking upon her.

A swath of hair slipped in front of her face and he reached in his pocket and pulled out a barrette, clipping it in.

She cracked a smile and touched it. "Do you normally carry these in your pocket? What else do you have in there?"

"This one is yours. I took it the night we kissed in your kitchen all those months ago."

She stroked his arm with her delicate fingers. "You never had to give me dresses, flowers, or jewelry to win my love, Justus. All you had to give me was this barrette."

Justus had wooed Page with expensive gifts because that's what Marco had taught him.

Her hand slid up his forearm until it traced the tattoo on his right arm. "This seems different somehow."

He turned his arm and looked at it. "I added another line. This one here," he said, running his finger along the curve. Each line was symbolic of the things he held important in his life: honor, courage, perseverance, loyalty, and sacrifice.

"What's it for?"

"You. Now the design is complete."

She touched it with her hand and blushed wildly. He could hardly get enough of the woman when she turned scarlet. *His* woman.

Page pulled back and straightened her shirt. "Does Adam have a job?"

He looked at her quizzically. "Why do you ask?"

She shrugged and reached for the stuffed rabbit, but Justus bent down and picked it up for her. "I could use a partner, Justus. Adam is a Healer, and that could be a tremendous asset. Relics are the ones hired as healers and consultants, but the gift he has would be unmatched. I often get cases from those who can't heal quickly. Chitah females have no Breed magic when they're pregnant and sometimes have complications. Shifter children are injured all the time. Adam could help so many people. It was just a thought tumbling in my head."

"I will speak to him," Justus decided.

Adam hadn't embraced the opportunities of a Healer, but working as a partner to a Relic might be a better opportunity for him. Even if it were temporary, Page would benefit from any assistance during her recovery time after giving birth. Perhaps helping Adam would make an impression on Novis, who in time might return the favor by putting the first spark in Page and making her immortal. A

Relic was genetically the closest to a human, so Breed magic worked differently on them and they could be changed into a Mage. Few ever were since the Mageri had a tight control over candidates they matched up with Creators. He had heard of some Relics choosing that life, but *very* few. Most would never consider it because they would not be able to have children and pass on their knowledge, thus being shunned by their own kind and ending their genetic line.

"Justus?"

"Yes?"

"Are you sure about this? I mean, I get that you've lived a long life alone and—"

"And I will be alone no more."

CHAPTER 30

WHEN JUSTUS TOLD ME THE news about Page, my knees buckled and I almost fainted. Shock might have been the operative word. Justus fathering a child was a literal miracle, yet it was not genetically modified, like me. This baby was *all* Justus and Page. Slater had given her fertility injections, and whatever was in that mix also allowed her to carry a Mage's baby without her body rejecting it. In the end, it was the simple act of his sperm meeting her egg and doing the tango.

Although in this case, it was less of a tango and more of a high-speed collision.

By the time they told me their plans, Justus had already moved her things in. I guess he wasn't expecting no for an answer, and he'd arranged for someone to load up the moving truck while his HALO brother drove Page to our house. I smiled when I peered into Justus's man cave and saw her afghan draped over the end of the bed. A couple of family photos graced the nightstand and her pictures were nailed on the walls.

When everyone had gone upstairs, I wandered into the nursery and closed the door. I took a seat in the rocking chair and clutched a musical bear in my hands, winding up the key in the back until it began to play a sweet lullaby. I admired the beautiful paintings throughout the room that Justus had created without my knowledge. As I stared at the crib, a tear trailed down my cheek.

The door creaked open and Logan closed it, kneeling before me with a stern look on his face. "Female, I can scent your sorrow through the hall," he said softly.

"This is what you're giving up with me, Logan." My lip quivered and I turned my head away. "This is what I had to give up, but nobody asked me if I *wanted* to. Samil just took the choice away from me, and I *hate* him for it." It was over; the tears were finally an onslaught of the grief I'd kept secret.

He smoothed his hand over my leg. "So... *that's* what this is all about."

"Slater's gone and whatever he knew about creating a child is gone. This will never be my future. But nobody asked me!"

He reached up and wiped away another tear. "Justus and Page do not know what fate lies in store for their young. He could have a short life. No parent wants to watch their children age and die."

Maybe Logan was right. Science could have given me a baby, but at what expense? It didn't matter.

"I think Aunt Silver has a nice ring to it, and you'll be hearing it a lot with this child and the ones my brothers will one day have."

I wiped my nose. "If they ever settle down."

He sighed and sat back, draping his arm over his bent knee. "This is true. I think Leo will be the one to settle first. He's often talked about having a large family. You will have your share of babysitting and after changing all those diapers, might be glad to send them home."

I smiled and placed the stuffed bear back on the shelf. "This is something I have no choice but to learn to live with."

"Nor do I have a choice. You may have marked your body with my name, but your name is an indelible ink across my heart. I love you, female. That means I go nowhere without you at my side."

My heart knew that Logan loved me, but I worried that this would split us apart. His Breed valued family and it was in their nature to have children.

He drew in a scent and his cheeks puffed out a little. "You're wrong, Silver. I'm attuned to the subtle changes in your scent and I know what you're thinking. Our lives will be enriched by the good fortune of others. You need not worry about where my heart lies. If this comes down to you wanting a child, then we will find a way to adopt. There may be children on the black market—"

"Logan! You wouldn't dare."

"Children are being sold to pay off debts, as was Finn. Our

home would be a better fate for a child than where they *could* end up going. There is nothing I wouldn't do for you, Little Raven. There is nothing I wouldn't give to you." He kissed the palm of my hand and then placed his hands over my stomach, softly stroking. "You would have been a wonderful mother, but you will make an excellent aunt. A child does not have to come from your body for you to be able to love it. You can still have children in your life without being a mother and be an influence on them. *Don't weep*, Little Bird."

He pulled me into his lap, curving his strong arms around my back as I listened to the thrumming sound of a purr deep within his chest.

"We're going to have to move upstairs," I said. "They'll want privacy."

Logan growled thoughtfully and sighed. "Since there are two hallways upstairs, Finn will take the one near the lift and we'll take the other. I *also* want privacy with my female," he said with mischief in his voice. Not to mention he was squeezing my ass and nipping my ear.

"I'm so glad Nero's gone," I whispered.

Logan leaned back and raked his fingers through my hair, studying my eyes. "I'm still looking into securing a building for all of us. Justus may not like the idea, but I suspect Page will prefer living in the city close to her clients. Justus will do what his female wants because that's what a male does when his heart is claimed." He kissed my nose and a smirk tugged at the corner of his mouth. "Have you spoken with your friend, Sunny?"

My heart sank. "Now that Nero's taken care of, she wants to have a ceremony and release Knox's remains. I told her I'd be there. The babies are coming soon and she needs this closure."

"Let me know the day. Leo and Levi will want to go. Lucian didn't know Knox, but he'll come if I ask."

"Don't go out of your way."

"Lucian is family and family sticks together. He will go if I have to staple him to the trunk of the car," Logan said in a deadpan voice.

I laughed softly and stood up, then wound the key on a musical toy. When it began to chime with a familiar nursery song, a smile played on my lips. Excitement swept away all the regret, and I thought about the joy of having a baby in the house.

Logan glanced at the crib as he rose to his feet. "They should put the bed in their room. Chitahs keep our infants with the parents for the first year to bond. Separating the child seems like a human thing to do," he murmured.

"They'll figure it all out."

He clasped my hand as we walked out the door. "Yes, and so will we."

It took three days of sleep for me to recuperate after Nero's attack. I'd finally begun working out in our training room with pull-ups and weight training. Page prepared shakes filled with all the nutrients my body lacked. I wish I could say they were tasty shakes, but Logan had to pinch my nose while I downed them. Simon and Justus had already weaned me from their light, allowing my body to recover on its own, which is why I'd slept off and on so much.

I slipped into a pair of sweats and a silly black sweater with a pink cat on it. Justus was more forgiving of sloppy attire when I was recovering from something, but I could tell by the slant of his brow that he would have preferred if I'd made an effort to look put together.

"What's going on up here?" I yawned and strolled into the dining room, which was alight with candles. Page sat to the right of Justus and to his left, Leo stared down at a stack of papers.

Leo cleared his throat and locked his hands behind his head. In the dim light, his hair appeared redder than it did in the sun. "The Mageri has arrested Cedric for his crimes in aiding and abetting an outlaw. Adam provided enough evidence through his contact to arrest Cedric for selling engineered weapons to Nero. His contact is still working on locating the ones who are creating them, but I have a feeling it's beyond our control."

"Did they have all the proof they needed? I know they're sticklers on written evidence," I said.

Leo placed his hands back on the table. "No. Things are changing, Silver. They have enough evidence to conduct an investigation and they're holding him while they check their sources. It's not protocol, but they don't want to risk him going anywhere. Although at this point, there's no way of telling how widespread some of the metal is. Adam seems to think the properties will fade over time, but it's speculative. The insider might be selling to someone else, so the Mageri is handling this arrest very differently."

"The times, they are a-changin'," I said, taking a seat at the far end of the table by the hall.

Justus rubbed his eye and glanced at the papers. "The Mageri sent Enforcers to Nero's compound. We found only four who were alive. All women."

"Mage?" I asked.

He nodded. "They hired a Sensor and discovered a grave of bodies buried in the back. Seven total—all human. We think it's possible they were one of us and Nero pulled their core light and infused it to his own. That would have rendered them mortal, and they would have no longer been of any value to him."

"Oh God," I breathed.

"They're not making the same mistake as with Ray and Cheri. The four that were released are under observation. They're receiving fair treatment, but there's no way to tell if Nero brainwashed them."

"Maybe a Vampire could question them," Leo said, folding the corner of one of the papers in front of him.

Justus made a small grunt as if giving the idea some thought.

"I think they've suffered long enough," Page interrupted. "You can't hold someone prisoner for what they might do."

"It's out of our hands at this point," Leo said. "We haven't been able to locate the Infuser who worked for Nero. Some of the people in the compound have given a physical description, so that will help. He visited on several occasions. It shouldn't be long before he's caught." Leo touched the gold HALO ring that all members of the organization wore.

"We made Adam an offer to join us," Justus added. "Out of respect for Novis, we decided not to approach him in the beginning, but he would be a valuable asset for HALO. I spoke with him this morning. He said he's done with this life."

I shook my head. "This was never the life for him, Ghuardian. It was the life he was forced into after his sister was killed. But this… this isn't Adam."

Page leaned forward with her chin in her hand, tapping her nose with a growing smile on her face. "No, but he *did* accept another offer."

I jerked my neck back in surprise. "What offer?"

"Adam is going to temporarily work as my partner. I need someone to manage my clientele. Some clients only require consultations and I can handle those on Internet conference calls, but I won't be able to treat the rest of my clients who are in need of medical assistance. I thought Adam would want time to think it over, but he agreed right away."

"Seriously?"

"I think Adam will be great. He has a good bedside manner; I watched how he was with Sadie. I can be the brains in the show with my innate knowledge, and he can be the brawn and fix people better than I ever could. I wish being a Healer were more prevalent among your kind; there are never enough Relics to handle all the situations that come up where medical attention is needed. Adam has limitations to work out, but I think in time he'll acquire some of the knowledge that I have. Perhaps he'll even go to medical school to catch up," she said, smiling at Justus.

He shook his head as if not believing it would be a long-term situation.

This was exactly the kind of job Adam needed. The gift of being a Healer only allowed him to fix people, but I knew Page would have higher expectations for his contributions.

Adam was going to be a doctor.

"Wow," I breathed. "Wow." I laughed and shook my head.

Page smirked and leaned back in her chair, hands resting on her belly. "He's moving back in with Novis."

"Where's Sadie going?"

Leo stretched and folded his arms on the table. "She's moving in with me, of course. We don't abandon our family to the streets. You have a houseful right now and we're going to be looking for something... larger."

He shared a private look with Page and Justus eyed them suspiciously.

Ah. Leo must have filled her in on their intentions to secure a building, but no one had mentioned it to Justus yet.

"I spoke with Sunny," I said, changing the subject. Silence blanketed the room and I twirled the mood ring on my finger, hating the finality of what was to come. This was probably in the back of their minds since Knox and Sunny were only humans to them. "She's having the ceremony for Knox. I'm going to drive with her to the coast tomorrow since Novis refuses to let her board a plane."

"Think again, Learner."

Anger surfaced. "Excuse me? Sunny is like family to me. This isn't up for debate."

He rose from the table and pushed in his chair. "You are not going with them alone and that's final. I'll have the car ready in the morning and we'll travel together. Page will stay here while we make the trip; she is too far along to be taking a long journey in the car. The risk of a traffic accident is too high."

Page didn't argue the issue. "Tell Sunny I'm thinking of her. I didn't know Knox like everyone else, but I can tell he was a respected man. Justus is right; I wouldn't feel safe on a long car ride. It's raining in some places and the overpasses might be frozen. I want you to both take it easy and call me when you get there so I don't worry. Justus? Don't roll your eyes at me," she said, pushing against the table to rise to her feet.

Leo began to chuckle and stacked his papers together.

"I was merely admiring the ceiling," Justus retorted, walking out of the room.

"The ceiling, my butt," she murmured, following close behind him.

When they disappeared around the hall, I heard the sound of reconciliation.

Kissing.

Page had her work cut out for her. Although, something told me she didn't *want* to change him. Their strong personalities complemented each other.

I turned my attention back to Leo. "How is Sadie doing after what happened at the court? I can't imagine she'd want to live in our world after having seen all that go down. That must have been frightening for a mortal."

"She's a resilient woman," he said, lacing his fingers together. "I sense she's lived a hard life, but she doesn't speak of it. She keeps a positive attitude. Sadie believes a person should influence the world and not be influenced *by* it. I will enjoy getting to know this remarkable woman."

"Your sister."

Leo lowered his head and pinched a tuft of his reddish-blond hair. "Yes, my sister. Adam's grown attached to her and I need to sever that," he said to himself.

"Why? Adam's a good man and he saved her life."

"She should be with her family."

"You mean Chitahs? She was born from your family, but she's human. You can't control who she chooses to be friends with."

"Her life will be difficult enough living in our world under these circumstances. Forming a relationship with a Mage would bring greater danger from those who oppose interbreeding couples."

"Like me?"

"No, Silver. That's not what I meant."

"Someday you'll figure out that you can't control other people's decisions based on your beliefs. I'd say life is too short for that, but for us, it's too long. It's way too long to be carrying around those kinds of prejudices. I know you accept me because of Logan, but I hope one day you'll accept me because you love me and nothing more. I know you're the eldest and looking out for your family, trying to keep trouble away, but just be careful how much you shelter them. Too much shelter not only protects you from the rain, but also the sun. We all need a little sunshine in our lives," I sang, rising from the table and giving him a close-lipped smile. "See you at the shore tomorrow, brother."

CHAPTER 31

ADAM INFORMED THE MOTEL HE would not be finishing out his stay. Part of him was going to miss that taste of independence.

He took a seat at the small table in his motel room and spun a box of cigarettes in a circle. It was the last pack he had purchased, and he decided it was going in the trash. Smoking wouldn't kill him, but Sadie had a point. He didn't want to be a weak man who needed a vice. Unlike Knox, it wasn't something he liked doing; it just smoked out the demons.

Saving Finn had awakened a sense of purpose in Adam. When Finn had gasped for breath and the color of life flushed in his cheeks, it'd had a profound impact. He'd brought the kid back from near death and now Finn would be part of Silver's family. If only Adam had been able to save his own sister, but something finally began to settle in him.

Acceptance.

Losing a sibling was difficult, but Annabell had been Adam's twin. They'd done everything together and he'd looked after his sister. She'd grown up to be a beautiful young woman with her whole life ahead of her—a life senselessly cut short in a dirty alley by who he later found out was a Mage juicing her light. It had taken away every shred of purpose in his life when he'd been left alone. Adam's entire family was in a cemetery. But had Annabell not died, Adam wouldn't have joined the Special Forces, met Knox, and eventually left to purchase a small house in Texas. He wouldn't have seen Silver that fateful night, running down a dark road. He wouldn't have been given his first spark by Novis, which had made him immortal. Knox wouldn't have met Sunny and she wouldn't be pregnant.

He wouldn't have become a Healer, and he thought about how many he might save during his own immortal life. Sadie was right in that fate only brought you halfway, but it was up to you to do the rest.

Maybe Annabell's death had a purpose, and that was to give him the ability to help others. The reason he jumped on the opportunity when Page made him the offer was that she hadn't made it out of pity, but need. She respected him and his abilities. In fact, it wasn't all about his gift. She expected him to assist with the lab tests and hinted if it worked out between them, she might teach him some of the Breed knowledge she possessed.

The longer he sat at the table of his empty motel room thinking about it, the more enthusiastic he became. Adam touched a scar on his arm and actually wanted this job to be more than temporary. The odds of her finding another partner again weren't good, and this surpassed the offers he'd previously received. It wasn't about money; it was about respect.

Adam had accepted her offer without hesitation and made the decision to move back in permanently with Novis. He now understood Silver's resistance in this world. It was tough to know the freedom of living on his own as a man, only to be thrust into a position where he was treated as a child. Novis gave him more freedom than Justus gave Silver, but there's a loss of pride when a man is dependent on someone else.

Adam didn't want to see himself turning rogue and becoming one of the men that HALO hunted down, and he'd come close to making that his chosen path.

He zipped up his leather jacket, stuffed his things into a small duffle bag, and jogged down the steps toward his motorcycle. The trip home was short, but the sun was shining and he could sense spring on his heels.

The cigarettes were left behind at the motel.

"Good to have you back." Novis held open the front door, welcoming him home.

Adam hung his jacket in the coat closet. "How's Sunny?"

Novis tugged at the long sleeves of his black shirt. "She has requested to go to the coast tomorrow and release the ashes. One of my men suggested a good location to have the ceremony. Have you eaten?"

"Can I speak with you privately?"

A few guards stood nearby and Novis waved them out of the room. "Come. We'll have drinks in the study."

They entered a cozy room with a small table by a window. Novis enjoyed his house being open and cheerful and made sure each room carried that vibe.

Novis placed a bottle of brandy and two glasses on the table. They each poured a small amount and took a few sips, looking at the rolling pasture of frozen grass outside before Adam began.

"What if I asked you for a favor?"

"Depends on the favor."

Adam rubbed the back of his neck and averted his eyes before looking up. "Would you be willing to make another Mage if I asked?"

Novis set down his glass and his clear-blue eyes glittered like crystal in the sunlight filtering through the window. He had a way of staring impassively at Adam that made him uncomfortable. It was a trait many of the ancient immortals had.

"And who is the intended?"

Adam gripped his glass and swirled the brandy. "Sadie."

"Sadie," he said flatly. "Is she aware of this?"

"No." Adam coughed and leaned back in the chair. "It seems unfair for her to be reunited with her family and have the life expectancy of a human."

"Tragic? Yes. Unfair? Such is life."

"That's a rosy way to look at things."

Novis wet his lips and stared out the window. "Is this a test of my patience?"

"Maybe the way the Mageri selects their candidates is screwed up. It's an arranged marriage based on who they deem worthy. Maybe I was the exception because you're a Councilman and the circumstances of my creation were... special. But Sadie would be a contribution to our world. She has a way of seeing things I think the Mageri could benefit from. You've spent years selecting warriors or intellects; maybe it's time you start choosing artists, free-thinkers, and people with heart."

"And what is your personal interest, Learner?" Novis studied him for a moment and tipped his head to the side. "I noticed the way you looked at her. Remember that she lives in the world of Chitahs and may have no desire to become a Mage."

Adam lifted his eyes. "So you'd consider this?"

"I've made no commitment. I'm only pointing out the obvious. How old is this woman?"

Adam thought about it. "I think twenty-four, if my memory isn't fading."

"Hmm. Too young. Does she know you're here?"

"Hell no," Adam blurted out, sitting back in his chair. "I don't want her to know."

After finishing his drink, Novis straightened his posture and put his elbows on the table, watching a redbird outside the window as it hopped on one of the feeders. "I do not wish to make a Mage in haste. This human is young and does not know our world. It would be foolish to offer immortality to a woman who does not have a full comprehension of what she is accepting. She would grow to resent you, and her anger would make her into a bitter Mage. It would lead her down the wrong path, and yes, I've seen this happen before in my lifetime. This is why the selection process now goes through the Mageri. The candidates are trusted humans who show great potential. They understand our laws and the politics between the Breeds. They do not come into our world blindly."

"You won't even consider it?" Adam cursed beneath his breath and stared out the window, shaking his head. "She might also resent the hell out of the fact she's getting old while everyone else stays the same."

Novis pushed the bottle of brandy to the side and studied him carefully. "Do you love this woman?"

"I hardly know this woman," Adam countered.

Novis smiled broadly and touched his lip. "I have known men

to fall in love in the hour of meeting a woman, so speak truthfully. Do you love her?"

Adam's voice lowered. "I care for her."

"I will make this bargain with you, Learner, as you have done a noble deed for the Shifter by saving his life. You have also impressed me with your acceptance to work with the Relic, and I want to give you something in return to show my appreciation. Allow this mortal to live in our world. If she still cares for you and continues to live in our world, then when she reaches the age of thirty, I will make her the offer. The caveat is that you must not reveal to her my intention. If you do, I will rescind my offer and she will live out her days as a human. You must love her as a human and she must love you as a Mage. She will soon come to understand the dangers of our world, and there is a chance she will decline my offer. If she accepts, she would become my Learner and be required to live within my home. If animosity exists between you two, it would displease me. I do not wish for you to sway her with the allure of immortality and guilt her with love. If you are uncertain of her feelings toward you, then be prepared she may not love you at all. You might feel differently by the time she is thirty."

"I would still want this for her. She's a remarkable girl, and damn if I'm going to sit aside and watch someone like her die."

"If I discover she is aware this offer is coming to her, I will remind you again that I will renege. She is much too young and unseasoned to bring on as a Mage. This much I know, as I myself was far too young. We'll see where things lie when she is thirty. Remember, she may not accept the life of a Mage. Be careful how freely you wish to give your heart. Don't start a relationship thinking she'll become immortal; that may not be the fate that plays out, and you would be left loving a woman who will perish in a short time. I would advise you keep a respectable distance and retain a friendship. Let's revisit this conversation in six years. Do I have your word you will adhere to my conditions?"

Adam felt a mix of fear and relief as his shoulders relaxed and he stopped clenching his jaw. It was stupid to think he could love a woman right out of the gate, but damn if he didn't have strong feelings for her. There was just something about Sadie that felt effortless, like they'd always known each other. Adam wondered if humans could also have kindred spirits. Knox once told him that he'd known he wanted to marry Sunny from the moment they met in the bar. Adam sure as hell didn't feel he deserved a woman like Sadie, but that's the kind of thing that gave a man hope.

Maybe Adam's feelings would erode with time, or she would find a man who had more to offer—like wealth and children. The one thing he wouldn't be able to give her was a family.

But it was a shot. It's the least he could do for a girl who had saved him without even realizing it—saved him in the best way that you can save someone.

He stuck out his hand and grinned. "It's a deal."

Novis just stared at his hand, as shaking hands was not a Breed custom.

"Won't kill you," Adam offered. "At least I didn't ask you to spit on it. The human in me doesn't feel like a deal is made unless two men shake hands."

Novis reached out and took his hand. "Then we have an agreement."

"Deal."

"How did I become so fortunate to end up riding with *you?*" I glared at my reflection in Simon's aviators.

He revved the engine to his Maserati as we tore down the freeway, heading to the coast. "Because luck be a lady, and you must have shagged her."

Justus was driving ahead of us in his Aston Martin because I'd taken too much time getting ready and he had a thing about punctuality. Leo had offered Adam and his brothers a ride in his spacious SUV. That didn't leave any room, so I'd agreed to ride with Simon. For the first thirty minutes, he blasted the Beastie Boys on his stereo and flirted with women he passed on the highway.

I glanced out the back window and watched a motorcycle in the distance get swallowed up by the fog.

"What are you looking at?" Simon asked, turning down the radio.

"Christian."

I hadn't seen him since our last conversation, and once again, he'd returned to skulking in the shadows. Only now his presence hardly seemed necessary after my display of power in front of the higher authority. Word had spread and to my surprise, for the better. I felt sympathy for Christian. Below the surface of brash words and indifference was a man. Unfortunately, the blood-sharing between us had confused his feelings toward me. I hoped in time it would fade, but I wasn't so sure.

The car slowed and I looked at Simon, who was rubbing lip balm on his mouth while making a right turn.

"What are you doing?"

"Fueling up," he said. "I skipped breakfast this morning and I refuse to stand by the bloody Atlantic Ocean with a growling stomach. We still have a few hours before kickoff."

"It's not the Super Bowl. Sunny isn't going to punt his ashes into the water. Can you show a little respect?"

Simon rolled the car up to a greasy spoon and muttered, "Yummy."

"You don't eat this crap. Keep driving," I said with a laugh.

"Afraid not, love. I have a few enemies in the city and don't want to risk running into any of them. Lard and heartburn it is." He stuffed his glasses in a middle compartment and got out.

I slammed the car door, my shoes crunching on tiny pebbles sprinkled across the parking lot. "This should be a memorable experience. Good thing you wore a shirt today," I said, pointing at the sign on the door that denied service to anyone without a shirt or shoes.

The misty weather had dampened the asphalt and fogged up some of the windows on the diner. We walked toward the door where a red light flickered, advertising they were open for business. I could see my breath, and the air was so humid it felt as if the moisture clung to my face. Most of the cars in the lot were big wheelers and white vans. The fog obscured the highway, but I could hear the cars rushing by as I rubbed my nose and followed behind Simon.

A bell jingled when we walked inside. The welcoming smell of coffee and bacon from the morning's breakfast rush made me take a deep breath. Heads turned.

I watched Simon saunter up to the counter in his suit. He wore slim trousers, a white shirt rolled up to the forearm, and a grey vest. He'd kept the vest unbuttoned for a casual look and I wondered why he always dressed down when he looked so good dressed up. A smart leather belt finished off the ensemble, one I'm sure he used more often in bed than around his waist.

He looked out of place in a diner where most men were wearing raggedy T-shirts, baseball hats, and baggy jeans. I wore black dress pants, a dark sapphire blouse, and a jacket. I took off my coat and draped it over a red barstool while Simon leaned on the counter and flirted with the middle-aged waitress.

She was a classic beauty, bright red hair pulled back and held in place with hairpins. Her teal dress seemed to fit right in with the décor and the white apron had a small ketchup stain.

"Why don't we grab a booth?" I suggested.

He dragged an irritated glance my way. "Do you really want to snuggle your arse in one of those ripped-up fart cushions?"

I rolled my eyes at Simon's inability to control the volume of his voice. After I took a seat to his right, the waitress placed two laminated menus in front of us.

"Order when you're ready. We're still serving breakfast, but the burgers are on the fire."

"No need, love. Fish and chips."

"We don't serve potato chips."

I leaned in. "He means French fries. I'll have a chicken salad."

Simon snatched my menu. "A chicken salad? Watching your weight or something?" He snorted and I lightly punched him in the arm.

"A chicken salad," I repeated. "Dressing on the side and if you have any crackers or something, that would be great."

"And to drink?"

"She'll have a vodka neat and I'll take a gin and—"

"Wait a minute, honey," she interrupted. "We don't serve

alcohol. So if you're trying to be funny, you can take your funny self into the parking lot and go to another diner."

"We'll have two Cokes," I said apologetically. "Sorry. We're on our way to a funeral and he deals with grief using humor."

She rolled her eyes dramatically, unimpressed with my perfectly legitimate answer.

"Simon, this is a human restaurant," I chided. "Can you tone it down for thirty minutes and act like a human?"

"So, you want me to spend my meal pining away over the miseries of life, wondering what I've accomplished and how none of it matters? Sounds cheery. Perhaps after that, we can talk about what I watched on the telly last night. It was a tough call between a movie about a giant ape and another with an Amazon goddess. The breasts win every time," he said with a wink.

"Oh, Jesus. Are you going to be like this the entire trip? If so, I'm going to send Levi to ride with you on the way home."

Simon shifted uncomfortably and pulled a sugar packet out of a slot. "I'm proud of you, Silver. Back at the jail. I think you did a real bang-up job."

"Thanks. Not sure if I'll ever be able to do something like that again…"

"Those blighters had it coming. It's a shame they were brainwashed by that manky bastard, but the show you put on was *spectacular*. Justice served on a platter. I would have hated to see what the higher authority might have done on their own. Probably slapped their bottoms and sent them on their merry way."

"You really dislike authority. Careful, Simon. Some of your opinions seem in line with Nero's."

"Corruption exists, Silver. Don't be naïve. Disliking authority is not the same as trying to bring it down with violence and bloodshed. Don't mix me up with those worthless pinheads."

"Maybe men like you are what they need. Why not work for the Mageri?"

He laughed like a hyena and several people shook their heads and gave us an ugly stare. Most of whom looked like truckers, but especially the guy in the booth to my right who was all but snarling at us.

"Seriously, love. You should have been a comedian."

"Maybe your influence is just what they need to shake things up. Why just do odd jobs for them contractually when you could get your foot in the door and really make waves? And I know how you love to make waves."

"Only on a waterbed."

I sighed and noticed the rotating display of sweets to my right. They had slices of apple pie and giant cookies. "God, look at that brownie. It's huge. I don't even think I could get my mouth around it."

"That's what she said."

I elbowed him and a man cleared his throat.

"Mind keeping it down? Some of us are trying to eat," a voice boomed from our right.

The jerk who'd barked the order had a full beard, orange baseball hat, and a belly that told me he'd spent a lot of time in diners like this. Mr. Beer Gut also looked like a man who enjoyed pushing people around. Perhaps Simon looked pushable.

Little did he know.

"How 'bout you keep your oversized mouth shut and piss off?" Simon suggested in a jovial tone, pouring a packet of sugar into his mouth. He'd lost a little of his British accent and almost sounded local. Simon manipulated his accent often. When we first met, he'd been trying hard to pass as American, but it had come out mottled. Then he'd found out how sexy women thought an accent was and totally played it up.

"Oh shit," I murmured as the man got up from his booth.

"Say that again, you little pissant?"

"Simon, no," I whispered harshly.

He swiveled slowly on his stool with his left arm still resting on the counter. He'd actually styled his hair nicely today with it slicked back and combed. The only thing he hadn't bothered changing was the tongue piercing.

Simon lifted his soft brown eyes up to the burly man who'd put his fists on his sides and scowled.

"I said keep your trap shut," Beer Gut growled. "This is a family place and people come here to eat in peace."

Simon's brow arched. "If you want to eat in peace, go home and eat in your kitchen. If you eat in a public establishment, be prepared that others around you might be engaged in conversations, some of which you may not approve. As for a family place," he said, glancing around, "I don't see any tots in here, unless you count the thirty you ate for lunch." He slowly poked his finger in the man's gut.

Oh God.

"Please, sir, we're on our way to a funeral and this is his coping mechanism."

"Silver, I swear to bloody hell if you say that one more time, I'm going to stop off at the nearest leather shop and show you how I'd *really* like to cope."

The man scorched me with his gaze. "Maybe you should find yourself a *real* man."

I bristled at his statement. "I have a real man. Do you have a real woman, or one of those blow-up dolls?"

Simon howled with laughter and let out an exaggerated snort.

Beer Gut grabbed a fistful of Simon's vest and yanked him off the stool. "Get the hell out of here."

Simon shoved his hands against the man's chest and knocked him back a foot or two. "Touch me again and I'll mop up this floor with your hairy arse."

"Why don't you two get out?" another man shouted from near the restrooms on our right.

I felt disgusted. Just because we'd laughed a little too hard? Was this the Twilight Zone, or had I forgotten just how intolerant humans could be? I'd been so wrapped up with all the prejudices that existed in the Breed world that I'd somehow forgotten how boorish humans were.

"We're going to enjoy our lunch and then we'll go," I announced. "Everyone go back to your seat and let's be calm, rational adults."

"Why don't you suck my dick?" the guy at the table suggested quietly.

"What did you just say to me?"

"You've done it now, boys," Simon announced, throwing his hands up in the air.

I was sliding off my stool to confront the man—although I had no master plan after that—when the guy with the beer gut snatched my left arm. In a quick motion, I knocked it away and did a maneuver that caught his arm in a lock. He bent to the side, groaning and trying to pull away.

"You shouldn't put your hands on a woman. It's impolite, and she might kick your ass for it."

When he reached out to grab my neck, I caught his wrist and stomped on his foot with the heel of my shoe. Then I shoved him backward until he fell against the front door, making the bell jingle erratically.

"Go sit down and quit stirring up trouble in here," I said. "Nobody here wants to see you throw around all your macho."

"What are you, some kind of lesbo?" The man at the table on the right heckled me.

I glared at Simon. "Well, this is nice and relaxing. Thanks."

He shrugged and took a sip of the soda the waitress had set down on the silver counter. "Looks like you're the one beating up all the humans," he muttered. "I'm just an innocent bystander enjoying my drink. I can't *wait* to tell Justus about this." His tone was gleeful as he lifted his shoulders.

"You better not," I said between clenched teeth. "Can we just eat?"

"Do you normally let your girlfriend do all the fighting for you?" Beer Gut bellowed, tossing his orange hat in an empty booth. When I saw the hat flying and his unwashed hair, I knew we were officially in deep shit.

The kind that required knee-high boots and a paddle.

Our heckler on the right stood up, muscles tightening in his thick arms. I noticed them when he took off his flannel shirt and showed off his wifebeater. He was tall enough to be a lumberjack, or at least the height I imagined lumberjacks to be.

His eyes locked on Simon, who was busy wiping a small stain on his vest jacket.

"What kind of pussy lets a woman fight for him?"

Simon leaned toward me privately. "I just love human insults from a man who probably has more lube inside the cab of his truck than in the engine. Bet he stocked up, waiting for the pornapocalypse. Is that the best they can do? Calling me a pussy is supposed to send a shudder to my immortal soul? You should hear what a gravedigger once called me; I still have waking nightmares about *that*."

"Simon," I said in a melodic voice.

"Did you hear me, pussy?" Lumberjack continued.

"'Fraid not," Simon yelled out, leaning against the counter on his elbows. "Doesn't seem many pussies heed to your call, does it? I can see why that would be a problem." Simon's eyes lowered to the man's crotch.

Both of the men looked like they could have been separated at birth with their scowls and scruffy beards.

"You wanna say that again?" Lumberjack stepped closer.

"Actually, no," Simon said. "Let's talk about your sheep fetish."

I did a mental facepalm and pinched him in the side.

"Ow!"

"Simon, please don't start trouble."

"I'm not starting trouble; I'm just giving it a little nudge."

"No nudging. We have somewhere we need to be."

Beer Gut shoved Simon in the chest and knocked the wind out of him.

"Don't do that!" I said, shoving him back. He barely moved.

The waitress leaned across the bar. "Hey, hey! You all take that outside. We don't want any trouble in here."

Simon lowered his voice, and despite all the chatter in the dinner and the sounds of forks touching plates, his words were deadly cool. "Touch me once more. Go on. Dare you," he said, the last part whispered.

The man stretched his arm out and barely touched Simon's chest with his index finger.

Simon snatched his hand, twisted it around, and broke his wrist.

He screamed and the heckler rushed at him with fists flying, but Simon was too quick and ducked, punching him in the balls. Three men who had been leaning out of their seat and watching the whole affair got up from their table, itching to kick some tourist ass.

"Whoa. I think you guys need to back off," I said.

"And why is that?" the one in the red shirt said, strolling toward us like he meant business.

I curled my lips in and balled up my fists. "Because I don't want to *hurt* you."

Simon unbuttoned his vest and draped it over his stool. "Come on, wanker. Give us a good show."

CHAPTER 32

"Oh my God," Sunny gasped. "What happened to you?"

I picked at the dried ketchup on my coat. "We had a little accident at lunch."

A blistering gust of wind blew in from the shore and I turned away from it. Sunny wore a black scarf wrapped over her head and a white coat.

"Where was Christian during all this?"

"Oh, I'm sure he was around," I said, tucking my hands in my pockets. "But he would have been disgusted if he'd had to save me from a handful of roughneck humans. I'm sure I would have never heard the end of it, so I'm glad he minded his own business."

She wrapped her arms around me and her voice softened. "Thanks so much for coming, Zoë girl. Can I call you that, just this once?"

I smiled. "Yeah, Sunshine. You call me whatever you want."

When she pulled away, her eyes were wet with tears and she dabbed the corners with her mittens. "I didn't realize it would be so hard. I've been doing pretty well lately. I mean, each day has gotten so much easier and I don't cry like I used to. But as soon as Novis pulled up and I saw the water..." She shook her head and looked up, letting out a mixture of a grunt and a shout of frustration. Then she laughed. "It shouldn't be this hard!"

We walked slowly, arm in arm, along a stretch of land that led to a rocky shore. The waves crashed violently against it with white foam and steel-blue waters. Everyone waited for us up ahead, but we were in no hurry.

"Sunny, can I ask you something?"

"Sure."

I sniffed and listened to our shoes crunching on the gritty path. Sunny's cheeks were bright red from the stinging wind. "Do you have feelings for Novis?"

A small crease formed between her brows. "Why do you ask?"

"Well, it just seems like there's tenderness between you two. At least on his end. I don't know him all that well on a personal level, but he doesn't really show compassion toward mortals. Except for you."

"He's been wonderful, although a little bossy about my condition. He's afraid every little thing might hurt the babies."

"That's what I mean," I said. "That's not the Novis I'm acquainted with. He's always tried to steer me away from associating with mortals because they'll die."

"We all die," she reminded me. "Some sooner than others."

"True."

Sunny stopped and turned to face me. A curl of her blond hair escaped from the scarf and circled in front of her face. She gave me a curious look and narrowed her eyes. "What is it you really want to say? I've known you long enough, girl. You have something on your mind, so spit it out."

"Have you thought about asking Novis to put his spark in you and make you a Mage?"

By the look on her face, I knew it wasn't a foreign idea. She'd given it some consideration.

"Novis made an offer for me to live in his home on a permanent basis. He confided in me one evening over a cup of tea that he'd like to hear the sound of children in the house. He told me a little of his family and some of the regrets he had. In his time, I guess men weren't hands-on fathers. All these centuries later, he says he's forgotten their faces, but he can remember their voices. He said he regrets not having kissed them more and wonders if they knew he loved them before they died."

I peered at the men and watched Novis tossing a rock in the water. "Wow. That's more than he told me. I just got the brutal end of the story about their slaying."

"Yeah, that too. I'm okay with our arrangement, but he's never made the offer to turn me into one of you."

"Maybe you should ask him," I suggested.

She looked up at the overcast sky and then stuffed her hands in her coat pockets. "I gave it some thought, Silver. But if you want to know the truth, I talked with Knox about it a while back. We wanted to grow old together. Now that he's gone, I don't have that dream anymore. But now I have the babies on the way. How fair would it be to them? I want to be human. I don't want to outlive my children."

"They might decide to become immortal when they're of age."

She tilted her head. "And who's to decide that? It's not easy to come into your world; there's no free ticket. What if they're turned away? What if they don't even want this life? That's a very real possibility because they may want a family of their own someday. I want to grow old. I want to be a grandma with white hair and wrinkly hands that my grandbabies poke at when they sit on my lap. I want to be a great-grandma if I'm lucky enough to live that long. I want to go when it's my time because…"

"Because?"

Her eyes glittered with tears and her lower lip trembled. "Knox might be out there somewhere, waiting for me."

I wiped a tear from my eye. "But you might fall in love with someone else, Sunny. You can't make that kind of decision over a man who's no longer with us. And how do you know he wouldn't want this?"

"Because it's what *you* want, Silver. You're afraid of letting me go someday. Don't selfishly hold on to something that doesn't want to be held. I want to be free to make my own choices and not be judged for them. I know it's hard to accept because immortality seems so appealing; we're all afraid to die. But this isn't something I'll regret. I'm going to be able to really enjoy every moment in my life because it won't last forever. Someday my kids will have to let me go because that's the natural course of things."

I held her arm and we continued walking. "You might change your mind."

"We'll see. Right now, this is what I want. I don't see myself changing my mind, especially when Zoë and Knox are born."

Sunny's Relic had confirmed the genders, and Sunny wasn't budging on their names.

"Are you sure you don't want to call her Wendy or Sarah?"

"Are you kidding?" she said with a small shriek. "Remember Wendy Robins from our old office? Oh my gosh, I'd never wish that fate on my daughter. To be named after a woman who slept with half the men and then got fired after spitting in the salad at the company picnic."

"That *was* kind of gross."

"Topic is closed. I've chosen their names and they both have special meaning to me. I'll be sure she's given the full story about her Aunt Silver."

"Just leave out the parts where I used to lay around with my cat watching romance movies all day."

She snorted. "Oh, like you don't still?"

"I want her to think her aunt is a kickass Mage."

"I don't know, Silver. I think she should know about her aunt who always spills her drinks when we go to the movie theater. And I especially want to tell her all about the time when her favorite aunt tried to shove me into a swimming pool when my apartment complex had a party."

"Don't forget to tell her about how her *dear old mother* grabbed my purse and pulled me in with her."

"Well, friends do everything together, right?"

We laughed and by the time we reached the group, they were all milling around and looking quite uncomfortable.

Sunny looked at the urn, which was sitting on a flat rock. Her upper lip began to swell a little and she stood beside Novis and faced all of us. "If you want to have a moment of silence or say something, go ahead. I really don't know what to say that hasn't already been said."

"Knox was a brother," Adam began.

He stuffed his hands in his jean pockets and hunched his shoulders as the wind blew from behind him. He looked nice in his black sweater and a knit hat that I presumed had belonged to Knox. Adam reminded me of a fisherman with the patchy scruff on his face. He stood at a distance to my right—eyes low, expression grim.

Adam clenched his jaw and looked toward the water. "The first time I met Knox, he told me to go fuck myself." Everyone chuckled. "That was his way of telling me not to cross him. Knox was a stand-up guy who always thought he was fighting for the right side. We couldn't have known back then what was going on, but joining HALO spoke volumes as to where his heart and head was. Knox believed in doing what was right and putting away the bad guys. If you were lucky enough to have Knox as your friend, then you knew he'd always have your back. That's what brotherhood meant to him. It wasn't about laying judgment on a friend, but backing him up no matter what. I'd made a decision to hunt down the man who killed my sister." His eyes flicked briefly to mine. "I had a conversation with Knox before he died and he told me no matter what I chose to do, he'd support me. I've chosen to let it go." His lips pressed tight and he nodded, taking a deep breath and folding his arms. "I hope wherever he is, he has my back on that one. I just wish I could have saved him."

Sunny lurched forward and held Adam. He kept his arms folded as she whispered something none of us could hear and her scarf battled against the wind. She kept talking and he suddenly cracked a smile and shook his head. Sunny brushed her hand down his arm and returned to stand beside Novis.

"Knox would have loved knowing you all showed up." She looked toward Justus and Logan's family. "He respected all of you. We talked about it privately, and while he may never have told you individually, I'm here to tell you that he had nothing but good things to say. He was proud of joining HALO, even though I was against it because I was afraid something could happen. Now I realize something can happen no matter what you do in life, so maybe it's better you do what's in your heart. I loved him. I *love* him. Most of you standing here are either immortal or will live a pretty long time. I hope his short life meant something to you," she said, struggling against tears. "Living forever means nothing unless you have a life worth living. Once you have that, it doesn't matter how many years you have left. Knox made me feel silly sometimes but yet loved all the time. He also made me grow up. He gave me children and family and I don't regret a single minute of our time together. So we're going to send him home and go order the most expensive dinner we can find around here."

A few grins touched everyone's faces, and Logan separated from his brothers and stood beside me with his hand on the back of my neck.

Sunny lifted the urn. Novis held her arm and helped her toward the rocky shore.

"Let's go," Logan whispered. "The wind is strong, but I can scent this female wants to be alone. She's in pain."

We headed back as Sunny knelt down and they began to pour his ashes into the ocean. Only Adam remained behind, watching solemnly.

Simon breezed ahead of us with long strides and Logan snatched him by the collar, looking over his messy hair. "I'm going to guess you're behind my female being covered in condiments."

"Can't help it if the woman wants to be smothered in my sauce," he said with a placid expression. Simon shoved Logan's arm away and walked off.

"Leave him alone, Logan. It's just his way. He doesn't want to admit that Knox meant something to him and this is how he's dealing with it. Justus and Simon have acquaintances but not many close friends. I guess most immortals limit their friendships because they don't want to deal with death anymore. I'm beginning to understand why. I hope I don't become that way."

"We all harden with time," Logan said. "It's a defense mechanism. You'll find it difficult to deal with the loss of someone you've known for five hundred years versus thirty. For a Mage, it must be a lonely life. But for Chitahs, we always have our children to make us forget. We age slowly and someday, Silver, you may have to let me go. You will outlive me."

I stopped dead in my tracks and turned around, watching Novis kneel behind Sunny and place his hands on her back as she covered her face. "Please don't say that, Logan. I'll find a way to make you immortal since you can't become a Mage. Who knows what science will be like in a few hundred years?"

He chuckled and held me from behind. "Don't hold your breath. I will love you after all this is gone. Someday we'll both perish from this earth and nothing will remain but the remnants of a planet that once held life. What matters is *now*. This moment," he said, brushing his hand over my shoulder. "And *this* moment, and the one that's about to come. I will not live with a morose Mage who dwells on death and bad tidings."

I laughed and spun around to face him. "Well then, nothing would cheer me up more than doing a little rollerblading."

His humored expression slid away and he arched a brow. "Ah. So you would send me to an early grave."

"You won't die, Logan. Only from embarrassment. Humor me in life and don't let me get too serious. Promise?"

His warm lips brushed against mine. "You have my word, female."

We walked toward Simon's car and I glanced back one last time. Novis was helping Sunny walk back to the car, but Adam remained behind. He sat on one of the rocks, staring into the ocean. The dull roar of the waves framed the moment in my mind and I wanted to sit by his side, but part of me knew Adam needed to be alone to say good-bye.

Novis had taken off his jacket and draped it over Sunny's coat. I wondered if anything would ever come to be between them, but I had my doubts. He clearly cared for her, but Sunny had chosen another path and would begin to age. Maybe it would be good for her children to grow up in a stable environment with a man who had years of practice being a father. His gift as a Creator had made him a mentor and he set an example for his Learners. But the one thing he lacked was compassion—an emotion a human was beginning to reawaken in him. Perhaps he'd be there to watch over her children as they grew up, and their children after them.

Logan held the car door open for me and I leaned in and froze. Sitting on top of my seat was a pub cap, but it didn't belong to Simon. Christian had bought the hat on our trip to Texas when we'd gone to question my mother. He wore it now and again to peeve me, but it suited him in a quirky way.

"What is that?" Logan asked.

I smiled ruefully, turning it in my hands. Christian wasn't just leaving me—he was leaving the life of a guard. It's something he'd mentioned on a few occasions and I knew life had something greater in store for him. I hoped he'd find what he was looking for, but I wished we had ended on a better note. But given our relationship didn't start on a good note, this seemed to be a fitting farewell.

"Christian won't be serving as my guard anymore."

Logan glanced around. "Are you certain? He might have just stepped away."

"No, he won't be coming back."

Good luck, Christian.

After an expensive dinner of lobster and every imaginable kind of seafood, I collapsed in a booth beside Logan and melted in his arms. Novis had spoken to me privately about Christian getting too personal and it becoming a liability. He'd meant to speak with him about it, but Christian was the one who had approached him. He hadn't told Novis where he was going, only that he wanted to do something that mattered. Of course, I'm sure the real version involved some colorful Irish profanities.

When I asked who my new guard would be, Novis had startled me by saying I no longer required one. After having seen my powerful display at the jail, he said it was superfluous to hire a guard with fewer skills than me. My abilities far exceeded any apprentice he'd hired in the past. As a Unique, he also wanted to arrange private sessions between us that went beyond what Justus could teach me. Novis planned to show me how to use my gifts in a way that only another Unique could.

He also said most of the city was buzzing about the events at the jail and few would try anything against me as rumors began to circulate of my power. It was hard to miss a green-eyed Mage with raven-black hair.

"Have you ever gone skinny-dipping in the Atlantic Ocean?" Logan asked playfully.

I laughed as the murmurs of conversation hummed around us. "Don't start that game right now. I'm about to pop from all this food."

"Rain check," he whispered, smiling wolfishly at me.

Simon stood up from our large table and announced, "Been a treat, but Silver and I need to head back."

I reached forward and used my energy to pull his keys into my hands. "Can someone else ride with Simon? I'm not ready to go yet."

Levi rose from his seat and Simon suddenly grabbed the back of Adam's coat. "Come on, princess. You're riding with me."

After Simon and Adam got their things together and headed out, I snatched another onion ring and held it to Logan's mouth.

He laughed and turned his head away. "Silver, I can't eat another bite."

"Not even from my hand?"

I started to pull away when he caught my wrist and devoured that onion ring like it was the last scrap of food on the planet. After licking each crumb from my fingers and causing warm tingles to erupt through my body, I reached for my glass of ice and began crunching on a few pieces.

Sunny returned from her fourth trip to the bathroom. She wore a tight maroon dress and black stockings. Sunny was already showing and carrying high. Novis held her chair as she sat down, then returned to the conversation with Leo about a trip he'd once taken to Alaska and some Eskimos he'd stayed with.

Justus's phone flashed for the fifth time, but he ignored it, listening to Leo. It was nice to see him put work aside and enjoy the moment.

Sunny made a fish face from across the table, puckering in her lips and widening her eyes as we giggled about the topics they were discussing.

I tapped an invisible watch on my wrist and mouthed, *"Do you want to go?"*

She shook her head and sipped her ice water.

Logan stiffened and I glanced up at him. I followed the direction of his stony gaze and caught a couple of guys ogling me, but not in a creepy way. My blue shirt was a V-neck with a little cleavage showing, something Logan had been admiring the entire evening.

"If he turns his neck one more time in your direction, I might twist it all the way," he muttered darkly.

"Look around, Logan. Most of the women here are over seventy or have five children attached to their hip. They can look all they want," I said, squeezing his leg. "I'm still going home with you."

An animalistic sound vibrated in his throat—the provocative kind. He slid down in his seat, causing my hand to move a little higher.

"Someone's in a flirty mood," I whispered.

"Must be the ale, or the scent of an aroused female in my presence. I haven't concluded which could be the culprit," he said with a growl at the end of his sentence.

My phone vibrated and I reached around to answer.

"Hello?"

"Oh, thank God you answered. Silver, it's Page."

"Oh, hi. We're just having dinner at a restaurant off the pier. Too bad you didn't come; the food was amazing."

"Silver, I'm in labor."

I sat forward. "You're what?"

Eyes turned in my direction and I plugged my other ear with my finger.

"It started early this morning but I thought it was a false alarm. It's gotten worse."

"How much worse?"

Justus stood up from his spot and leaned forward with his fingers pressed on the table.

"I don't know. It's getting close. I can't call a Relic—Justus doesn't let anyone down here because of security and I don't know how to work all these alarms."

"Oh God." She was right. She'd never figure out how to disable them and let someone in through the double sets of security doors Justus had set up. She didn't have the access and neither did Finn.

"Learner?" Justus almost shouted.

I looked up at his wide eyes. "Page is in labor. But she can't get anyone inside because of the security and you never allow anyone down there without permission."

"I went out the front door," Page continued, "but I couldn't get through the second set of doors."

Justus flew out of his seat and literally ran through the restaurant and out the main door.

"Does anyone have any suggestions?" I asked.

Novis shook his head. "If he hasn't put her information into the retinal scan, she won't be able to get out without disabling the alarms."

Crap! The alarms could only be disabled through an identity verification. It wasn't as easy as punching in a code.

"Simon. Simon went ahead already. Someone call him up and tell him to get his ass over there. He's got access."

Novis pulled out his phone and got up from his seat.

"Page?"

"Yes, I'm here."

"Sit tight. They'll be there in a couple of hours. Can you hold out?"

"I don't know—I've never had a baby before! Everyone's different and I can't check to see how dilated I am. I've delivered around forty babies, but I don't know if I can do this," she said in a frantic voice.

"Oh, you can do this, Page. You're *so* doing this and you won't be doing it alone."

Everyone got up from the table, threw down money, and headed out.

"Can you get here faster? Maybe a plane?"

I laughed. "I don't know if that would be faster unless we hijacked it, and I can barely drive a car. Is Finn there?"

She held her breath and released it. "Yes. He's freaking out."

I covered my face. "He's going to have to man up; you tell him I said that."

"Man up!" she yelled out harshly.

I smiled as Logan opened the door for me. "You'll be fine, Page. Women have been having babies for millions of years. Just remind yourself of that. Some women squat down in the cornfield and out pops a baby, then they go back to—"

"I'm not delivering my baby in a cornfield! This is not funny, Silver."

"I'm trying to lighten the mood. Do you think panicking will help? Just stay calm. Think of it from a Relic perspective and what you would do to make your patient comfortable. Give your instructions to Finn and make sure he does exactly what you tell him. I don't care if he has to rub your feet."

"Gee, that would be kind of nice."

"Do you want to stay on the phone with me?"

Leo started the engine and everyone buckled up.

"No. Just keep your phone on. Finn will call you if something goes wrong."

"Nothing's going wrong, Page. Positive thoughts. Just let nature do its thing. Labor can last for hours, so just relax. Justus will probably be there in fifteen minutes the way he drives that damn car."

Levi turned around with his phone against his ear. "Novis has a trusted Relic he's called up and she's swinging by the house. She'll be waiting outside for whoever shows up first to let her in."

"Did you hear that, Page?" I sighed with relief. I was nervous and excited all at once, but just wished we were closer.

"Yes, I heard. Please hurry. I don't think I can do this alone."

"Okay. Make sure your phone is charged. Be there soon."

I hung up and leaned forward to look at the speedometer. "A little faster, Leo."

"Silver, there are sharp curves on some of these roads and this is a vehicle not meant for top speeds. I'll go as fast as we can without getting arrested, but any faster and none of us will get there."

I sent Justus a quick text message that a Relic would be waiting. His response was: *I know.*

Levi's thick arm flew back and he snapped his fingers at Lucian, who was sitting in front of me. "Swap out. Now."

Since Logan and Lucian needed more room, they sat in the middle and I sat in the back seat on the right side, Lucian directly in front of me.

Lucian unbuckled while Levi crawled between the seats and fell onto Logan's lap.

"Ahhh," he said, turning around so it looked like *Santa Logan* might give him a gift this year. "I love ya, Lo, but let's keep this between us."

Logan leaned his head back and shoved Levi into the seat once Lucian crawled up front.

"How's it going back there, honey?" Levi turned around and I looked at the dimple in his chin.

"I don't know. Everything's just happening so fast."

"Novis said he's taking your girl home."

Without having realized it, I began rubbing at the Chitah bites on my neck. Sometimes when I felt worry or fear, they burned. I curled my legs up with my back against the side panel and watched Logan. He ran his fingers through his messy hair and turned his gaze out the dark window.

"Leo, how about we bump up the priority of securing a building for all of us?" Logan suggested.

Leo's eyes flashed up in the rearview mirror. "I may have found a location on the west side. Levi, do me a favor and call Sadie. Make sure she's still at home and tell her to stay where she is. I'll drop you off and then I need to head back. I don't like the idea of leaving a female alone all night."

Levi turned around and began texting.

CHAPTER 33

"Silver. Silver, wake up."

"Huh? What?" My head bobbed and a few doors slammed in the quiet vehicle.

"We're home."

Those two words worked like five espressos. I climbed out of the car and sleepily rubbed my eyes as I stumbled toward the garage. We didn't have the device to open it and Justus must not have seen us on the monitors. I opened a lockbox using the fingerprint detector and punched in the code. My Ghuardian had James Bond envy because no other member of HALO went to these extremes.

"Call if you need anything," Leo yelled. He got in the SUV and backed out.

"Lucian's not coming?" I asked as the door lifted.

Logan chuckled and ducked under the garage door, stepping inside. "Chitah men revere pregnancy and infants; few want to actually see one being born."

A chill swept over my body as I remembered Logan had been there for the birth of Sadie. This was familiar territory and it must have brought back terrible memories of his mother's death. His fingers linked with mine and we walked around Simon's car toward the elevator hidden behind a sliding panel. I activated the doors and we descended to the tunnel below.

Neither of us spoke a word as we moved swiftly down the hall. Justus had left his Aston Martin parked out front and the tires and frame were uncharacteristically covered in dirt.

After the going through the security doors, I entered the house, and that's when I began to get scared. It was quiet.

"Finn?"

Logan closed the door behind us and took off his coat.

"They must be downstairs," I said in a breath, jogging toward the hallway.

We hurried to the lift, and as it lowered into the training room, Logan gripped my hand.

The first thing I saw was Finn pacing around the floor with his arms folded. I hopped off the lift and didn't like the concern on his face.

"Is everything okay?"

He shook his head. "She was screaming."

I caught sight of Simon lying on one of the weight benches. The hallway to our bedrooms was dark and empty. I apprehensively passed each door until I reached Justus's room on the far right.

"I can't, I can't," I heard Page breathe.

"Give her something!" Justus shouted.

I slowly turned the knob and peered in. A Relic, who looked to be in her fifties with dyed black hair and of Spanish descent, crossed the room toward me. Her red lipstick didn't seem to fill in the lines and her face glistened from the heat of the room.

"Ghuardian, your energy is leaking," I said. "Turn the heat down."

I could see Justus rubbing his face and pacing at the foot of the bed. Page was turned on her left side with her back to me, hugging a pillow. Adam leaned forward in the chair beside her, brushing back her hair.

"I'm Silver," I said in a quick meet and greet. "Page is my Relic and friend. How is she doing?"

The Relic stepped outside and closed the door behind her. "I'm Elsa. Novis must be a good friend to you because I don't usually work outside my clientele, but he's always been good to my family. Page is not doing well. She's having a difficult time with the labor. Why doesn't she have her own Relic?"

I glanced at Logan and back at Elsa. "The circumstances of her pregnancy are delicate," was all I offered. "Um… she may look nine months, but the pregnancy went a lot quicker than that. She's around five months or so."

Elsa's eyes widened. "*Ay Dios mio.*" She touched her cheek with her hand. "Your friend, Adam, told me he's a Healer, but he's not able to heal what isn't broke. If she hemorrhages, he might be able to help, but he said he's never tried his gift on a Relic before. They're too close to being human."

"Is she pushing yet?" Logan asked, easing up to my left and rubbing his jaw.

Elsa was about five inches shorter than I was and had to tilt her head back to look up at Logan. "The contractions are coming every five minutes. I was called here on short notice and didn't come prepared for a cesarean. I hope it doesn't come to that, but if you want to know the truth, I've been having difficulties picking up a heartbeat from the baby," she said in a hushed voice. "I don't have a fetal monitor with me because I didn't have time to go to my office. My partner is out of town, and Novis didn't want a second person involved. There's a possibility we may lose the baby, if it's even still alive."

I covered my mouth and lowered my eyes. Page had known this was a possibility because she had no idea what effects the drugs Slater had given her might have on her fetus.

"Can you take her to a hospital or call someone?"

She shook her head. "Human hospitals are out of the question. It's too late for that. If we load her into the car, she could give birth on the side of the road and I won't be able to see. It's cold outside and the bumpy car ride mixed with the stress of her contractions could be worse on the baby as well as the mother. Another Relic may not get here in time. Call Novis and see if he'll send someone else out to help, but I wouldn't hold my breath. You live too far from the city."

"But she said it was an active pregnancy," I argued. "Lots of kicking."

Elsa nodded. "Then maybe that's a good sign. Say a prayer if you believe in God. The hard part is about to begin and I need that man *out* of the room," she said, pointing her finger at the door. "He's upsetting me and I can't concentrate."

I opened the door and went in, then gripped Justus by the arm. His skin was so hot it burned my fingers to touch him. "Ghuardian, come out and let the Relic finish her job. Having you here is going to stress her out. I know you're concerned—we all are."

Justus glanced sideways at me and I felt his skin begin to cool. He walked around the bed and told Adam to move. As Justus knelt in front of Page and held her hands, Adam approached me, rubbing the back of his neck.

"She's not doing well," he whispered. "I've never delivered a baby, so I don't know how much help I can be."

"Please stay," I urged. "They need your skills."

He shook his head and combed his hair back. "I don't know if it will work, Silver. All gifts have limitations."

I gripped his arms and leaned in tight. "Adam, it's not just your healing ability that makes you stand apart. Elsa needs an assistant, and you're the only one I know who can keep a cool head when things get crazy. I mean, my God, you watched me transform into another person and still managed to fix me up!"

Page moaned and I watched Justus whisper something to her as he brushed back her damp hair.

"I need everyone out," the Relic announced, clapping her hands once. "Someone needs to bring down a pitcher of ice water, glasses, and also some hot water. I have what I need to sterilize my equipment, but I need to clean up when the baby comes. Also, grab some towels or sheets you don't care about getting ruined."

I glanced to my left and Logan exited the room. "I'll go help," I said to Adam.

He shaped his mouth like a small *O* and blew out a quick breath. "Go on, woman. Do what the doctor asks."

"That's the spirit."

Justus walked around the bed and stalked out the door. Elsa opened a large black bag and began pulling out instruments. Page clenched her teeth and screamed.

"Adam, go hold her hand and make her sit up," Elsa said. "She needs to start pushing, but only when I say."

I left them alone and as soon as the door closed, her scream shattered the silence.

"Oh God," I whispered. "Please let it be okay."

The reality hit that Page was mortal and aside from the baby not making it, women died in childbirth. That was a reality. The

Relic knew her stuff, but part of me wanted to take her to a hospital. The only problem was, Breed women never gave birth in human hospitals. A record would be created on the child and there was a risk of them being discovered because of all the blood tests and possible abnormalities that would show up since they weren't human. A Relic was as close to a human genetically as it got, but the risk of getting caught was too great.

"Now that the cavalry is here, I'm going upstairs. I can't endure the sounds of a wailing woman," Simon announced.

"Do you need me here?" Finn asked.

"No, go upstairs and get something to eat. It's probably better if there are fewer people around. Can you ask Levi to give Novis a call? Tell him there are complications and we may need another Relic."

I had doubts it would do any good; her labor was moving along too fast. I walked to the far wall on the right and sat down, hugging my knees. The lift descended and Logan stepped off, heading toward the hall with a stack of towels and sheets. I hadn't even noticed until that moment that across the room, Justus was swinging his heavy sword in a series of swordplay techniques. The blade swirled over his head and every muscle in his arms bulged as he swung it down. He lunged forward and spun around, slicing through the air. I could only imagine what he must have looked like on a battlefield.

Logan took a seat on the floor in front of me and we did a little shifting around until I slid my left leg underneath his right leg and wrapped the other one around his waist.

"What happened with your mother?" I asked in a quiet voice.

"She had a difficult labor that lasted thirty-two hours. In the end, she hemorrhaged and the midwife wasn't able to stop the bleeding. She died before Sadie was born. There were difficult decisions made in order to get the baby out."

"How did your father react?"

Logan shook his head. "He raged. Then something switched off and he held no more emotion. He's not the man I once knew."

The sound of the heavy sword cutting the air chilled me to the marrow. I lowered my voice and tucked my hair back. "I don't think Justus will survive this if something happens to Page."

"His frustration is a heavy scent on my tongue," Logan agreed. "I lost my mate and her unborn child—I know exactly what that kind of loss is capable of doing to a man. Be prepared, Silver. If the delivery does not go well, it will affect him profoundly. The grief and rage will become a dark place that only he can bring himself out of. I would not feel right with you living in this house with him."

"He's my Ghuardian; I couldn't abandon him."

"Perhaps this would work out for the best. We could get a place of our own and Justus would have his home here. I don't want there to be a dark influence on your life, Silver. That's exactly what is moving through this room, and it's suffocating my senses. It's a foul, earthy scent that will quickly consume him. He may be a respectable male who has spent his life working for HALO and doing what is just, but never underestimate the power of grief. It led me to some dark places."

I lowered my head, leaning against Logan. Justus had once told me that not all endings are happy, and he was right. A happy ending was an oxymoron. My heart sank as I realized life was throwing another unexpected curveball.

The lift descended and Levi held a pitcher in one hand and large steaming jug in the other. "Who needs all the damn water?" He eyed Justus with caution and his nose twitched as he set them down. Logan got up and hauled them to the bedroom.

Levi sat to my left and patted my knee. "Are you holding up?"

"No."

He put his right arm around me and I leaned into him. "Nothing bad is gonna happen. Women have babies *all* the time. Trust me. Once the bun is out of the oven, everything will be back to normal. Well, except you'll be changing a lot of poopy diapers and Justus will probably be slaving away, bringing her pancakes in bed," he said with a chuckle.

I laughed softly against his chest. "Justus can't cook. He'd burn those bad boys."

"Maybe I'll stick around and cook the Levi breakfast special."

"Now I'm afraid."

He pinched my arm a little. "Hey, now. My waffles will make you weep tears. True story. I've seen it happen."

When he reached around and pressed my cheeks into a smile with his rough hands, I knocked his arm away and felt guilty for laughing. Guilty, because when I did, Justus glared at me over his shoulder.

"Nothing to worry about," Levi continued. "When all this is over, we're going to move into a big-ass apartment building so none of us will be apart. Sadie's excited because she won't have to live with any of us and gets her own space. I don't know what the hell is wrong with living with me. Finn turned out okay."

"Aside from the fact he's now belching and leaving his laundry all over the floor, he's absolutely normal. You definitely worked your magic in making him a Cross brother."

"If it passes the smell test, then there's no point in putting it in a hamper. I don't even own one of those things."

I leaned away and looked up at him. "I'm willing to put down money that you're going to end up meeting a guy who's a neat freak. Then what?"

Levi shrugged. "Then *he'll* pick up my dirty shorts."

"He may not want to touch those shorts with a pair of rubber gloves doused in alcohol."

"Then he'll have to see my way of doing things."

"He might seek comfort in another man's arms. Someone with a big… hamper."

Levi belted out a gravelly laugh. "Silver, you've already planned my mating and divorce."

Logan appeared from the hall and everyone tensed. Justus lowered his sword and wiped away the beads of sweat on his forehead. Logan's blond hair was disheveled and he rubbed his cheek thoughtfully as he kept a watchful eye on Justus. Logan looked incredibly tall and formidable, still carrying himself in a way that would make any stranger question his intent.

He walked in my direction and gave me an imperceptible shake of his head.

Something was wrong.

The sword clanged on the concrete as Justus threw it down and stalked toward the bedroom. I waited for the sound of him opening the door but heard nothing.

Page's feral scream made my hair stand on end. There was agony and pain in that cry, enough that Levi covered his face and rubbed his hands angrily, fingernails scraping through his hair.

Logan squatted down and wiped his face. "It doesn't look good."

"What's happening?"

I inhaled deeply to catch my breath and leaned forward, gripping his knee.

He held his hands stiffly up to his face and pressed his index fingers against the bridge of his nose, rubbing the corners of his eyes. "There's blood. Adam can't do anything to help her until the child is born. He doesn't want to risk hurting the baby with his energy. They're forcing her to push hard to get it out. Adam said she refused pain medication early on, so there's nothing they can do to comfort her."

Another scream echoed in the hall and tears stung my eyes. I launched to my feet and Logan gripped my hand. I snapped it away and met Justus in the hall. He had his arms folded tightly against his body and his forehead resting against the wall.

I came up behind him and held his shoulders, leaning against his strong back. He'd lost control of his Thermal abilities and the heat radiated off him. We could hear Adam shouting to push, and Elsa saying something unintelligible. Page's screams weakened and it suddenly became eerily quiet.

My heart quickened and Justus stepped away from the wall. I could visibly see his heartbeat against the fabric of his shirt. Logan came up behind us but kept his distance.

We continued to stare at the door and heard the sound of slapping. Other than that, it remained quiet.

No chatter. No screaming. No crying.

Silence.

There are times in life when the most jarring sound is silence. I backed away from Justus when I felt his energy swell. Page's pregnancy had gone too fast; her body hadn't had enough time to adjust to carrying a baby to full term.

"She'll be fine," Levi whispered again, this time his voice

uncertain. I felt his hand smooth over my back and I had a sick feeling in the pit of my stomach.

I heard the quick sound of skin rubbing against skin and the sound of objects tapping against a metal tray. Minutes ticked by.

When I glanced at Logan, he lowered his head solemnly.

The doorknob turned and Elsa appeared. Her puffy hair fell in messy strands from a loose bun that once held it. She lifted the end of her long shirt and bent forward to wipe the sweat from her face. "There were complications," she began. "Once the bleeding started, I couldn't stop it."

I heard the sound of Justus's heavy breaths.

Elsa rubbed her eye with the palm of her hand and I could hear a faint trace of distress in her voice. "Page is all right, but the baby… I'm afraid the baby didn't survive."

It felt like a sledgehammer to my heart.

"Adam was able to heal Page and she's resting. I'm going to give her fluids due to the blood loss… and I'll administer sedatives. She's going to be upset. Mothers should never have to bury their children. If she wants to hold it before I take it away, then it's up to her. It might be better if she didn't lay eyes on it; that's something you can never erase from your memory."

A chill ran up my spine when I thought I heard the haunting sound of a baby's cry. *Had I imagined it?* Elsa cocked her head and we heard it again.

She swung open the door and Adam faced away from us, leaning over the end of the bed. Elsa moved beside him and we stood frozen at the door. I reactively gripped Justus's arm and felt paralyzed when I saw the bloody towels wadded up in the trash. Page looked ghostly and her eyes blinked open as she struggled to lean forward and look.

The Relic was working on the baby, clearing its airway and grabbing a swaddling blanket. We couldn't see anything, but Adam peered over his shoulder and had a wide, excited grin.

Finally, we heard the screeching wail of an angry infant. *My God, what a set of lungs!*

Elsa lifted the tiny bundle and carried it to the other side of the bed, placing it in Page's arms.

Adam strolled up with a grin I didn't think he'd ever be able to erase.

"Stubborn," he said. "Just like you, Justus."

I turned around and picked up Max, who had wandered in and was slinking around our legs. After giving him a kiss on the ear, I handed him to Logan. "Let's leave them alone."

CHAPTER 34

THE RELIC MOVED ABOUT THE room, discarding the bloody towels and sterilizing her equipment. Justus felt his heart finally slowing down, and relief consumed him. Adam helped set up the IV line so Page would regain her strength—she'd almost died. Adam had been able to heal her internal injuries, but she was weak from the blood loss and they didn't have any available for a transfusion. The Relic rolled her eyes when Justus asked her to go get some.

Justus stood to the side, allowing the Relic to work diligently. He watched Page's brown eyes as they soaked in every inch of that baby. Page cradled the infant in her arms, stroking his soft hair with her right hand.

"I'll leave you two alone for a minute, and then I'll be back to check on the baby and finish up in here," the Relic said. She didn't seem aware that Justus was the father. How could she? It was impossible for a Mage to have a child.

Until now.

Adam followed behind her and the door closed.

"Come see," Page said, inviting him closer.

She'd never looked more radiant. A fresh sheet had been draped over the bed and the baby was swaddled in a thin white blanket that showed the top of his head.

"Pull the chair over so you can sit down," she said, pointing toward the wall.

Justus robotically dragged the chair to the edge of the bed and took a seat. "He's alive?"

"No," she replied.

His heart plummeted in his chest.

Page smiled. "But *she's* alive. It's a girl."

"I thought I'd lost you both," he said in an exhale.

"Justus?"

He looked up and an angelic smile lit up her face. "She's got your hair." Page brushed her fingers across the baby's scalp. "She's a blond-haired beauty." Then her eyes flashed at him. "If you're going to reject her because she's not a boy…"

"Page, be silent. You need rest and I want to hold my child."

Justus took the tiny infant and turned her around in his large hands.

"Hold the back of her head for support," Page instructed.

She was so small and delicate—Justus realized this was the first baby he'd ever held, and it made him nervous. Her pudgy nose and puckered lips made his heart beat fast. He could see Page in her newly carved features—he could see himself. In his arms, he held a mirror of their love. Justus quickly began to strip away the blanket.

"What are you doing?" Page asked, moving to sit up. "She'll get cold."

"I want to see her."

He set the baby on the bed and pulled the blanket away, counting each of her fingers before kissing her palms. She started to shake and cry, and as much as he wanted to comfort her, that sound filled him with fatherly pride.

Life.

His child.

He counted the tiny toes on her right foot and kissed the sole. When he moved to the left foot, he blanched.

"What's wrong?" Page sat up and leaned over, concern splashed across her face. "Justus, what's wrong?"

How could this be? His heart picked up a frantic beat and he felt the blood rush out of his head.

"Justus, what is it? You're scaring me," she said, gripping his arm.

On the sole of his little girl's foot was a mark.

A Creator's mark.

Not *his* mark, because when the first spark goes into a Mage and they become immortal through energy and light, a rare few receive the gift of a Creator. Each newly born Creator carries a mark that is unique from the one that created them. It's distinct so that their progeny will inherit that same symbol. No two Creators share the same mark, so it's easy to track a Mage's lineage.

He rubbed the pad of his thumb across the baby's foot—as if he could wipe it away.

"She's a Mage," he breathed.

"*What?*"

His eyes glazed over. "She has a Creator's mark."

"Maybe it's a birthmark. Babies are born with those all the time."

He shook his head. "Look at it. The markings are distinct and not the same coloring."

No wonder he had felt a swell of energy from Page during her pregnancy. Now that the baby was born, he could sense her energy was different.

Page held the baby's fingers and sighed thoughtfully. "She's so pretty."

"Will she grow?" Justus hesitated, fear slicing through him at the implications.

Page spoke in a knowing voice. "Yes, she'll grow. She grew inside me and she'll continue to grow. She's part of us both—Mage and Relic. If I put on my Relic hat, then I'm guessing her growth rate will slow down as the years go by. A Mage's core light is what keeps you immortal and hers is too weak, being so young. When she reaches full maturity and her light is the strongest it will get, she'll probably stop aging and become one hundred percent Mage, just like her father. I just wonder how much of my knowledge she has in her, if any."

Justus leaned forward and kissed the mark on the bottom of the tiny foot. He began to have visions of his daughter growing up strong and fearless—a warrior as well as a beautiful creature who was as intelligent as her mother and as noble as her father.

After wrapping up the little bundle, he lifted her into his arms and cuddled her close against his neck. She was warm and soft, so light he was afraid to take both hands off her.

"Should we name her? I was expecting a little boy," Page said with a short laugh. "I have all these blue booties and hats. Oh, lordy. Poor little girl."

Justus sat in the chair beside Page, smelling the baby's soft head and pressing kisses to it.

Page tapped her nose thinking. "What about Elsa? We could name her after the Relic. Or maybe Tara. How about Winnie? I had three top boy names picked out and now—"

"I've chosen a name," Justus announced.

"Oh, you *have*?" Page said. "No discussion about this? It seems like I should have a little input, given I pushed her out of my body."

He loved that woman's attitude. Justus smiled and held the baby in front of him, watching her yawn and wiggle around.

"Months ago, you told me men never gave you flowers. It's why I began sending you orchids. They're delicate flowers, but it seems you didn't find them pleasing. In a conversation we had in your kitchen, you said offhandedly that no man had ever given you a rose."

"A rose with baby's breath," she said with a chuckle. "I don't like those little weed things."

Justus held out the infant, placing her gently in Page's arms. "I've chosen the name Rose. I want to be the first and only man to give you a Rose. I can do little about the baby's breath; it comes with the package. Je t'aime, *Mon Ange*."

Page tucked the infant in her left arm, brushing her finger over her chubby little cheek. "Rose," she whispered. "Rose De Gradi."

"No," he interrupted. Justus had inherited the name of his Creator because that was the tradition. But Rose was a Creator and could keep her own name. He didn't want her to have Marco's name. "I give her the name Rose, but she'll take La Croix as her surname."

Page smiled with uncertainty. "Are you sure?"

He brushed a long strand of bangs away from her face as she kept watching him with those beautiful doe eyes. Justus looked down at the baby and his voice deepened to a serious tone. "Rose La Croix, daughter of Justus and Page, you're going to become a remarkable woman someday."

Something had been bothering Justus and he wrung his hands

nervously. He took a deep breath. "Would you consider becoming a Mage?"

Page continued stroking the baby's head. "I would. I want to stay with you for as long as I can. If Rose will become immortal, which I'm certain she will be, I want to be there to help her with all the questions she'll have in life."

"I'll call Novis," Justus said, rising to his feet.

"Wait a second!" she exclaimed. "I need to get my girlish figure back. Why don't you give me a year or two? Unless you have a problem with older women…"

Justus belted out a laugh. He might have been changed over when he was twenty-seven, but by no means was she the older woman in this situation.

"I'm serious, Justus. If I'm going to be immortal, then I need to get rid of all this baby flab and you're going to help me train. Don't laugh at me. I mean it."

He smothered his grin. If it were his choice, he would turn her that very night, just as she was.

"She's a Creator," Page marveled. "I wonder if in five years she'll have the ability to give the first spark to someone else. Wouldn't that be something to have my own child become my Creator?"

Justus shook his head. "We'll talk to Novis and get his advice. She'll need guidance on how to use her gift. I am honored you would choose this life, Page. I will wait for as long as you need."

Page wiped her brown hair away from her eyes and smiled. "Can you call the Relic in? We need to finish a few things in here and I'm going to need some sleep."

Justus had experienced a mix of fear, loss, and elation all in one evening. He pressed a soft kiss to Page's forehead, stroking her cheek and slowly pulling away. He took a minute to soak in the moment—to photograph it in his head. *This* was the moment his life had changed and the gratitude he felt for the fates was immense. He'd spent years feeling his purpose in life wasn't family or love, but honor and justice. Putting men away and upholding the laws. Now he was beginning to see he could have it all.

In small moments.

Six weeks had passed since the birth of Rose La Croix. The night of the birth, I had sat with Adam in the dining room and we'd shared conversation over a cup of gourmet coffee. I couldn't help but notice he hadn't been able to wipe the smirk off his face since saving Rose.

"First baby?" I asked.

"I hope they don't all go that way. Feel me? There was a minute there I didn't think she'd make it." Adam looked all swashbuckling, reminding me of the man I'd first met back in Texas. Maybe it was just seeing the hope glimmering in his eyes that had been lost for so long.

Adam recounted what happened during the birth. He said after a valiant effort to save her life, Elsa had finally covered the baby's lifeless body and left the room. He didn't think his healing light would work on an infant so small, but since it had successfully helped Page, he gave it a shot. Upon the first gasp of breath, he began clearing her airway and rubbing on her like the Relic had been doing to stimulate her to cry.

Adam stayed with us for two days to care for Page. He followed her instructions on what she needed, checking her vitals and making sure that she took it easy. Page wanted to recover quickly so she could care for the baby. Justus didn't hesitate in taking his duties as a father seriously. After each feeding, Rose would go into her daddy's arms so he could warm her with his Thermal heat and rock her to sleep in the nursery.

I'd never seen him so gentle.

I don't know if Christian ever called Justus and smoothed things over, but when Page began receiving flowers and cards, one card stood out. The envelope was addressed to Justus, not Page. It was black with an embossed design on the front, an infinity symbol in silver.

The only thing written inside was: *May your new light forever shine.*

There was neither a signature nor a return address, but I knew it was from Christian Poe. It was his way of apologizing, and because it was kept with the other cards, I had a feeling Justus had finally forgiven him.

Logan cooked our meals, which I had no complaints about except for the night he decided to make anchovy pizza. Finn looked a little out of place but delved into the extensive library in our home, devouring all the books on law he could find.

Page said the baby was old enough to be around a large group of people now that she was six weeks old, so I decided to host a dinner party to celebrate. Logan and Levi helped me in the kitchen as we made enchiladas, burritos, quesadillas, and more guacamole than I'd ever seen in my life. The Cross brothers were invited, along with Simon, Novis, Sunny, Adam, and Sadie.

All showed up.

It was a spectacular dinner—one of the best we'd ever had. Simon told raunchy jokes that made Sunny roll her eyes more than once, and Levi demonstrated just how many burritos one man could consume.

I made a mental note not to ask him to stay overnight.

Sadie soaked it all in. She'd been getting to know her brothers and the week prior, we'd gone to Northern Lights to watch her perform. She had an angelic voice with just the right amount of rasp. What I loved was how she didn't have a need for a band. She sang a song without her guitar and still had the audience in her thrall. I couldn't help but notice the glittery look in Adam's eyes as he watched her. After her performance, Logan insisted she begin playing at the Breed clubs. The pay was better and to be honest, I think he was so proud of his little sister that he wanted to show her off to the world.

It was also nice to have a group of girls in my core of friends—it wasn't just me surrounded by a bunch of men anymore. Page wasn't ready for a girls' night out, but we had plans in the summer to do something out of town. I didn't think she'd be able to leave the baby, but Justus convinced her to agree. He had complete confidence he could care for that child by himself.

At least for a weekend.

After the last enchilada was scooped out of the dish, everyone retired to the living room. Simon collapsed on the flokati rug, his arms and legs stretched out as he moaned and groaned at the ceiling.

"I haven't eaten like that since my trip to France in 1923. I feel... punished."

We had pulled in extra seating to accommodate everyone. Justus and Page cozied up on the leather sofa facing the monitors while Logan and Levi made themselves at home on the couch facing the fireplace. Lucian sat in a leather chair to the left, staring at fish swimming by on our screensaver. Sadie plopped down in a green swivel chair next to Adam, who was doing his sexy lean against the wall.

After Levi raised the topic on the latest Breed crime report, Novis followed me into the kitchen to help with the drinks. No alcohol would be served at this gathering, so we made several cups of cocoa and hot apple cider. I dropped an oversized marshmallow into a cup, listening to the chatter in the other room.

"Did Justus talk to you about Page?" I asked.

"He did. And before we get to that, you missed your training session yesterday."

"Sorry. I had to run to the dry cleaners and then I got wiped out."

He skeptically arched his brow. "Wiped out?"

I shrugged. "Everyone is entitled to a day off."

Novis had begun working with me on my Unique abilities, testing my limits and helping me learn how to harness that energy. But between his sessions and Justus's—which had been ongoing since the birth—I was exhausted.

"I will allow you to take a day off, but it would be courteous to call and give me notice so I can rearrange my schedule."

"Sorry about that."

He stirred a spoon in a cup. "I have another assignment for you. This one is more than a messenger role—I need you to speak on my behalf at an upcoming event."

Butterflies violently hurled themselves against my stomach in panic. "What event?"

"It is a speech I'm to give in front of the Mageri regarding Nero and the events that unfolded in front of the higher authority. I'm unable to attend as I had already made a commitment to an old friend and will be traveling out of the country that week. It's nothing to trouble yourself over. I'll give you the speech and you can memorize it."

"Speech?" I exclaimed, my eyes wide, my voice shrill. "I have to make a speech in front of people?"

"Just a few hundred."

I spun around and gripped the sink. "Oh my God. I think I'm going to be sick."

Novis laughed and his face brightened as he lifted the tray of drinks. "Only kidding, Silver. You said I needed a sense of humor, but where has yours gone?"

"That's not funny," I lied, still coming down from shock.

"I do have an assignment. Your duties as my apprentice are still ongoing. This is why it's imperative for you to be proactive in learning how to use your gifts. I have the utmost confidence you can take care of yourself."

"Well," I admitted, "Logan hasn't confessed to anything, but he's unofficially taken over as my guard. The last run you had me go on, I caught him lurking in the shadows. He's not as smooth about it as Christian was."

An enigmatic smile crossed his expression. "Come. We have thirsty people waiting on these drinks."

I eyed him suspiciously as he turned the corner. When I entered the living room, I set my tray on a small table and began passing out the drinks. Sunny returned from using the bathroom, looking more pregnant than ever.

She stopped and Novis handed her a cup, steam swirling in front of her face as she took a sip. My eyes skated down to his hand resting on her belly. It was remarkable how a human had restored what he'd lost in his immortal life—humanity. Another man beneath the layers began to emerge—not just a wise man of authority, but a friend, a mentor, and someone who opened his heart to others.

Sunny touched the engagement ring Knox had bought for her. She wore it on a silver chain around her neck to keep him close to her heart.

Novis had established a close friendship with Sunny and had welcomed her family to live in his home for as long as they wanted.

Maybe they were good for each other, even though it wasn't a romantic relationship. I tried not to think of how she'd soon age and her children would be grown, because dwelling on the end of things never allows you to enjoy the beginning. I had to be positive about the privilege of seeing her descendants and being able to tell them the beautiful and tragic story of Sunny and Knox. Maybe I had to believe everything happened for a reason. Logan had once said that every event in our lives leads us to a greater destiny, even if we don't always understand the purpose. I was beginning to see some truth in that.

"Come sit beside me, Little Raven, and rest your feet." Logan tugged at my hand.

"Don't you want cocoa?"

"I already have something sweet," he said with a suggestive arch of his brow. I collapsed in the space beside him and sighed.

Finn relaxed against the wall in front of us, and Max sauntered up to him, flicking his tail left and right. Finn didn't like my cat, and Max seemed indifferent about it. They engaged in a staring contest as Max sat down and growled. I watched my brother as he stuck out his tongue at the black cat and tossed a marshmallow at his head. After it bounced off and hit the floor, Max took a few licks and walked away.

Leo eased into a chair beside Lucian to my left. He placed some papers on a small table in front of him. "I've purchased a building on the west side of town. This is an amazing location and it won't require much renovation to the building, outside of security. There's an underground garage with two levels, so there'll be plenty of space for parking. We'll have six floors, and the walls can be knocked out to make the homes the size we require. Some of us need the space," he said with a chuckle. "I'll let everyone look over the layout."

Page handed Justus the baby and he set her on his lap. Rose was dressed in a pale yellow nightgown with tiny daisies on it. Justus played with her toes and spoke to Leo without looking away. "Why not just give us each our own floor?"

Leo counted on his hands, looking about the room. "That would leave an odd man out. We'd have Levi, Lucian, and Finn. That's four when you include me. That leaves us with only two floors left and two couples," he said, looking at Logan and then Justus. "Sadie will be left without her own space."

"I'll stay with you," she piped in. "I'd like the company. Unless you don't want to listen to your baby sister playing her guitar. I get it." She smiled and played with a braid in her hair. I couldn't help but find her amusing, because even at our dinner party, she wore her boots. She called them her lucky heels.

"I have no problem with that. One day, I may look at expanding with another floor, if possible. Is everyone in agreement? When Sadie finds a mate, she'll move in with him, as is usually the custom."

"Mate?" Levi said, sitting up straight on the sofa and making fists with his hands. "I don't think she's going *anywhere*."

"Uh-oh," I whispered to Logan. "Sounds like the big-brother instinct is kicking in."

Sadie crossed her legs and smiled expressively, putting a blush on her cheek. "Just remember, boys, I'm the one who decides my own fate. You'll accept whomever I give my heart to, and nobody had better even think about scaring him off. I don't plan on getting hitched next week, so you can put that out of your head. I'm not even sure how many men would want to marry a woman whose only skill is playing the guitar and baking a pecan pie."

Adam leaned forward. "Did you say pecan?"

"Yeah, why?"

He chuckled and crossed the room, lifting one of the cups and sitting on the edge of our sofa. "Nothing. It's just my favorite pie," he said, taking a slow sip.

Levi scorched Adam with a glare.

"Bloody hell," Simon murmured from his spot on the floor. "Just shag her and get it over with."

All the girls burst out laughing and the men shook their heads.

"I love baking pies," Sunny chimed in. "I have a fantastic recipe for an apple pie that's orgasmic."

I stifled a snort when Novis's cheeks bloomed red.

The baby began crying and Justus held her up so her feet stiffly touched his legs.

"Justus," Page said, tugging down the back of the multi-colored knit hat that covered Rose's pretty blond hair. "She's too young to stand."

"Nonsense," he said. "She *wants* to stand. Look at her smiling."

Rose cooed and Justus smirked at his daughter with the cherub face and big brown eyes.

Justus hadn't changed. Same shaved head, designer clothes, imported cologne, and a fancy Rolex—even though a Mage didn't have need for a watch. His muscles were an example of what a man could look like with the right conditioning. His eyes still sparkled cobalt blue and his Charmer ability seemed to have no effect on his woman or his daughter. Novis suspected Rose was a Blocker, or had inherited whatever resistance Page had to Justus's charm. Rose would cry and pout at him, but sometimes I think that little baby knew she could make Justus the kind of father he was meant to be. Even though he hadn't changed outwardly, something was different about him—a youthful spirit that shone in his eyes that I'd never seen. He seemed more alive and in the present than ever before.

Simon rolled over and finally sat with his knees up, watching Justus help his daughter stand. "She's a charmer, that one."

Justus's eyes became volcanic. "Bite your tongue. That's one gift I wouldn't wish on her."

Simon laughed. "With Page's looks and your attitude? Yeah, as if men won't already be chasing her. That one you're going to have to keep an eye on, mate. She's going to break hearts."

"Adam, do you think you can take a picture of us?" Page asked. "Silver told me you're quite the photographer and I'd like a family portrait."

He smiled with his dark eyes. "You bet."

Rose let out a happy squawk and Justus lifted her up and kissed her cheeks.

I no longer felt sadness about the fate I'd been handed. I knew I'd have children in my life through others, and that was enough. Not everyone is meant to have a spouse, a child, a home, or all the things promised at an early age. We must take what we are given and make the most of it. My life was about finding purpose and opening my heart to let others in, even if it meant losing a piece of my heart in the process. Loss was part of love.

Logan nuzzled my neck and I gave him a warm kiss, touching the tiny laugh lines at the corners of his mouth. His amber eyes glimmered in the soft light and I felt a deep reverence for this man who had turned his life around, all for love.

All for me.

Adam had been right all along: Some men do stick around.

Maybe Justus had a point that there are no happy endings, but there's always a beginning—a new start filled with hope and love.

Sadie glanced across the room at Adam as he sipped his warm drink and set it on the table. He winked at her and she laughed quietly, shaking her head and twisting a small thread from her dress.

Sunny sipped her cocoa from a loveseat to my right while Novis engaged in a serious conversation with Justus. During their chat, Novis placed his hand on Sunny's stomach, feeling the two lives kicking within her. He smiled at her briefly and resumed his chat. Sunny was learning it was okay to laugh again—that life went on and Knox would live on through her memories and her children.

I watched Justus as he kissed his baby sweetly on the cheek, whispering something in French.

He was my Ghuardian, my mentor, and in some ways, my father. Nothing in life is permanent, and while I knew I would someday face losing people who meant the world to me, they had become the very definition of who I was.

Family.

Friends.

Home.

This was the life I was meant to live. These were the people I was meant to love.

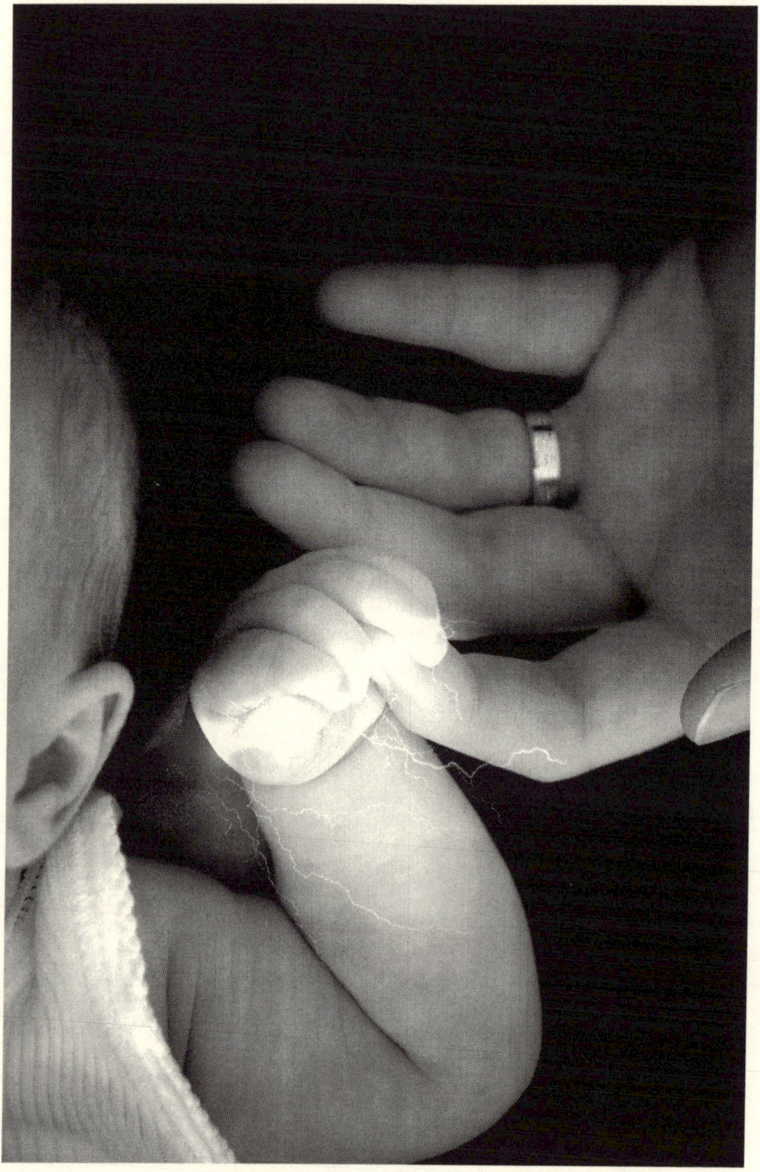

Printed in Great Britain
by Amazon.co.uk, Ltd.,
Marston Gate.